Evil for Evil

Volume 1

J. B. Alijewicz

First Printing, 2019
ISBN: 9781696782487

Cover by: Rey Reynoso

Editing by: Catherine Langholff
Jessie Kalish

Acknowledgements

I would like to thank everyone who encouraged, inspired, and pushed me to finish this book. Without you all, this might have taken another eight years to complete. You are all blessings in my life, and I am grateful for you.

First, I must thank my loving husband, Jon. Thank you for always forgiving me when my head is constantly in the clouds and for your unfaltering support.

To Sean, for listening to me endlessly spin nonsense in my indecisions, changing the story dozens of times.

To Lora, who sat patiently, giving advice as I read aloud less than stellar writing.

To Amanda, for convincing me to make my single story into an epic series.

To my cousin Rey, aka Tato, who without hesitation, selflessly designed the book cover and graphics.

To Catherine, who has been my biggest helper and kept me calm when I felt overwhelmed.

To Candice, my long time best friend, for never letting me think badly of myself.

Prologue

Scratching nails echo in the hollow, dark cave. The old man's knobby fingers twitch with desperation to make a sound, his twisted body lying half alive. He sputters, choking on blood, trying to cry out. The creature ripped out the old man's vocal chords, making it impossible to warn the others. This is his last chance. Clinging to life, he has to make the impending catastrophe known. His wet, red hands paint out a single word in his blood on the stone. He surrenders his soul to the beyond, knowing there is nothing else he can do.

Chapter 1

A fierce wind blows over rolling emerald hills into a small merchant village. Practical huts, made for function and not show, line the muddy main road, cutting through the town. The people dress in the same manner as the huts, bland, colorless and practical.

One person among the crowd stands in drastic contrast to the rest. A man wearing a metal mask pulls his bright green cloak tighter around himself. The silver and copper hides more than half of his disfigured face. The metal reflects the sunlight and flashes with the smallest movements. The parts that are not covered reveal sharp and angular features. Lifting the hood over his head, he conceals the small black symbols running down the back of his neck. His tattered black gloves have holes, exposing chapped and calloused hands.

He crouches down in the mud surrounding the stables. The end of the sword he wields buries deep in the soft soil, keeping him balanced. His boots are caked with grime while he watches the people go past with practiced disregard. The road buzzes with conversation and shopkeepers trying to peddle their wares. Despite the activity, fewer people roam the street than usual. The masked man wonders if the frigid weather or his presence has scared customers away.

The growl of his stomach reminds him once again of his hunger. He can almost taste the roasted animals hanging upside down by a nearby stand. The smell reaches his nose more seductive than any woman. Licking his dry lips, he tries to remember the last time he had an actual meal.

"I have brought you something to eat, sir." A dirt-ridden young girl extends her bony arms. In her hands steams a tankard with a savory stew.

Uldon almost smiles. He reaches for the pewter mug, and the green sleeve falls away from his arm. The girl only sees it for a moment: the metal crest burned and embedded in the man's forearm.

"Magdonna, no!" a woman shrieks, pulling the girl's hand away before she can have any contact with the man. The stew sloshes out onto the floor as the mug falls.

A weaker man than Uldon might have wept at the loss of such a rare chance of sustenance.

The round woman drags the little girl away. Her brown eyes stare with pity into his and the moment of intimacy pierces through him. A full cycle has passed since anyone has made eye contact with him. He grabs his forearm, as the crest burns white hot against his skin.

He prays it is not so. He raises his eyes again to the tiny figure, and the metal scorches. Taking his hand and covering the crest, he hopes he can stop what it is doing. *Why her?* Uldon wonders with deep regret. He knows his job well and laments at having to destroy her.

Four nights pass and Uldon begins worrying the others had not received his message. He plants himself at the stables and stays cemented to the spot, waiting. He doesn't know how much he can trust a messenger when they want nothing to do with their kind. Uldon had grown so anxious the last few evenings; he almost went to the deed at hand on his own.

"Uldon."

He turns to a familiar voice. Two figures draped in rich green cloth come bounding toward him on jet-black horses. Onlookers' jaws drop as the two men enter the small merchant village. Some ignore them, while others place "closed" signs in front of their shops. Others even shriek at having three of the green-cloaked men in their small town. Both men pull back their hoods revealing symbols down their necks although not as visible as Uldon's.

"Now, Uldon, you look dreadful," the larger of the two men says, smiling. His mess of red hair clashes with the green cloak. His beard and bushy eyebrows leave very little of his pink skin showing.

"We got your message," says the second, his face stern and eyes suspicious. His dark hair stays exactly in place while he wrings his pale hands. "Are you sure? This isn't where you were supposed to be stationed. For goodness' sake, this is a town of merchants."

"I was only passing through on my way to the mountains," Uldon explains to the twitching Aldon.

The two men tie their horses in the town stable. The other horses pale in comparison to the shining, black and regal animals. They will have to walk from there. The keeper does not dare ask them for payment, nor does he even acknowledge them. His lack of hospitality does not even faze Eldon and Aldon as they stride out into the open street.

"Are you sure," Aldon asks again, his eyes becoming shiftier, "the crest burned?"

"There was not a doubt in my mind."

Walking shoulder to shoulder, they make their way up the main road, weaving through the town. Shops, carts, and patrons line both sides of the road, but the townspeople push out of their way. They part to let them through, not wanting to even bump into them by accident.

"Good day to you now, fine sir!" the redheaded man bellows to a boy, whose face blanches white as a sheet. Eldon takes long strides, his shoulders pushed back as he walks down the center of town. "Good morrow, my lady.

Lovely robes." As he speaks, he waves to the woman on purpose, showing the crest on his arm. The woman who owns the cloak stand faints.

"What are you doing, Eldon?" asks the dark-haired man.

"I think it's quite funny, don't you, Aldon?" Eldon winks at his friend who wrings his hands with more fervor.

"Not at all," Aldon replies. "I don't enjoy being a social outcast." He frowns as they walk farther down the road and people clear the area.

"We don't have much farther to go," Uldon says. "There is a tavern around this corner. That's where we have to go." The bile rises in the back of his throat at the very thought of leading them to the young girl.

"Now really, Uldon, I was only half joking when I said you looked terrible. When we get to that tavern, I'm getting you some food."

"Good luck getting them to serve us," Uldon sighs.

"Oh, I think we can arrange that," Eldon smiles, winking at his friends. He pulls his sword from its sheath as they approach the pub. He kicks open the door with his massive black boot, spilling daylight in the dark tavern.

Eldon's shadow looms in the doorway. People quake at the sight of him. He stands over six and a half feet tall, covered in thick red hair. Every inch of him is rippling muscle and calloused skin. The thick body armor under his cloak adds to his bulk. He holds his sword before him. His face shows no expression.

The room is so quiet the patrons can hear the mice chewing on their crumbs.

"Food! Now!" he bellows.

People close by hand him their food, half eaten, desperate to appease him. Eldon smiles to his comrades, showing the missing molar in the back of his mouth. Aldon wrings his pale hands, as they sit at the first table, causing the people to scurry away. The rest of the room does their best to turn their backs and ignore them.

Uldon had become accustomed to the cold outdoors the last few nights, and pulls back his sleeves, finding the pub's heat and odor stifling. He squints, letting his eyes adjust to the dark, smoky room.

"Who is it then?" Aldon asks, looking around the room. "It must be him over in the corner."

Across the pub, a strapping young man swallows his food whole, without any regard to the tense atmosphere. The young lad has the sharp expression of someone who could quickly mature into a dangerous man one day. Eldon appraises him as though hoping there will be a great deal of fight in him.

"If only," Uldon says, worn. A discarded turkey leg lies on the wooden table. Even though his stomach churns, he starts to chew the meat from the bone in front of him. "Right over there." He points discreetly to a young, scrawny girl cleaning the tables. Her shoulders slump in, making herself as small as possible. Her face is cast down. Uldon's eyes shine with tragedy while watching her spindly arms haul a basin to clean each table.

"You aren't serious!" Eldon sputters, his lip trembling, "That child is much too young! It won't be a fight. It will be a slaughter. Besides the age, that little urchin is female! Female, Uldon. You must have been mistaken now."

"There is no mistake. I wish it were so."

Uldon sincerely wishes she had not walked up to him, and he had never seen her face. He toiled for hours over whether he should send word to The Order or merely ignore it. But he knew if he ignored it, it would have been treason of the worst kind, turning his back on his brothers.

"Well, there is nothing we can do about it. And we must obey the oath we have taken, even in situations like these." Eldon's complexion turns distinctly green. "You two are much too weak to do this. I must," he says, pushing back from his seat, and drawing his sword once again.

He approaches the little girl. She studies this red-headed giant with much less fear than the rest of the people in the room. Her eyes reflect awe more than terror. Eldon breaths heavily, dreading what he has to do.

"What is your name, child?"

Everyone in the room freezes, holding a breath. Every eye watches the exchange between the giant and the mouse.

"Magdonna, sir."

Eldon points his sword at Magdonna.

She freezes in place, her breathing uneven.

"Outside child. Now."

"No!" the girl's mother yells.

"Quiet, woman, or I will run you through," he spits with venom in every word.

The woman cries silent tears, covering her mouth to not make a sound.

"Magdonna, you will listen to me. Outside. Now."

With trembling hands, she puts down her scrubbing basin and rags. Eldon still holds the sword pointed at her, walking outdoors into the sunlight. Uldon follows, his heart beating against his ribs. Eldon directs her to a large clearing. He stands enormous and fierce. His steady hands don't betray even the smallest indication of the dread of his actions.

The girl shivers in the cold, her arms wrapping around herself. In the daylight, Uldon sees her shabby clothes. Her unwashed hair lays tangled under a handkerchief keeping it from falling to her face.

"We must do something!" a man hollers, about to charge Eldon.

"I don't think so," Uldon says. Both he and Aldon draw their swords. "No one interferes unless they wish to die today."

The crowd gathers in a circle around the scene, furious, on the edge of rebellion. The child looks up at Eldon with tears in her eyes, her breathing ragged. Her eyes shift to the faces in the crowd. Not a single person moves to come to her rescue. She watches the sword lift high above her, the sun glinting off the blade. The girl holds her trembling hands to her heart.

Uldon's stomach churns, the anticipation of what is to happen making his skin prickle with unease.

"Papa, I will be with you soon," she says, calmly.

She closes her eyes, with tears streaking down her cheeks. She tries her best to stand completely still.

Eldon brings down his sword. The crowd shrieks and covers their eyes, horrified.

Eldon's sword comes down on Magdonna's sloped right shoulder. Magdonna jumps, expecting the impact, but it never comes. The side of the blade gently comes down on her shoulder, light as a feather.

"Magdonna," he says, lifting the sword once again and touching it just as lightly to her left side. "You have been chosen and found worthy. Now with these witnesses and your brothers, I induct you into The Order of Kalrolin."

The crowd's expression slowly shifts from absolute alarm to murderous outrage. But not even one attacks. No one so much as speaks up.

Magdonna stands still as a statue, much too stunned to speak. She tries to take a step, but her legs don't have the will to move. She wonders if they might collapse from underneath her if she forces them to do so.

Aldon rummages through a bag under his green cloak and pulls out a second vivid green robe. He hands it to Eldon, who kneels in the mud, wrapping it around Magdonna. It's far too large, and the cape swallows her whole.

"I'm so sorry," He whispers so low, no one can hear. He closes his eyes and breaths out. Opening his eyes, he gets up, and motions for her to follow him.

Chapter 2

A young Darklandian man, almost the same shade of gray as the sky, weaves through trees and clouds on inky black wings. The sky turns a darker shade of gray with each passing moment. Soon, it will be pitch black in the Darklands, long before it even dims in the land of the Blood Ones. He flies far above the sky so as to not be discovered, his clawed hands clutching a large leather-bound book against his chest. His shoulders shift as his bat-like wings stretch from his muscled back and he glides on the wind. Ebony hair whips around his pointed ears and almond, coal-colored eyes scanning the ground, making out the distinctive geography, providing his location.

Once far enough in the land of his people, he descends, assured that it is safe to walk. If he had landed in the land of the Blood Ones, he would have surely been attacked, with cries of the people yelling "Creature". His bare talon feet tread on the clay ground. His wings fold neatly behind him as he rolls his neck. Tattered pants are kept up by a rope tied around his narrow waist.

Even with the old man dead, he had thought for sure, someone would have discovered the book missing. A serpentine smile stretches across his face. Instead of stopping to wonder why it had been so easy to steal the text in his arms, he boasts at his intelligence, his pride inflating. Tucking it under his arm, he makes his way through the forest of black, curling trees. The fog hangs low on the ground, and the sky slightly darkens to a rich gray. Even the excellent weather seems to be congratulating him on his conquest.

He skulks into the thickest part of the Darklands, to the stone temple.

For a moment, he stares at the temple. Unevenly-fashioned large slate rocks create a drafty and ill-constructed shelter. He had never seen it with his own eyes before. At one time, the temple was a place to respect those who had passed to the great beyond, but its use had diminished long ago. His kind do not care for those who died.

At the threshold, two massive Darklanders block the intruder trying to enter the splintering doors of the temple. Their stance widens as they fold their thick arms.

The loner bares his pointed teeth. His face transforms into something monstrous. His features stretch forward, making his face less human, more feral. His teeth grow longer, and the whites of his eyes become red.

The guards respond by spreading their wings and pushing out their broad chests. Their faces also stretch to long snouts and sharpen in defense. Their teeth and claws grow longer. Each guard is three times his size, but the thief has no fear, his lean, long frame unmoving.

"Tell the Old One that I am Warrick," he sneers quietly from his now long-muzzled face. "I have what he wants."

Both are skeptical. Many Darklanders had come to the stone temple claiming to have what the Old One wanted. It was never true. They ventured there seeking fame or fortune, but above all else, power. One guard leaves to inform the Old One, the bounty hunter named Warrick, waits outside the temple doors.

Warrick stands for only a tense few moments before being motioned to enter. He gives the other guard a smug expression as he glides past him, his features returning to normal now that his anger has abated.

He strides down a long dark aisle, the ceiling almost touching the head of the massive guard in front of him. At the very end of the long corridor looms an enormous room.

The only source of light in the whole temple flickers softly from a single long stem candle in the very center. From what little he see, designs and symbols decorate the interior walls. Firelight dances unevenly, skewing the features of the Old One approaching them. Warrick sets eyes on him, and bares his teeth, his upper lip pulling back with a hiss. Crouching low, Warrick readies himself to attack. The Old One appears not to be of their kind, and he suspects he has been tricked.

"I know what you are looking at," the wiry old man says. "Isn't it a convincing disguise?"

Warrick stands his ground, almost certain the old man is a Blood One. His claws extend, ready to shred him to ribbons. The Old One's skin holds pigments more brown than gray. All his teeth smile back flat and crooked. His eyes twinkle light blue rather than yellow or black. The features of his face and his ears are rounded, and his hair waves, long and light. His skin possesses the most realism. The Old One has a frame of wrinkles around his eyes, and his skin sags on his face and arms. He does not possess the waxy sheen of their natural look. The tunic around his shoulders completely covers the wings folded close to his back. His shuffling steps unnerve Warrick, who prefers the slow, measured movements of their kind.

"If I just walked freely in The Land of the Blood Ones, I might not even be recognized," the Old One says smiling, but the emotion doesn't reach his eyes.

Clutching the book, Warrick's eyes narrow. The old bag before him speaks too much. His tone and manner suggest he lacks the instinct of self-preservation, allowing himself to be in a room alone with someone much younger and stronger.

The Old One smiles with a wicked glint, "You won't do a thing to me, young one. I have thousands of equinoxes on you." The old man crosses the room and snatches the book from Warrick in one quick movement.

Warrick jumps back, his features sharpening and his brow pulling low over his eyes.

—

The old man waves his hand at Warrick, "Calm yourself. If I wanted to kill you, you would be dead already," he says, scanning the yellowed pages of the book.

To Warrick, the book possesses no unique quality. The faded black cover and discolored pages appear like any other.

The Old One skims his fingers through the crinkled pages. Slowly, a genuine smile creeps on the time-worn male's face. Soon, the grin gives way to light chuckling, almost echoing in the room. "You did indeed bring me what I wanted."

The Old One starts mumbling to himself and pacing in the expansive space. A slight hum resonates from the book, and Warrick feels buzzing across his skin. The Old One brings the book over to the single candle, getting a better look at the pages. When he lifts his head back up at Warrick, his face has distinctly changed. His eyes have turned black, and his features are noticeably more angular.

"The mercenary Warrick. Is that your real name?"

The young thief nods without saying a word. Every muscle screams to flee, but he tightens himself, forcing his body not to move.

The Old One studies him carefully, his mouth twisting with consideration.

"I expected you to be much older. Well, *Warrick*, how would you like to become my new apprentice?"

Warrick takes a slow step back, "No. I just want my payment."

The old creature's lip curls, smiling once again, "That was a rhetorical question."

With a flick of his knobby hand, the doors to the temple bolt shut. Warrick spins around in desperation.

"You aren't leaving. You never will."

Chapter 3

The landscape stretches before the four travelers without an apparent end. The chilly air pushes the long grass of the rolling hills. Trees dot expanses of plains, broken by numerous dense forests. They weave their way around the land, taking the cover of trees whenever possible. The vivid blue sky is almost cloudless. Only if Magdonna looks left would she see a hanging dark sky. She knows the Darklands are to the North, where the creatures live, and to stay as far away as possible. The tension in her chest loosens slightly, as she is glad to see they are not going north.

This is the furthest Magdonna has ever been, and it should be gorgeous to behold. But instead of excitement, she sits with vacant eyes, clutching tightly to a man she barely knows. Magdonna has never ridden a horse before and knows it is a mistake to do so now. The height seems far too unreasonable, and with the way the horse jerks and bumps, she fears plummeting to the ground. Her tiny hands ache from clinging to this stranger's cloak so desperately, but she doesn't dream of letting go.

Uldon wonders what Magdonna must be thinking. When she had first come up on the saddle with him, he was surprised how easily she could be so close. With The Order's reputation, he thought for sure she would have been more apprehensive about being in such close proximity. They had taken her from her home and family. How lonely and alienated she must feel. She had not said a word, and she seemed frightened when they first began their journey.

Uldon watches Eldon who rides far ahead to make sure no hidden dangers approach. Aldon stays behind in case someone or something tries to attack from the back. Uldon accepts his responsibility of keeping a close watch on the girl. The trip back to The Order's land is riddled with dangerous risks. The creatures spy to see who the next young member will be, hoping to snatch them up when they are young so they can never grow to be warriors against them.

"I'm very sorry, Magdonna," Uldon says after half a day of silence.

"For what?"

Uldon balks at her assertive tone, "For taking you from your land, your home, your mother-"

"That woman was not my mother," she says with seething hate. "I'm not sorry at all to never see her again."

This tiny girl speaks with such confidence. He can't believe the words are coming from a child. Thinking back, he remembers her expression in the clearing, almost peaceful. She thought she was going to die then, but she didn't beg for her life or cower in fear. Grown men groveled in the face of death, but this seedling displayed dignity. She stood up taller than she had before. A thought crosses his mind.

"You whispered something in the clearing; it was too low to hear. What was it that you said?"

She becomes quiet again, shifting in the saddle, her eyes hard. Uldon does not blame her for not wanting to talk to him. To his surprise, however, after some time, she speaks.

"I was telling my father I would meet him soon, in the great beyond."

———

He stays silent, wanting to ask more questions, but also wanting to respect her privacy. Uldon doesn't speak. If she wants to tell him more, she will.

Magdonna heaves a heavy breath, finally dropping her tight shoulders.

With that small sound, Uldon knows the wall between them crumbles.

"When I was born," Magdonna begins, "my mother died giving birth to me. When first I heard this news, I felt guilty. If I were never born, then my mother would still be alive. My father loved me, but I knew he was sad. I had taken his wife. He never saw it that way, but I did. It was just the two of us running the pub, and we were happy, for a little while, before he became sick. Father didn't tell me he was ill, even though he knew. He was afraid that once he died, I would be cast into the streets, so he married a woman who always drank at our tavern. I was angry when my father married her. I didn't know why he did it."

Magdonna stops and Uldon's jaw shifts. She is sitting behind him and he wonders what expression she is making. Is it the same peaceful expression as in the clearing or something harder or sad? To his surprise, he hears her continue.

"She was loud and rude and terrible. One night he finally told me the truth about why he wed her. I was so sad, but I had to pretend I knew nothing so others wouldn't suspect. I could never show my sadness or weakness in any way. My new mother was shocked the day he died. He did everything he could to hide his illness from her because she would have never married him if she knew. After that day, she treated me more like a live-in servant than a daughter. She would often talk about marrying me off for money or selling me as a servant. She always had men at the house, and they would treat me just as badly. They would order me around, beat me. Some days – the good days – she would just ignore me completely.

"The first day you came to town and came in for food, she turned you away, and she told me stories about the Green Cloaked Men and them being cursed. I had heard similar stories told by men in the bar. But when I saw you, you didn't seem scary, just sad. But then I thought, maybe being cursed or dying was better than the life I was leading. I wanted to be back with my father. When I thought the red-haired man was going to kill me, I thought this was a gift from my father, a way out. But now I see he has other plans for me, a different life."

Uldon's ears burn, not believing what he has heard. So much tragedy has befallen this young girl. He doesn't say a word, not having the heart to tell her this isn't her way out, just a different disappointing life.

"Elmore, you old fool. Where are you?" Dawsley squawks, pushing aside a flap of fabric leading to Elmore's room.

Dawsley's green robe covers his ornate, filthy armor. His dark eyes dart side to side, his nostrils flaring. A small sheen on his dark brow shines in his frustration. Dawsley has the air of a distinguished gentleman, with mahogany skin and gray at the temples of his dark hair. He carries himself tall with confidence and authority.

The coarse cobblestone room remains untouched. The blankets on the animal skin cot lay smooth and set the same as the day before. A few clothes, green cloaks, and belongings litter the small wooden shelf, which leans against the wall. The lone thin window facing the outside lets in a stream of light. No sign that Elmore had come back to his room. The worry for his friend taints his seething anger.

"Has he not come back yet?" Asks Ylmore, considering the room from the hallway. His bony body follows a very prominent nose.

"This is just like him," Dawsley says. "We gave him one simple thing to do, and he botches the whole operation."

Ylmore leans his wizened body more on the single crutch he walks with, and uses the other arm to wrap his green cloak around him tighter.

"He should just retire with dignity, like you, Ylmore."

Ylmore frowns, deepening the lines of his face, "If I could, I would still be out there, fighting. The thrill of battle!" Ylmore pulls aside his robe with a dramatic flourish, exposing his ribs where nasty claw marks dominate his skin. Dawsley shields his eyes from the gruesome scar tissue. "It was one hundred equinoxes ago ; the sky was black as pitch-"

"For the love of decency, old man, stop exposing yourself! We have all heard that story at least thirty times, and every time the creature gets bigger."

"No respect for your elders," Ylmore snaps, pulling the robe back over him.

"That is it. Four days is enough! If he does not return by sundown, then we are sending out a search party in the morning. After all, he can't be playing around when he is in possession of Kalrolin's Journal."

"I wouldn't worry too much, that book couldn't be safer than with Elmore. He would die before anything would happen to it."

Dawsley shakes his head and becomes quiet. That is exactly what he fears.

Chapter 4

The travelers ride into the night, the horses sprinting until daybreak. Magdonna dares not even close her burning eyes for a moment. The cold air scratches her throat with thirst, but she doesn't make a peep.

"We don't have much longer," Uldon says, reading her mind. "We will be at The Order grounds very soon. If you look carefully, you can see it on the horizon."

She strains her eyes against the rising sun but sees nothing. The longer she stares at the hills, the more everything blurs.

"We are approaching our checkpoint; we have to walk from here."

Far ahead, Eldon jumps off his horse and waits, shaking the blood back into his numb legs. Magdonna's eyes search the land again. How can there be a checkpoint in the middle of bare soil? The horse comes closer, and Magdonna believes her eyes are playing tricks on her. The green hills start to move as though bugs crawl underneath the surface of the grass. Blinking hard, she tries to get her eyes to focus. It is not until they are almost on top of Eldon that she makes out the tremendous green towers shrouded in the same color fabric as their cloaks and the land. Her eyes adjust, noticing a few other men walking around the tower. Uldon pulls Magdonna from their horse. Her legs wobble slightly from numbness, and she grabs Uldon's arm to find her footing. Aldon arrives last, annoyance written clear across his face from the long ride.

———

"Welcome back, Uldon." A handsome youth smiles politely. Magdonna's cheeks burn. The boy isn't much older than her, with a face too lovely for a male. She shies away, only daring to make small peeks at him.

"Now what do we have 'ere?" a weasel-featured man asks. His sandy hair curls untamed, and his eyes are like two jewels, even brighter green than the cloaks or the land. "Whattya doin' bringin' creature bait to the o'der? A bit too skinny to be appetizin' if ya ask me," he jokes, scrutinizing Magdonna.

"Meet the newest member," Eldon booms with a hint of melancholy.

"Great Kalrolin! You surely pullin' me wank! It-it can' be!" He stutters with anger at the very idea of them making such a morbid joke.

"I would rather have nothing to do with your wank, so I am certainly not pulling it."

"But she is much too delicate," the good-looking boy protests, ignoring their vulgar exchange.

Magdonna casts her eyes to the ground, embarrassment blooming in her chest at being spoken about as though she is not there.

"It can't be." The handsome one sets his eyes on Magdonna, his expression softening. Magdonna can't help but notice his river-blue irises set in large eyes. She finds herself staring, unable to pull her own eyes away.

"I'll tell you one thing for sure, Nolan, she is much more durable than she appears."

Uldon appraises Magdonna with an expression her father would give her sometimes.

Her chest tightens.

"We had a full day and night's journey without stopping for food, rest or relief and she didn't complain once." Uldon's eyes turn to his travel mate, "Isn't that right, Aldon?"

Aldon's expression turns sour.

"Hahaha! Gettin' shown up by a mini lady like tha'!"

Uldon crouches down next to Magdonna. She gets a better look at the metal mask on his face and wonders how he lives with it always there. It shines silver with copper scrolls. She wonders what his face looks like behind it.

He speaks kindly to her, "If you need anything, this is the time. It is safe to stop here for a little while before we head to the center of town. We have everything in the tents. This is a stopping point, so there is food and drink and a place to relieve yourself. Take your time. You will need the rest." Uldon smiles.

Magdonna weakly smiles back, and turns from him, swallowing back her trepidation.

The green tents are virtually invisible to her. If Uldon had not pointed them out, she never would have seen them. She walks over to the tents, feeling their gazes press on her shoulders.

The center of the town bustles more active than Uldon has seen in a very long time. Men fire orders at each other while younger members run about with stern expressions.

"Uldon! Thank the great beyond you have all come back," Dawsley says, running over to their group.

"What is going on?" Eldon asks, his bushy eyebrows pulling together.

Aldon sinks in on himself, his eyes darting from place to place even more anxious than usual, while Magdonna positions herself behind Uldon, trying to remain invisible.

"It's Elmore," Dawsley says. "Instead of hiding Kalrolin's Journal, I let him take my place; he is always complaining about having nothing to do. But now he is missing, and the checkpoint guards on the south end said that when he left, he didn't have any provisions with him. That was nights ago. We sent out a search party, but he could be anywhere. Uldon, you are the best tracker we have. Without you, there is no way we will be able to find Elmore or the book."

Uldon deliberates for a moment, looking down at Magdonna who is thoroughly confused, back to Dawsley, then Aldon wringing his hands, back to Magdonna, and finally Eldon.

"Don't worry, Uldon, I will take her," Eldon says, concern written all over his face. Magdonna steps out from hiding behind Uldon.

"What is that?" Dawsley asks, seeing the little girl for the first time.

"This is the newest Order member," Aldon volunteers bitterly.

"But she is a girl! We don't have women in The Order!"

"We do now," Eldon says.

"My crest, I don't have time for this." He shakes his head, frowning. "Uldon, we must go now. I have to get a few more people. Meet me at the south checkpoint."

Dawsley gives Magdonna one last confused glance, then with a flick of his robe, strides away.

Uldon's mouth turns down abruptly. "Magdonna, I'm going to have to leave you for a little while, but Eldon will take care of you. We shall meet again," Uldon says quietly to Magdonna before turning away.

Reluctantly, she shuffles beside Eldon, who smells of stale drink and salty sweat.

"Come now, child. You have to meet Gallowgrave. He has been waiting for you."

Magdonna soon comes to realize there is seldom any color in The Order's town beside shades of green. She notices a tent or building covered in the dyed fabric one moment and the next it blends into the surroundings. There are perhaps hundreds of armored and cloaked men roaming the mud roads of this town. From what she can tell, the organization of the tents and buildings has no rhyme or reason. Had Eldon not been guiding her, she would have become lost and desperate.

Just when she thinks they are never going to stop walking, Eldon comes to a halt in front of a large stone building, also covered in camouflage. In the very back of the building is a long thin tower, the fabric waving slightly in the wind. From the reverence on Eldon's face as he stops by the door, Magdonna guesses the weighty significance of this building. She swallows hard, not knowing what to expect.

Eldon's large hands creak open the door.

Chapter 5

Thick, sickeningly bitter clouds of smoke billow, in the largest room Magdonna has ever seen. The walls burst with large brightly colored beautiful tapestries. Toward the back of the room, long steps lead down to a lower level. A cauldron burnt with use spews a rank stench over a fire that throws odd shadows on the stone walls. Thin windows set high let in light cutting the darkness. A tiny man, bald as a boulder and leathery brown, hops back and forth between the cauldron and another table spilled over with herbs, odd colored liquids, and ancient books. His back faces them as he stares intently at his measurements.

Magdonna has never met a real sorcerer before and she wonders what she is doing there. The tiny man halts, his back becoming bolt straight.

"I know why you are here. I have been expecting you." The little man turns around with an expression as serious as death. Magdonna's heart jumps into her throat. "You who have been chosen by Kalrolin himself, you who-" The old man breaks suddenly, squinting his eyes and bouncing up the steps with an agility of a much younger man. He takes his hand and pulls gently on his beard. "Why cobblestone and mirth!" chirps the old man. "Aren't you a girl? At this age it's a bit hard to tell, boys look like girls and girls look like boys, but I'm almost certain you are a girl. What are you doing here? Where is the new oacling?"

Eldon wryly answers, "For someone who was expecting us, you do seem surprised. This is Uldon's oacling, Magdonna."

Uldon's oacling? Magdonna has more questions than answers, and it eats away at her. She assumed once they had reached the City of the Green Cloaks she would have an explanation.

"A girl! A girl in The Order! Why the last time that happened was...why I'm not quite sure if that has ever happened!" The old man races across the room back toward the door. As Magdonna turns, she notices the entire wall, besides the door, is floor-to-ceiling shelves of books. The old man leaps light as air onto the bookshelf, climbing each row, muttering and pulling books out, flipping through pages, and tossing them to the ground. His legs and arms sprawl out like a spider. He climbs down and sits with his legs crossed amongst the books, biting his nails.

"You will have to excuse him," Eldon whispers. "The old man has sipped a few too many of his potions. He has been known to confuse it with soup."

Magdonna hopes he is joking.

"Yes! I knew it was here!" Gallowgrave pops to his feet, pointing at a page with a large toothy grin. "The Great Kalrolin decreed that there would be a day when The Order will be changed forever. A new era will be born! A member to the Order like no other will be chosen."

"Now that tells us nothing."

"What little you know! Magdonna, with you comes the beginning of a new time. A New Era!"

Magdonna sits before the cauldron, watching Gallowgrave pace.

"I'm not going to lie, Magdonna. The Order is no place for the weak or women. Why you have been chosen is yet to be seen. Do you know what we do, Magdonna? Why the Order exists?"

She shifts slightly. "You fight the creatures." Magdonna knows nothing else. No one ever talked about The Order of Kalrolin, exactly who they are, or even who Kalrolin was. There only existed superstitious stories about the Green Cloaked ones.

The Old man sighs.

"There was a time, long ago when we were revered. But now, we are mere ghosts with our own scary stories." Gallowgrave lifts one bony finger to point at a tapestry painted on the wall. In the first painting, a smiling wizard clutches a book. "Kalrolin was a powerful sorcerer, the most famous and well known of his time. Many coveted his power, but he took on only the very best students.

"You see the problem, Magdonna? Jealousy and animosity existed. A potential student begged Kalrolin to let him be an apprentice, but Kalrolin saw darkness in him, and turned him away." His hand sweeps to another painting of a lad clutching the book slinking away into the shadows. "The young man was not going to take this lightly, so one night he stole the book of Kalrolin's spells, taking it into hiding with him."

The old man points to a new picture. The boy casts spells, but all around him, the lush green lands turn black.

"With the book, he enslaved, killed, and stole. The self-indulgent and dark magic he was practicing was taking its toll, turning the land around him into nothing more than darkness and ash. Even the animals and people were affected by his black magic, wickedness seeping into their flesh, turning them evil." He gestures to a new picture, a picture of The Darklands. "The people's hearts became black, turning against each other, feeding off their kind, drinking their blood.

"Kalrolin, who had been looking for the man for cycles, noticed the land turning and knew he was there with the book. Even as strong as Kalrolin was, he was no match for this new dark sorcerer and the army of people that were loyal to him, either out of fear or love of chaos."

He points to a new picture of Kalrolin standing in front of a large fire and wisps of magic flow out from the flames. They stretch out like vines across a map of all the land of Solum Cowdh. Her eyes follow the trails they make like winding roads.

"That was when Kalrolin set out to find himself warriors, to help him on his quest. Through a spell he cast, he was able to seek out the bravest, smartest people to fight. He called them The Order because that was what they were supposed to bring about. To protect his warriors, he made a magic crest that he embedded on all of their arms. It gave them strength and sheltered them from danger and dark magic.

"The night they attacked to retrieve the book, the evil one knew Kalrolin was coming. He had transformed the people of the land into hideous, bloodthirsty monsters. These creatures were strong, with wings to fly, claws to tear and sharp teeth to bite. The battle lasted for nights. Many died. Finally, it was a duel between Kalrolin and the boy who stole his book, who by now, was a dark wizard. He had even transformed himself so he could be stronger against Kalrolin. Today, you know that same dark wizard as the Old One. He lost and was greatly weakened. Kalrolin placed a spell so he could not leave the stone temple in which he lived."

He points to a picture of them fighting. "Kalrolin won and got back his book, but the creatures were too many to destroy. Kalrolin and his Order fled the land to recover. But it was far from over. The Dark Sorcerer had his creatures search to find the book while drinking blood from innocent prey."

Magdonna's eyes grow wider with each new painting.

"Kalrolin decided the book had to be protected so only the pure of heart could get access to his spells. That's when he decided The Order had to continue. Kalrolin enchanted the crests to burn upon finding someone worthy, so other members could find successors and make The Order stronger to resist the creatures. In doing so, he unintentionally made members of The Order outcasts, believing that if you were chosen, it was a curse because it's a life-threatening, thankless job. We give new members the option of joining or dying. There are only two options. Most think of it as die now or get slaughtered in battle later. But we give the choice.

"Those who join are expected to protect the book and fight the creatures to save our kind. You leave everything behind. The Order is your life. You cannot marry or have a family of your own. *We* are your family. It is a brotherhood stronger than blood. You can never leave except by death.

"Now that you know what is expected of you, Magdonna, we will give you time to decide whether you are going to accept your fate, or choose to go to the great beyond."

Magdonna stands with her jaw set, her fists clenching. Her heart thumps so loudly it pounds in her ears. "I don't wish to die," Magdonna says with her voice shaking. "But if I must, then I would rather die bravely than take the coward's way out. I accept your invitation to the brotherhood. I will fight, and make my father in the great beyond proud that he raised me."

Uldon has found Elmore.

The men in The Order hang their heads low at the wrinkled body of their fallen brother. Deep in the vast caves, he lies twisted and alone in the dark. The only thing more disturbing than seeing their mentor and friend lying

motionless on the cavern floor is the last word the old man
had written in his blood.
   "TRAITOR"

Chapter 6

The shackles dig deep into Warrick's wrists and neck. After struggling for nights, his body slumps in resolve. The Old One didn't need to chain him because the opening of his small room throbs with magic. If Warrick had been able to free himself, just walking out of the open door would throw him back with so much force he would hit the back wall. Warrick knows the Old One had restrained him to degrade him, to make him feel like a pet.

He must have been mad to get involved with the Old One's affairs. The decrepit creature's reputation pales in comparison to what he had been experiencing. Warrick should have been aware, that the most sinister enemy doesn't look dangerous at all. The Old One appears as fragile as an aged Blood One. The Old One's lack of outward intimidation should have warned Warrick that something sinister lay beneath.

"Warrick, I do believe you have been in there long enough," comes the brittle voice of the elderly Darklandian. "I have food for you."

The rich, rusty smell of blood wafts over through the doorway. Warrick can't resist the scent, so he steps closer, forgetting his chains, which pull him back. Though he can't see him, Warrick knows the Old One monitors his every move, prepared to punish him if he acts out.

Craning his neck as far as possible, he barely manages to see the main room of the stone temple. A low fire dances where the long candle used to burn. A large stone basin sits above the flames, warming a thick dark liquid. Warrick's tongue runs along the bottom of his lip, his saliva pooling. His eyes fixate on the bowl.

A light chuckle startles Warrick.

"That is our first problem. If I had desired, I could have slashed your throat. You would have been none the wiser with the way you are lusting after that blood. You need to hunger for something much more than blood if you want to become powerful."

Warrick positions his features so they don't reveal a single thought.

"I have heard your name before, and you fascinate me. The rebel loner that has no alliances, who steals and kills without blinking an eye." The Old One strolls closer, inspecting Warrick like a prize horse. "You have proven yourself by getting Kalrolin's Journal when others have failed."

Warrick pretends not to listen to the old man like a petulant child.

Warm chuckling fills the room once again. "You have so much to learn if you are going to become my most trusted pet."

Warrick spits at his feet as a metallic roar erupts from deep in his chest. His face transforms into something monstrous. He strains against the steel chains, clawing and snapping at the air.

"That will not do."

With yet another flick of his hand, blood showers the wall behind him. Three slashes embed Warrick's chest. The shock snaps him back into stillness.

"The sooner you learn to listen to me, the sooner you can eat. Until then you can starve."

Warrick's muscles ache already. He had seen creatures that had died of thirst, their shriveled twisted bodies petrified to stone. No one in The Darklands can think of a more painful or gruesome death. It was a horrible mistake coming here, one he could never take back.

—

Chapter 7

Gallowgrave and Eldon's jaws hang slack at Magdonna's answer. It takes Gallowgrave an awestruck moment too long to respond.

He clears his throat, "Well then, Magdonna, if you are genuinely accepting, the first thing we do is give you your crest, and a new name, to start your new life. Uldon must be here for that. You see, Magdonna, the crest lets us know who to induct next. It tells you. The crest also chooses the right student and teacher for one another. Uldon's crest burned when he saw you, but if you had met Eldon, or any other Order Member for that matter, you might not have been chosen. Uldon's crest discovered you, so now you will learn from him. He will be your teacher, mentor, and brother for the rest of your life. This is part of your sacred oath. When, or if, you get the calling to become a teacher, it is betrayal to ignore it.

"He will also pick your new name. Because his name is Uldon, that means his students will have the last name *lan*. There is an order you see. The oldest generation is *more*. Then their students are *sley,* followed by *don* and this most recent generation *lan.* After *lan,* it will be *ius.* Not everyone inducted is the same age, and some Order members never find new members, while others find many. In the case of Uldon, Aldon, and Eldon, Dawsley found them all.

"I understand you came in through the east checkpoint. You have met two of your new brothers in your same generation: Nolan and Keelan. I'm sure you know whose mentor Keelan is, just by hearing his mouth," Gallowgrave gives Eldon a cockeyed grimace, but Eldon doesn't look the least bit reverent. "Nolan's mentor died in battle three equinoxes ago." Gallowgrave bows his head in respect. "So Nolan is his mentor's mentor's responsibility now."

"So, that means his mentor now is a *sley*," volunteers Magdonna.

"You catch on quick. Yes. His mentor is Beasley. He is our blacksmith, and Nolan has also taken up the trade. But don't always expect to do what your mentor does. There will be a time when you shall find your skill."

"What is Uldon's skill?" Magdonna asks curiously.

A light flashes in Gallowgrave's eye as he says, "Tracker. You can run, but you can't hide from Uldon."

Magdonna can't think of possessing any valuable skill. Maybe she will end up disappointing everyone. Uldon choosing her must be a mistake.

The doors slam open, and Magdonna jumps at the sound. Uldon's long steps carry him across the room in seconds. A wave of relief washes over her.

"We have a problem," Uldon says, getting down to business. "Dawsley is arranging a meeting." At that moment, a drum resonates loudly. "We must take our places." He turns his attention to Magdonna.

Eldon straightens and replies to an unspoken question, "She accepted, Uldon. You would be proud of your student, if you saw how quickly and bravely she took to her calling."

"There wasn't a doubt in my mind." He half smiles. "Come, Magdonna, your place is with me," says Uldon.

As she looks into his warm, brown eyes, just like the day she first met him, she knows deep down her place is with Uldon.

Uldon stands at attention next to Eldon and Aldon. Magdonna shifts awkwardly in front of him. Dawsley doesn't need to quiet all the men in the central stone tower. They know something is wrong and Dawsley has the answers. The members press shoulder to shoulder, trying to make the most of the limited space. The tower contains a sea of green and metal. Each member stands on the stairs facing the depression in the ground. Beside Gallowgrave's cauldron, Dawsley takes deep breaths, watching his men file in until at last, they all stand at attention.

"Men," he calls. "I have grave news. Elmore has died a valiant death." Murmurs of sadness and shock spread, but Dawsley continues even louder. "He was trying to conceal Kalrolin's Journal when a creature attacked him." The noise increases as he keeps talking and shouts above their voices. "The Journal is nowhere to be found and is believed to be in the hands of a creature. Be settled!" The room quiets. "We have one safeguard, which we placed equinoxes ago."

The space stills as they are taken aback by the news.

"Did you know about this?" Eldon asks Uldon, his face scrunched.

"From the looks of it, no one knew," Uldon replies.

Murmurs spread through the crowd.

"All is not lost," Dawsley continues. "But what is most disturbing of all, perhaps, is that Elmore knew something about his attack. Because his dying message was 'TRAITOR.'"

At that last word, the room falls silent once again. From the corner of their eyes, they scrutinize their companions. They can't believe someone they lived with, fought with, and spent every part of their day with would betray them.

—

"One among us is an ally of the creatures. We do not know who, why, or how this happened, but I tell you this now, we were prepared. We have outsmarted whoever is betraying our brotherhood. Trust me when I say we will find whoever it is, we will not show mercy, and he will regret the day he crossed his brothers." He lets the words hang in the air. His gaze shifts from face to face, as though he is hoping the traitor will crack under pressure. "You are dismissed, we will meet again."

Some leave more quickly than others, but everyone can feel the shift in The Order. Where there was once trust amongst each other, now a seed of suspicion has been sown. They exchange sharp glances around them. Even if one among them is not the traitor, they have been lied to by Dawsley about an unknown safeguard.

"We had a common enemy that kept us all brothers, but now, without that, who knows what is to become of us?" Uldon says.

Eldon has no words. His miserable expression says it all, as he claps Uldon on the shoulder before leaving the stone building. Only Gallowgrave, Uldon and Magdonna remain.

"If only you had come to us under less dire circumstances, Magdonna. We are going to have to retrieve the book. This is a dark time to be inducted into The Order," Uldon explains.   Uldon's permanently sad eyes catch Magdonna and he sees compassion and understanding.

"Nonetheless, you have accepted, and now it is my job to turn you into the great warrior I know you will be," Uldon continues.

Magdonna's face lights with excitement and something deep inside Uldon aches with melancholy.

Chapter 8

20 Equinoxes Later

"I think you are finally ready Warrick. It's been a long and hard road-"

"Twenty equinoxes."

"Has it been that long? I lost track."

Warrick hasn't lost track at all. For the Old One, this time had been an amusing little game. Warrick had endured equinoxes of imprisonment, forced submission, and virtual starvation. After a time, when the ancient creature believed him too weak to rebel, he let him help with his spells. It was then they noticed pages missing. The most formidable spells were torn from the middle to the end of the Journal. Kalrolin's most perfected spells were gone. Most importantly, the incantations the Old One needed to be free from imprisonment were all missing. The Old One launched a full-scale attack against The Order and all the Blood Ones for deceiving him. There had been a bitter fight ever since. The Darklanders acquired more ground and people were run out of the villages closest to the border. But the Green Cloaks were always one step ahead. And the Old One had taken his frustrations out on Warrick.

"Yes, Master."

Warrick runs his tongue across his flattened teeth and keeps his eyes on his new strange hands and feet. It had taken him a while to learn the transformation spell and even

---

longer for him to get use to the mechanics of his changed limbs. It wasn't enough the Old One took his freedom, but forced him to modify his face, his body and even the color of his skin.

"You have become such a loyal little pet. You will be going out on your own, and I trust you to do my work. Remember: I still own you."

"Of course, Master."

The Old One never lets Warrick forget that he owns him. He can inflict excruciating amounts of pain without having to be anywhere close to him. His eyes shoot over to the long braid of his own hair interwoven around a large staff.

"Bring me back the pages, and I will be all powerful and rule over all the Blood Ones. Then you may have your justice against the Green Cloaks."

Warrick takes to the skies, his revenge so close, he tastes it.

Uldon's ears are keen, to the ring of a blade slicing through the air. He dodges the edge that threatens to sever his arm clean off. He sidesteps again and swings his sword, blocking the next onslaught. He now faces his attacker. His eyes turn to steel, his concentration unwavering.

Elan smirks with haughty eyes. Lunging forward, Uldon feigns a straight attack but shifts left at the last possible moment. Elan dodges the sword, predicting his attack and grabs Uldon's wrist, twisting it back behind him. Uldon's sword crashes with a clunk to the ground. Pain shoots up his arm, and a groan escapes his lips.

Uldon stamps his heel down hard on her foot. She yelps, loosening her grip enough for Uldon to break free.

Breathing heavily, he ducks, grabbing his sword. He braces himself, now on equal footing with his attacker. They circle each other, swords before them. With wild fire, Uldon swings his sword, each strike more forceful than the last. Elan can't keep up, and Uldon's sheer strength causes her sword to fly into the air. Her breath catches in alarm, now defenseless. Uldon raises his free hand and beckons her to come at him again, daring her to attack.

Even unarmed, Elan charges with a guttural battle cry. In the blink of an eye, a slick dagger is pulled free from their sleeve. Uldon's complete surprise shakes his concentration. He has no time to defend himself as the point of the blade collides with his stomach. With just the force of the impact, he slams to the floor in total astonishment.

His adversary's mouth turns up in a smirk, holding out her calloused hand. Uldon gladly accepts it.

"That's the third time this week that you have beaten me, Elan."

"It's because I had excellent training," she says with a smile.

"Did Nolan make you this?" he wonders, picking up a clouded pewter dagger from the ground.

"Of course. It took him longer to dull it down for practice than it took to cast. He is making me a custom pair. He lost a bet... owes me a favor."

Uldon frowned. "Perhaps if you had a hidden dagger made for you earlier, you wouldn't have been left so defenseless." Sickening regret tugs on his chest every time he sees the eyepatch over Elan's face. Her eyes looked so deeply into his the day they first met; now only one returns his gaze. Neither one of them would ever forget her first battle against the creatures. She has a permanent reminder.

"I would lose my eye again if that meant it would save your life a second time."

She appraises him with such intensity; Uldon casts his eyes down and rubs his fingers. "Magdonna," Uldon squirms.

"Elan. It's Elan. That's the name you gave me. And it's been long enough so you should stop calling me by my old name," she protests but glances down at her feet, shrinking away from him. "I'm not a little girl anymore," she adds softly. "When are you going to see that?"

Elan meets his gaze, holding his eyes for much too long.

"Elan," Uldon breathes out too exhausted. His lips tighten, as if he would rather fight a thousand creatures to avoid a conversation long overdue. Uldon pulls away from her close proximity then looks at anything but her. Still at the corner of his eye, he can see her cave into herself and her cheeks stain pink.

"I'm going to Nolan to see if my daggers are ready." The tightening of her jaw tells Uldon she is going to give him the cold shoulder again. Elan practically sprints away.

He sighs, exasperated, running a hand down his face and slumping his shoulders.

The Order's land, once so confusing to Elan, now has a familiar flow. The fabrics covering the buildings tap against the stone. The oaclings walk in lines, going to and fro from their lessons. She nods casually at the other Order members passing by, making her way across the village to the blacksmith shop. Elan whips around the corner and with smooth steps sits on the large bench beside the blacksmith. The heat of the room is sweltering compared to the outside. Nolan wears a thick leather apron with black gloves. His skin shines with sweat as he stands beside a blazing flame puffing black smoke. The uneven cobblestone floor has weapons lined up, and more items hang from the wooden beams of the roof and walls. The iron glows as orange as the flames engulfing it. Over the years, Nolan's arms have become thick with muscles and burn scars. His blond curly hair flops forward over his river blue eyes as he works; the black tattooed symbols run down the back of his neck.

"Is it ready?"

"Good afternoon to you as well, Elan," Nolan chastises without taking his attention away from his work. "I do wonder at times if women had raised you, would you still be as brash."

"I'm not brash. I just like getting to the point." She smiles, but keeps her glance shrewd.

"Not long before you are forty equinoxes. Are you ready?"

Elan doesn't want to think about the eve of her fortieth equinox. She will be an adult in The Order's eyes. She touches the back of her bare neck, knowing it won't be like that for very long.

"Yes," Elan says. As much as she tries to hide it, her "yes" sounds more like an "I'm not sure."

Being an adult means she will be leaving headquarters, become a nomad for a time, and scout the land either for trespassing creatures or new members. Most had permanent places assigned to them, but not for the first few equinoxes. Uldon will be with her for a while, but then they will have to go their separate ways. They might send someone else to accompany her, or they might not be able to spare it. It is a lonely way of life, but necessary to have as many eyes and ears out in the land as possible.

The deadliest, most hardened Order members go to the Darklands. She knows for sure she would not be assigned there. The ones who stay in those cursed lands Elan has only seen a few times. They spend their lives hidden in the gray terrain. When they report back, it is brief, and they leave as quickly as they come. Their will and souls are as hard and fearsome as the creatures themselves. Many die or those who return for good are badly injured, never to be the same physically or mentally.

—

Retired members spend quiet days relaxing, helping teach oacling classes or running menial tasks and errands. They are free to do whatever they wish with their time, but mostly they like to gamble and tell tall tales of their glory days to new oaclings who sit listening with awe.

Nolan would never know the struggles of being a nomad. As a blacksmith, he needs to stay at headquarters. But it must be lonely for him as well. Everyone else will leave him behind. Keelan already left but still comes back from time to time. He is always quick to come back when he knows there is a victory party.

Nolan's large, blue eyes try to meet Elan's single shifting one.

"Elan?" croaks Ylmore as he approaches. "You're here again? You might as well have taken up being a blacksmith with as often as you hang around this place."

Elan gets up immediately to give Ylmore a seat. His bones crack as he settles in. "I'm such an old man. I can't even cross the main buildings without getting winded. Ah, to be your age again, Elan. To be almost near the eve of my fortieth equinox! I remember being so excited to go out on my own. I will never forget my greatest battle." With a swoop of his robe, he exposes his sunken, boney torso covered in scars. Elan can't hide the disgust on her face. "It was one hundred and twenty equinoxes ago. The night was black as pitch-"

"I think you might have told us this story before," Nolan interrupts. "Doesn't it sound familiar, Elan?"

"Yes, it does ring a bell," Elan says with a tone far too polite.

Ylmore *humphs* at them both as he covers himself again, gets up from the bench, and manages to teeter out.

The sword Nolan hammers sizzles as he tosses it into the cold water. He walks to a small wooden table at the far end of the room. Elan can't help but creep up behind him, a hint of a smile at the corners of her mouth. Nolan carefully unfolds a small piece of tattered, gray fabric holding two daggers. Elan's breath catches as she gazes at the metallic

—

45

knives shining from the firelight. They are buffed into a lustrous polish, sleek and small. Her hand shoots right to them. Just as she suspects, perfectly weighted.

"You are an artist, Nolan."

She can't stop staring at them.

"They are one of my better creations," he says, standing straighter than before. "These are not just any daggers, Elan. I used the metal from old crests to make them."

The idea is both morbid and intriguing. When a member of The Order dies in battle, the brothers do their best to remove the crests so that whatever magic that makes them work does not fall into the hands of the creatures. Elan often wondered what they did with thousands of generations of crests. Certainly, they were recycled. That means the metal used for these daggers holds the magic of Kalrolin. Her eye becomes wide, wanting to try them.

"It must have taken you forever to make them. I know I won a bet, but this is much finer work than I expected."

"Consider it a birthday gift," Nolan says.

"Thank you. They are a much better gift than I deserve."

"I wouldn't say that," Nolan says, barely audible.

"It's nearly half day. They should all be in the auditorium by now. You must be tired, hammering metal since daybreak."

Nolan nods just as Beasley enters.

Beasley and Nolan exchange polite head nods. Nolan places his hammer down on the anvil with a clang. "Elan and I are going to the arena, Beasley. We shall meet again."

Beasley's girth does not leave much room for the two to stay anyway. He swings his arms and belly around, trying to make his way through the clutter. Sweat gathers on his bald head. He nods at Nolan then he gives Elan a crinkly, nearly toothless smile as they go.

They walk to the building in complete silence. The blacksmith shop occupies a spot close to the arena and armory for efficiency.

The arena looms enormous, built of stone, and constructed longer than it is wide. Weapons are mounted on the walls beneath high windows that let in light. A few fires always burn in hearths receding into the walls. Barrels, targets and an elaborate obstacle course pack the inside. An older oacling cranks a handle with gears for moving targets. They spin and dive, mimicking the movements of a creature. The air permeates with the musky scent of bodies in motion. They kick up debris as they walk around the hay-strewn floors of the building.

Elan and Nolan stroll to their usual corner. Their friends have already settled into the spot as if they had been there all day. Lelan and Jordon weigh the weapons in their hands, inspecting each one with critical evaluation. Tresdon leans lazily against the wall, adorned in haphazardly placed armor. His playful eyes twinkle with amusement. A smile stays on his lips while he crunches on an apple.

"Tresdon," Nolan says, surprised. "I thought you weren't to report back for another day."

"I'm not," he says between swallows of food he snatched from the food tents, "If you see Dawsley, I was never here."

Elan sighs at her hopeless friend.

Lelan drops his sword and confronts Tresdon. He straightens his back, lifting his chin, trying to get the most out of his less than average height. Lelan's brooding hazel eyes bore into Tresdon's, "How could you even say things like that? You should have stayed at your station a day longer and reported to Dawsley the moment you came in. You're violating procedure and disgracing us all. The members of The Order of Kalrolin have dignity, honor-"

"And most have a total disregard for personal hygiene," interrupts Tresdon dramatically, holding his nose.

Everyone except Lelan bursts into laughter.

47

As much as Elan agrees with Lelan, she doesn't support him. She won't allow it to go to his head. If she encourages him, he will go off on how her armor isn't worn to regulation or her eyepatch isn't straight enough. Lelan is the only one Elan knows in The Order that listens to Ylmore's repeated stories with rapt attention.

Jordon doesn't take his focus off his blade as he speaks, "Lelan, you are lower in rank, so that is no way to talk to a superior. You should know that more than anyone. And Tresdon, you should have waited an extra day. Our mentor taught us better than that. You shouldn't disgrace his memory. The least you can do is let Dawsley know you are here before he finds out on his own."

Lelan pouts, grumbling something under his breath. Tresdon rubs the back of his neck and has the decency to turn pink with shame.

Jordon is always the voice of reason in their group. The only one that lets Lelan know to calm down his hot temper, to convince Tresdon and Keelan not to let a wild boar loose in the oacling rooms, to patiently show Elan for more times than she can count how to properly skin a rabbit. Elan suspects that out of anyone else one day he will lead The Order.

Tresdon smirks, "Got to love these rules! I am younger than Lelan but higher in rank! Maybe I should order you to do a few laps around the arena, huh?"

Lelan bursts out, "That's not the way it works and you know it!"

Elan stops laughing and whips out her dagger, pointing it at Nolan who had been sneaking up behind her. "Don't – even– think– about it."

"Putting that dagger I gave you to good use already. Good to know." Nolan smiles.

Eldon's laugh booms from behind them, making Elan jump as he struts over.

"What are you doing here, Tresdon? Aren't you supposed to report tomorrow?" Eldon asks, shaking his finger in mock disapproval.

"With all of the members in The Order, how does everyone know exactly when I'm due back?"

Before Lelan shoots Tresdon a smart remark, the war drums roll.

Chapter 9

"Elan, get to Aldon's left flank and Eldon on the right! Serdon, Nolan, and Kingsley, fan out when we get to the village. Uldon, stay close to me," Dawsley orders. "Mosley, you know the land. The smoke signal came from the south by the River Weeds."

"That's only a few lengths from here," Uldon says.

"They are getting closer to our headquarters and stronger and their numbers are increasing." Dawsley appraises his few companions, with a wary gaze. Ever since the book had been stolen he always had a hint of suspicion behind his eyes.

For equinoxes, they'd monitored every brother, interrogated and searched, but were no closer to finding the traitor. One thing was for sure, however: he still dwelt within their company. The creatures knew too much about their plans and hideouts. Many had died because of the treacherous man who leaked their information. At the very least, Elan suspected Dawsley knew who the traitors weren't. He had only told select members the location of the hidden pages. They hadn't been discovered yet.

"Elan, stay close to me," Uldon orders.

Elan nods once but her heart beats twice as fast. It is not only the battle upsetting her, but also the threat of losing Uldon. The crests protect them, but only so far. They can't bring someone back from the dead.

They ride over the land on the jet-black horses of The Order, rushing to the small town being terrorized by the creatures. The thrum of the hooves beats hard against the lush terrain.

The smoke billows high above fires burning the village's houses to the ground. Screams of people and metallic roars of the creatures ring through the air. They kick at their horses' side to go faster, and the beat of Elan's heart mirrors the weighty stampede of the stallions.

Elan spies dozens of large muscled creatures gliding overhead. Their ebony wings spread wide as they circle the village like a dark cloud. With one hand holding the reins, she draws her sword.

Two Order members stationed in the village have sweat beading down their brow. Their sword arms shake, and their green robes are stained with splashes of red. Creatures continuously dive down at the men, slashing claws, and snapping teeth.

Women and children run for cover as men try to fight the Darklanders off. Blood spills from between fingers clutching their necks, others lay dead on the ground. One creature is so busy terrorizing the village that he doesn't even notice the Green Cloaks coming. Elan and Uldon ride to the aid of Order members. Elan's sword rises high as the wind pulls on her face. With one quick swipe, her blade slices one of the flying creatures. Her eardrums almost burst from the roar erupting out of the creature's elongated snout. Her horse bucks back, but she holds on tight.

"Thank Kalrolin, you arrived," one of the Order members says, gasping for air.

"You can give us thanks later when we win," Uldon cries, already dashing away to fight more creatures.

The creatures don't need weapons; their razor sharp claws and piercing teeth wreak more than enough damage. The fact that they are also much bigger than her own race gives them another advantage. Elan refuses to believe the old stories claiming the Darklanders were once men.

Something solid slams Elan across the face with such force that stars burst in front of her eyes. Her ears ring as the village spins so fast she nearly falls from her saddle. A

—

creature laughs wickedly. Its long hair and sharp teeth drip crimson as it flaps around her. It propels a giant arm and her armor screeches as it claws her shoulder. Acting on instinct, Elan spins her sword, whipping it around severing the hand that moments ago scratched her armor, it now thuds sickly to the ground. The creature bellows, tucking his wrist hard against his chest and takes to the air, leaving a trail of red.

"Elan," Uldon calls. "Help that family!"

A female creature descends, trying to steal bags of grain, clawing at a frightened man and his cowering wife and children. The children wail, tears streaking down their cheeks as their father has nothing but a rake to defend them.

Bounding toward the creature, Elan lifts her sword high above her head and stands in the stirrups to get more height. The blade soars through the air. Elan rips the creature's wing, and the creature crashes to the ground with a painful scream. Elan swings her leg around the horse, sliding off the saddle. As the beast lurches up, Elan sees that the brawny female towers almost an oxenlow tail taller than herself. She swipes her massive clawed hand, and Elan jumps back, just in time to feel the force of the air brush pass her stomach.

The creature advances toward Elan. Though she dodges, a claw catches Elan's wrist. This time the Darklandian successfully knocks the sword from her grasp. Elan drops to her knees, and the mud-soaked ground saturates her pants. Her elbow hits hard into the back of the creature's knee, causing her to lose balance and fall. Elan crawls through the muck groping for her sword. But the female creature snatches and pulls Elan's ankle, holding her in place. The beast gleefully twists. A lightning bolt of hot pain shoots up Elan's leg as she stifles a scream.

"Your blood will taste like sweet victory," the female growls.

Elan's heart pounds. The rusty scent of blood on the creature's breath slithers across her face. Elan pats her sleeves, trying to release the daggers from the holder. She pauses, hearing a sickening crunch and squish. The creature's face falls as a sword bursts from her chest.

Uldon stands, shaking with rage. His expression breaks at his mud-soaked oacling. Relief has never felt so euphoric as she watches the daylight reflect off of his mask. Uldon hoists Elan up from the mud, throwing her arm around his shoulders. He puts his own sword in his holster while he retrieves hers from the ground. Heat runs up the back of her neck as Uldon carries her to safety. The creatures flee in cowardice one by one. The chaotic sounds of the fight begin to die down, leaving silence in their wake.

Elan wants to protest that she is not a weakling and she can walk. Embarrassment tightens her throat. Uldon lowers her on a small patch of grass.

"Are you alright?"

"Yes. I can walk. She didn't break it. It's just twisted. I could have handled myself back there, Uldon," she defends.

Uldon shuts his eyes tight. His face pales, shaking his head.

"She had you. She could have killed you, Elan. This is all my fault. I-"

Uldon stops abruptly, and the hair on her neck rises. Something is amiss. The wind picks up, and the temperature drops. The grass on the ground crackles with static. Her feet and fingertips prickle with some unknown change in atmosphere. The remaining creatures must feel it too because the sky clears as the clouds overhead dim. The clouds swirl then spiral. Something in the distance descends from the shadows.

Elan's eye widens, and Uldon turns swiftly to scan the horizon. Elan blinks faster, trying to clear her vision. She beholds a being she has never seen before, hovering close to them.

A man with ink black wings glides between the clouds. Elan's jaw drops, and her lips tremble. In the pit of her stomach, fear coils. This being is neither a man nor a creature, but something in between. His hair and irises shine blacker than the stallions they ride. A thick leather belt around his hips holds tattered pants in place. His flawless body radiates as though a light glows beneath his skin. His teeth and ears aren't pointed like a creature's. Almond shaped eyes set deep in an intense face stares at them, menacing and cold. His bat-like wings expand to their full capacity. He has feet instead of the large talons. He stretches long thin fingers, with nails instead of sharp claws. His most unearthly feature is his hands, sparking the way Nolan's metal does when hammered.

"What is that?" Elan asks. Elan stands up, hardly noticing the bolt of pain in her left ankle.

"Whatever it is, I don't think it's on our side." Uldon draws his sword. He catches the eyes of the other members, they don't need words. This demon needs to die. Elan takes labored breaths as her body tightens like a coiled spring. She clutches the ground beside her until her fingers brush the leather hilt.

Every citizen in town backs away or takes cover, trying to save their hides. The Order members draw their weapons, keeping them at the ready. They don't move, silent with trepidation.

The glowing man chuckles at their confusion. He quivers his hands ever so slightly, and the ground beneath them rumbles, cracking, and breaking. They stumble, muscles tense, and disbelieving, as the land shifts. One member runs at the strange man screwing up his face. He stops as though he has collided with an invisible wall. The man's sword falls from his grip and he grabs his chest suddenly, falling to the grass, spitting blood.

The rest of The Order members quickly turn from stunned silence to burning hate. They sprint in unison, advancing with swords raised. The ground shudders even more, but it does not deter their path. With great agility, Elan flies over the terrain.

He is so close. Elan can see every detail of his striking face. He smiles without humor, lifting his hands then pushing his palms out. A ripple of power bursts forward.

54

They are flung back with thunderous force, slamming into the ground. Elan pushes up, her body aching. She scrambles up once again to attack the glowing man, but her feet stop dead in their tracks. Panicked, Elan looks to her brothers for help, but just like her, the souls of their boots refuse to lift from the grass. Some drop their swords beside them as they pull at their legs, willing them to move, but they don't budge.

The powerful being snaps his hand back, and their swords fly away. He takes his time, as though savoring their powerlessness. He closes his hands into fists as crushing unbearable pain surges through her body. Elan grits her teeth, taking deep, steadying breaths, trying to stop convulsing. Some cry out, others won't give the sorcerer the satisfaction.

"I have a message for you," he begins. "Give the Old One the pages to Kalrolin's Journal or prepare for us to take more prisoners. We will no longer show you mercy by merely killing you."

A flash of light reflects from Uldon's metal mask seems to catch his attention. He pauses. Recognition crosses his face. As the odd sorcerer opens his hands, the pain dissipates.

Uldon averts his eyes, panic-stricken.

The ethereal man's feet touch the ground silently, tentatively creeping to Uldon.

Elan's breath hurries as she notices this creature singling out Uldon. The thing steps closer to him and she panics. Like a wild animal, she tugs at her legs to get free as he glides closer to Uldon. Then Elan stands straight as an idea forms. She pulls at the holders under her sleeve. A sigh of relief escapes her lips. Her daggers have not flown away like the swords.

The strange being's eyes rake over Uldon, transfixed.

Elan forces her hand to steady. If she misses, that thing will kill her and Uldon instantly.

His side is exposed as he leans in closer to Uldon and folds back his wings. His long-fingered hand grabs Uldon's

—

55

chin. Jerking his face from side to side, the expression of confusion shifts to understanding.

Uldon struggles, hitting the winged man with fists and trying to pull away. But this being is too strong. The strikes might as well be a soft caress.

The strange man's chest expands as he inhales. His nostrils flare, and his head pulls back. His features twist in revulsion. He tightens his grip, and an ear-shattering roar erupts deep inside him. His eyes turn red.

Elan throws out her arm, flicking her wrist. It whistles, flying to its target and hits him straight and true. Elan's eyebrows lift in disbelief.

A jolt of confusion stops the winged man. He whips around to his side, finding the source that disrupted him. His blood streaks down his left side. He gapes at the small knife sunk deep into his side. His mouth opens wide, as his eyes bulge. His chin lifts, following the angle of the dagger right to her.

Heat and rage swirl behind Elan's eyes, but also triumph. Her arm remains frozen after delivering the landing blow. Her body tenses with anticipation. She studies his every move for the smallest indication of what he might do. She doesn't even care what happens to her so long as his attention is no longer on Uldon.

He takes a step in her direction but staggers. Another rivet of blood rolls down his side and to his thigh. Grabbing the handle, he pulls. His muscles coil with the effort but it doesn't budge. With each passing moment, blood pours from him. His eyes glaze over and he blinks slowly. All his power seems to drain from his body. The spell keeping each of The Order members in place weakens, as he shakes his head like he is trying to stay awake.

Elan feels lighter as she wills herself to move to fight back.

The sorcerer forgets about Uldon and he takes his chance to run. But the smallest stir of the air causes the sorcerer to turn toward him again. Roaring in protest, he throws out his hand and strikes Uldon. His mask is hurled into the air and lands far away from him. The Order members take advantage of his distraction and close in.

The monster can't stay. He has lost too much blood, he stumbles back. His wings spread wide, with one giant swoop, he flies away.

Some run to the bleeding Order member, but Elan runs to Uldon, falling before him and embracing him in her arms. Her throat closes and her words are strangled.

"Uldon, please wake! Uldon, you can't leave me! Wake!"

The Order members watch in silence as she clings to him. She sees his face without the mask for the first time. It is a grizzly sight. Chunks of flesh had been clawed off his pink face. He has no eyebrow, and his right eye is misshapen. Elan's body shakes as she tries to hold back her tears. Her head spins, turning her stomach sick. She had never cried in front of anyone while in The Order. She didn't cry when they burned the crest into her skin at only twenty equinoxes old. She had not cried her first day before battle or even when she lost her eye. She could stay strong for anything, except losing Uldon.

Chapter 10

Warrick's wings strain to carry him to the center of The Darklands. It takes too much effort, he has lost too much blood. He drank from a lone drifter on the way to The Darklands, but the wound drained him almost at once. If he doesn't improve, he will have to travel the rest of the way on foot.

Warrick's mind reels with the events that had taken place. He knew the man in the mask. That Green Cloak did not recognize Warrick, but Warrick knew him. He had to go back to their land and finish him. All of Warrick's life had been building to this pivotal moment.

His breathing labors as he staggers across the gray terrain. The floor beneath him tilts. Warrick knows if it were not for the magic coursing through him, he would be dead. He pushes to go a little farther without rest. Stopping anywhere would leave Warrick exposed to every danger in The Darklands.

Finally collapsing against one of the knotted trees, he succumbs to weakness. With urgency, he pulls at the weapon lodged in his side. But the dagger won't yield. Gritting his teeth, he tries again. A groan of anguish rips from his mouth. He pulls until it finally slides from him.

Warrick turns the tiny object that had inflicted so much damage. He had surrounded himself with the dark spells he'd learned from the Old One. Nothing should have been able to penetrate the barrier protecting him, yet this tiny blade had. Examining the metal, he can feel the electric hum of sorcery from it.

If it can glide past the Old One's darkest magic, then the metal holds Kalrolin's power. Warrick mumbles a few incantations over his wound, and his skin does not knit back together as wholly as he intends. All of his weight leans into the tree trunk, allowing himself a few more moments of rest. His injury stops bleeding, but exhaustion seeps into his bones. A wicked idea crosses Warrick's mind, as he clutches the dagger. The bat wings beat against the air, lifting from the ground once more.

Elan sits by Uldon's cot all day. She doesn't leave to eat or rest. She stays, wanting to see his sad brown eyes again. Something inside her broke on the battlefield, and she doesn't know if she will ever go back to normal. Elan distracts her mind by counting her every breath. She prepares herself to stay as long as it takes until Uldon wakes. She studies him with longing. What would she do without him? Elan can't bear the thought of him never waking up. Many times she wanted to reach out and hold his hand, but restrained herself. She had already bared too much of her soul on the battlefield. Her open display of affection had earned her criticism from other Order members. At the time, she had hardly noticed it, but now she restrained herself, hyperaware of their judgment.

Uldon's eyes flutter open. Elan jumps, leaning in, trying to detect any damage.

His expression warms as he sees her grief-stricken face.

"How are you feeling?" she asks breathlessly.

"I've been better," Uldon whispers weakly. He notices the familiar single window and dark brown curtain to his tiny quarters. Cool metal rests against his face.

Elan grins widely. The relief is so complete, she thinks tears might slip away again, but holds them back.

"I thought I had lost you."

"It will take more than that to kill us, Magdonna. We still have Kalrolin's protection."

Elan's eye darkens at the sound of her old name once again. Her stomach falls to her feet. Magdonna was the name of the little girl she was, not the woman she is now. Uldon props his body up on his elbows as he lies in bed.

"Uldon, I couldn't stop thinking about if that battle was going to be the last time I spoke to you."

Uldon sighs, closing his eyes, and shudders. "Every battle I fear losing you. If you died, how would I go on living?" He gazes at Elan with a mix of hurt and grief.

A shock of lighting and a rush of euphoria sweeps through Elan. She sits, awestruck at what she heard. The words had come from Uldon, but Elan felt like he drew those exact feelings from her heart. After his touch with the great beyond, he finally sees her. The room is bitter cold, but heat spreads from her chest. He feels the same way about her. She knows it. Nervous and dizzy with joy, she leans in, wanting to take his hands in hers.

"The guilt would kill me," Uldon forces out.

As quickly as the elation appeared, it evaporates. Her happiness drops like a stone. Her ears burn and a wave of shame chokes her. All-consuming darkness replaces where her heart should be.

"Your guilt?" she asks. Her voice is weak.

"I wish every day that I had never met you. I keep thinking if I had just ridden straight through your town, or if you hadn't seen me when I entered the eatery, you could be leading a normal life now."

She pulls in air. Her throat closes, and her lungs struggle.

"How can you say these things, Uldon?" The words come as barely a whisper. "I have no regrets about the day we met. I wouldn't be leading a normal life if I stayed in town with that woman. Being with you and The Order has made me happier than I have ever been in my whole life." She swallows. Elan has never felt so vulnerable before. She has never been this honest with anyone. Elan can't understand why loving Uldon hurts so much.

His brown eyes glisten with tragedy.

"Uldon, I-"

"Don't speak, Elan."

He says it with such command it feels like a slap to her face.

"If you go on, you must remember that whatever you say, you cannot take back. You threaten everything that we are to each other. Is that what you want? Things will never be the same between us."

Biting down on the inside of her cheek, she holds her tongue. Why can't Uldon love her more than just his oacling? Their relationship could change for the better if he loved her and she would be glad for it, never to go back to the way they were.

For the first time, Elan realizes for certain Uldon can never return her affections. The devastation leaves her reeling. She didn't know pain existed worse than an injury received in battle. No pain can quite match its tenor. She controls her expression with immense effort. Elan can't stand to be around him a moment longer and wants to hide with embarrassment. She refuses to crack in front of Uldon and shows no weakness. In his eyes, she must seem pathetic, and she doesn't want pity.

"Very well then, Uldon. We shall meet again."

Elan walks briskly from his quarters, almost running away from the dwelling of her brothers. She pulls her hood above her head, covering her face in shadows. Other Order members walk past her, she tries to keep her face hidden. There is no place to go, and no horses to flee. She goes past the center of The Order's town and does not stop until she reaches the river. On the outskirts of their domain, grass and trees remain unaltered by civilization. No Order member has any need to be so far from the buildings. The watchtowers stand in the distance.

The fertile soil of the riverbed nourishes the grass, it grows almost as tall as Elan's waist. She disappears into it, her cloak the same color as the ground. Her knees buckle beneath her, and she hangs her head, taking shelter in the weeds. Elan hugs her knees to her body. A small sigh of pain escapes her chapped lips. For a little while, she can be invisible. Maybe they won't find her for a long time, or perhaps this pain growing inside her will swallow her whole, so she doesn't have to return to Uldon's rejection.

Eldon barges into Uldon's room as if he owns the space. His massive body fills half of Uldon's tiny sleeping quarters, but he pushes himself in anyway.

"It's good to see you awake."

Eldon's smile doesn't reach his eyes, and right away Uldon reads his trepidation.

"Just cut to the news, Eldon. It's written all over your face. There was a meeting without me, wasn't there?"

Eldon squirms like an overgrown guilt-ridden child, "Yes."

"Why didn't you wait until I was awake? Or perhaps you thought I would not?"

Lines of worry dominate Eldon's usual buoyant expression. He pauses for a long moment, looks outside the curtain to his room and leans in, speaking more quietly this time, "What happened on the field today bodes most unfortunate for you."

"What do you mean?"

"Because of today's events, some believe you to be the traitor."

"What?!" Uldon screams.

Eldon hushes his brother, continuing to speak low and rushed.

"The strange creature with the great power... he seemed to know you, Uldon. He even walked right up to you. Now, Mosley was the most adamant in believing you are the traitor. He said that the creature with powers must have recognized you somehow because you were conspiring with the Old One."

"That's insanity," Uldon yells, outraged, his eyes large.

Eldon clasps a dirty hand over Uldon's mouth to stop him from shouting.

"Now what's more insane is the fact that others agreed with him. Serdon piped up saying that you had to have been on the creature's side because none of us had ever seen him before, so how would he know you."

Eldon looked over his shoulder again, leaning in more so that Uldon could smell the drink on his breath.

"He also asked how you were still alive. He could have destroyed you with all his power, yet he just struck you. Nolan, Aldon and I defended you, of course. Dawsley had enough sense to quiet us all down and told us not to speak of it again. Nolan and I wanted to warn you, but it was a direct order from Dawsley not to tell you. But I had to tell you. Everyone seemed on the verge of rebellion. They may have been trying to discredit you. There has been so much talk about Dawsley's successor that they may have wanted to take you out of the running. Either way, I would watch your back from now on, Uldon."

"How could my brothers turn on me so quickly?" Uldon finally says after Eldon apparently believes it safe to remove his hand.

"These are dark days, when we can't trust each other." Eldon shakes his head. "Dawsley went to talk to Gallowgrave to see what we can do now. This new creature is a real threat. We have to stop it, now, and Gallowgrave might have a plan."

Both remain silent, the room thick with tension.

"So, tell me, why *did* he recognize you?" Eldon's expression shifts between suspicion and self-loathing.

"I don't know."

"You can trust me, Uldon. Have you met before?"

"I have never seen him before!" Uldon shouts. His blood boils at the thought that even Eldon doesn't believe him. Uldon can see the slight squint of Eldon's eyes and how he stands a little farther back than before. He feels a well of hopelessness, even his very best friend seems to have doubts.

"Where is Elan?" Eldon asks suddenly, as his eyebrows raise and his face lights. "I thought for sure she would still be here. She didn't come to the meeting because she refused to leave your side. You raised a fine oacling. She was quick with those daggers. If it hadn't been for her then we would have been in serious trouble."

Uldon suspects Elan slipped away to the river. She'd liked to go there as a child and often wandered to that spot when she needed to think.

His insides wrestle with a wide range of feelings for her. When he looks at her, he sees the little girl in the village and hurts for her. Guilt plagues him, he wonders if he had done anything unintentionally to cause her infatuation. He hates himself for adding to her troubles.

Right now, he does not have time to think about it. The attacks in their lands take precedence. A creature unlike he has ever seen threatens them, and he faces accusations of being a traitor. She will eventually get over him, he hopes, for both of their sakes. And Uldon wonders if they could ever go back to the comfortable relationship they once had.

—

64

Chapter 11

The Old One has been waiting far longer than he should have to. His features twist in an angry grimace as he decides, Warrick needs reminding of who is in charge. He stumbles over to his cauldron, where a long staff is propped up beside it. A long braid of raven-black hair twists around the top. Clutching the staff, malicious intent sparks in the Old One's eyes.

The aged creature sighs with melancholy when he hears the thud of two feet hitting the ground. The familiar pacing of Warrick's steps echoes in the stone temple.

Warrick wraps his wings around himself, covering his wound. He knows that the Old One expects Warrick to have a few scratches from battle, but he would be suspicious of the severity of that one.

"You certainly cut it close. Next time I expect you to be quicker about returning."

"My apologies, Master. There were a few more cloaked ones than I had estimated."

The Old One's eyes widen. "I thought so. He wasn't lying to me after all," he says, pondering the idea. He muses to himself, ignoring Warrick. "There is a reason there were more members, Warrick," the Old One finally says aloud. "We were right on top of their headquarters. I didn't send you directly there in case it was a trap. With all your training, I knew you were more than capable of handling yourself."

Warrick's heart races beneath a calm exterior. The Old One had sent him, aware of the dangers, without a single warning. Warrick's jaw clenches.

"Of course, Master."

The Old One turns. Warrick toys with the idea of attacking him now. He imagines the sound of the Old One's neck snapping. His eyes blaze, murderous.

"I am quite unhappy with you, Warrick. Most unhappy. With all your power, you have not gotten me a single page, nor have you brought me back a prisoner. At the very least you should have brought a single green cloaked one, so I could question them."

Some followers of the Old One had brought back Green Cloaks before to be questioned. He felt no pity for their suffering. Besides the fact that he found the Green Cloaks loathsome, they received treatment no worse than what Warrick had already endured at the hands of the Old One. Better them, than the wizard turn his wrath on him.

The Old man walks over to his staff. As Warrick's stomach knots, he knows what's in store for him. "You might need some reminding that you must do much better to impress me."

Warrick will not be harmed again. Now is his only chance. Warrick falls to one knee, his head bowed and his hands on the ground. Warrick's sizeable right hand conceals the tiny dagger hidden there.

"Master, I have brought you something, a gift. May I give it to you before I receive my punishment?" His tongue stiffens in his mouth. He must remain calm so as to not give the Old One any cause for suspicion.

Warrick knows his position of subservience will please The Old One. He had to witness the Old One's perverse delights in his ability to break a creature's will.

—

"Yes, my pet. What have you brought me?"

The Old One stands in front of Warrick, placing a hand on his head. Warrick's hand curls around the dagger, his heart pumping in his chest. He only has one chance. If he gets caught, he will be tortured to death. He will take the risk, if it means freedom. Quick as lightning, Warrick jabs his arm out, under the Old One's breastbone. The point of the dagger slices effortless into his flesh.

Blood sprays out, and the Old One has hardly enough time to express his shock before Warrick stands, pressing the knife deeper, cutting to his heart. Warrick's hands bathe in scarlet. He would have never believed a dagger holding Kalrolin's magic could inflict so much ruin. The Old One's protective spells and power drain as quickly as his blood.

The surprise on the Old One's face, shoots a thrill through Warrick. Many equinoxes he dreamed of this moment. The Old One is helpless in his hands. Euphoric pride and amazement swells in him as the tables have turned. This powerful creature, older than legend, comes to ruin by his hands.

"Never again will you control me, you old madman."

Warrick allows him to fall to the ground, gasping and bleeding out. The Old One will not live. The dagger pierced his heart. Warrick runs to the staff. He snaps it over his knee, with a wicked grin. If the Old One were not dying, Warrick would never have been able to even touch the staff. Warrick spits on the ground where the Old One struggles.

Before leaving the stone temple, he quickly snatches the leather-bound book, eager to escape. The Old One lies in a pool of his blood, which is increasingly getting larger.

Warrick savors the scene before him, his vengeance temporarily satiated, watching him writhe. Now he can pursue the vendetta that has haunted him, most of his life. With the knowledge of where the Green Cloaks live, Warrick plots to return.

He spares one last glance at the dying creature before him, enjoying his pain and defeat. But he will see a much more significant enemy dead before the end of the day.

The great drum pounds across the lands. Its particular rhythm calls all members to a meeting. Eldon walks into the infamous stone building with Uldon. Those in battle that day give Uldon mixed expressions ranging from anger to pity. Everyone but the watch guards and Elan attend. Just as Uldon starts to think that perhaps she won't be coming at all, she enters through the doors. Her place is beside Uldon, but she instead finds Nolan and accompanies him.

From where Uldon stands, he notices her face, hard and expressionless.

Dawsley stands in front of all his men, holding out both of his palms for silence. The few conversations with hushed voices stop at once.

"I am sure that word has gotten around about our battle in the village by the River Weeds. We are facing a threat greater than we have encountered in a long time. The Old One has taken himself a student. We don't know who or what he is, only that he possesses great dark sorcery. He is neither man nor creature, but something in between. If it were not for the protection of Kalrolin's crest, then two of our members would be dead."

Uldon notices Elan almost turns her head to look over at him, but doesn't.

"This meeting was called so that all will know about this new being's existence and to warn you all to take extra caution. Beware of a thing as pale as lunya light with wings of a Darklandian. His hair and eyes are blacker than the evilest of hearts. Gallowgrave is going to do his best to protect us."

Gallowgrave bows his head as he stands by his bubbling cauldron. "We will send word to those out in the land. Be safe. Don't take unnecessary risks. We will meet again."

Elan watches people disperse, causing Dawsley to weave through the crowd to get to Uldon, Aldon, and Eldon. Elan observes Dawsley pushing his way to their ranks.

"Nolan, I must go. We will meet again," Elan yells over her shoulder.

"We will meet again," repeats Nolan, sputtering apprehensively and blinking rapidly.

Dawsley clicks his tongue. "You should have been with your mentor, Elan."

"My deepest apologies." She bows once out of respect.

"Aldon, Eldon, Uldon, and Elan, please come with me." They follow obediently, walking deeper into the room toward Gallowgrave and his cauldron as the last of The Order members leave.

"Gallowgrave, if you would not mind?"

At Dawsley's request, Gallowgrave mumbles a few words. He dips his fingers into the bubbling liquid before him, but it does not burn him. Lifting his hands out again, he spreads his fingers, and a wave of power brushes past them. A goopy, yellow, opaque substance covers the walls and ceiling.

"I don't know who I can trust anymore," Dawsley begins. "But I believe that I can trust my oaclings. What we talk about now never leaves this room. Gallowgrave has sealed us off from the outside. No one can come in or hear us. I didn't want to tell everyone else in The Order, but we are in serious trouble, more than we have ever been before. Please tell them what you told me."

Gallowgrave nods his head. They listen intently as if the words from Gallowgrave hold their fate.

"If The Old One has taken a student then it could mean the end of The Order. The Old One's dark magic is second to Kalrolin's magic, but that is all. Even the magic I create will never be as strong. We had a fighting chance because the Old One was weak from his confrontation with Kalrolin and did not have the book. But now with the book and with a student who can roam freely, this new being will almost be impossible to destroy. He can be injured or weakened, but it will take so much more to kill him. The best we can do is to contain him."

"What do you mean by that?" Eldon demands.

"We can use his magic and his strength against him. We can use a binding spell that binds him to The Darklands forever. It is a binding spell similar to what was used to entrap the Old One to the stone temple. Those that are sorcerers are conductors for magic and can bend it to their will. Anyone can make a spell or a potion but if you are not born a conductor you will never be able to do anything with it. Some are stronger conductors than others. This new being is like a blazing beacon. This spell will cause his magic only to be directed in one specific place. Instead of being able to conduct his magic out, it will be used like a rope to create the bond."

"No," Uldon says. "That's not good enough. He deserves worse than to be bound to his own home. I say we bind him to the caves those monsters killed Elmore in. He will have to live in the place where The Book was stolen and Elmore was viciously murdered. He won't see his land ever again. And what's best is he will slowly starve, taking equinoxes to die. There is no animal other than the crows that go to those caves. He toyed with us on that battlefield as though our lives meant nothing."

"I agree," Aldon says. "If we bind him to The Darklands he can still conspire with the Old One. If he is in the caves, we can make sure no creature ever comes near him."

"You are right. We shall bind him to the caves. It's a fitting punishment," Dawsley confirms.

Elan speaks up, "How are we going to get him on our lands and to those caves? Unless he is ordered there by his master, he has no reason to go there again."

"He will have reason to go if there is something there that he wants," Dawsley says. "Like perhaps the missing pages to Kalrolin's Journal."

Understanding crosses their faces.

Dawlsey stiffens.

"We still have a spy in our ranks. What if it accidentally slips that some of the pages were hidden deep in those caves? We could start a false rumor. The traitor will go back to the Old One, and he will send that new creature of his to go and retrieve them. We only need to watch and wait for him. We can get teams to watch the mouth of the caves and ambush him. We can put-"

Before Dawsley can finish his plan, he hears the drums again. They aren't the rhythm of a meeting, or a battle, or a warning. Their rhythm announces complete danger.

The North guards beat hard on the gigantic drums with wooden mallets as a cloud, sparking with magic, rolls across the land. Everything the mass engulfs leaves the forest in twisted, mangled destruction. Far above the cloud hovers neither a man nor a creature. The guards know the thing they were warned about approaches. His wings push against the air, keeping him in the sky. He holds in one arm an immense leather book.

Every Order member clamors to the armory, getting shields and swords, daggers, and chains. The north point guards grab their bows and shoot wildly at the being, but the arrows are deflected away from it. The soldiers head to the north checkpoint, creating a united front, ready to fight to the death.

The being's eyes scan, cold and calculating.

Elan's heart stops, seeing the beast again. She is petrified, frozen in place, unable to pull her attention away from him, as the more he surveys, the more impatient he appears. Elan can tell that the control on his magic and temper is slipping as his features stretch and his teeth sharpen. Realization dawns that he is from the Darklands and not one of their kind turned evil.

"Dawsley!" his voice screeches into the dimming light. "Where is the one you call Dawsley!"

Elan watches Dawsley stand in the crowd along with all of his brothers. Some clear away from him, but others try to hide him. Elan's head twists in the bustle, unable to find Aldon, Eldon or Uldon. They had separated in the commotion. All of the men's face are set in determination. She knows that any one of them are ready to give their lives in Dawsley's place.

"I am Dawsley!" he booms, cutting through the now unnerving quiet amongst them. "I am here. If you are looking to destroy me then I warn you that I will not go down without a fight."

"Nor will he go down alone," shouts Eldon.

A sneered reply drips from the apprentice's lips, "I don't care for *you*. I seek another. But I know that you are their leader, and I have a bargain to strike with you. I have Kalrolin's Journal. And I will return it to you under one condition: I want the masked one."

Elan's heart stops then kicks back in, beating in her throat.

"If you give me the masked one, I will spare you all, at least for now, and I will give you back your precious book. But if you don't, then I will come looking for him in your lands, and anyone who stands in my way will not die a peaceful death. I am willing to show you mercy. I will even give the masked one a fighting chance. You have till sun up to make your choice. I will return for my answer."

72

A sound almost like a thunderclap echoes all around them, and in the same instant, he disappears.

Chapter 12

An argument explodes after the monster leaves. Around Elan, everyone yells and argues suggestions and opinions. Some are ready to throw Uldon to the powerful creature immediately. Others think giving into his demands shows weakness. Frenzied disorder erupts, but Elan can do nothing but witness the scene before her like she is a million oxenlow tails away.

"Calm down. Everyone! All of you!" Dawsley demands.

No one is listening. Everything is chaos. Dawsley is on the verge of ripping his hair out when Gallowgrave spreads out his arms and snaps the tips of his fingers. Everyone's lips seal. Their tongues glue to the ceiling of their mouths.

Although Elan hadn't said anything, her mouth remains immobile.

Gallowgrave's eyes blaze. "Since when do we give in like cowards to any creature's demands? If we give in to him now, what is next? And who is to say he won't destroy us all anyway even after he has gotten Uldon? We don't even know if that is the Journal. Why would this creature have it and not the Old One? We are a united brotherhood, and here you are turning on each other. Have you all completely lost your minds?"

Gallowgrave releases their mouths.

"Even if there is the smallest chance that the creature is telling the truth, then I am willing to sacrifice myself for the good of The Order," Uldon gets out first.

"No, Uldon you can't!" Elan says desperately.

"I won't let you do it Uldon," Aldon agrees.

"How can you be so selfish?!" Mosley asks with such force, spittle catches in his thick mustache. "We are talking about the greater good, one man for everyone else's safety."

"Why does he want you anyway, Uldon?" a voice from the crowd asks.

"That's a good question," another says.

"How does he even know you?"

Elan's eyes shine as Uldon screws up his face. His fingers pinch the bridge of his nose. He doesn't answer. He shuts his ears and storms away, pushing through the wall of bodies. Dawsley stops anyone from following Uldon, but as Elan rushes after him he allows her through. She shoves her way through, needing to be near him. The evening sky darkens. There is only so long before the darkness turns back to light and they will have to make a decision. Elan finally catches up to Uldon and grabs his arm. Uldon stops, but keeps his back to her.

"You can't do this."

Uldon peers down at her with melancholy Elan knows all too well. It is the same sad look she had seen on the day they had met. It is a look she has not seen in his eyes in a very long time.

"This is what we do, Elan. I tried to fight it, wish for something else but gave up. What's the point? There is nothing more to us than The Order. There is nothing in our life except to die for this cause. And if I don't, then my whole life has been meaningless."

"It doesn't have to be that way Uldon. It can be better. You can have more to life than this."

Elan stretches higher on the balls of her feet. She closes her eye as a tear rolls down, and she kisses Uldon, light as a feather. Uldon doesn't stop her, and when she feels his hands on her shoulders, she wants him to pull her in

—

75

closer. Something in her stomach flutters nervously. Instead of pulling her in, she feels the pressure of him pushing her away. He shakes his head slightly and looks down at the ground.

"No, Elan. It will only make things more difficult, not better."

He doesn't set eyes on her again as he retreats from Dawsley and the others.

Uldon hides in the shadows of the arena. The building blocks the wind in the spot where he stands. He takes deep breaths and thinks about what Elan said to him.

Wanting anything more than to be utterly obedient to The Order is treason. He remembers when Jordon joined. He had a beautiful young bride but had to leave her. Jordon's life could only be that of a warrior and protector. He never saw her again. One has no loves, no loyalties other than The Order.

"Uldon, there you are," says Eldon. Uldon emerges from the shadows bravely. "Dawsley has another plan. He has called us all back to Gallowgrave's tower. Where's Elan? Didn't she come after you?"

"I think it is perhaps best if we leave Elan out of this. She is my oacling and has become overemotional and is not thinking clearly."

Eldon nods. "If that's what you want. Come, now. They are meeting us in the stone tower. Dawsley is still calming everyone down."

As they walk across the main buildings, Uldon's thoughts get the better of him.

"Eldon, when you were called, you left behind your parents, five brothers and two sisters. How did you deal with that?"

Eldon stops walking and squints, his eyes at Uldon.

"I'm just curious to know. It wasn't easy leaving my mother all alone. How do you remain so unaffected by it all?"

Eldon starts walking again and keeps his head straight as he speaks. "The way I saw it, Uldon, was that I was leaving to protect them. I would have died, if I didn't accept the invitation. I thought that even though I could never see them again, I would do my best to protect them from evil. Why do you ask after all this time, Uldon?"

Uldon doesn't answer because they've already arrived at the main tower. Aldon is the first one there, running his fingers through the books on Gallowgrave's table. He retreats from the table, coming to both Uldon and Eldon.

"It is a madhouse out there. Everyone is looking for you, Uldon. Some are ready to offer you on a silver plate to that creature. Some brotherhood we are. You can't even trust these strangers," he says, his voice thick with bitterness as he wrings his hands. "Was Elan not with you?"

"Uldon said she is becoming too emotional."

Aldon pouts, "That's the problem with having women in The Order. I always thought it was a bad idea."

"Don't forget that she has been braver and stronger than even you," Uldon defends.

"Of course you would defend her. Kalrolin only knows what you two have done during your private training sessions that you should be so close."

Uldon's stomach turns. "What is that supposed to mean?!"

"Enough!" Dawsley interrupts as he comes striding into the room with Gallowgrave, just as annoyed. "What is happening to my men? Everyone is at each other's throats! I need us at least to stick together. And how dare you speak about Uldon's oacling in such a manner! We all know that they are both completely admirable and loyal to The Order."

Aldon bows immediately to both Uldon and Dawsley, "Please forgive me. I was speaking out of anxiety. I didn't mean to insinuate such disloyalty. Elan won't be joining us. She is not taking the news well."

"That is understandable," Dawsley agrees, but frowns deeply. Dawsley bows as well, accepting his apology.

Apprehensively, Uldon lowers his head.

Gallowgrave bends over his cauldron, mumbling the words to a spell. He dips his fingers once again, and the thick yellow magic covers the walls. "I don't know what the Old One could be thinking. He has some trick up his sleeve. Why would he send his servant here for Uldon? And why would he let him bring the book here if that *is* the Journal? We are continuing with our plan nonetheless. Once he is bound to the caves, we can question him on his master's motives. But this time we have bait. We have something that the Old One's student wants more than the missing pages."

"Are you suggesting we use Uldon as bait?" Eldon asks, appalled.

"We aren't suggesting it, we are telling you to," Gallowgrave says. "If we can get him to the caves, we can bind him there, and I can hide in the shadows. That thing won't see me. I must prepare the spell as soon as we leave here. The binding spell is much more complicated than I had originally thought. We must find a beast to kill. The greater the life force, the more we can bind him, and the stronger the spell will be."

Uldon bites the inside of his cheek. He had been willing to give his life for the Order but if this did not work it would be more than *his* life in danger. It would be Gallowgrave and everyone else in the ambush that would suffer if they were not successful. Uldon had a bad feeling about what they were about to do. He exhaled a lengthy breath from his nose, forcing the words from his mouth. "I am willing to do this," Uldon says.

"I knew you would be," Dawsley says, approvingly.

"Won't he think this might be a trap?" Aldon asks.

"I have a feeling this thing thinks he is too strong to be destroyed. His pride will be his downfall. Look, how easily he came here, as though he had all the power. He won't see it coming if he still thinks he is in control," Gallowgrave explains.

"It's agreed then," Dawsley interjects. "We tell the creature that we want the book and that we are willing to give up Uldon. You two will be by the caves. We will be close by, but if anything seems to go wrong.... Are you sure you can do this, Gallowgrave? You said he was stronger than you."

"I will do my best."

"Very well then. We tell the members that we have decided to give you up. No one must know our real intentions because the traitor might catch wind. We shall meet again!" Dawsley says triumphantly.

"We shall meet again!" they all repeat in unison as Gallowgrave takes down his spell books and they all go their separate ways.

Elan stares into the darkness. The whole camp knows by now that Uldon has decided to give himself up for The Order. Elan is still in shock. She can't bring herself to move from the bench in the blacksmith's space.

Nolan finds her in the dark, alone and unmoving. He places a large hand on her shoulder. He doesn't say a word. The sky outside becomes steadily lighter.

"He's going to meet him by the caves, alone," says Nolan.

Dawsley had already told the creature that Uldon would be willing to fight when he came at first sun up.

Elan jumps to her feet without warning. Nolan's hand snaps back from her shoulder.

She clenches her jaw. Her shoulders straighten. Running from Nolan, she gives him one last look, which says *goodbye*.

Warrick savors his moment of victory. He smiles greedily to himself. He will have him at last. The nightmares and contemplations that have plagued his every moment are now happening. He is so much stronger than the days he had thought about ripping that Blood One's throat out, but he will not drink even one drop of his filthy blood.

Warrick knows with certainty that they are going to lead him into a trap, but he does not care. Even if he dies today, Warrick will take as many of them down with him as he can.

"I will avenge you, Hessarro. Finally, you can be at peace," he whispers, closing his eyes and envisioning Hessarro. His wings spread, he leaves the cover of woods, headed to the caves, where his destiny awaits.

Gallowgrave sits mutely in the caves, with his trusted cauldron piping excitedly over a rapid flame. The beast they had captured and slain, lay before the lavender potion. It is a giant oxenlow they had found grazing in the fields. He hopes the animal is enough to make the binding spell strong enough. He paces in the dark, damp caverns. Gallowgrave waits with fluttered breath, in the pit of his soul sits utmost foreboding.

Chapter 13

The billowy clouds thin, and the bright blue sky of new morning turns pewter, a storm is about to break. The picturesque landscape becomes less inviting. Uldon looks back at the jagged caves, knowing where he needs to lure the creature. He must be close because Uldon can sense the same static on the wind as the first day he appeared. Uldon draws his sword, and his eyes scan the clouds for black wings. He spins around, not wanting to miss the creature's descent to the ground.

"I'm already here," comes an icy voice.

Uldon spins to face the Darklandian wizard.

The sorcerer's body relaxes, almost stepping lazily. He either does not care that he will be engaging in battle or is overconfident. Uldon doesn't know which, but he does know he hates this thing. He hates its long frame and artificial Blood One features and the way it acts. Mostly, he hates the way it speaks: slow, measured and accented.

"Well, I'm here. Where is the book? What do you want?"

The pale man's eyes open larger in shock. His face shifts, incredulous. "You will have the book once you are dead. I will inform the others where to find it." He takes a deep breath. "You don't remember me, do you? Well, perhaps this will refresh your memory."

The strange man's features shift and change to the face his nature granted him. He drops his façade. His features sharpen along with his teeth. His eyes and features become cat-like and reptilian at the same time. His skin darkens to a drab slate. The Darklandian stands with held breath and arms at his side, waiting in anticipation. Uldon can tell that the beast is expecting a reaction.

"I don't know what game you are playing at, monster. But I am not afraid of you," Uldon bites.

The creature's jaw actually hangs open and his eyes pop from his face. Outrage seems to be replaced with fury. His face twists as though confronting rotting remains.

The Old One's student finally manages to form words. "I wasn't sure if I had killed you equinoxes ago. I thought perhaps you lived but hoped that you had died. More than your face, I recognized your scent on the battlefield. That sickening smell is not something one easily forgets. But apparently, I have escaped your memory. I'm the one that ruined your face!"

Uldon swallows. When Uldon saw him on the battlefield, there was nothing familiar about the creature. How could he have forgotten? He had endured thousands of fights since then. So much time had gone by, Uldon forgot there was a time when he didn't have to hide his face. All he remembered from that day was the mask the village had given him. He remembered now, and every small detail came back to him in vivid clarity.

"I have come to avenge Hessarro, and I will lose my life to do so!"

His powerful legs propel him far above Uldon and he dives down, picking up speed. His claws hook, and he exposes his teeth. Uldon manages to slice his shoulder but is pinned to the ground with the monster's weight. Uldon's arms burn with effort as he uses the broad side of his sword to push on the Darklandian's chest and stop his teeth from clamping down on him. Uldon tucks his legs and gets his feet on the creature's stomach and kicks with all his might. The creature falls back, but not as far as Uldon is aiming. He grunts in dismay, realizing that he had not pushed him close enough to the mouth of the caverns.

The creature claps his hands together and interlocks his claws. Uldon suspects this is not a good thing. A buzzing, whirling red light surrounds them. Murmured words hiss around Uldon as he begins to feel a change in his body. Now is his only chance, before the creature has a chance to finish whatever spell he is planning. He must run to the caves and lure the monster in so Gallowgrave can bind him.

Uldon sprints for the opening of the caves. Just before getting to the entrance, Uldon's limbs jerk and a scream rips from his throat, his body feels as though it is being torn in two. He drops on the stones just outside the mouth of the first cave. He pushes up, fighting through the pounding in his head. Uldon crawls on his hands and knees, trying to get inside to Gallowgrave's hiding place. He won't signal for his brothers to protect him, not yet. He would rather endure the pain then let them get caught up in this monster's evil magic.

He ~~Uldon~~ hears the heavy footfalls of the creature advancing on him.

Uldon focuses on getting into the cave, so when he hears a roar of protest, he doesn't know why. The spell on his body abruptly releases. Armor clangs and he turns behind him to see the swoosh of green from an Order Member's cloak. Perhaps one of them didn't want to wait for the signal. Then he recognizes the mousy brown, hair so familiar to him. His breathe catches.

"No, Elan! What are you doing?! Get out of here!"

Uldon scrambles to his feet, frantic. The rest still hide, watching from a distance. They should come at any moment to save her. He can't have this ruined.

The creature grabs Elan and flips her to the ground, but his eyes don't leave Uldon. Elan struggles to her feet. With a flick of his clawed hand backward, a ball of black magic hits Elan in the chest.

Elan's arms clamp around her body tightly. Her knees stiffen, immobile. Her face reddens as she struggles to breathe or move, but something holds her straight up, as though puppet strings keep her standing.

Uldon's locks eyes with his enemy before sprinting into the dark caverns. His boots fly over the rocky terrain.

The sorcerer bolts after him, gritting his teeth. His dexterous talons help him grip the soil beneath him as he sprints into the darkness, so he gains on Uldon fast.

Spots start to appear in front of Elan's eye. She needs air. Much longer and she will blackout completely. As the creature gets farther away, her legs and arms loosen. The protection of the crest fights off the dark magic. Finally, she can breathe as they both disappear into the caves. She gulps greedily at the air, taking in so much her lungs hurt. She must go after them. If she doesn't, she risks losing them in the labyrinth of caves.

She is about to charge in when a strong hand grabs her upper arm. She regards a mass of red and green. Eldon is grave. "You can't go in there, Elan. Leave it alone."

"No. You will not stop me."

"But you don't understand—"

Elan doesn't bother to listen as she slips her arm from his grasp. She knows she is swifter than most and runs into the caves as Eldon yells her name.

Uldon, at last, reaches Gallowgrave hunched over his cauldron. His breath scrapes against his dry throat. He has led the creature to their trap. Gallowgrave starts his incantations as his hands begin to glow the same lavender color as the potion before him. The liquid sings, taking on the life of the slaughtered Oxenlow.

Uldon halts as he comes to the place where the creature is to be bound for all eternity. Everything falls in shadow except the rays of sun that somehow seep through the stones and Gallowgrave's fire.

The Darklandian startles, gaping openly at the scene before him. Cruel amusement makes him smile. A laugh bubbles from his lips.

"This is what you have planned for me? This twisted old Blood One that you call a sorcerer? You will die by my hands before he can finish even one spell!"

The creature charges. Uldon dives down, just missing claws trying to scrape the unruined part of his face. He tumbles to the other side of the cave from the beast. Uldon straightens his body, tense and prepared for combat. They run toward each other and collide, and the wind is knocked out of him.

Gallowgrave begins to perform the spell, franticly chanting.

Uldon pushes the creature against the stone wall as pieces fall off and scatter.

Elan turns a corner and sees the smoke and light from a fire under a cauldron. Uldon grapples with the creature, avoiding his snapping teeth. Realization dawns on Elan as she stands cold, realizing her mistake. They must have decided to go through with their first plan to bind him.

Gallowgrave abruptly stops speaking. He must have finished the rest of the ritual. He places one hand on the stone. He stretches out to set his other on the Old One's apprentice to bind him to the caves.

Elan sees Uldon peek over to her from the corner of his eye. He manages to push the creature away and turns to yell, "Elan, get out of here, now!"

The creature does not hesitate, taking advantage of his distraction. Faster than possible, the creature's arm blurs. His razor sharp claws clamp on Uldon's neck, slicing into his throat. Blood showers. Uldon convulses under the monster's grip. He tosses Uldon's body aside like a rag doll, and Uldon crumples to the ground at Gallowgrave's feet. Gallowgrave turns ashen, his mouth hanging open. Uldon's blood spreads in a circle around them.

Lightning shoots from the top of Elan's head down to her toes. Elan's head overflows with the events that had only taken seconds. Uldon's blood coats the creature, and he laughs with manic glee. She squeezes her eye tightly. Her chest compresses. The armor she wears weighs down her shoulders, turning her knees to rubber. She opens her eye. The evil cackle rings in her ears. Her devastation turns to burning fire. Elan won't wait for this thing to die a slow painful death in the caves. She will inflict as much pain on this creature as she can now, by her own hands. As her blood turns hot and her vision blurs, she knows the evil monster will pay. She charges with her sword aimed ~~down. She will cut him~~ low in his gut ~~and pull the blade upward,~~ to rid ~~ridding~~ the creature of his insides.

He is almost too ecstatic to notice her roar. The beast snaps back to awareness and crouches low, ready to spring defensively. The blade aims poorly at his abdomen. Elan sees him sidestep the edge. He is next to her now. She slams her shoulder into his chest. The sheer force of the impact slams his body back into the stone wall again. Elan's heavy breathing hisses through her teeth. She pins him, pressing every bit of her strength to keep him in place.

Gallowgrave runs over with his hands outstretched and still iridescent. His hand comes closer and tries to clasp the Darklander's arm. Gallowgrave has his other hand placed on the stone.

The creature laughs at her struggles to keep him back. With a simple flick of his wrist, a white flash of pain spikes through Elan's knee. Unable to support her weight, she stumbles and falls. With a thud, Elan's head strikes the ground. Through blurring vision, the world disappears as the darkness engulfs her.

Elan can hear the bustle going on around her, as she slowly comes back from the dark. Her knee and head ache. A sore spot, she doesn't remember getting, throbs at her side. She tries to force her eye open but finds herself too weak to manage it. Elan doesn't smell the musky scent or cold air of the caves. She doesn't know where she is, but can tell she is no longer in the caverns. Muffled voices call out her name, and she screws up her face, fighting off unconsciousness.

"Elan? Elan, can you hear me?"

The smell of sweat and stale ale hits her nostrils. It's Eldon. He had warned her not to go into the caves. Everything comes flooding back into Elan's memory. It is her fault that Uldon is dead. She longs not to wake up and face the reality that Uldon died because of her actions. If she had listened to Eldon and had not run in there, then she would not have distracted him. He would still be alive.

Had they failed the mission? Is the creature bound to the caves now? After she had passed out, Gallowgrave must have succeeded because she is still alive. The monster would have killed them both if Gallowgrave had been unsuccessful. But Elan does not hear Gallowgrave's ~~voice~~ amongst the chattering voices. Perhaps ~~Gallowgrave~~ he had died protecting her. The possibility makes her despise her existence.

"Elan, can you hear us?" Gallowgrave asks.

88

At the sound of his voice, Elan's eyes flutter, fighting to open. He is not dead! At least he is still alive. His face begins to focus. But he does not look happy. Gallowgrave takes a step back frightened, as Elan touches a sharp pain now peaking in her knee. How long had she been out? Elan is about to ask what is wrong when she notices she can see everything in the tiny room. Everything. She doesn't need to turn her head more than necessary to see the whole space. Sitting up causes the room to spin. She covers her left eye. She sees the room. She blocks her right eye. Everything should have plunged into darkness, but she sees the room as well, as she had before she lost that eye. Her heart pounds as she grips her blanket.

"Gallowgrave, what has happened?"

A roar echoes in the hall outside and through the separating wall.

"He must be awake," Eldon says.

"Yes," agrees Gallowgrave as he strokes his beard in deep thought.

"Is that the creature?" Elan's brow comes down low over her eyes. "What is happening?" She asks again more insistent for answers.

Both Eldon and Gallowgrave's eyes shift. Eldon takes a gulp and his neck bobs.

"There was a complication in the caves," begins Gallowgrave. "I was so close to binding him. My hand was on the stone, and I reached out to touch the creature's arm. It would have only taken me a moment to touch both at the same time to bind them. You fell, and you knocked into me. My hand came off of the stone, and I frantically tried to keep myself balanced." He stopped, casting his eyes down and shaking his head, as though he had tried to defend himself from a horrible crime he knew he had committed.

"Then you are saying you never got a chance to bind him, but we somehow captured him?"

"I'm saying that I did not bind him to the caves." Keeping his head down, he speaks his words to the floor. "I accidentally bound him to you."

Chapter 14

Warrick wakes from a deep sleep. His head throbs. A cold stone floor lays beneath his body. All he remembers is the caves and the tiny cloaked one falling and the sound of his head against the ground. The old Blood One lost his footing as he knocked into him. Without thinking, the old magician flailed his arms and grabbed him for support. But that is it. Warrick had somehow blacked out.

Just as he is wondering where he is, he hears voices.

"It's awake."

"Shud we le' Gallowgrave kno?"

"No, you simpleton, he is with Elan now. We just need to watch him. I don't think he will go anywhere."

Warrick leaps to his feet. He nearly screams as his left knee shocks with hot pain and almost buckles underneath him. He doesn't have time to worry about his injury – it must have happened in battle. His head whips around, and he finds himself caged. Three sides are thick iron bars, but the wall behind him is stone. There is nothing in his cell except a pile of hay in the corner, which he suspects functions as a bed, and a bucket tucked into the other corner.

Warrick straightens his back and turns a humorless smile at the guards before him. This primitive cell will not hold him. His body tenses as he runs at the bars, ignoring the sharp bolt of pain propelling up his left knee once again. Something tugs around his midsection, getting stronger the closer he gets to them. He stops in surprise. Warrick's legs

——

struggle against an invisible barrier. He cannot go any farther. He roars in defiance clawing at the stone ground trying to get leverage, while not putting too much pressure on his left knee. An invisible rope comes from behind the wall, keeping him from going any farther.

"My Crest! He isn't going anywhere," says a short, broad man. He has the nerve to walk right up to the bars. Warrick fumes, less than a half an oxenlow tail away, but can't get any closer. He settles for just glaring at them instead. The partner he speaks to is the complete physical opposite, long and thin. These guards must be a joke. Even if they had better physiques, they are no match for his power. A mere two Green Cloaks and a rudimentary spell will not hold him.

Warrick cannot reach the bars, but he can still use his magic. These weak men won't stand a chance. In a hushed voice, he recites a few words and hurls his hands out. The unmistakable pulse of magic waves beneath his skin, but the men stand unaffected.

"Whatcha doin' there wit your fingers, creature?" the beanpole asks.

Warrick gapes. Both should have slashes as if whips had hit them. Instead, they watch quizzical and unaffected. He fervently tries the second time, with only the smallest sparks of magic igniting his fingers. Warrick's temper flares and he screams and thrashes, but stops because the pain in his knee and side are excruciating. He crouches in the corner, imagining all manner of violent revolt.

"He cannot be any farther from you than seven Oxenlow tails. We have him in the cell next to us. We are in the guard's room."

She refuses to believe Gallowgrave. "That's not possible. How can you bind the Creature to a living person? There must be a way to undo this. There was a spell that created it. There must be a spell to break it." Elan's voice starts to get louder.

"If one were to exist, we don't have it. All his magic was taken from him and converted to create this bond. It was originally intended to bind someone to something inanimate, but there is no documentation of binding two living beings. Also, the spell was made much stronger than intended." Gallowgrave stops, taking a deep breath and forces the words from his mouth. "Uldon died, and the spell took on his life force to strengthen it. These events are unprecedented. Just look at your eye!"

Eldon hands Elan a highly-polished silver plate. The Order has no use for reflective surfaces, and Elan almost doesn't notice the difference in her face. One of her eyes is the same dark brown it has always been. But her new left eye shines black as the Creature's. Elan's hand shoots up, wanting to claw the otherworldly mutation out of her face. But Eldon's massive hand holds them back. His face drips with pity.

"What are you saying, Gallowgrave? That I have to live attached to the Creature that killed Uldon, who has killed hundreds of our kind? I'm going to find a way to slay the beast right now and be done with this!"

"You think it is that simple?" Gallowgrave sputters. "You think we didn't think of that before you woke? You two are bound. You hit your head and sprained your knee, and the Creature has the same injuries now. You have an injury on your side that the Creature had acquired. If we bring any harm to it, then you will also suffer."

"Then I will take my own life and see if he dies too."

Gallowgrave heaves a tired breath, "If you do that, you are potentially setting it free, while your life ends."

A large lump forms in Elan's throat as she controls her breathing, "I should have died in those caves anyway. Not Uldon."

—

Her sentences hang in the silent air.

"It is my fault for going after him." She swallows back her grief, keeping her voice steady. Right now, she will not fall to pieces.

"What's done cannot be undone. We have to find a solution. I must talk to the Creature."

Gallowgrave stands and leaves. She sees him slump as if he is about to have the weightiest conversation of his long life.

Warrick sits in the middle of his cell continuing to glare at the men. There is no other course of action to take, so he just tries to make them as uncomfortable as possible. The stocky one seems to be ill at ease, but the beanpole remains oblivious.

A new set of steps pad toward them. Warrick turns to his right and finds he can reach the bars to the side of him, but not the front. He wonders why they would cast such an odd spell. The slight form of the wizard from the cave creeps into the cell room.

The frail man keeps a safe distance, as if he is gauging the Creature's prowess.

"Let me out," Warrick hisses.

"You, Creature, will not be going anywhere ever again."

"You are planning to imprison me here forever? Torture me?" His eyes dance, crazed. There is nothing they can do to him that hasn't been done before, he has lived through it all, endured.

The foolish wizard shakes his head, "We aren't planning on hurting you at all."

"We aren't?" the stocky one asks alarmed.

The old goat's nostrils flare, as his agitation is palpable. "Please leave. I must speak to it alone."

With reluctance, they shuffle out the door to what is apparently a hallway.

Warrick sizes the bony Blood One up. If his magic were working, he would have been out of these confines and consuming his blood in one movement.

Remaining blood stains the Creature's skin. And Warrick doesn't miss the Blood One's lingering observations and his face paling at the crimson stains.

"I don't know how you found us and I don't know why your master sent you here to single out Uldon. I don't know what game you are playing at, Creature, but it is over now. You killed our brother. He was a man of great honor and dedication. As much as we would love to get rid of you, Creature, we have an unexpected problem."

"I don't care about your problems," he spits.

"Of course you don't, but this is also your problem, and you might be interested in knowing it."

His curiosity gets the better of him, and Warrick shuts his mouth long enough for the Blood One to continue. He jerks his chin up as permission for him to speak.

The sorcerer carefully lowers himself and sits on the dusty floor. His movement makes Warrick notice the nitwit's feat are bare. He narrows his eyes and recognizes the off kilter oddness the Old One once described of someone who had done too many spells that have gone wrong.

"I cast a spell that was supposed to bind you to the caves. I'm sure you know what binding spells entail, being a student of the Old One." The wizard says *the Old One* like they are unsavory words.

Warrick nods, still suspicious and on guard. He won't let him know his knowledge of binding spells is much more extensive than Warrick wanted.

"Well unfortunately for both you and one of our members, you have been bound to each other."

Warrick's eyes narrow. That isn't possible. "I don't believe you," he spits in a hushed voice.

"You don't have to believe me, Creature. You will find out soon enough." The wrinkled blood sack stands and dusts off his tattered clothing, "I'm sure your master will be looking for you soon. We will have attacks to worry about. You both still need to heal. You will be left here until we can figure out what to do with the both of you. Death isn't an option, Creature, so be prepared, because I'm sure the life you will lead from now on will not be a pleasant one."

Warrick isn't going to tell the aged man that the Old One is dead. He isn't frightened in the least. He has avenged Hessarro's death. He is still alive and unharmed. There is no possible way his life could get any worse than being with the Old One.

Elan tires of staring at the same three walls and curtained doorway.

Beside Gallowgrave and Dawsley, she had nothing to distract her thoughts during the last few days. Her mind always drifts back to Uldon. When both men came and went, she acted emotionless. In the night, she let go of the reins of her self-control, weeping openly. Things would never be the same ever again. A once permanent part of her had been snatched away, she doesn't know how she will function. Breathing in and out had been a thoughtless task before Uldon's death. Now, taking in air seemed like a laborsome task. When her eyes close, an image of the masked face she had adored so much materializes. He would never smile at her again or spar with her in the training auditorium. That life with him is now over.

—

Her thoughts would get interrupted most nights, faintly hearing the Creature, just a stone's throw away, pacing and limping, mumbling incantations, or breathing fitfully in its sleep. The magic Gallowgrave worked on Elan's injuries mends her body quickly. She wishes he would slow it down and she could stay there forever, avoiding the inevitable.

The sun shines through the window, lightening the quarters. Elan sighs, throwing an arm over her eyes. She will face the murderer that killed Uldon. Not only will she have to face him, but she will have to see him every day for the rest of her existence. The prospect makes her stomach churn with nausea. Uldon's death happened faster than her mind could register. A small part of her doesn't want to accept her current reality. Her head whips to the side.

There it is again, the scraping of his feet against the stone. He paces. Elan supposes he is as anxious as she is, locked away and knowing you are meeting the enemy you can never leave.

Both Dawsley and Gallowgrave wait at her door before the light fully reaches the sky.

"We thought we would let you in on what we have decided," Dawsley says.

Elan wonders what it will be. Will they kill her and take the chance of it not working? Will they banish her from The Order? Will they bind both her and the Creature to the caves to keep him contained?

"We have decided to have both you and the Creature stay on Order land," Dawsley decrees.

Elan blinks, dumbfounded, listening, but she doesn't know if her ears are deceiving her.

"You were to become nomadic because your fortieth equinox is near, but we cannot have you alone with such a dangerous being. We will not abandon you to deal with this alone. Even if he cannot harm you physically, we want to keep a close eye on him. And there still might be some answers we can get from him."

Gallowgrave gives Dawsley a guilt-ridden expression before continuing.

"I'm also sorry to say this Elan," Gallowgrave says. "But we can use this unfortunate situation to do something good. By keeping him here, the Old One can't use him as a weapon."

Elan's forehead becomes creased. "Is this the only way?"

"Trust us. If there were any other way to handle this situation, we would. I can barely stand the thought of doing this to one of my descended oaclings," Dawsley grunts.

"Then I must trust the decision you have come to," Elan says, resigning herself to her fate. "I will give this a try."

They escort her to the cell. She leans most of her weight on an old crutch, trying as best she can to look unscathed. Her body is stiff and sore from being in bed, unable to move. The chamber of the Creature is cast in dusky light, as the sun crawls higher across the sky.
The Creature crouches in the furthest corner, still in shadow. Elan makes out the silhouette of his figure as he slinks out of the darkness. Her body recoils as he draws near to the bars. She fights the instinct to back away. She won't show this thing her fear or apprehension in any way. Her heart pounds at the memory of his grinning face over

Uldon's dead body. Seething hate runs through her veins. The desire to destroy him wars with her self-preservation. But she cannot harm him in any way. Had they been in another situation, she would have loved nothing more than to rip his heart from his chest.

His head is down, and he lifts his eyes to them slowly. She sees his face contoured oddly compared to her kind, foreign and very much out of place amongst those around her. His body unfolds from being crouched on the ground. When he stands Elan notices his stature for the first time. He is a bit short and lean for a creature, but still taller than Dawsley.

His pitch-black eyes meet each of theirs one by one, leaving Elan for last. As his gaze turns on her and she looks directly into those grotesque irises, she feels the unmistakable burning sting of the crest on her arm.

Chapter 15

Elan pulls her eyes away quickly. She deludes herself, believing that she imagined it, but knows she hasn't. The burn still lingers on her skin. The crest on her arm demands that she take this creature as her oacling and fight in The Order. This isn't possible. As much as she wants to lie to herself, she knows that she had not imagined it.

Bile rises at the back of her throat. He had killed the man she had loved. She wants to harm this demon anyway she can. To ignore the calling to take him as her student is betrayal. She resents being an Order member for the first time in her life. Her face remains immobile as she studies the Creature, giving none of her thoughts away.

Dawsley speaks first, carrying authority in his tone, "What did the Old One want with Uldon? And where is the Journal?"

The thing behind the bars replies with a simple pointed toothy grin, his eyes mocking.

Dawsley's voice deepens, "So, you aren't going to talk? I doubt you will be so confident for long. Most of your power has left you. Gallowgrave's magic is stronger than you now. You also need blood. It has already been a few days. And if you don't talk, you are not going to be fed. Your counterpart will still eat and not be hungry, but you, on the other hand, will be perpetually starving." Warrick doesn't look alarmed, but Elan knows Dawsley hopes the threat will persuade him. "You can't go anywhere that Elan doesn't go."

Elan feels his appraisal carrying not even a hint of interest. Then, turning, his eyes slide away.

"Also, you cannot harm Elan without injuring yourself. You will stay here on Order Land, where we can watch you."

The Creature spits at Dawsley's feet. A rumbling sound of anger emits from his throat.

Dawsley's arms shake with the effort not to strike the Creature. A muscle beside his jaw ticks. He strides toward the door, motioning with his hand for both to follow.

As they walk down the hall, Elan follows past her chamber door. She stops. An unfamiliar tightness squeezes around her middle, uncomfortable and very unwelcome. They pivot, puzzled, as she holds on to her stomach with one hand, and the crutch with the other. She takes another step and the twisting increases.

"I had forgotten," Dawsley sighs. "You can't go much farther than this from the Creature."

Elan balks at the information. She puts all of her effort, into moving her lips, to make words. The true gravity of her situation, dawns on her.

"I am imprisoned here. I'm allowed to stay, but I will be isolated from everyone."

Gallowgrave's face falls, "We are preparing a separate dwelling for you. You can't stay here; too many Order members come and go in this building. You both will be far enough away from the center of town so the Creature won't be up to no good in the nighttime hours, but close enough so we can keep an eye on you. Just be patient. For now, you stay here, but we promise to take care of you." Gallowgrave places a hand on her shoulder, "Be careful of him, Elan. Leaving him here with you puts me ill at ease. He can't harm you physically, but there are other ways to inflict pain. Be strong. We will come back soon."

Dawsley and Gallowgrave exchange an anxious look, before they leave her standing alone.

"We've found it!" Lelan calls across the grounds to Dawsley, who approaches.

An excited crowd surrounds Lelan and Jordon, cheering and clanking their swords. Everyone roars, exuberant. Clutched in Lelan's hands, the sizeable leather-bound book is so familiar to them all.

"That Creature was true to his word, surprisingly," Jordon says to Dawsley. "We found it not too far from the caves, just leaning up against the rocks. We gave him Uldon, and he gave us the book."

With relish, Dawsley retrieves the book from Lelan's hands. Tears threaten to streak down his face. As the pages drop open, his face is alight. He touches the yellowing paper and reads the scribbled letters. Slowly, his face drops as he flips through the pages with fervor.

"This isn't Kalrolin's Journal! He has tricked us all."

Fenix's heavy feet follow the path to the temple. He had once been a guard at the Stone Temple, but had seldom been called upon since Warrick was now the Old One's pet. Even if Fenix is taller and broader than most other Darklanders, he could not conduct magic like Warrick. His use had been demoted to that of an errand lackey.

He stands just outside as an uncharacteristic silence sets his teeth on edge. As Fenix approaches the wooden doors, the splatters of blood on the handle don't escape his attention. He is slightly concerned, but not troubled. Blood is a part of their everyday lives, and some is bound to spill.

The doors don't need locks, not when two powerful spellworkers reside there. He creaks open the doors. The scent of congealed blood wafts from the inside. His sight adjusts to the inky darkness quickly. Taking a step, his foot squishes and slips beneath him. The floor shines in syrupy garnet. A body lies in the center of the pool of blood.

Fenix runs to his Master who has a dagger in his chest. His hands shake, horrified by the scene before him. He kneels beside the body. He yanks the knife out, and a small trickle of blood follows it.

Fenix's mind is a whirlwind of questions, thoughts, and concern. His hands hover over the body, not knowing what to do. A low, almost inaudible sound of breath and a slow heartbeat breaks the silence. He can't believe his senses; his master is still alive. Gently, he lifts his master's body and places him into his room on a bed made of soft grass covered in a large blanket.

Fenix needs to clean his wound and bring him blood to replace all that he has lost.

"Master, I will be right back. Please hold on until then."

Elan sits in her room staring icily at the crest on her arm. She wants to dig her nails into her flesh and rip the metal out. She would tell no one the crest burned. No one would know.

Shoes slapping rapidly on the stone floor echo down the hallway. Elan sticks her head out to see Dawsley marching up toward her, his eyes blazing, and fists clenched. For a wild moment, she believes he knows about her crest and he is there to accuse her of treason. Her fingers tremble as she holds the curtain back from her doorway. But he strides right past her into the cell. Elan follows, her curiosity getting the better of her.

Dawsley halts at the bars, the veins in his neck popping. Elan imagines it takes every effort for him to speak instead of producing inaudible screams.

"Gallowgrave was right. You didn't even have Kalrolin's Journal to begin with-"

"What are you talking about?" The Darklandian clenches his jaw.

"Don't you dare interrupt me! You deceptive cobe! I just knew the Old One would deceive us! You never had the book. So he still has the Journal and Uldon is dead, but we have you. The Old One didn't predict us trapping you. Whatever plan you devised, it won't work. You will starve, waste away and rot," Dawsley spits. "And I will take pleasure in it."

Elan is glued to the spot. Dawsley's rage is only an echo compared to what Elan feels. The beast never had the book. They are not a single step closer to their goal. Uldon died for nothing.

The Darklandian comes up to the bars, pressing his face as close to Dawsley as he can.

"I hope you never find that Journal! May the ground of Solum Cowdh open up and swallow it whole!"

A burst of pure pain smacks Elan square under her jaw. She doubles over holding her face, tears streaming down from her eyes. She forces them open long enough to see the Creature on the ground of his cell, wiping the blood from his mouth as he grins, licking his lips. Dawsley cradles his hand with the other.

Elan moans miserably. Finally, Dawsley notices her behind him, and his anger ebbs from him. He rushes to her with fretful eyes.

"To the great beyond with this spell!"

"I'm fine! I'm glad you did it," Elan protests. She gives the Creature a hard glare as he smiles and his fingers grace his swelling face. It hurts to speak, but a small sadistic part of her relishes that the leech can feel the excruciating throb. The rusty flavor of her blood sits on her lips.

The beast inhales deeply. He propels himself across the cage, mad eyes fixed on the fresh blood trickling down her chin. His face stretches long, and his teeth become larger and sharper. Elan backs away, retreating from the room as Dawsley tries to shield her. She hears the Creature roar and thrash against the bars.

Elan shuts her eyes tight and covers her ears. The ravenousness of his face depicts the pure evil he is. For the rest of her life, she is bound to this creature, this monster, and there is no way out.

Fenix waits anxiously beside his master. Healing balms and plants cover his wound. The leaves' strong mint odor fills the room. Despite Fenix cleaning the wound and changing his bandages every day, there is little improvement. He knows no magic to help and isn't even sure if he can perform a spell if he did.

The stillness breaks with the sound of flapping wings. They are not the bat-like wings of their kind, but the soft swish of feathers. Apprehensively, Fenix steps away from his master. He creeps slowly to the outside door. He can smell the birds and no one else, but still has the intelligence to be on guard. There perched in the clay soil, three blackbirds stand side by side, watching Fenix with curiosity. There is something much too perceptive about these creatures, and Fenix feels goosebumps on the back of his neck as their beady black eyes seek his. In front of them leans a large package wrapped in the same green fabric as The Order. It's bright against the gray terrain, with a white piece of paper pinned to it.

Fenix slowly kneels to take the package. He opens the note and recognizes the handwriting immediately. In scrawled letters, he reads.

I believe you are missing something.

Fenix unfolds the coarse fabric to reveal Kalrolin's Journal.

Chapter 16

Elan hangs her head under the scrutiny of watching eyes. Every Order member has come to view the bizarre parade go by. Dawsley leads as Elan follows with the Creature trailing behind. He leaves as much space between them as the spell will allow. He hides behind a large burlap cape and hood, covering him from their sight. Gallowgrave stays on the end, watching the Creature closely.

She can feel the weight of judgment on her. Not a voice heard nor a grunt uttered breaks the shocked silence. Her shame keeps her from making eye contact with anyone. If her friends are there, she does not know. She has not even heard from Nolan. Even her fortieth equinox had come and gone with no mention of it from anyone. She is officially an adult now in the Order's eyes, but she has not been formally accepted as one. The back of her neck remains uninked with the symbols of adulthood.

She feels as though she is walking to her death rather than to her new home.

Home. What a mockery of the word.

A sack hangs around her shoulders containing her few belongings. They trudge through the thickest of the town until they approach the outskirts of the center. The cold wind whistles through the few trees. It doesn't escape Elan's attention that they are following close to the river, the place where she used to feel most at peace. The small stone house ahead of them sits at a distance, but not as far as she had suspected. Looking over her shoulder, she can still see the men and almost hear their voices carry across the long grass.

The stone building must have taken days and nights on end just to finish. The brown, terracotta, gray, and cream rocks are embedded in hard clay and hay. The sides and roof are adorned with green sheets flapping slowly in the wind. Not too far from the building is a small wooden outhouse. Elan wonders if they all desired her exile so much that they created this separate place for her as soon as possible. She can think of more than a few Order members who would be pleased to see the only female member excommunicated. Even so, she can't blame them for hating the one that contributed to Uldon's death. No amount of their disdain matches her self-loathing.

Dawsley stops at the front of the wooden door to the small dwelling. The Creature stays farther back, not allowing himself to get too close to the others. He remains aloof, keeping a cold exterior. Gallowgrave catches up and opens the door.

Elan steps inside with Gallowgrave and Dawsley. The Creature stays outside the door in protest. His back straightens, and he folds his arms.

"Aren't you going to come in?" Dawsley huffs irritably.

"Without being properly invited?" Warrick asks with sarcasm. "I wouldn't dream of being so rude."

"Suit yourself."

Elan loosens a breath with relief at the Creature's unwillingness to enter. His voice crawls over her skin, leaving her sick. Even with her hate, guilt still nags at the back of her mind for ignoring her calling to make this vile thing her student. If only she could destroy the Creature, and end it all. The rage and desire for vengeance almost takes hold of her. She swallows it back, assessing her surroundings.

The room they stand in is the largest, containing the hearth to her left with a cauldron resting inside. The room is thin and long with one window on the far end. To her right,

Elan notices two rooms facing the hearth, without doors. Fabric is pulled to the side of the entrances. Elan suspects the spaces were built to let the warmth of the fire spill into their quarters. Each room has a window facing outside with wooden shutters. The one closest to her has a perfect view of the river.

Elan is astounded at how much thought and effort they put into this lavish home. None of the Order members had their own hearth. More guilt than she thought possible crashes down on her shoulders.

"I can't accept this."

Elan marches away from the stone house and the center of town. She can't face them. All of the open air still does not help her breath. Picking up speed, she puts more distance behind her. She hears the rustling of the long grass as someone else follows. Spinning around, she expects to see Dawsley or Gallowgrave. But her heart turns cold to see the monster stumbling behind as if being yanked by a rope.

"You look surprised to see me," he hisses, irritated.

Elan can't believe she forgot that she will never be alone to think. There is no getting away, even for a moment. She turns, squeezing her eyes tight.

"Are you an imbecile? Just because you can't see me does not mean I'm not here. I will always be here. That constant reminder that you failed your friend."

Her ears ring and her body flushes in anger. One moment Elan tries to block him out, the next something snaps, and she flies across the long grass, hands positioned to strangle the Creature. Knocking him to the ground, she presses hard against his throat. The veins pop in the Darklandian's neck and temples as he tries to pry her hands off. His claws scrape against the metal on her arms. It's hard for her to breath, but she refuses to let go. She gasps and gags, inflicting harm on herself, but can't find the logic to care. Her lungs burn for air. The Creature's eyes bore into hers as if his searing gaze is enough to hurl every hateful word that exists. Elan becomes light-headed. Her vision blurs. Before she blacks out, the air buzzes and bends around her.

Gallowgrave blasts her off of him, screeching, "You have completely lost your mind!"

Gallowgrave hobbles over to her, ignoring the Creature. He helps Elan up from the ground and whispers to her in a low tone, "This is what he wants, Elan. He wants to upset you, to drive you to madness. But you must be strong and not let him. You are one of the bravest Order members I have ever known. You have the will to stand up to him, to not let him know he is getting to you. I know you can do this."

The Creature has already gotten back on his feet and he circles them. His chin tucks in as he stalks them, his brow low over his eyes.

Elan can't help her heart rate picking up. A slow chill goes down her back as he watches them. Even though she knows well he is not a danger to her, she still has the ingrained reaction of defense and fear.

The Darklandian smirks as he rubs his bruising throat.

Gallowgrave leads Elan back to the house with the Creature following unwillingly, slinking silently behind them like a cat.

"We must go and let the others know of their future conduct now that Elan is out of the armory quarters." Dawsley orders Gallowgrave. "Elan, you have been in the armory awhile. Wash up, get settled and report back to Gallowgrave's tower. You are still a member of our ranks. You still have work to do."

"Yes, sir."

"We shall meet again."

Gallowgrave and Dawsley retreat, glancing back every few steps.

Elan doesn't bother acknowledging the Creature. She steps into the house and chooses the room with the window facing the river. Green fabric is slung over a rope line, creating a make-shift curtain to the entrance. Taking the edge of the cloth, she slides it over. She folds and sets aside her remaining two cloaks and another set of armor. Looking at her sword, she wonders if she should keep it close to her. With haste, she tucks it into one of her cloaks.

The small room contains a small shelf pushed against the stone walls. Tucked in the back corner is a bed, which is nothing more than a giant sack stuffed with hay on a wooden platform. Even this is a luxury, because in her usual quarters, there would be just a tightly pulled cot. For a moment, she double takes when she discovers a small white piece of paper on her bed. Elan approaches the small folded parchment. Her fingers open it with the utmost care, wondering what it could possibly be.

She reads the paper, her chest aching.

Elan,

I took a chance and thought you would pick the room with the view of the river. Dawsley ordered all of us not to see you when you were in the armory. We were even told that we can't get near you once you leave. Unexpected things happen in battle. Jordon, Tresdon, Lelan and I don't blame you for what has happened.

None of us knew what they had planned, so how could you? I wish you strength in this time. Know that you still have friends.

Nolan

The letter does little to alleviate her guilt. Elan wishes they would hate her. She doesn't deserve their mercy and friendship after committing such an odious mistake. She places her face into her soiled hands, trying to block out the world.

Elan pulls back, noticing her dirty hands, clothing, and armor for the first time. It's been over a quarter cycle since she has washed. Dirt and even blood permeate her cloak and armor. Her stomach lurches. The scenes from the caves flash in her memory. She needs to clean the violence and death from her. Pulling aside the curtain, she sighs, relieved to see that the savage Creature still refuses to enter. She grabs the cauldron on her way out.

Leaving the hut, Elan finds the Creature with his claws deep into the ground. His legs strain to pull with all his might to get past an invisible barrier. The tendons rise on his legs and arms, the muscles in his back knot and shift. A roar thunders out of his stretched mouth. He goes nowhere.

He hears the slam of the door as Elan closes it behind her. He stands, breathing heavy with the effort of trying to escape. Standing upright, he sets his jaw, his nostrils flared.

"I will find a way out of this entrapment," the Creature promises. She walks away, ignoring him. He has no choice but to follow. "Even if it means risking both our lives, I will be free again."

Elan continues toward the river. The rush of water instantly puts her at ease. Such a small, familiar sound has been a more exceptional comfort to her than all the words someone could give. Dipping the caldron into the river, her hands sting from the cold water. She hauls it back. The water sloshes with her movements. She places it in the hearth carefully so as to not wet the wood already set. Taking one of her swords, she strikes it against flint to create a spark. The dry wood ignites, and the warmth of the fire presses against her.

The Old One's apprentice leans against the doorframe, but doesn't enter.

"You can wash off the blood and the smell of the caves, but you can never wash away what has happened."

Elan follows Gallowgrave's advice and does not listen. She removes her cloak then unlatches her armor on her arms and torso. She feels lighter now without the metal. As she yanks her boots off one at a time, she wiggles her toes, stretching. Elan dips the corner of her robe into the warm water to wash the dirt from her hands first. The prickle of watching eyes runs up her neck.

She turns on the Creature, "Aren't you going to give me privacy?"

"Do I bother you?" He steps into the front room.

The smooth, measured way he moves and the accent of his voice unnerve her.

Living in the Order didn't give anyone a chance for modesty, but she was always kept separate when possible. She plans on taking the cauldron with hot water to her room, though it would be more comfortable to stay in front of the fire. She turns her back to him and removes her baggy shirt. Thick fabric winds around her torso. A high-pitched hiss pierces the air.

"You're female!"

Her fists ball up. "Of course, I'm female. Are you sure *you* are not the imbecile?"

"There are no female Green Cloaks."

"There obviously are."

"Don't toy with me, tiny female! You are not a Green Cloak. This was a trap. If my life depends on your safety as well, I am as good as dead anyway."

"I can take care of myself," she says, trembling with rage.

"I sincerely doubt that. Had your sorcerer not interrupted, I would have killed you as quickly as the masked one."

Hearing the wretch speak about Uldon so callously makes her erupt. "Don't you dare talk about Uldon!"

"Uldon? Is that so? Now I understand why you ran after him." He gives her a condescending leer.

She fights not to retaliate. Her muscles lock.

"Is your bed not as warm without him?" he whispers.

Her nails dig into her palms. Anger builds, rippling through her.

"Don't you ever disgrace his name again," she says, dangerously low, staring into his eyes as if just the expression could sear his soul. But instead of burning the Creature, the flesh on her arm scorches even hotter than before, demanding her to listen to the calling she has ignored.

The Creature grabs his forearm, staring at Elan's metal crest.

Elan holds her breath. He knows her crest burned.

And he is the only living being who she can't hide it from.

Chapter 17

"What was that?" he asks, reaching to grab her arm so that he can take a better look at the source of his pain.

Elan jerks her arm away. "Nothing you have to be concerned about."

"I do if it's going to be burning my arm every few days," he snaps.

Cold hits Elan's heart, squelching her burning rage. She had forgotten that the first time the crest burned he must have felt it too.

"It only occurs once in a while," she invents, leaving the answer vague enough so if it happens again he can't catch her in a lie.

Her eyes cast down, not daring to look into his face. Her attention returns to the cauldron, blocking him out. Before she can even remove the first layer of wrapped fabric, the Creature leaves, shutting the door firmly behind him. Elan can't help but irritate him more. "What's the matter? Do I bother you?" she yells out, mimicking his same tone. A sadistic pleasure tickles her, knowing she has unnerved him.

After Elan has washed and changed, she leaves the small stone house to find the Creature sulking miserably in the long grass. His back faces the center of Order land, and he gazes into the long stretch of land that gives way to forest trees and hills.

Elan says nothing to him because she knows he can hear her shuffling along the grass. He will have no choice but to follow her anyway, even if he is pretending she isn't there. After a few moments, she hears an irritated grunt as he rises to follow.

Taking long strides across the grass, she heads to Gallowgrave's tower. Her adversary's steps are silent, and Elan doesn't hear the Creature so much as she feels his oppressive presence.

The town notices her arrival as she approaches. They all seem to disappear one by one. By the time she reaches the central buildings, the dirt streets are as deserted as a ghost town, but she can still feel them watching curiously. Elan can't help but wonder what the Creature thinks, being on enemy land and seeing their inner sanctum.

The smell of meat cooking wafts past her as she crosses the food tents on the way to the tower. Elan's stomach growls aggressively. Her preoccupation with the events of the last hours has wholly distracted her from hunger. But now Elan holds her stomach, starving. She must wait until after she meets Gallowgrave so instead of stopping, she presses on.

The smoke from the blacksmith's fire puffs in the background. Her eyes travel to the shop. A wide opening with an awning covers the inside in shadows.

The large wooden doors to Gallowgrave's tower groan loudly as she shoves them open. As usual, the hazy tower lingers with an unpleasant stench. The Darklandian takes his precious time coming into the tower, delaying the meeting as much as he can. Once he passes her with disinterest, she shuts the doors behind them.

The Darklandian's nose crinkles upon entering, giving the cauldron a look of utter disdain. They walk closer, but the Creature abruptly stops.

"You can go on, but I'm staying right here," he says, low and cruel. "His magic reeks of incompetence."

Elan doesn't understand but doesn't ask questions. The more he keeps his distance, the better. She averts her gaze when he speaks, her face cast down. Gallowgrave pours over books in the center while Dawsley leans over the table gripping the edge impatiently. The Darklandian is still murderously ill-tempered, watching them from farther back.

"I'm ready for my new duties," Elan says.

Dawsley's eyes flick over to their problem for a split second before he speaks, "You are to do oacling chores until further notice."

Elan blanches. "You jest."

"This is what is best for you." Dawsley does not make eye contact, keeping his gaze down on the splintering boards before him.

Elan can't hide the shame she feels of being told to do the work of the oaclings, her body wilting.

"Of course, you won't be with the oaclings at the same shifts because we don't want them anywhere near the Creature." Dawsley twists his lips.

"What good am I to the Order if I'm merely doing oacling chores?"

Dawsley turns to finally face her. "The work they do is vital to our community, and you are here to serve. After the sun hits the highest point, I expect you to report to the fields. I have already informed Hemsley that you will be joining him."

Before Elan can protest his decision, her stomach rumbles.

"No arguments. Get something to eat before you meet him. You are in for a lot of work today." Dawsley flicks his hand to dismiss her.

"But Dawsley-" Her stomach betrays her once again and squeaks, interrupting her words.

"That's an order, Elan." Dawsley's tone is firm, leaving no room for argument. "And the other members have all been warned to keep their distance. They come close to you at their own risk. The Creature can still hurt us, but we outnumber him and can restrain him. Now go. Hemsley will report back to me if anything strange happens."

"We will meet again." Elan bows begrudgingly. She turns around and strides away, leaving Dawsley and Gallowgrave alone once more.

Dawsley waits a few moments longer to make sure they don't turn back around before speaking again, "This is awful news, Gallowgrave."

"I don't know how the Creature got one of my books, but it is one of my very own that he left by the caves," Gallowgrave says clutching the fraudulent book. "My theory is that the traitor gave it to him to deceive us. There would have been no possible way the Old One would have let his servant take the real book to us."

"That proves my theory. If the Creature stays, he will know the traitor when he sees him and expose him with that recognition."

"I still feel guilty not telling Elan the real reason we are letting her stay on Order Land," Gallowgrave mutters. Wetting his lips, he frowns.

"You know Elan as well as I do. She would do anything for the greater good of The Order. She would not blame us for doing what we must." The higher pitch of his voice tells Gallowgrave that perhaps even Dawsley does not believe his own words.

Gallowgrave shakes his head in agreement, but still feels repulsive at exposing her to such an evil.

Elan leaves Gallowgrave's tower, sparing one more fleeting glance at the blacksmith's. From a distance, Nolan lifts his hand in a gesture of hello. Elan gives one quick nod of recognition, as her expression softens.

"I see being the only female of the Green Cloaks means you don't have many cold nights." The Creature's voice comes from much too close behind her. Her face hardens once again, striding toward the tents. Grinding her teeth, her heart pounds in her ears.

The closer she gets to the food tents, the more her anger evaporates. At least a dozen fowls are lined up on a spit. A vat of vegetables and stew simmers over a massive fire. Mosley is on food detail, and he enjoys every moment of yelling at people who try to sneak in for thirds. His bushy blond mustache twitches from side to side in irritation.

The smell of spices, meats, vegetables and something else she can't detect makes her salivate. Her stomach aches in anticipation. There are only a few Order members on kitchen duty, but most back away and leave the moment she approaches. An evil grin spreads across Mosley's face as his eyes follow Elan.

"Got yourself in a real mess didn't you, Elan?" he asks with wicked glee.

She keeps her temper even though her face burns. She grabs a plate, keeping her head down and trying to steady her shaking hand.

"Of course, I always knew having a female in our ranks would be our demise." Mosley gives the Creature a dirty look. "Perhaps Dawsley isn't up to the job of leadership any longer. Maybe someone else should take over, someone more qualified. If I were in charge, I would throw the both of you out. Look at you. You're just as much a freak as he is.

That new creature eye of yours should be ripped out and cast into the fire." His face becomes purple with anger as he slams a sharp cooking knife into the table. "Vile mongral," he spits in the same direction where the Creature stands.

The beast growls, pulling back his top lip and exposing his elongating upper teeth.

Elan forcibly slaps food down on her plate, ignoring their exchange, going from one table to the next as Mosley's voice carries over. She breathes evenly through her nose and out of her mouth.

"If you had any dignity or loyalty at all, you would quit on your own, Elan. Who knows who else will die because someone is trying to protect the girl."

At this, Elan throws her plate down and glares at him so intensely Mosley stops laughing. He throws her one more snarl and turns from her.

Elan finds the table furthest from where Mosley stands and collapses into her seat. He was the last person Elan wanted to see. The worst part of what Mosley said is that he might be right. How can she stay here and face everyone? Uldon told her he wished she had never become an Order member. Maybe he was right. If she weren't here, perhaps Uldon would still be alive.

Elan sinks her teeth into a massive bone covered in fleshy meat, chewing angrily. She swallows without tasting. One, two, three bites then swallows. One, two, three bites then swallows. One, two, three.... Elan stops. She chews slowly, letting the flavor sit on her tongue a little longer. Something isn't right. Mosley must have prepared the food differently. There is an unpleasant bitter taste. She puts the bone down and breaks a piece of dark bread. It doesn't take but a moment for her to notice the bread's unpleasantly coarse texture. The food is different. Everything is grating with an odd aftertaste. Elan is furious that Mosley cooked such detestable food.

The Creature scrunches his nose, standing back from Elan's plate of food.

Sniffing the food curiously, it doesn't even smell as appetizing as before. Tossing the food aside, Elan decides she has had enough to eat, but her stomach still feels empty. Walking to the garbage, Elan cannot remember a time when she did not clean her plate. After discarding the remains, she slams her plate into the scrubbing basin beside it.

She freezes and sniffs. A rich scent that Elan can't place catches her attention. Beside her, the Darklandian pulls a prolonged intake of air. With her curiosity peaked, she walks back over to the food tables, looking for the source, but the smell only fades.

Mosley watches Elan closely as she inspects every piece of food. Elan can't find the delectable scent. Striding away, she passes the garbage bins once again, but surprise catches her. The aroma seems to be getting stronger. Her interest gets the better of her as she peers inside the open bin. Behind the rotting stench of uneaten bits of food is something bizarrely alluring. Flies swarm as she tries to see past the garbage.

The bits of chopped oxenlow and other animals' remains sit at the bottom, dripping fresh blood. Elan's heart pounds, not because she is disturbed by the grizzly sight, but because she is elated. Confusion quickly takes the place of joy. Jumping back, Elan tries to put as much space between herself and the bin.

The speed of her steps increase, but the Creature keeps up with a smug expression of understanding on his face.

"I was wondering why my hunger pains have not been as severe as they should have been. I suppose we are connected even when it comes to hunger. Your magician didn't know."

"I don't know what you are talking about," she spits, keeping her eyes down. Just the sight of him makes her lip curl.

"You are so transparent. I could smell it too. That mouthwatering scent that makes your heart beat faster and makes you a bit mad."

120

"I smelled nothing."

How much she wishes at this very moment to be rid of him for good, to slash his throat and watch him die slowly.

"You liar. You have it too now. Just like me, you are infected." Elan stops. A dark shadow crosses his expression. "Congratulations, Green Cloak, you have experienced your first bloodlust."

Chapter 18

The Old One opens his eyes to a shadow-filled room. The familiar smell of hay and the residue of old spells creep into the Old One's consciousness. Pain spikes from his chest. He gingerly places his hand at the source of the agony. A sticky paste saturates his wound.

Warrick was going to die a slow painful death for his treason. The Old One wants to leap from his bed, hunt him down, and make him pay. Spreading out his fingers, he forces his weak voice to speak, trying to heal himself. Nothing changes.

The Old One finds his guard, Fenix, walking through the opening to the room, holding more medicine. Fenix nearly drops the bowl in his hands as he rushes to his side. His words tumble out with questions much too fast for the Old One to keep up with.

"Master, what happened? Where is Warrick? Why did he not save you?"

An overwhelming current of rage causes the Old One to roar, "You are never to say his name to me again! That traitor has taken the book. He did this to me. We must talk to our informant."

Fenix blinks, his eyes glazed over with the flood of information, "The book was returned by the cloaked one who is loyal to us. But there was no explanation."

"Do you have the dagger that cut me?"

"Yes."

"Bring it to me, along with the Journal." An agonizing pull in his chest spikes as he barks the order.

Fenix falls over his large clumsy feet to bring the items and stumbles back into the room. Fenix extends his arms and bows his head, crouching low. The Old One weakly clasps the book and opens the pages with care, validating its authenticity. He holds the slim dagger in his hands, and Kalrolin's magic pulsates through the metal. The Old One wonders how Warrick had come upon such a rare and powerful item.

"You send the word out – that mutinous filth has a price on his head. The bounty hunter will now be the hunted. Let all know that I am still alive and he has not bested me. Wherever he is, we shall find him and have him dragged back here, alive."

Fenix has never seen such wrath from his master and trembles at the judgment awaiting Warrick.

The day had been dull and very unproductive. After meeting Helmsley in the field, they did minor repairs and preparation for the next phase. When the air would become warmer, they could once again grow food. Elan fed the few animals they kept and cleaned up the filthy stalls. The work was degrading and the experience was only made worse by the Creature who stood by and watched with disdain. Elan knew she shouldn't be complaining. She deserved it both for her disobedience and the consequences it had caused.

Elan now stands in silence at the oacling education building, organizing their books.

The Creature watches at a distance, having no choice but to follow. His current silence unnerves her more than his previous instigation. He follows her with cold calculation. Elan's eyes meet his with suspicion. He runs his hands across the books and creeps along the isles with a mischievous stare. Remaining calm, she ignores him, steadying her hand as she places each book.

Elan struggles to keep her mind occupied with the tasks at hand, but can't stop her emotions from swinging back and forth all day. Dual desires war within her. The ache and the sadness of loss linger with the overwhelming hatred to destroy Uldon's murderer. All the while, the ever-present nagging of want pulls at Elan's stomach. She finds herself thinking about those bloody remains. A hand rubs her aching belly, as her mood turns more cross than usual.

Elan's body cries out its desperation for sustenance as they make their way back. Once again, she passes the food tents. More Order members sit in the food tents eating their last meal for the evening.

She almost marches past the tents because of so many Order members milling about. Her appetite gets the better of her, and she comes closer. She hasn't eaten all day, and her head swims. The crowd separates. The eyes of every Order member scrutinize Elan as she makes her way to the table. They back away from her and the Creature. Elan sees Jordon, Tresdon, Lelan and Nolan from the corner of her eye. They gape, wide-eyed and mute. She takes her plate and fills it again with food.

The Creature holds his head high. Hateful grumbles and nasty expressions are aimed at the leech lingering behind her. But his eyes shift, alert, and his shoulders tense as if ready to strike if he needs to. He keeps his hands positioned at his sides. The shadow of a sneer touches his face as his eyes dart.

A sense of déjà vu fills her as she brings the full plate of food to the furthest table. The Creature sits beside her. A twinge of relief makes her breathe easier. At least they are treating her like an outcast instead of throwing stones. She concentrates on her plate. The prospect of nutrition fills Elan with wild need.

"Why are you trying to ingest this slop? This isn't what you need. It isn't what *we* need," he whispers so no one can hear.

Her hands curl into fists.

"There is no *we* and this food is exactly what I need."

She sinks her teeth into the warm bread and fights to keep herself from gagging. She chews and manages to swallow. Taking the leg of a bird, she rips a piece off. Consuming the meat is more tolerable than the bread, but still tastes unusual. She takes a long draw of ale, hoping the liquid will ease the food down. Her face twists as the acrid liquid hits the back of her tongue.

"Fine, Tiny Female. Keep fighting it. It will only get worse for you. Each passing hour will only get more excruciating. I can handle the allure of blood. But I doubt you will be as strong against the beckoning. The longer you abstain, the more difficult it will be for you. I wouldn't want to be one of your Green Cloaked friends once you finally snap."

"Shut your mouth."

The Creature's eyes are as cold as stone, but she can still see a small lingering evil thought expressed on his face.

A stool across from her slides against the dirt ground. Startled, she holds her breath as Jordon sits and puts his plate down. Every Order member pauses to watch.

Before Elan responds, Jordon speaks first, "I'm not afraid of a creature by himself, nor am I so disloyal to leave a friend when they need my support the most."

Lelan puffs out his chest and strides over. He pulls out a seat louder than necessary. "I shall join you too," he shouts, slamming his plate down on the table. He throws the Creature a scowl before turning his attention to Elan.

The Darklandian glowers at their new company. He stands, departing from the tents as far as the curse will allow.

It doesn't take long for Tresdon and Nolan to follow suit. The usual ruckus group sits in uncharacteristic silence.

"How are you managing, Elan?" Nolan asks, while pushing his food around with a spoon.

"I'm fine. I can handle this."

"We've missed you," Lelan pipes in. "At first, we were told to stay away. Then later we had orders that we could come near you at our own risk. Is it true? You receive each other's injuries?"

Elan nods.

Tresdon throws a glance over to the Creature standing far beside the tent wall. The Creature flashes his teeth at him with a low hiss. Tresdon laughs without humor. "It seems like you have been bound to a real charmer." And he gives him a sarcastic wave which only causes the monster to seethe further.

Their faces twist in disgust as they turn their attention back toward the table. They speak to her but don't make eye contact. Their attention stays on the plates before them.

"Did you all do something wrong?" Elan demands, clutching her utensils in a fist.

"Of course not," Lelan protests, his usual stern expressing turning even more affronted. "Why would you say something like that?"

"Why won't you look me in the eye?" Eyes, she had meant. She has two now.

The air around them becomes uncomfortably quiet. Even Tresdon who is always talking and joking hangs his head like an admonished child. He pretends to be very interested in cutting his meat into tiny pieces. Elan squirms in her seat. Jordon takes his time chewing.

"Thank you for still being here for me, even if I don't deserve it."

All of them finally look at her with startled expressions. Underneath everything she sees the pity in Jordon's and Nolan's eyes the most.

"Shouldn't we go?" comes the Creature's biting tone from close behind her.

His voice splashes down her back like ice water. She grips her fork. Elan reminds herself again that stabbing him will only be counterproductive.

As Tresdon's sharp knife cuts into a hardened slab of meat, the Creature walks close behind him and collides with his elbow. Tresdon's blade slips, slicing his other hand. A line of red oozes from his broken skin. His knife clangs to the table as he wraps his finger with the edge of his cloak.

But he isn't fast enough. It isn't a substantial cut, but Elan sees a thread of deep red and smells the sweet perfume. Her heart races, and saliva pools in her mouth as her body responds at once. Something evil inside her wants her to propel herself across the table and drain him of every drop of blood. Adrenaline pumps through her veins as though she is amid battle, ready to strike.

"You beast!" Tresdon yells at the Creature.

Elan spins away, holding her breath. The farther away she walks, the more she feels her sanity returning to her.

The Creature doesn't need to say a word for Elan to know he silently mocks her reaction. She halts, almost causing the Creature to bump into her.

"Don't you dare do anything like that again."

"I won't need to do anything, Tiny Female. The moment you go into battle and one of your friends is injured, your first thought won't be to save them. It will be to drain them. You remember that."

Elan tenses. She had wanted human blood. In this intellectual battle of wills, the Creature's manipulation seemed to be working. The crest's magic must have some flaw, causing it to burn. There is no possible way he would be chosen by Kalrolin to fight in their ranks. Something so vile and unscrupulous would serve no use to them.

Elan's head snaps up at the sound of drums. It calls for everyone to meet immediately at Gallowgrave's tower.

"What fresh torment is this?" Elan groans, not ready for more bad news.

Chapter 19

Elan stands at the back instead of taking her place by Eldon, and Aldon. Uldon should have been there too. His absence has not gone unnoticed. Elan pushes back the throbbing rising in her chest. He would never stand in his place again. The last time they held their ranks, she refused to be next to him. Elan grits her teeth, unwilling to reveal her emotions. A soldier doesn't linger on death or a loss but moves on with their life, remembering their comrade well.

It feels as though someone has ripped a vital organ from her body and the rest of her fights unsuccessfully to function in its absence. The Creature beside her single-handedly obliterated her only love, and here he stands, practically unharmed and toying with her.

Gallowgrave's hands grip each side of the cauldron as he gazes deeply into the swirling blue and red. The contents reflect off his dark skin. His eyes fixed as though in a trance. Neither Gallowgrave nor Dawsley has said a word for a long time now, but each member waits patiently.

"I have been watching the lands, with no movement from the Old One," Gallowgrave begins. "Then this afternoon the cauldron called to me. When I considered its depths, the information it yielded was most surprising."

He pauses, with everyone's curiosity overflowing.

"There was an assassination attempt on the Old One. It was unsuccessful."

There is a collective intake of breath. The Creature stiffens, as the muscles on the side of his jaw throbs. Elan smirks greedily. He must be distraught that someone tried to kill his master.

"The Old One has been betrayed by his kind. A creature dared to try to end his existence."

Murmurs of surprise ripple through the crowd and Elan's eyes widen. One of the Old One's own kind wanted him dead?

"The Old One wants the traitor alive. He has sent his most deadly servants after him. The one they are looking for is a bounty hunter named Warrick."

"We have heard of him before," Dawsley speaks up. "Though none of us has ever seen him, stories travel fast. He is a tracker that could rival even Uldon's skill, and a thief. From what I understand, he is a rogue. He has no allegiances or rules. However, there have not been rumors about him in equinoxes, and he was assumed dead."

"I have heard stories told of him too," Mosley speaks up. "He would just as soon slip a knife into his comrade's back as to an enemy if he could gain from it. But he is as slippery as ice and twice as cold. His face is as much a mystery as his stories."

"Perhaps he thought that killing the Old One would mean he could get the book on his own and ransom it for a reward."

"You may be right. The book would be useless to him unless he knew how to wield magic and very few still know how," Gallowgrave answers. "But this is good news for us. The Old One is weakened, and we have a better chance now than before to get the book. We need to double our efforts in the expeditions. Dawsley will set up a larger team."

Crowds of Green Cloaks rush forward, brave enough to go to The Darklands.

"We must join the expeditions," Elan hears the Creature whisper to her.

"Why in the great beyond would you want to join the expeditions?"

"Because I want the Old One dead perhaps more than any of you remaining Green Cloaks," he purrs. "I tried to kill him. I'm the one he is looking for. I am Warrick."

Elan's forehead creases. She can't trust this fiend. He must want to go into battle so he can entice her with the blood on the field. Or perhaps he wants to be back in his land so he can turn on The Order and return to help his master.

"How do I know you are not lying so that you can get back into your homeland?"

"Because I can tell you exactly how I attempted the murder. I don't know how anyone could have survived. But that old creature is proving much more cunning than death."

Doubtful, Elan answers, "No. I refuse to even entertain your idea."

The Creature's chin lifts as his back straightens. "You... You... stubborn shrew," he sputters, low.

Elan ignores him, holding her tongue from giving him a proper lashing. Her body aches and though it isn't late, she longs to rest, not fight. Sleep will help her forget the growing pains of hunger.

Dawsley spots her in the crowd and makes his way through.

"It's going to be a madhouse with all that has happened. You should get rest. Come back tomorrow morning."

Elan bows, accepting her orders. "We shall meet again."

"I have something to say," the Creature intrudes.

"Whatever you have to say to me, Creature, it can wait until tomorrow," Dawsley dismisses him.

The Creature tries to follow his retreating form but can go only so far before he must stop. Elan has already started going the opposite direction of Dawsley. She leaves through the large doors toward the darkness of the cabin.

Elan swings open the door to the cabin. She strikes her flint, coaxing a fire in the hearth. The only light in the room comes from the fireplace, and it throws the room in dramatic contrast. Elan tosses off her armor. Fingertips knead her temples as she shuts her throbbing eyes. Her thoughts spin uncontrollably. She squeezes the muscles on her arms and legs, trying to loosen the tension. Rolling her neck, she finds little relief, physical or mental.

The Creature leans in the doorway once again. "It's not going to go away, you know. Our bodies will just become brittle and less willing to work unless we eat. Now that you smelled the blood, you long for it more. We won't be able to function."

"Stop saying 'we.'"

"Let me feed," he croons. "It will be better for both of us."

"So you are saying we should go out and find an innocent person and feast on them? That is not going to happen."

"What if the person we feast on isn't so innocent? Would you be alright with that?" Elan frowns at the mischievous glint twinkling in his eyes.

Elan waits before answering. She wants to tell him she is never going to participate in any of his plans. But then she remembers Tresdon's blood. Elan is afraid of herself. If it means protecting her friends then just maybe she would be okay with it, as long as they were truly evil.

"I might be alright with that."

The monster snickers, "I knew you would answer that way. Are you going to decide the person then? Who are you to make the choice? You Green Cloaks are not innocent. You have murdered so many. You kill my kind without even asking why or without even a thought as to whether they fit your definition of innocence. Not just my kind, your own as well. What do you think happens to those who don't accept becoming a Green Cloak? You are no better than I, yet you want to stop me from feeding for survival. None are innocent, so then anyone should be fair game."

Elan knows if she hears his mocking voice a moment longer she will not be able to restrain herself from hurting him. "I'm done with you for tonight. I must rest."

Closing the curtain behind her, she leaves a small opening to let the fire's warmth into her room. The bed cradles her body like a haven as she lies down. The water of the river roars quietly outside of her window. She pulls an extra cloak over herself and closes her eyes. It takes only a moment for her to fall asleep, even with her thoughts spinning.

It feels like Elan has only blinked when she awakens hours later in total darkness.

She doesn't know what woke her. The sky is still dark and spotted with innumerous orbs. The crippling pain in her stomach increases until she can take the sharp, hot, daggers in her stomach no longer.

Stumbling out from her room, she staggers into the night toward the water's edge. Whether the Creature has been awake all this time already, or if it had also awakened from the pain, she doesn't know. He follows behind her through the tall weeds. The land clears until she reaches upriver where the water runs cleanest. Dipping her lips in, she takes large gulps of the frigid water, hoping to alleviate the pain, but it only makes it worse. The churning disgusts her, and she doesn't know how much longer she can hold off. She retches up the entire contents of her stomach. Her body clenches involuntarily.

Elan turns to the Creature. For the first time she sees how much paler he has become and the sheen of sweat on his brow. He must be a mirror image of her, irritable, hungry, and weak. It has been about six nights since the Creature has eaten. She doesn't think she can last another day. They will both suffer a horrifically, painful, slow death unless they drink blood.

"We can't go on like this," Elan says to the Creature. "We need blood. Tonight, we feed."

Chapter 20

Warrick watches the small female soundlessly creep across the hills far from Order Land. They had snuck out under the violet night in search of blood. She knew the shift changes for the watchtowers and precisely when and where to leave without being seen.

His spirit is haughty. Breaking her was easier than he thought. These weak willed beings would not last an evening as one of his kind. The farther out they walk, the more Warrick wonders what town they are going to descend upon. He doesn't see any smoke or firelight close by. His mouth salivates at the prospect. The land stretches out into hills and forest, but no towns. Quite suddenly, the Female stops on the edge of a clearing in the woods.

Warrick squints inquisitively.

"Must it be blood from a man or woman? Can't you take the blood from a beast?"

Warrick frowns. "The beasts in our land are poisoned with dark magic. So are we. That is why we need fresh blood so that the fresh blood can dilute the poison. Because we are said to have descended from your kind, at one point, we cannot take animal blood without it reacting badly. We must take blood from a man or woman."

He watches as the Tiny Female presses her lips into a hard line and closes her eyes, shaking her head, "I refuse to accept it. You are bound to me. I am not bound to you. We don't know how this spell works. Even if I obtain the same injuries as you, why am I also feeling your hunger? There is obviously a physical connection, but I ate our food, and you did not react badly to it. It just tasted terrible. I am willing to try even if it puts both of us at risk."

Warrick is skeptical of her train of thought and folds his arms across his chest.

A single oxenlow silently crosses the long grass, winding its way through the trees. He watches as she pulls an arrow from the quiver on her back. She sets it in her bow and Warrick watches her arm shake as she pulls back the taught string. The tiny female releases the string with a snap and the arrow flies and successfully shoots the oxenlow down. Something about the way she holds her pose after making the landing blow sparks a strange sense of recognition.

Rushing, she flies over the terrain then bends over the Oxenlow as Warrick watches.

He frowns down at her hovering over the great smelly thing, "You could kill us both by resisting, you know."

"I could also save us. We don't know how this spell works. If I drink the blood, then it is not in your system, but at least I'm giving us both something we crave."

"The craving may subside, but the contaminated blood in my veins does not become diluted. We will still feel the effects of the dark magic coursing through me, damaging my body." His voice shakes, and his volume raises with impatience. This female is infuriating.

The oxenlow's dead body cools with every moment they argue. "I'm doing it." As the Green Cloak leans her head in closer, she pulls out the arrow that had killed it. The blood gushes from the opening. Her head kicks back as if disgusted. The blood smells delicious and he can see it unhinges her. Putting her mouth to the wound, the blood spills from her lips.

She pulls away. Her mouth stains red, and she gags.

Warrick jumps back, outraged that the tiny Blood One might empty her stomach there on the ground.

"What are you doing?"

"It tastes terrible, even worse than the food."

Warrick gloats vindictively, "You see, the only way for us to survive is if you let me drink from one of your kind. I promise not to kill them. We just need food."

Warrick's mouth stretches wide with his satisfaction.

Elan won't even think about drinking any more blood herself. But she does not have faith this creature will drink without draining some poor unsuspecting victim. Even if he had the will to stop, he might just kill someone for the sport of it, to torture her with guilt. A spasm of pain slices through her chest. The beast places a hand over his heart.

"Are you having a bad reaction to me drinking the animal blood?" Elan worries, her lip trembling. She can't imagine feeling worse than she does now.

"No, this is all just an effect of me not drinking. First, come the stabbing pains, but that is nothing compared to the stiffening ache in your joints. From there it only gets worse. The skin starts to become tight and dry up. Painful cracking of your skin opens sores. It continues to constrict your whole body, making it hard to breathe. Your muscles start to atrophy, twisting your body in gruesome positions. But there is no mercy of dementia or deterioration of our brain. All the while your mind knows what is happening. You can feel every bit of pain with vivid clarity."

"No matter what you say, no matter how much danger I put myself in, I refuse to hurt another one of my kind to satisfy our hunger."

"Then you have sentenced us to death."

Even to Elan it seems she sentences herself to death. She should have died instead of Uldon. This is the least she can do. Die and be with him in the great beyond. Elan stops in her thoughts. Even in the great beyond she would not be able to face Uldon. The shame of causing his death would be nothing compared to the rejection she already received from him. She could not die without somehow making things right with The Order. What would Uldon think of her if she left her family behind? She still had Jordon, Tresdon, Nolan, Eldon, and Lelan to think about. Her family.

Elan swallows hard. She needs to live but can't allow the leech to drink from a person. She knows what she has to do, but shakes at the prospect.

"You need blood. But I can't trust you not to drain a person for every last drop. And I know that you want to live." Elan stops, almost backing away from her choice. "I have blood. And I know that if you drink mine, you won't kill me. My death is yours as well."

The Creature stands frozen. The only part of him that changes are his eyes, widening. For the first time, his cold mask slips, and he expresses bewildered shock. His clawed hands almost tremble as she moves her cloak from her left arm. He can hear the blood pulsing through her veins. His jaw slacks.

Elan's skin crawls while the Creature slides closer. He takes hold of her wrist. His hands are smooth and cool like the underbelly of a snake. He is close to her now, the closest he has ever been. She tenses, uncomfortable with the proximity, but holds still. Her lip curls as he gets closer. His fangs gleam as he opens his mouth to take a bite. Elan braces herself. His teeth are so sharp that it does not hurt as badly as she expects. Two very small driblets of blood roll down the Creature's left wrist as well. Yes, of course, he would receive the same injury. This assures Elan he will be careful. He might lose too much blood himself if he bites down too hard. Elan starts to feel light headed.

"That's enough, Creature!" He doesn't stop, taking long draws from her wrist. "Stop! You could kill us!" She wonders if he can even hear her, or if he is too drunk on her blood to notice. Why did she think the Creature wouldn't murder her? He had taken Uldon's life, and now his selfish hunger would kill them both.

The horizon starts to tilt and spin. He is going to drain her dry. She is too weak to push him off. His hands clamp down tightly on her arm. Where did he get the strength? Dragging in air, she finds it hard to breathe. "Let go!" Small dark dots start to bloom before her, and her eyelids become heavy as she fights to keep them open. If only she had brought her dagger or her sword, then she would be able to stop him. Before she blacks out completely, the Creature finally pulls away. She doesn't understand it, but despite the spinning, Elan feels better. She falls to her knees, too weak to stand, holding her wrist.

"You stupid monster, you could have killed us!"

"Well, I didn't."

The Darklandian rips a piece of his brown sack cloak, tying his wrist to hold back the small openings. Unexpectedly, he takes Elan's arm and does the same to her.

"I have to take care of myself, don't I?" he asks with the first real grin Elan has seen him give. She knows he isn't smiling out of kindness, but at triumph of getting what he wanted. Goosebumps run up her back, and fear makes her shiver as she realizes she just might have made a pact with a demon.

The whole walk back, Elan can't stand to look at the Creature's smug superiority. She had cracked and let her enemy drink her blood so they could both survive. She can feel a distinct difference in her body. The blood has helped them both. He had not taken enough to reverse the adverse effects of the starvation completely, but already her joints hurt less, the stabbing pains throughout her body had left.

She still feels a small pang of hunger from eating minimally that day, but at least she no longer feels her hunger doubled by the Creature's.

But now she is cold. Much colder than she has ever been in her life. Taking her hands, she hugs them under each arm. She longs to go back to her bed and get warm by the fire. With each step she takes, her feet seem to drag like stones. She has no energy left. The loss of blood is so significant that she feels deflated.

Looking at the Creature, she notices how much better he seems. His form is fuller than it had been before. With just one meal he has drastically changed. Elan assures herself that now the Creature has drunk, she will be able to eat again since she satiated the craving.

Elan regrets looking at him at all because she feels the crest burn on her right arm again. He can feel it too because he places a hand on his forearm, with an almost threatening glare.

Going back into the cabin, she studies her crest in the firelight. Her skin around the metal turns pink. The crest physically burns her skin. She rips a piece of fabric from her cloak and dips it in a bucket of cold, clean water kept in the corner of her room. Taking the material, she wraps it around her crest. The fresh water is only a momentary relief before the cold wears off. One more time she dips the fabric in, but this time ties it tightly to her forearm. No one can see what is happening to her. Now both of her arms can expose a terrible secret. Thankfully, they had just started the frost phase, and she would not have to worry too much about it, but she wonders how long her crest will continue to bother her. She hopes, at some point, the crest will give up telling

her to induct the new oacling. It is unlikely, but she wishes
for that possibility nonetheless.

She crawls into bed, hugging herself, wishing that by
daybreak things will be better.

Chapter 21

The thudding of a heartbeat makes Elan jump. She runs through the woods trying to find its source in the dark. She searches madly with desperation. That heart must be someplace. Tracking it down, she sees a figure in the woods, and the heartbeat grows stronger. Her eyes glisten as fangs jut from her mouth. She grabs the person from behind and sinks her teeth deep into their neck. As the person screams, she realizes the voice sounds too familiar. When she releases, the person turns, and she sees Uldon standing before her, blood gushing from his neck, just like she had seen in the caves. She screams and screams and screams as his body falls to the ground covered in red. Ringing in her ears blocks out all sounds.

Elan pops up, covered in sweat. Her hands shake. It was just a dream. She touches her teeth making sure they had not grown overnight. They haven't. It's not real. Uldon's face is etched in her mind though. Taking deep breaths, it is a while before her pulse calms.

She gets up on wobbly legs, her lips chapped and her mouth as parched as dirt. Pushing her dream aside, she remembers reality. The Creature has eaten, and now it is her turn. She looks forward to the prospect of food and water. Today is going to be better than the last. It has to be.

After getting ready for the day ahead, she walks out of the cabin and around the back. The Creature's hands strike at the ground and toss something backward and forward. Coming closer, her face turns to disgust. His claws keep catching and releasing a small field mouse as it desperately tries to escape. His eyes are bright like a barn cat as he is held amused.

Upon seeing Elan, the Creature stops and observes her with a critical analysis. He puts the mouse back on the grass and it scurries desperately away.

"We have to go to report for the day's duties."

The Darklandian frowns as he gets up and follows her.

As they make their way back to the Order town, Elan quickly grabs a tankard of ale and bread. She will start off slow this time. This will work. It has to work. Elan swallows back the ale without it so much as touching her tongue, but she can still taste the putrid flavor on the back of her mouth. Her face turns sour. She tries the bread, breaking a small piece and swallowing it whole. The flavor makes her stomach twist. She didn't know bread could taste like a rotting animal carcass. Once again, she holds her nose and just swallows a small piece. With each intake, her stomach turns, but knows she can't live off of nothing. Once she cannot stand to take any more, she tosses the bread to the ground.

Elan's breath quickens. The animal blood tasted terrible, but unwilling to see if human blood would be any better, she won't have much more time to live. A half cycle at the most.

From the corner of her eye she sees the Creature give a self-satisfied smile. He must be so thrilled to see her suffering like this. The horrible leech is enjoying every displeased expression she makes.

"Let's get to the chores," Elan orders, leaving her plate and the remaining food and drink on the table.

It has been two days since the Creature drank. Elan's pull for nutrition demands her attention. By the second evening, she doesn't even bother to go back to the large food tents. She knows by now it is a lost cause. Her body aches again, just when she had thought that the effects of hunger had subsided slightly. While lighting the hearth of the stone cabin, her body sags. Even her armor weighs heavily on her shoulders. Struggling to keep her eyelids open, she puts her day clothes aside, plopping herself down on her bed.

They had upturned the land all day to keep it fertile. The Creature seemed to be much more at ease than she the last two days. He almost looks healthy now – his skin had darkened, and is less pale than it had been before he took blood from her. A rosy tint colors his cheeks as he watches her work.

He drank until nearly satisfied that day, but she is far from it. Her hunger and thirst for blood had lessened after he drank, but now it had returned, more fierce than before.

Elan doesn't know anything about this binding spell. Gallowgrave may have made a mistake when casting it. She slowly starts to feel less and less like herself and more like a ravaging irritable creature.

Elan wanes more each day. She turns her hands over. Had they always been so boney? The emaciation sets into her body much faster than what is normal. She fades while the evil being thrives. Soon he will consume her until nothing remains of herself, just a twisted version of what she once was.

Even as she and Hemsley plowed the soil, she had heard his heart beating loud and clear and couldn't help but remember the blood that gushed from Tresdon's hand. And she hated herself for remembering the dream of drinking Uldon's blood. She even indulged in sick fantasies of going over and having a little sip of Hemsley's blood. After all, he had more than enough. Maybe he wouldn't mind sharing a bit with her. Even more frightening still were her thoughts of going to him and taking his blood by force. He would be unsuspecting of her draining him.

She catches herself indulging in thoughts of something that can never be. As Elan now rests in the hut her mouth pools with saliva, and she clears her head. A knock at the door makes Elan jump. Without thinking, she answers as an automatic response.

Elan freezes as the door swings open; the Creature stands just outside. His body is a mere silhouette in the darkening horizon. His eyes are so black they reflect the orange of the fire from the hearth, making them two burning coals in his head. It gives him a supernatural appearance.

"I'm still hungry."

Elan frowns and clamps her fists.

"You felt better, didn't you?" He stalks closer. "After I had blood, you felt relief, did you not?"

Elan doesn't want to answer him. She is still starving but had felt momentary ease after he drank her blood.

"I just need some more. Once I have more blood, then you will feel better again. That is the solution. As long as I am full, you will be too."

Elan wavers at his spoken truth. She had felt normal for a little while when he had taken her blood. He just needed more, Elan decides. That is why she craves everyone else's. He isn't full. Once he is satisfied, then she can regain her sanity. But she faces the same dilemma. He couldn't go and get blood from anywhere but her veins. She has to sacrifice some more of her blood. Elan is not sure she has enough left. And after he drank from her before, he wasn't able to control himself. But she can't deny what she needs.

"No. You almost lost control last time. I lost more than I thought. If you aren't very careful this time around, you could drain me. I need a bit more time to make more blood."

"You will be fine. We need blood."

Those sentences send shivers through her. He stalks closer. She backs away, raising her hands as if to ward him off.

The Creature approaches, slow but determined.

"I assure you, you will feel better, and I won't kill you."

Elan knows undoubtedly he means the opposite of what he says, but she is so famished she only half cares. He snatches her arm again. She pulls to get away from his grip, but he latches on. Her limbs don't have enough strength to move.

Some small part of her does want the momentary relief of when he drinks and doesn't care if it kills her. She braces herself as he sinks his teeth deep into her flesh. With the first gulp her head spins, with the second one they both fall to their knees. If the Creature does indeed get her same injuries, he must be feeling his body shutting down too. Her voice refuses to work, and her mind reels, too disoriented to articulate her protest.

After only two gulps, the Darklandian stops. He staggers back from Elan, holding his head. Two driblets of blood flow down his left arm. He doesn't look back at Elan as he stumbles out the doors. Elan clamps her hand around the small openings trying to stop the blood flow. She doesn't even have the will to crawl into her bed. *Yes, this is it,* she thinks to herself in half delirium, *he will keep taking and taking until there is less and less of me. I will be nothing more than skin, bone and a memory.* She slowly drifts off to sleep, unable to cling to consciousness.

Elan's eyes open slightly to see the room lit. Even sleeping next to the hearth all night, the chill seeps into her bones. Unwillingly, her body pushes against the stone to get up. Elan runs a hand through her knotted hair. As she pulls away, strands sit on her palm. Repeating the action, more tangle in her fingers. Dried blood streaks down her arm and stains her palm red.

After cleaning her arm, she dresses with sluggish resistance. Elan puts on twice the clothes she usually would, trying to conserve her body heat. Even with the extra layers, her armor swims around her.

The Creature's small replenishment of blood the night before was enough to keep her less desperate than usual. She is weak, cold and a bit disoriented, but not mad with need.

The Old One's apprentice stands outside the door. The last living thing she wants to encounter this morning is him. She trips as she walks out the door and falls on her hands. The Creature stands, watching her. He frowns, annoyed, and says, "I didn't want to get hurt."

Falling and hurting him would make her very happy indeed. She glares at him, and her crest burns again. Gritting her teeth, she takes in air and grabs her arm. The Creature does the same too, looking ruefully at her crest. Elan imagines he wants to rip it from her skin to stop the burning permanently.

Elan peeks at his right forearm and sees a red circle forming there. It burns her skin literally, and so it burns his. The pain recedes from her arm slowly. Dusting herself off, she gets to her feet. She heads out with the Creature in tow.

An oacling stands at the bottom of the north tower when they arrive. His eyes fill with fright. His feet stick in place, almost shaking, before the Creature. Oaclings rarely stand watch at the top of the towers. Usually, they are at the checkpoints below, so his presence is expected.

When Order members arrive, other oaclings take their horses and lead them to nearby stables. More oaclings set up the small tents that provide immediate necessary provisions for those who have traveled very far. Elan remembers when she had first come and used those tents herself.

Elan and the Creature climb the steps of the tower and stand watch silently. In one corner of the tower are spare blankets for cold nights and in another corner a bow and arrow for emergencies. This tower too is draped in green.

The green fields stretch out for a long way before the land gradually turns dark gray. She knows if they were even higher, they would see the ground meet the water. But the tower can't be too tall. Even in green, one would notice a massive tower in the landscape. Silence envelopes them for a long time before the Creature speaks.

"This is a terrible system," the Creature says, scrutinizing the massive animal skin drum. A cumbersome mallet leans on its barreled wooden side. "Won't people know where you are when they hear the drums?"

Elan sighs, "Even the closest village to us is too far to hear anything. Besides, Gallowgrave cast a protective spell so that only people on Order land can hear the drums, just in case someone is too close by."

"Then why wouldn't he just do a cloaking spell for the towers and everything so no one can see it?"

Elan huffs in frustration. "He does to an extent. I don't know how magic works. He must have his reasons for doing it this way."

She says it with such finality she hopes he will not ask another question.

The Darklandian leans himself against a wall, crossing his arms and smirking, "I know full well his reasons. He can't. He isn't powerful enough."

Elan deliberately doesn't respond.

"That's another thing I don't understand. Why is your wizard here instead of in the Darklands trying to defeat the Old One? He would be much more help there than here."

Elan's face screws up, suspicious that he is gathering information to take back to his kind. Elan wonders why the traitor hasn't told him all this already. He had found their land quickly enough, so he must know about their defenses. Since they are safely on Order land and not leaving soon, she decides to answer him.

"I was told that when he was younger, he would leave for many nights to defend our land. At that time, he was still an apprentice. His teacher would stay here. Gallowgrave now stays to protect the book and also our oaclings. Protecting the book and our young ones are the most important thing, so that is why he has always been here."

"And yet he even failed in doing that," he says, goading her.

"Gallowgrave's magic is much subtler, that's why you think it is weak," Elan says, trying to defend him. "He helps us by making new enchantments on our crests, keeping the protective spells on them strong. Order members are sent out, but when it is our shift to return for one cycle of rest, Gallowgrave can strengthen them and add new spells when he discovers them."

He doesn't ask any more questions, already seemingly losing interest in the conversation. Frowning deeply, he turns from her and sits on a small rounded bench in the tower, positioning himself in the direction of his homeland. Elan notices his hands ball into fists and then relax.

Being in the tower keeping watch forces Elan to concentrate on her empty stomach. The longer the stretch of time, the more the thought of blood consumes her.

The Creature sits back a little further, humming something under his breath. Elan, willing to take any distraction, tries to listen intently to the tone. It's not an unpleasant melody, almost catchy. Unconsciously, she starts to hum the tune as well.

The Creature stops abruptly and straightens in his chair.

"Why are you humming the melody to an old folk song of ours?" he spits.

Bile rises at the back of her throat as if the melody she hummed was poison in her mouth.

"You were humming it," she snaps back.

His eyes narrow for a moment, then he leans toward her. His expression opens, almost kind, if it were not for the dangerous calculation in his eyes. His lips turn up slightly at the edges, and he softens his voice.

"Would you like to hear it?"

Before Elan can answer, he starts the song anyway. The moment he begins the haunting tune, she regrets it immediately. The words, so disturbing and bizarre, make her feel ill at ease and do nothing to help her forget her hunger.

> *The bones grind against the stones*
> *The buried bang away*
> *There is no love, no loyalty*
> *Just a price to be paid*
>
> *The collector waits for none*
> *Watch for him to come*
>
> *The darkness chokes the singing lark*
> *The blood bathes my hands*
> *There is no hope, no place to hide*
> *No sanctuary to stay*
>
> *The collector waits for none*
> *Watch for him to come*
>
> *The-*

"I think I have heard enough," Elan says sharply.

"As you wish."

He stretches out his legs and crosses his ankles, falling back into lazy ease.

He doesn't need to sing the lyrics any longer, he just hums the melody, but Elan thrums her fingers against her leg, distressed. She doesn't know why, but something about that song stirred something inside her. A vindictive joy in hearing the suffering of others taints the way the Creature sang the song. But the first notes he sang were beautiful and comforting. Maybe she isn't wasting away at all. Perhaps because they are bound, she is turning into a creature herself, slowly and steadily. She touches her teeth again and wonders if her incisors have always been so sharp.

Chapter 22

The next morning goes by in a hazy blur of events. Elan had another nightmare. She tossed and turned most of the night.

Elan scrubs every dish and utensil at the food tents. Once in a while, a flashback of the dream she had passes before her eyes. She is thankful that Mosley is not on kitchen detail this time around. Semore, another retired Order member, not as chatty as Ylmore, had been cooking and left her and the Creature to clean the pots. She labors away slowly, weak and tired, cold and hungry.

The world is a detached and foggy place in Elan's eyes. The cur does nothing to help and watches. His eyes always observe with little indication of his thoughts. But Elan believes she knows his motives. He wants her blood. If he tries to drink from her again, it could be downright disastrous. Elan knows he won't try it unless he wants to put them both in a sleep they won't awaken from. But his imagination must be running wild just like hers. Everyone in a short radius is possible food. Each thump of a heart is maddening. She can hear the flow of blood rushing through their veins. At any moment, she might snap and sink her teeth into one of her brothers.

She abruptly stops cleaning and looks into the eyes of the Creature who has been doing nothing but staring at his potential meal. She gives him a threatening snarl.

Amused at her efforts, the corner of his mouth lifts.

Then her crest blazes. If she had put her arm into a blazing pyre, it could not have been as hot. Both Elan and the Creature scream and double over.

Members are milling about the large food tent, socializing. Alarmed, they all turn, rising to rush to her aid.

Elan plunges her arm into the soapy cleaning water. It ceases to scorch her.

As Order members rush to her side, she shoos them away. They can't know about her crest, but worst of all they can't be anywhere near her right now. There are too many heartbeats.

"Elan?" Elan notices Eldon's voice at once. He parts the crowds to get to her. "What is wrong?"

"I'm fine. I just burned myself on a pot. Go back to what you were doing."

The small crowd reluctantly agrees as they give sideways glances to the Creature. Eldon is the only one who remains unmoved.

"Are you sure you are ok? You don't look well. Your skin is pale. And have you lost weight? Have you been sleeping alright?" Eldon holds his eyes on the Creature, his mouth a straight line. Slowly he pulls his gaze away.

"No. I'm just fine," Elan says, trying to straighten up and forcing a light smile.

Eldon evaluates her once more before he lets his shoulders drop and hangs his head. He looks hurt. He meets her with a tragic expression and places a hand on her shoulder, in a rare show of affection, "You know if you ever need anything, Elan…"

Elan swallows back a lump and responds, "Thank you, Eldon."

"Alright. Be more careful with those pots," Eldon says to her retreating back, but throws a suspicious scowl at the Creature.

Once he walks far enough away, the Creature stands close to Elan. She wants to back away from him. He leans in. "You are hiding something. That thing burning your arm, you lied to them about it. You didn't even tell the Pungent

One. It must not be something common as you had said. What are you up to?"

"Why didn't *you* tell them? You could have said I was lying." Elan fumes that he didn't. It somehow makes her feel indebted to him.

"I don't like you, but I dislike them even more. If you have a reason for your lies and I am forced to choose a side, I would choose you over them. You are not telling them you are feeding me. And so, you keep my secret, and I will keep yours. Even if we decide to find a food source elsewhere, I promise not to tell. No one has to know about our arrangement. But you better know how to fix this. I will not have my arm burn me every day. My patience only goes so far for your kind. Just because I hate you less doesn't mean I don't hate you at all."

Elan doesn't take well to his threat but keeps her mouth shut. He is buying her a little more time, and she is not going to refuse it. Elan continues her job, not even daring to raise her eyes to his face, in case it happens again.

By the evening, Elan deliriously moves without thought. She has no more blood to give the Creature. They both must go to bed hungry. Walking sluggishly, Elan barely makes it back to the cabin. Her stomach gurgles and growls in protest. She holds her belly, remembering the days when she took having a full stomach for granted. A throbbing pain begins a steady rhythm in the back of her skull.

Instead of the Creature disappearing to the back of the cabin as he usually does, he follows her in. Elan is too tired to argue and too apathetic to care.

"You are just going to try and sleep?" the Creature accuses.

"That was what I was planning on doing, yes."

"You can't pretend forever that we are fine. We are wasting away, Tiny Female, you faster than myself. We are both starving. Now more than ever it is apparent that we must hunt. If you do not let us do so, then I have no more blood, and you condemn us to death. We have gone over this many times already. There are plenty of towns close by, more than enough people to drink from."

For the briefest of moments, Elan is filled with euphoria. But then she sees the Creature's face alight with triumphant glee. He looks primal and even frightening. Taking deep breaths, and closing her eyes tightly, she remembers that blood means having to kill someone. There cannot ever be any yielding to this impulse no matter how tempting, not now, not ever. Elan repeats it to herself, forcing her mind to believe it. But she is not perfect and she doesn't know how much longer she can last. A burn at the back of her throat rages, dry and in need of a cure.

"Don't fight it, just give in. It's instinct."

"Your instinct, not mine!"

The Darklandian clenches his teeth and the muscles on the side of his jaw pulse. His nostrils flare, and he breathes heavily through his nose.

"I'm going to sleep," Elan makes her way to her room. "You can stay up all night and complain if you wish." She gives him one last hard look but regrets it instantaneously as the crest on her arm burns again. Each time is more scalding than the previous. She clasps her arm closer to her body, holding back her screams of anguish. Beads of sweat roll down her forehead. He grabs his arm as well, looking ruefully at her, too angry to even utter words to express his loathing adequately.

Elan does not want to speak, does not wish to have another argument or bear with him a moment longer. Her body is sore, starved and drained. She closes the curtain to her room and falls on her bed.

The next day, Elan goes from chore to chore, numb, too weak to do much of anything. She can think of nothing but eating. Throwing dirty clothing into the soapy water, she scrubs each article.

Elan begins to think seriously about what the Creature said the day before. If he would be willing not to tell anyone of her crest, then he wouldn't tell about them feasting. They could get away with it. In secret. They could go into a town and find a criminal or a drifter. No one would miss them. In fact, she would be doing everyone a favor.

It is such a simple solution to her problem. He can eat his fill. She would find relief. She can live while someone undeserving of life will die. It has been nights since she has even attempted to eat solid food. She must hold her nose to gulp down the foul-tasting water.

Elan dives far into her planning when she realizes what she is doing. She is considering letting the Creature murder. Uldon would have been disgusted with her.

But Uldon is no longer here, a voice in her head whispers to her. And the voice sounds very similar to the Creature's. *This will be our little secret, just like your crest burning. We keep secrets for each other. After all, your survival and mine are linked now.*

Shutting her eyes tight, Elan thinks she is going daft. When her eyes lift, the Creature watches her with a puzzled expression. What had her face revealed of her secret thoughts? Frowning deeply, anger bubbles inside her.

This is all his fault. The way she feels, and her doing oacling chores, and Uldon's death. Her sanity slips away, she blames this creature. On top of that, she is now indebted to him for not saying anything about her crest.

Furiously slamming the clothes down, she storms off, knowing even this can't make her escape him. After only a few yards her heart beats faster to pump what little blood remains in her body. Her muscles strain. Her eyes roll back, and she is about to pass out when arms hook under her armpits to catch her.

Elan sobers up, seeing the Creature's face above her. Her desire to push him away almost overrides her acknowledgment that she needs his support to stand. She grunts a disgusted noise and tries to pull away but stumbles.

All Elan remembers next is a single, unfocused glimpse of her room, the sound of the river and the smell of the soft hay on her bed.

Elan jumps awake. Her body shakes. Her hand has a problem steadying itself as she closes her eyes trying to force them to stay still. What she is about to do is beyond insanity. She wraps herself in multiple cloaks. Her steps are soft. She creaks open the door, but as silent as she thinks she is, the Creature already begins to lurk around the corner for the source of the creaking door.

She swallows as though she is trying to push back the words that are about to come from her mouth. Elan cannot wait a moment longer. "The nearest town shouldn't take long to get to."

The implications of what she says make a grin nearly spread across his face. He knew she would break eventually. Warrick tries his best to hide his glee. He walks on a tightrope. It's a balancing act. Anything he does or says could make her change her mind and he won't risk it.

"Lead the way," he croons, as the thought of what is about to happen gives him great satisfaction.

Elan walks past him, her body slumped over in defeat. Warrick walks close behind with a bounce in each step.

Chapter 23

Elan can't believe it is so easy to slip by the guard again. But she doesn't have to worry too much about being seen. The guards focus on the sky for what is coming, not the ground for who is leaving.

The sun set a long while ago, and everything for miles is dark. They had walked on foot the whole way. Elan has newfound strength, propelled by the idea of being able to feel relief from this unrelenting burden. A long dirt road becomes cobblestones as more homes and shops come into view. The buildings became plentiful and cluster together.

A chill of regret runs through Elan. There are families, women, and children asleep in their beds right now. Little do they know that a creature lurks in their town. The people she had made an oath to protect she is now putting within reach of a creature who has been starving. He can snap at any moment. If she can't stop him or can't run away fast enough to pull him back, they could be all dead in an instant. As Elan imagines that scenario, all she can think is how savory the blood would be. *Yes, just think of it as a banquet. You couldn't help yourself. It's not your fault at all. It's instinct. What you are doing is for survival.* The Creature's voice in her head tries to reason with her. Cold sweat starts to accumulate on her brow. If they are looking for a drifter or someone who deserves to die, then they have to go somewhere where wickedness dwells.

Elan had never been to The Rusty Bucket on her own before. Technically, she wasn't on her own now either. She can see the warm light escaping from under the door and through the shutters of the windows. The green cloak would provide them with little advantage and most likely cause more trouble.

Elan stops the Creature. He wears the same sack cloak he had the day they had left the armory. It covers him and is a neutral enough color not to draw attention. Before they enter, she takes her cloak and puts it inside out. She doesn't want to attract attention. They are to slip in and slip out undetected. The Creature watches Elan, anxious to eat. From behind the door there are voices of men yelling and harlots laughing. Glasses clink, and footsteps trample along the ground.

Elan enters first, opening the door and keeping her head down. With so much commotion, no one even notices their arrival. Elan and Warrick weave their way through the mess of people to find the darkest table in the furthest corner.

Every sense goes into overdrive. She can feel the warmth of each body that passes and hear their heartbeats. The patrons' blood rises to the surface of their skin as they blush from too much drink. Subconsciously, Elan's tongue runs over the top of her lip.

"Who is it then?" the Darklandian asks, leaning over. "We can't stay here too long. We might get overzealous and attack in front of everyone."

Elan wipes the saliva from her mouth and strokes her bottom lip. "It is a bit hard to choose. None of these people look very appetizing."

Aside from the possibility of blood, Elan doesn't want to have her mouth on any one of these people to drink their blood. Elan stops. She wouldn't be drinking anyone's blood personally. The Creature is the one drinking. She is not a creature, but she feels like one. She touches her teeth again to make sure no fangs are growing there.

She scans the room and finds a lone man sitting at the bar with a small sack. He is middle-aged, round and poorly groomed. His boots are very worn. He is a drifter.

That's the one. He is perfect. He is not a local. No one would miss him. Just wait until he finishes his drink. Follow him out. We will eat, and you can go back to normal. Only this once. It won't happen again.

Warrick settles himself into the table the Tiny Female had chosen. He is surprised that it has taken her this long to finally be here, to take action. The Old One would starve Warrick for cycles telling him that it was for his own good. That making him abstain from feeding would help him endure for survival. He is used to the torture he is experiencing. But the Tiny Female should not be as used to this as himself. Her willpower impresses him, almost as much as it infuriates him. But in the end, he was successful.

A loud shout makes Warrick jump. He is hiding behind his cloak as best as he can and is fairly certain he could kill anyone of these Blood Ones with his bare claws, but the sheer quantity of them is enough to make him flinch. He is surrounded and anxious to drink.

His gaze falls back to the Tiny Female sitting next to him. Warrick sees the look in the female's eyes that he has seen on hundreds of creatures. The glint in her eyes, the deep breaths, dilated pupils and steely concentration means she has picked her prey. Following her gaze, he sees their intended meal. She doesn't need to say a word. Right now they are of the same mind. They will wait for the perfect moment. It isn't too much longer.

The drifter tilts his head back and drinks the last of the ale in his cup. He slams it down on the bar and begins to wobble his way out.

Elan and the Creature get up from their seats and leave soon after him. Her new coal-black creature eye takes less time to adjust to the darkness.

The man slowly drags his feet on the road. He stops to hike up his bag on his shoulder. The streets are bathed in black. He shuffles across the stone walk.

They close the space between them. She is almost within arm's reach as they creep up soundlessly. Elan's palms sweat the closer they come to the man.

The Darklandian quickens his gait, catching up to the drifter. They are far enough away from the bar now, they could pull the drunken man into the ally. He is so intoxicated there wouldn't be much of a struggle. The Creature peers over his shoulder at Elan, and with a clinical response, she nods her head.

Lightning fast, the Creature descends upon him. He snatches him by his arm. The man opens his mouth to exclaim in surprise, but before he can, the Old One's apprentice claps a hand over his face. He drags the man kicking and struggling. Part of Elan witnesses this, horrified, and wants to stop the Creature. But a much more significant part of her is thrilled by it all. She follows close behind and watches as the Creature opens his teeth. The light gleams off of his fangs, and the man has a moment of sobriety as he can see what is happening to him.

She sees the man's frightened face. The shock and panic etched there. But what catches her attention is an item that falls from his bag. A new doll drops to the ground. Its yarn hair and fabric limbs sprawl out. Something inside of her snaps. A moment of clarity wakes her.

This man has a family someplace. A little girl somewhere very far off waits for her father to come home from a long journey. This man will never see his daughter again. Perhaps every day of her whole life she will wait for her father to walk through the door of his home.

"No," Elan says as she charges the Creature with the speed of an arrow, slamming into his chest. He isn't pushed away so much as caught off guard. She is so weak it is not her strength that makes him let go.

The man screams as he runs to the main road, falling all the way. "Creatures! Creatures!" he yells.

Elan gets a start when she realizes that he must have thought she is one too. Elan hears the clopping of boots pounding the stone. She looks out the alleyway to see the two Green Cloaks stationed in that town. Elan's stomach drops. She will be found.

They are in no shape to fight off anyone. They run to the opposite side from where they had entered, the cold air stinging their faces and their lungs stabbing with pain. They still hear the pounding of feet. The Green Cloaks are far behind, but they will catch up soon. Elan already slows, her legs unstable. They duck down another ally, then another.

Elan and the Darklandian stop and press their backs against a very narrow alleyway.

"I think they went this way," one of the Order members calls to his companion.

Both Elan and the Darklandian hold still as statues as the two Green Cloaks pass. Elan's heart pumps so loud she is sure they can hear it.

"Let's try this way," one says, pointing. "They might have flown off by now."

They leave, running the other way. As soon as the Green Cloaks' footsteps die away, Elan and the Creature slip out. They silently make a run for it in the opposite direction. Once they are out of the town, they veer off the main road and hide in the shadows of the trees.

They both gulp huge breaths. The Creature slams a fist into the side of a tree. He leans on the trunk. His face becomes hard, as a growl rumbles from his chest.

Elan bends forward with her hands on her knees. She squeezes her eyes tight. She had tried to kill an innocent man so that she could live and this pain would stop. But after she would not have been able to live with herself. Crazed with hunger, she didn't even think about running into her fellow brothers. Caught up in the moment of what she wanted, she didn't consider the consequences of her actions.

Elan used to wonder how creatures could have been just like her once, when creatures were so evil. But looking at herself now, she understands perfectly well. Creatures may have been tainted with dark magic all their lives, and it is in their blood, but there had to be something in the nature of all men that made them instinctually wicked. She could see how survival would drive most living things to almost anything.

Elan's breath becomes ragged. She manages to choke out, "I should have never done this."

He bites his lower lip. The tendons in his neck strain.

"Now what are we going to do?" he hisses after a while.

Elan hugs herself as if she can physically stop herself from falling apart. He must be breaking too. All she can do is prolong the inevitable. But she still fights against it.

"I can't spare much. Just take a little bit more from me, and I will figure something out. I'll force myself to eat regular food if I have to so my blood can sustain us. But for now, this is the best I can do. We will go back to the cabin, you can drink from my veins, and we will think of something in the morning. We have to."

The Darklandian does not look the least bit convinced. He regards her from head to toe. He shakes his head slowly with apprehension.

She struggles back to the cabin wondering if they will wake up in the morning.

"Elan? Are you in there?"

Elan manages to pry her eyes open slightly. Small rays of light coming through the window's shutters cut through the darkness of her room. The fire has died out, and little puffs of smoke linger. She is in her bed cocooned with extra blankets. Her head feels like a boulder as she carefully sits up. The room spins and Elan holds her mouth, thinking she might throw up the water she drank the night before.

The door squeaks open, but she doesn't hear it shut. The curtain swings open, bringing in blinding brightness that is quickly blocked out by a massive form.

Elan recognizes the stench at once.

"Why are you still sleeping?" Eldon asks. "It's almost midday. You were supposed to report to the fields hours ago you-"

Eldon stops cold. She knows what he sees. She saw it herself in the reflection of the water when she took a drink last night. Her skin is so pale it is almost translucent. Her cheeks sink in, and deep purple bruises darken underneath both eyes.

"By Kalrolin's magic! What has happened to you?" Eldon asks, as he kneels down to get a better look. Elan can hear his heart pounding. She hates herself for wanting his blood so severely and leans into the sound.

"I'm fine. I just feel slightly beside the dusk. That is all." She turns from him, closing her eyes, trying not to notice his veins straining on his neck.

"Slightly beside the dusk? This is no mere illness. We must get Gallowgrave here at once."

The last person Elan wants to see is Gallowgrave. He will find out about her crest, with his magic. He will somehow know how desperately she craves blood too.

"I'm fine, Eldon!" Elan pleads desperately.

"Not another word from you. I'm getting Gallowgrave here right now." Eldon flees. Elan wants to run but knows she is too weak to go far. Even if she could run, there is no place to go. She can do nothing more than wait.

Elan doesn't want to be anywhere near the cabin, feeling cornered. Gallowgrave and Eldon stand above her, not missing one detail of her sickly face.

Gallowgrave eyes her tightly as she fidgets under his gaze. Her hands curl in to hold the sleeves of her cloak down. She does not know what she wants to hide more: the fact that she is ignoring her calling, or that she willingly let a creature drink her blood.

"You look thin, Elan, and pale. Have you not been eating?" Gallowgrave folds his arms in front of him, waiting for an answer.

He knows. He knows that she craves blood. How does he know? Her heart races and she stops breathing as she holds her sleeves even tighter.

"I'm sure you didn't know that Kalrolin's crest keeps you from most illnesses," he says to her quietly as he sits on the floor beside her bed. "There is something else going on here."

Faster than a viper strike, Gallowgrave grabs her right arm. She struggles to release his grip, but he sees the green cloth tied there. Elan's eyes cast in shame. He takes the material wrapped around her forearm and exposes the crest. Her skin blazes bright red and puffs up around it.

"Great, Kalrolin! What is going on?" Eldon yells.

"Elan and I need to speak alone. Eldon, please report to Dawsley and tell him that Elan will not be doing her chores today."

"But Gallowgrave-"

"Go."

Gallowgrave makes sure Eldon is far enough away then shuts the door and closes the shutters.

"Did you think you could hide this for long, Elan?" Gallowgrave asks, his nostrils flaring. "Do you think you are the only Order member in history to ignore their calling?" He doesn't wait for her to answer but keeps belittling her. "How have you been eating? Well? Or maybe not so well at all?"

Elan doesn't understand his change of subject. How could he have known that she wasn't eating well? It has nothing to do with her crest. Her expression must have said it all because Gallowgrave's eyes grow alight with understanding.

"Perhaps you thought you could deal with the burning on your arm forever? But you can't ignore your food tasting terrible, or the body aches. Kalrolin's magic binds you. What you are doing is not only treason, but it is punishable, not only by our rules but also the magic in your crest. You have found your oacling, yet have not said anything to us. The last time you left our land was when you went to the River Weeds village. Were they there? Have you been hiding it that long? Under the circumstances, you cannot train your oacling directly, but you must tell me who it is, otherwise your situation will not change."

Elan's mind stops as everything comes together. So that is the real reason her food has tasted odd. Her food hadn't tasted strange when she was first in the armory. Her crest had not burned yet. She had come close to losing her mind.

"I can't tell you." Elan wants to get well so badly, but she doesn't know if she can confess this secret making her deteriorate mentally and physically.

"You must. Duty and magic bind you. I know it is hard condemning someone to this life. No one ever wants to pluck someone from their land and bring them here, but you must be strong and know there is a reason you were chosen as a mentor. Kalrolin's magic picks the perfect teacher to lead each oacling."

"You don't understand," Elan protests, swallowing back a lump.

"I know I can't relate. I have never had an oacling, but you must do what is right. What you're supposed to do."

"This is much harder than that. Please, if I confide in only you, you must help me and not tell a soul," Elan begs without pride.

"You can trust me, Elan. That is what I am here for."

Elan lowers her voice and nervously checks the windows as she says, "It is that Creature, Gallowgrave. My crest burned the very first time I looked into his eyes. He is supposed to be the newest member of The Order of Kalrolin."

Chapter 24

Fenix doesn't want anyone to know just how weak the Old One has become. He has been keeping him safely shut away as he recovers. He doesn't like the idea of bringing in the most dangerous creatures in all of The Darklands to find Warrick. The Old One must be very bad off if he couldn't rely on his magic to locate him. Fenix paces, wondering if he should just tell the impending visitors that there was a mistake and their services were no longer needed.

A knock on the door startles Fenix. He had thought for sure he would have heard their approach. Perhaps this is an audition of their skill. He carefully pulls open the door. Three creatures stand back, much farther than necessary. They are courteous, giving Fenix his space and not expecting an invitation to enter. Or perhaps they are defensive, standing back in case it is a trap.

Stepping out, Fenix soundlessly closes the door behind him.

Three creatures stand before him. He knows them well. Crank, Snur, and Ichbone.

"You called us. We came. Who do you want dead?" Crank asks, standing in front. He holds his head higher than the other two. Crank's very slight form enhances his sharp features. His glossy black hair touches his shoulders. His jagged fangs are uneven, and his eyes shift.

Both Snur and Ichbone are at his flank. Snur watches with his jaw slack and his eyes glazed. His sunburned, dirty hair is streaked with gray, and one arm is much thinner than the other. He has a tool belt with knives swinging around his waist.

Ichbone's bald head shines, and he has a severe underbite. Out of the three, he appears the most intimidating. The ridge on his forehead juts out, dramatically pronounced. Iron chains and spikes are draped haphazardly on his shoulders.

"We want someone back alive, not dead," Fenix explains.

Crank snickers maliciously, "We don't do alive."

"You will if you want these." Fenix holds up a small pouch. He rattles the bag so Crank can hear the glass beads inside. All three of them exchange impressed looks. "You only get them if you deliver."

"Shouldn't I at least get half now and half later? We could use them now." Crank leans forward.

Fenix clutched them tightly. "Because it is so important to the Old One that this creature is found, you will get only three now. Only a taste of what we have to offer."

Crank turns to his company. Ichbone nods his head once, but Snur shrugs, seeming unimpressed.

"Take it or leave it." Fenix's temper rises the longer he has to deal with them.

It doesn't take much longer for Crank to respond.

"You have a deal. Who do you want?"

Gallowgrave licks his lips before answering, obviously not knowing how to respond. Elan hopes the Creature can't hear their hushed voices.

After a long stretch of silence, Elan finally speaks, "Do you think this is an effect of the binding spell? Kalrolin would have never wanted a creature in his ranks."

"I don't know." Gallowgrave begins biting his nails and mumbling to himself. "For now, let's keep it a secret. You have told me you found your oacling. Your crest will stop burning."

"There is more, Gallowgrave. The Creature told me that he was the one that tried to kill the Old One and that he is Warrick. He said he wanted to go back into the Darklands to finish what he started. I believe he is lying to me, in order to return. He may be up to something."

Gallowgrave bites his nails with more urgency, "Of course we can't believe him. The Creature was the Old One's student. The Old One must have favored him in some way. He was even taught magic. But there is one thing I know for sure. Don't let your guard down. Don't trust him." Gallowgrave stops and thinks for a moment. "If he is telling the truth, it won't take long for him to be hunted down. We will know if he is telling the truth if someone or something comes to kill him. Even all of our secrecy and protective spells will be no match for possibly hundreds of loyal Darklanders trying to find him. Not to mention the traitor. I wonder how much he has told the Old One already? Or what they are planning? It's maddening not knowing."

Elan swallows loudly. Creatures wanting to harm him would also mean she would suffer. *If* he was telling the truth. Her life depended on that small *if*. For the first time, she hopes that the Darklandian is being deceitful.

"We don't want any more suspicion around you, there is enough as it is. We know nothing for certain. We will give you something simple to do the next few days. You should be able to eat now. You have told me about your crest. Get your strength up. Report to the library as soon as possible. Can you get up?"

Elan's mind wipes away all concern with that last sentence. She can eat again. No more suffering, no more wasting away. The body aches will stop. She can return to normal again.

"I can manage," Elan says with determination.

Gallowgrave nods. "I will head out. We don't want anyone seeing us leave together. We shall meet again."

She nods and doesn't wait long before finding the strength to walk out into the bright morning light as fast as her body will allow. Her head floats, detached from reality. She has to get to the tents.

"Creature?"

Going around the back, she finds him curled under his cloak, sleeping beneath the little warmth of the sun. He doesn't look well either, sullen and weak.

Without opening his eyes, he says, "What in all the land makes you think you can just call me whenever you will? Leave me."

"That is fine with me. I will just start walking, and then you can be dragged along the ground." Nothing was going to delay her.

Sitting up quickly and scowling, he wraps his cloak tighter around him as he follows her back to the center of town. Her muscles don't want to work. The cold cuts through her skin and she presses on. Nothing will stop her.

Elan can't arrive at the tents fast enough. She doesn't even glance at Mosley as she piles her food up once more. The members dining don't exist to her because she is ravenous. She plops down at the furthest table again. The Creature sits beside her, facing out. He will not turn his back to anyone.

"This isn't going to work," The Creature sneers. "It will taste terrible again. Why do you keep trying? We have to go back to that village."

"Absolutely not." Just the thought of trying again made her skin crawl. She had been something else entirely that night. "We are never doing that again. I will eat and build my strength. Don't forget that if I waste away, you don't get your blood."

The Creature clenches his jaw and looks away. His eyes shut, and he sighs.

She anxiously holds a cup full of fresh water. Bringing it to her lips, she only takes a small sip. Relief makes her bold as she gulps down the life-giving liquid. It is fresh and crisp, alleviating her thirst. She slams the empty cup down, feeling triumphant. She holds a small piece of bread between her fingers. This could mean life or death to her. Slowly bringing the bread to her face, she sniffs at it. Placing it in her mouth, she chews. It is soft and moist and delicious. She takes another bite. A cascade of relief falls on her. The Creature was not taking over her as she suspected. She is indeed still herself and not a monster that would have to take the lives of others for survival.

The Creature watches aghast and instantly looks hostile at seeing how she isn't gagging. His mouth becomes a hard line.

Her relief is short-lived as her mind begins to work again. If she isn't turning into a creature, then she had seriously considered murdering a person for blood. She cannot believe how close she had come to killing someone for survival. A chill runs down her spine. Elan had never known she was capable of such thoughts and she came very close to fulfilling them. She can't believe the lengths she would go to save her own life when faced with death.

But she isn't going to die, not yet anyway. She tries to comfort herself with this thought. Elan stuffs her face, swallowing so hard it hurts her throat.

The Creature watches her, disgusted. His lip twitches. "Lovely table manners."

Elan is too relieved to be annoyed by him. Every morsel is delicious. She just keeps repeating to herself that she won't have to resort to killing others for food. She isn't turning into a creature, and she isn't wasting away. Her life is still her own, to an extent. Elan wants to eat more, but her stomach has been so empty lately that eating more would be impossible.

After a while, the worry that creatures may be looking for him overshadows her joy. Now that her primary matter has been taken care of, her focus turns to the other dangers she still faces. There could be a hoard of creatures looking for him, at this very second, if this creature is Warrick.

"Are you really who you say you are?" Elan fixes on him intently, for the first time not worried her crest will burn. Her eyes bore into his as if doing so will tell her if he lies.

"Would you believe my answer either way?" he replies coolly. His eyes shift, startled by her direct stare. He squirms uncomfortably.

"Maybe. We will know for sure if other creatures come looking for you," she whispers low, hoping no one can hear.

"Why give them the upper hand? Waiting for them seems too passive. I say a preemptive strike would be best. We should go to The Darklands before they come here."

"We could only do that if I believed you are Warrick, and I don't believe you are."

"Well, Tiny Female, it appears as though we have to start trusting each other a little."

"Me, trust you? You are a murderer and every chance you get you try to manipulate me," she fumes. Her gaze becomes intense and fueled by hate.

"Remember, I am keeping a secret of yours. You should think if I weren't trustworthy I would have told them what happened to your arm," he taunts, refusing to look away.

"I know you are only using it for collateral. I'm sure you are only waiting for the perfect time to say something. But at this point, it doesn't matter. I have taken care of it."

"So soon?"

"Disappointed you lost your bargaining chip?"

The beast's nostrils flare, his lip curling.

"Am I interrupting something?" Nolan booms with an edge of irritability.

173

The Creature leans away from Elan and she sits back as well. She did not realize they had bent in so close to one another. An outside observer might think they were conspiring instead of arguing.

It had been odd to not see Nolan for so long. She used to see him every day. Lifting the corners of her mouth, she gives him a weak smile.

"Yes, you are," snarls the Creature. "Move along, blacksmith." He cocks his head to the side quickly, shooing him away.

Nolan frowns as he sits on the other side of Elan. "Gallowgrave said you had a late start this morning and you will be assisting Beasley and me tomorrow. It's simple work. I was told you were ill. You don't look so well to me. Should you be doing chores at all? Maybe you should just rest for a few more nights. We don't want you getting worse."

Elan hears the Creature snort beside her.

"I will be fine. Thank you for caring so much, Nolan." She gives him an encouraging smile, but it only makes her cheekbones jut out and doesn't help her convince Nolan she is okay.

"Okay. See you tomorrow," he says, stilted, as though he is being careful.

Nolan and the Creature exchange looks of mutual hatred as he walks away.

"I don't like that one," the Darklandian says, watching Nolan.

"You don't like any of us."

"That one more than any of you. There is something about him I find particularly disagreeable. His wide gait and statuesque face, angers me, and the way he observes you and is always around like a constant pest." The Creature watches Nolan's back as he goes.

Not really caring what the Creature thinks, she doesn't bother pursuing the matter further. After nibbling on a few more pieces of bread, Elan finally decides to head over to the library.

The oaclings' morning classes just finished, and Elan takes the books scattered about the desks and brings them back in small piles. Even the slightest effort tires her.

The Creature yet again sits at one of the desks as he flips through some of the books without much interest. Elan finally feels satiated after so long, making her thoughts much quieter and focused.

Elan walks behind the high shelves and puts each one back in sequence by subject. Elan peeks at the Creature through the opening in the racks and sees him studying one of them already on the table more intently than the others. He opens the page and grimaces.

Once she rounds the corner to retrieve more books, the Creature turns away and feigns disinterest.

Elan frowns at his strange behavior. Taking a few more books, she walks around to put them away. She goes to the desk where he lounged moments ago. Picking up each book to return them, she quickly flips through the pages to make sure he was not trying to ruin the Order's educational texts. In each one, pages rip and yellow with age.

Not overthinking the incident, she continues her job, but the Creature doesn't open a single book again.

They spend the whole day not speaking a word to each other as Elan wrestles with her thoughts.

The long quiet day gives Elan too much time to think about what had happened the night before. The desperation of her hunger almost led her to do the unthinkable. She had gotten just a small glimpse of what it was like to be a creature. She had only dealt with the desire for a cycle. What if she had to deal with that maddening thirst her whole life?

She doesn't want to think about it. She doesn't want to sympathize with their kind.

As she starts to put one of the other books away, she finds the text he was gripping so intently. This time, instead of checking for any damage caused, she studies the pictures. Inside there are illustrations of slain creatures and the glorified drawings of the Order members who killed them. The depictions of the Darklanders are crazed. It describes their weak spots and the fastest and slowest ways to kill. The browning pages indicate that it is one of the older books in the library. Right away, she knows these pictures are inaccurate. They show the creatures with armor, knives, and maces. Elan can't understand why this one was off the shelf. It is outdated. Why would a mentor choose to give oaclings incorrect information? Creatures don't forge armor.

Elan begins to wonder how much the Order even knows about creatures, other than how to kill them. Taking a deep breath, she remembers something the Creature said. That they kill for survival, for food. She wonders if young creatures are taught right away how to kill, just as their oaclings are taught to defend themselves. In her mind it is different. The creature young ones are killing. The Order young ones learn to protect their kind. She justifies herself over and over with this fact.

We are surely better than they are. We are the good ones, she says to herself.

That night, Elan sleeps soundly. Hunger doesn't plague her nightmares. In the morning, she feels rested and more like herself.

Just after the sun comes up, Elan and her sulking tormentor arrive at the blacksmith's shop. Beasley and

Nolan are forging and grinding the swords and blades. The room is filled with smoke. Even with the large opening to the outside, the fires still create an oppressive heat. However, Elan is grateful for the warmth rather than resentful.

Nolan turns his attention to his two new arrivals and gives a warm smile to Elan. "We are making the swords and armor. All you have to do is keep the fires hot. Just keep heating the metal in the fire and then throw it in the cool water. After a little while, do it again. You do that three times before moving on to another piece," Nolan explains.

Elan nods. Over the equinoxes Elan had spent on Order land, a significant portion of her time had been spent at the blacksmith shop watching Beasley and Nolan work. Even oaclings helped forge weapons a bit. Each time the metal was plunged in, the fire made it stronger. So each time it comes out from the flames, it is better than it was before. It was a lesson they were all taught growing up – one of Dawsley's favorite things to say. The metal comes out of the fire stronger than before. The same could be said about being an Order member.

Elan gets right to work, taking off her heavy armor and setting it aside. She puts thick leather gloves over her hands, going all the way up to her elbows. Beasley hands her one of the newly hammered swords. She places it into the fire, waiting for it to get white-hot. It doesn't take long, and she throws it into the cold tub of water just outside the opening. It steams, and the water sizzles as a cloud of vapor rises. While Elan enjoys this job, the Creature watches silently from a chair in the corner.

Secretly, Warrick wrestles with his thoughts. He thinks about what the Tiny Female had said about possible bounty hunters seeking him out. He smiles to himself, wondering what pathetic excuses for assassins the Old One plans on sending.

Warrick scans the armor and weapons laid out. With nothing better to do but sit in a corner and observe, he watches the Tiny Female working fervently. Her hair sticks to her neck as she sweats from the fire. For lack of entertainment, Warrick has to admit, he observes her often. The few moments the Tiny Female forgets he exists, like right now, she has a spark. His stomach twists and he has to look away.

The Fat Blacksmith is absorbed in his work, grinding, hammering and heating then repeating each step. He takes particular pains to be careful and weigh the balance of each weapon. Warrick appreciates a hard worker who takes pride in his craft. Even he could see the light in his eyes and the joy of creating each item from the metal.

Warrick's attention unwillingly turns to the Blue Eyed Man. There is something Warrick does not like about him at all, but he cannot tell what. He works just as hard as the Fat Man, and the weapons he makes are perhaps of even more exceptional quality, but his toil is not out of joy. A hardness underlines his face as he works, except when his attention turns to the Tiny Female. Warrick does not miss the softening of his expression and his river blue eyes seem to shine when he watches her. Just as he suspects, the Tiny Female labors away, oblivious to him. She doesn't return his stolen glances. Slinking satisfaction settles in his belly at her lack of interest. Perhaps Warrick can use this to his advantage. Yes, there are possibilities of knowing the Blue-Eyed One's weakness. He smirks.

"Elan, we must speak. Now."

Elan lifts her head and sees Dawsley standing rigid. The tendons in his neck pop as he restrains his anger. Elan has no idea what she has done, but knows she shall pay for it dearly.

Nolan and Beasley freeze in place as they watch the exchange between Elan and Dawsley. A thick air of tension strains between them.

Putting down her things at once, Elan follows Dawsley. He races across to the other buildings. Elan suspects they are going to the tower, but when Dawsley turns to go to the arena, she is even more puzzled than before.

Elan sees the Creature dawdling behind her, rolling his eyes and shoulders slumped appearing bored out of his wits.

Dawsley finally stops in the open space of the training auditorium. It is dark, as usual. The building, however, is oddly empty. They make their way to the far end of the building.

"I had an interesting conversation with Gallowgrave not a moment ago. Do you have any idea what it was we talked about?" Dawsley's voice echoes slightly.

Elan wants to curse and hit something. Gallowgrave had told her that she could trust him.

"Answer me."

"I can guess what you were talking about." Her words drip with bitterness, and she doesn't have the confidence to look him in the eye without scowling.

"How could you do this? You have a sacred oath to uphold."

"We don't even know if it's real or because of the spell," Elan defends shaking her head slightly.

"We can't take that chance. It must be done, even if I don't agree with this in the least and I would rather cut off my arm than see this creature become an Order member-"

The monster's head jerks to them, hostile, "What are you talking about? You won't ever have to worry about me becoming a member of your little society. If I were not stuck to your female, I would not even be here."

Dawsley looks incredulous. A tick jumps on the side of his jaw. "None of us have any choice in the matter, Creature. Kalrolin's magic chose you. It is sacred and our highest law. We usually give the oacling the choice of accepting or death. In your special circumstances, there is no option. You are one of us now."

"Never!" the Creature sputters with denial.

Dawsley goes on, "You will begin his training this instant, Elan. You should have started a long time ago."

"You are completely mad!" The Darklandian really did look at Dawsley as though he were some kind of vile insect. "Nothing you are saying is making any sense. And I refuse to take orders from anyone, especially from the tiny female. I have nothing to learn from her."

Dawsley chortles a quick humorless laugh, "Do you think you have a choice? Magic enforces the penalty for not following our laws. The crest on Elan's arm won't allow it."

Elan sees the realization dawn on his features as his eyes fall on her metal crest. The Creature shoots Elan an accusatory scowl. His fists clench and hissing breaths escape his teeth as his eyelids squeeze shut. His words explode from him. "Well, you are not sticking one of those metal things on me. And I am not becoming her student." He throws a condemning finger pointed at her.

Elan wants to grab his hand and bite down hard on his reproachful hand.

"You are bound to Elan. So if you don't play along, Creature, she will suffer and so will you."

The monster quivers with fury. Every muscle strains against his skin, taut, tight. His chest rises and falls with his rapid breathing. He begins to move in a frenzied pace back and forth, muttering to himself.

"I will not wear a symbol of allegiance to murderers. I may be bound here, but you do not own me nor am I one of you!" he roars.

Elan watches as the Creature becomes unhinged. His eyes flash, crazed. Elan finds herself taking a step back from him. For the first time, Elan is truly afraid of the Creature, and she leans back more. He always seemed to hold tight reins on his behavior – controlled – but now he resembles a wild wounded animal.

"Whether you want to be one of us or not, Creature, you now are, crest or no crest." Dawsley frowns then adds sarcastically, "I shall spread the happy news to the other members."

Dawsley turns on his heel, not looking back.

Chapter 25

The Creature rages, kicking at anything he can find and trying to free himself from the leash of the spell by repeatedly trying to push the limits of their allotted distance. He pulls against the invisible rope connecting them and flaps his bat wings, but he cannot go any further if she does not move.

The ground beneath the Creature is marred with claw marks. He breathes heavily and sweats from the effort. After catching his breath for mere moments, he begins to struggle again, trying to escape.

Elan sits with her legs and arms crossed defiantly and watches him, just as angry and hopeless with the situation as he is. Equinoxes could pass with him struggling to get free, and his efforts would be in vein. He had to know this, but still he fought and raged. Did he want to get back to the Old One that badly? He must want his power back, and some evil deed or scheme awaits him. Her stomach churns at the thought that this Creature is in line with the Old One. He was his student, and this Creature condoned the Old One ripping through her homeland. This same creature tried to convince her to let him feast upon her kind, and she very nearly did. The Creature is a murderer and wicked to his very core. The fact that he is now her oacling is a cruel twist of fate.

Shoving herself up off the ground, Elan stomps over, and the Darklandian staggers forward. There is a glimmer of hope in his eyes at the advancement. He lights up for the briefest second from the gained forward motion, but his expression falls seeing Elan walking toward him.

The Creature takes a long hard glare at Elan. Perspiration beads on his brow while he slows his ragged breathing.

She musters up enough contempt to make her words acidic. "You are a creature. You don't belong here or in our ranks. I will train you because I have to by our laws. But I will not force you to learn or follow my instruction because I don't care if you learn. This isn't where you are supposed to be. You will never be one of us."

"Agreed," he replies with just as much venom.

She turns from him, disgusted that he is now her brother in arms.

Elan is supposed to be training the Creature. But instead, she has been practicing herself in the most secluded part of the arena. She has not been in a single battle in over a cycle. Her body is sluggish with the stiffness of disuse. Repeating every position she was taught, she uses every strike Uldon had shown her. With each movement, she remembers Uldon. His words of instruction rings in her memory. She sees all of her lessons as a child as she worked with the wooden sword, and remembers the day he finally let her use a real one. Elan even recounts every second of the last time they were here together. She had been so stubborn and mad at him. But that was a waste. Had she known she would lose him so soon, she would not have wasted her time being petulant.

The drums for a meeting thunder. Her thoughts reluctantly turn to Dawsley. Elan will not be going to this meeting. She knows the news he is about to tell them. He will inform every Order member that a creature that tried to kill them, and perhaps slaughtered many of their brothers, is now a member. Many will feel the way Elan does. Betrayed. Others will not believe the news, even coming directly from Dawsley. What will happen when they see the Creature now, knowing the truth?

Warrick exhausted by his ire, could do nothing but sit on the ground and seethe. He watches the Tiny Female practice all day and doesn't understand how Blood Ones use sharp pieces of metal as efficiently as they do. Warrick unwillingly admits her fighting skills are more impressive than in the caves. As she moves in the arena he thinks she looks concentrated, deadly. He supposes her emotions had gotten in the way of her focus that day. He had killed that vile man, apparently someone very close to her. He takes a moment to wonder just how close. His suspicious eyes narrow as he watches and ponders her character.

A highly polished sword hangs on the wall and looks different than the others. Vines and leaves intricately engrave the metal. The blade looks so sharp that it cuts the rays of light touching its edge. His curiosity gets the better of him, and he gets closer. Warrick sniffs at the metal and apprehensively taps the broad side of the blade with a claw, and the metal pings. Warrick takes hold of the hilt and picks it up off the wall. It's lighter than he expected and as he swings, it glides through the air. Warrick's hand tingles as if the sword had been missing from his arm all his life. The weight of it, the speed, and the silver ring of the blade through the air hums a sublime harmony. Even the sunlight reflecting off the metal mesmerizes him. Moving it backward and forward, the light from the closest fire dances on its glossy surface. As he tilts it toward himself, he sees his reflection and finds his expression smoothes from a scowl.

"What do you think you are doing?" the Female demands. "Where did you learn to hold a sword like that, Creature?" she asks, shaking slightly.

"I never have."

Stalking closer, she holds the sword at her side. Her face is determined and fierce. Her arm lifts and Warrick only has a half a second to defend himself as the blade speeds toward him. With reckless abandon, she attacks. Warrick instinctively knows what to do. His limbs move all on their own, blocking her advances. The sword swirls around him. The Tiny Female stops, her nostrils flare and her shoulders curl forward defensively, but she doesn't continue to fight.

"Where did you learn to use a sword like that?" She asks with an edge sharper than his sword.

"I don't know. It just felt right." Warrick doesn't understand himself why he feels like he was born to use a sword, though he had rarely even touched one. He scrutinizes the weapon in his hand as though he can find some hidden magic within it.

Elan doesn't want to say it aloud. She doesn't want to say that the Creature fought with fluidity. The form is nothing like Elan has ever seen. It is distinctly different – the way the Creature made it artful, the way he dances with the blade. She doesn't know how to react, how to take this revelation. Perhaps Kalrolin is telling Elan that she must induct him.

He was born to be an Order Member.

Crank, Ichbone, and Snur leave a pile of blood-drained bodies in their wake. Besides being full of blood and stronger than ever, they have information. To them, the information is far more valuable than anything else at the moment.

The people in the Blood One town had seen a dark cloud on the horizon just over a cycle ago. The darkness had ripped the trees apart and turned the sky an ashy gray. Only powerful magic could have done that. Observing the place where the villagers said they found the gray clouds and the twisted trees, they find only a few broken branches, scattered. This is not what their victims described at all. But still, something sets Crank's teeth on edge. These woods hum. His body can sense what he can't see.

"We stay here," Crank barks at them. "We stay and watch. I can feel something strange in these woods."

"Me too," Snur grunts.

Ichbone rubs his chin in agreement.

They catapult themselves up high on the trees, leaping from branch to branch. They get as high as they can go, getting close to the trunks and wrapping themselves in their wings, keeping their heads low. In the shadows of the leaves, they look like uneven knots on the tree trunk. They will be patient and watch.

All good things come to those who wait.

Elan had waited until the sky deepened to violet before leaving the training building to avoid everyone. The Creature and Elan practiced all day separately. The time had flown by with the complicated thoughts that occupied her. She had assumed the Creature would get bored after a while, but he had not. He had only become more hypnotized with the blade each hour. His accuracy and speed made her shiver with instinctual forewarning.

After secretly making their way back to the hut, Elan lights a fire. She rubs her icy hands together, and for the first time wonders what the Creature does on cold nights like this. Where does he sleep?

A light rapping on the door makes Elan's eyes wide. She swallows as she takes soundless steps to the door. Perhaps it is the Creature wanting entrance. Elan doesn't know why she is so worried. He can't hurt her without hurting himself. Standing by the door, she listens carefully for the shuffling of his feet. Holding still, maybe he will think she didn't hear the knock, and he will just walk away. Someone pauses behind the door and she listens to them take a breath, and almost sees the cloud of air as they breathe out into the cold.

"Elan?"

The voice makes her jump. Her nerves calm as she opens the door.

"I should have known you would come here after hearing the news," she sighs.

Nolan practically has to squeeze his way through the door. "I was watching your cabin to see when you would come back. You could have left the training building any number of ways, but you can only come in through this one door. What is going on? The Creature is one of us now?"

"That's perceptive of you to watch the cabin door. Maybe you should become a tracker."

"Don't try and change the subject. It's not like you to be indirect." He puts his hands on his hips and his mouth is a hard line.

He is right.

"Fine. I didn't tell Dawsley that the Creature is my oacling. I don't even know if my crest only burned because of the binding spell," Elan sighs. She takes another deep breath before blurting out, "As if I wasn't an outcast enough already, I needed this." Elan presses her hands to her eyes. "You must be so ashamed of me for keeping this a secret."

Nolan's annoyed expression turns to one of pity. "I'm not actually." He stops and sits casually on the bare floor. He takes a deep breath before continuing. "I'm almost impressed. I never thought it was possible for you to ever go against the Order. Even under the circumstances, I thought you were almost as much of a die-hard as Lelan."

Elan smiles. "No one is as dedicated as Lelan." Elan sits on the floor as well, crossing her legs.

"No, really. I mean it. I remember when you were first starting out. It was like you had to prove something because you were the only female. You fought harder. You became tougher. You read every book. You followed every rule. You listened to every instruction Uldon gave. It's nice to know you have something that you strive for more than The Order."

Elan tried to ignore the way her stomach twisted at Uldon's name. Nolan had no idea that she had wanted something more than the Order for a long time. Though she was happier with this life than the one with her stepmother, she had wanted to love and be loved by Uldon. Something piques Elan's curiosity.

"So I'm assuming your motivation to stay here isn't love of The Order. What's your dream, Nolan?"

Nolan's gaze drifts far off.

"I… always thought that I would have a family. My father had taught me everything there is to know about animals. I thought I would be breeding and training horses with my own family. I would not be trapped in some militant anti-monster brigade. But I suppose we have no choice." His voice hardens at the last sentence.

Elan isn't surprised with Nolan's bitterness. Many Order members feel the same. Elan can't relate much. Her life had miserable before being inducted. Here, she has friends, brothers, and security. And though she is seen as an outcast by many of the other members, this is her home. This is her family. She had been taking it for granted.

"How is everyone else reacting?" Elan asks.

"Just as you would expect. Jordon is quietly contemplating, Tresdon is verbally outraged, I'm confused, Eldon is in complete denial, and Lelan is ready to become best friends with the Creature now that he is our newest 'brother.'"

"He can't be serious." Elan fumes at the thought that Lelan could forget this Creature killed Uldon.

"I'm afraid he is."

Elan knows Nolan is trying to protect her and not tell her the worst of it. He didn't even mention Mosley and Serdon. They most likely are ready to hang her and the Creature or exile them to the most dangerous parts of The Darklands.

"Are you coming back to the blacksmith shop tomorrow?" Nolan's voice is quiet and his attention is on the ground, almost like he is shy to be asking.

Elan forces a smile, "Most likely not to work. I will be avoiding everyone for a while. Leaving very early in the morning to go to the training building, staying in the far corner away from everyone, then staying late to avoid anyone on the grounds. But you know I will be visiting at some point. It's going to be a rough day tomorrow."

Nolan smiles briefly and then gets up to leave.

Elan says goodnight as she stands by the door watching him go. She is grateful to have a friend like Nolan.

As she turns, the door closes behind her. But she catches her breath in surprise, backing away. She thought she was returning to an empty room, but next to the hearth stands the Creature.

"How did you get in here?"

"The window, of course. The door isn't the only way in and out. I thought he would never leave," the Creature says, stalking closer.

"How long were you listening? What are you doing? Why are you even in here?" Elan stamps her foot.

"I'm hungry."

"You just drank yesterday evening," Elan protests, her face getting hot with a mixture of anger and fear.

"I only had a sip remember? I couldn't take much more. But you have eaten more than your fill today, and we are both noticeably stronger. I just want a bit more."

"You can't have anymore." Her voice shakes, but her face is determined.

"Come now, Female." He smiles wide, his sharp fangs, prominent. "I won't bite hard."

Elan watches with trepidation at what the Creature does next. He takes a piece of fabric and wraps it tightly on the indent of his left arm. She looks down at the bend in her left arm. That's where he plans on sinking his teeth.

Warrick stops suddenly at her pale face and dilated eyes. He has seen that look before. She is either going to run or attack. From her expression, he believes it to be the latter. Her fear of him satisfies Warrick. Her heart beats wildly. If it keeps up that rhythm then when he pierces her skin she will bleed out, killing the both of them. She must be calmer for it to be safe. Reluctantly, he steps back.

He studies her set expression and her body starts to loosen.

"Perhaps this is a bad time," he says, completely agitated. "But I will need to eat again, and soon. After I am satisfied, I believe I can go a while without feeding. I went as long as half a cycle before it started to get bad. We don't want to get back to that state, however."

The Creature strides past Elan to walk out the door.

"Creature?" she calls as he turns the corner of the hut.

He smiles to himself before facing her again to answer, "Female?"

"You can take a bit more, but after that, you can't have any more for a while. Agreed?"

"Very well." Warrick licks his teeth. If it meant he could feed now, he would have agreed to just about anything. Warrick walks back into the cabin.

She holds out her arm, but her heart rate continues to race. Her eyes flick back to the door, licking her lips. She is probably concerned that her friend will come back.

"Female," Warrick begins, "Your heart rate is much too fast. If I take blood now, you will lose it too quickly, and you don't have much you can spare."

He sits on the stone ground on the opposite side from where Nolan sat, annoyed. Warrick watches the fire, turning his attention away from her, listening and waiting until her heart rate slows.

Elan regards him, wondering if he is up to something by not insisting as he had in the past. As he sits close to the fire, frowning and keeping warm, her inquisitiveness gets the better of her. She had heard that dying of starvation for creatures was the cruelest and most painful of deaths, and she had gotten a glimpse of what that meant. The body aches and craving were excruciating enough. And he had mentioned everything that happened to a creature's body when they were lacking a meal of fresh blood. At the time, she assumed he was trying to frighten her.

"You told me once in the beginning how bad it was not to have blood. We know that dying of starvation is a painful death for your kind. Is dying that way the worst fate for your kind?"

The Creature frowns, studying her cautiously. He answers hesitant, seeming to ponder his words even while he says them.

"Yes, it is the most excruciating way to die. And it is a slow death. It isn't just about thirst, but being poisoned and it getting incrementally worse each passing day. Even amongst our kind, you don't even starve your worst enemy. Such cruelty is nightmarish. You only experienced the very beginning stages."

He does not go on. Elan can tell this is not something he wants to talk about in detail. He closes his eyes and shakes his head as if trying to cast out a terrible memory. She doesn't miss how he goes rigid, either from fear or anger.

Elan twists her face in indignation. She wouldn't have lasted another day. Had Gallowgrave not come to tell her she could eat food again, she is confident she would have found another way back to that village. A little doll would not stop her nor would an entire legion of her other brothers in arms. How did creatures live every day like that?

For the first time, she thinks of creatures as having needs just like herself. They needed to eat. They needed to sleep. She had always considered them as objects or something below insects. But they are much closer to her kind than she ever thought before. Another thought comes to mind as she sees him sliding closer to the fire to get warm.

"How do you stay warm at night?"

He cocks an eyebrow at Elan, mystified.

He replies with measured words as is the Creature's custom, "When it gets frigid, I sleep on the roof, next to the chimney. The stones heat up from the fire."

"Oh."

Warrick smirks. "Where you worried about me all alone outside?"

Elan's temper flares. "I don't care at all."

Her heart rate picks back up, and the Darklandian rolls his eyes, releasing a long suffering sigh.

"Have you been friends with that one long?" He asks flicking his hand to where Nolan sat before, his face twisting in displeasure.

Elan instantly calms at the thought of her best friend. Kind-hearted, shy Nolan. "Yes, he was my first real friend when I came here. He was one of the few that showed me compassion when I first came, instead of treating me like a pest or oddity." Elan stops herself. She is saying too much, giving him too much information.

The Creature shifts, his face crumpling, agitated. A small grunt emanates from the back of his throat and he jumps to his feet as though he cannot get up fast enough.

"Wait. Aren't you going to…" Elan holds out her arm.

"I'm not very hungry anymore," he spits.

Without any further explanation, he strides out the door.

Elan raises her eyebrows at his strange behavior. She tries to listen for him climbing up on the roof but hears nothing. *He must be there,* she thinks, even though as hard as she strains, her ears can't make out a sound.

Elan goes to her room, leaving the curtain to her room open to let in warmth. Elan falls asleep, still trying to detect any sound at all from the Creature, but never does.

193

Chapter 26

Gallowgrave runs to his tower as fast as his legs can carry. It is early, and the sun begins to touch the horizon. Once inside, he slams the door shut, running to his cauldron and mumbling the words to put a thick protective barrier on the whole inside of his tower.

Dawsley comes out from the shadows of the tower. "It's a good thing you called me. We have to find another way to get information from that Creature. Trying to starve him for information hasn't worked. He must not need blood anymore because Elan eats and he is linked to her."

"I'm glad you made it, we have urgent things to talk about," Gallowgrave interrupts, fidgeting. "The Creature and the traitor must somehow be working together, even under our very own eyes."

Dawsley's face drops. "That's impossible. What has happened?"

"I went to make sure that one of our pages was still safe. The Creature has spent so much time on our grounds. I needed to know everything was alright."

"Please don't tell me, Gallowgrave." Dawsley shakes.

"I'm afraid so. When I went to go check, I found this in its place."

Gallowgrave hands Dawsley a folded page. As he opens it, there is nothing in the middle but three black crows, their wings almost touching, creating a circle.

"If the Old One does have the missing pages, then he will have all the spells he needs to be free of the stone temple. He will be able to come into our lands within a few cycles. With the book and his freedom, we don't stand a chance of destroying him." Gallowgrave wrings his hands as he stares down at the birds.

"You are wielding that sword wrong, you know," Elan criticizes.

"I'm using this thing just fine. I don't need you to tell me I'm doing it wrong," the Creature defends.

Elan exiles them once again to the farthest training spot. The area is bereft of any other Order members, who want to keep as far away from the Creature as they can.

"Really?" Elan walks over to the wooden swords used for practice and tosses him one, and she takes another. "Let's see how you would fare in a real sword fight. No dirty tricks, just swordplay."

"You do know that this is completely irrelevant. In a real fight, no one is going to care about rules and the proper way to do things."

"There are more efficient ways of using the sword without having to use as much strength. You will get tired much too quickly, whereas I will be just fine."

"I doubt that." The Creature strikes and Elan blocks his attack easily. He swings it around and once again she stops the wooden blade from touching her.

It's Elan's turn. She strikes and the Creature blocks it as well, but she lunges low almost right after, and the end of the stick makes contact with his stomach. He looks at the point of the stick ruefully. His upper lip quivers as Elan smirks.

The Darklandian pushes back his shoulders and rolls his neck. He sets his feet wider apart. This time he fights harder, and Elan defends and counterstrikes. The Creature begins to look worried the longer Elan holds him off. She does not even break a sweat and her breathing remains even. She swings the stick around again, and it taps his neck. He bares his teeth before his face pulls in determination. The Creature puts more force behind his movements, fighting back fiercely. She can see the exertion in his limbs, how he is using more effort, to make her stand back. Her small frame makes her more elusive than him. Elan sees his eyes squint, his nose wrinkle and his upper lip pull up from his teeth. His features are changing with his heightened adrenaline.

Elan only sees a flick of his eyes to her knee before he moves. His leg hooks around hers, pulling it from underneath her, making her slam to the ground. Her lungs rock in her chest as her back aches sorely. She was winning and he knew it. He couldn't stand the idea of her besting him so he took a cheap shot.

"That's cheating," she yells, getting back up on her feet.

"That is what a real fight looks like." And the Creature had the nerve to lean forward, getting close to her face and smirking.

Elan's rage spikes in her chest. Faster than the Creature can react, Elan steps behind him, pulls his arm forward while pushing his opposite shoulder. He swings around and collides with the floor, his wings crushed under him. She draws her real sword from her scabbard and points it to his neck.

"If this had been a real fight, I could have killed you a long time ago," she mocks, her pride inflating.

The Creature's alarm flashes only for a moment before his angry mask slips back into place.

"Am I interrupting something?" a voice calls, approaching from the other side of the auditorium.

Elan jumps, putting her sword away quickly as the Creature gets back on his feet.

"Elan," Dawsley says striding over. "I would like a word."

The Darklandian raises his eyebrow.

"Alone," Dawsley says.

"If only," the Creature chides. He picks up the wooden sword and starts to practice again.

Dawsley takes Elan by the arm and leads her a bit farther away. He goes as far as the spell will allow. He turns his back on the Creature, speaking low.

"We have a problem. The missing pages of Kalrolin's Journal are scattered everywhere. Most are on our grounds, but some are not. Gallowgrave and I both felt uneasy about their safety, so he checked on them to make sure everything was still in its place. But last night, Gallowgrave found that one of the pages was missing."

Elan's eyes become rounder with each sentence.

"The Creature must be conspiring with the traitor. We have gone so long without any pages missing, twenty equinoxes without a problem, then when the Creature comes on our land, we are missing a page."

"But that is impossible. He hasn't left my sight even for a moment. He can't go anywhere that I'm not."

"Think hard, Elan. Have you seen him speaking to any of the members, even briefly? Was there a time you were even for a moment distracted, and he was not in the same room as you or out of sight?"

"I can't think of anything, not even..." Elan stops and thinks. He is out of her sight every evening. He says he sleeps on the roof by the chimney, but she has never heard him there before. Even last night when she tried to listen to his steps they did not come. The traitor might come and visit him in the evening when she is asleep. Maybe the traitor even brings him provisions to keep him warm. "Just at night. He doesn't sleep in the hut. That is the only time I can think that he is out of sight."

Dawsley rocks on his feet slightly, chewing his bottom lip. "All I know for sure is that there is some suspicious business going on and I know it has something to do with that Creature. Keep a closer eye on him. We don't want to let him know that we are on to him. We have secrets of our own."

Dawsley glances back over to where the Creature practices. He clenches his hands into fists before marching out, leaving Elan alone on nanny detail.

Elan studies the Creature warily the next few days. He is much smarter than he appears. She does not even know for sure if he was lying to her about never touching a sword before. That is impossible. No one could have so gracefully maneuvered such a cumbersome weapon on their first try. And what about the way he speaks? Most creatures don't say more than a few sentences, but he has a rare eloquence compared to others of his kind.

Elan assumes the Old One taught him well. He knows magic and is very articulate. Elan is sure that he knows how to read and write both modern and ancient language. She had seen him pick up books in the education center, and he looked at the pages with comprehension. In addition to reading and writing, she is positive that deception was also in his lesson plan.

She hates to think that one of her brothers is working with this Creature, but worst of all working with the Old One. Elan has to stay alert, on her toes, to be one step ahead of him if she can.

For the hundredth time that day, the Creature stops practicing to return Elan's intense scrutiny, and she turns away, pretending not to stare.

"I think we are done for the day," Elan announces.

He puts back the wooden sword and sluggishly comes toward her. She tracks his every move. Everyone had already left for the evening so she didn't fear having to walk past more probing stares.

Elan hopes to walk in the shadows and hide as they make their way back to the stone cabin.

"Hey, Elan!"

Elan cringes at the call. Lelan. Of course, it had to be him. Lelan runs over with a set expression. She does not have the patience to deal with him, but steels herself for the interaction.

He nods at Elan before turning his attention to the Creature.

Without any preamble, Lelan speaks, "I wanted to say that I don't forgive you for killing Uldon. But with that said, I also want to say I understand why you did it."

Elan thinks she is going to be sick right there in front of Lelan. She had to have been hearing him wrong. Just when she thinks she imagined those words out of his mouth, he continues.

"It was in battle. We all go in knowing the possibility is death. It was a fair fight-"

"If by 'fair fight', you mean your kind tried to ambush me and entrap me while I came on my own," the Creature interrupts.

Elan startles, then snaps back, "You had magic. We had every right to even the playing field. Or did you forget that?"

Lelan clears his throat peevishly at the interruption of what Elan imagines is a perfectly planned speech, but continues as if there had never been a break in his monologue.

"-and one person was the victor. That is the way it goes. Though you were working for the Old One, I still acknowledge you as my brother in arms, by the decree of Kalrolin's choosing. Once you become an Order member, you have a completely new life, and everything before is erased. If his magic has chosen you, then I trust that it is right." Lelan bows, waiting for the Creature to return the gesture.

Elan stares, her mouth hanging open, utterly speechless and sickened. The Creature is vile. Elan does not understand how Lelan could see him as anything else. Not hating him betrays the memory of Uldon.

The Creature opens and closes his mouth like a fish, his expression open with shock. Then his face changes to one of utmost disgust. The Darklandian spares a glance at Elan as if to check her reaction to see if this is a joke, but by her expression, sees it is not. The Creature gives a low, quiet growl as he strides past Lelan.

Elan knows he will have to stop soon if she doesn't follow, but honestly, right now she would rather be in the Creature's company than Lelan's.

When they reach the stone hut, Elan doesn't go in right away. If the traitor comes every night to conspire with the Creature then maybe if they stayed up late enough she could catch him close to the cabin.

"We should get some fresh water from the river," Elan suggests.

"Don't you have enough? And besides, it is dark, how do you expect not to fall into the icy water and drown?"

She had wanted to stall him somehow.

"Half of that cabin is yours, you know. It is warmer inside than just on the roof."

The Creature chews over her words. He lifts his chin, looking down at her with trepidation.

"Though the offer is very generous, I decline."

Of course he would decline so that he could have more time with the traitor, Elan thinks.

"Alright," Elan says. "Have a good night then."

Elan walks in and pretends to get ready for the night. She lights the fire and puts her things away. She stays awake, straining her ears until the lunya has passed half the sky. Quietly, she tiptoes outside the hut. The air slices at her skin. Elan's height makes it difficult to see on top of the roof so she walks a distance away to get a better look. Sure enough, there is an uneven lump on her rooftop next to the chimney. It doesn't seem as though the traitor is coming tonight.

A bird caws, making Elan jump. Turning toward the sound, she sees perched up on a tree branch three blackbirds staring at her. Their eyes are shiny, reflecting the little light of the blackness. Elan doesn't know why but the birds give her a feeling of foreboding. Not wanting to be under their intense gaze a moment longer, she rushes back into the cabin and pulls the blanket around her.

Chapter 27

"Get up!" a sharp voice snaps at her.

Elan jumps back, as the Creature crouches over in the darkness of the front room. The fire has died down, and dampness clings in the air. For three days now, they had been getting up before dawn, doing oacling chores and working on the Creature's sword skills. They would only leave to go to the education center when the oaclings needed the training room. Nolan had been bringing Elan food and spending time with her while the Creature barely spoke to either one of them. He would sulk farther off or ignore them while still in their company.

Dawsley and Gallowgrave both checked up on her from time to time to make sure she was keeping up with watching the Darklandian. But she never had anything new to report. She never saw any other Order members by the hut, and Dawsley and Gallowgrave were keeping watch at night.

The Creature had not drunk her blood or even asked after his strange reaction a few nights ago. She is thrilled that he isn't leeching off of her.

"I thought you would like to know the sun is coming up soon. If you want to avoid everyone again, then I suggest you get up now."

"This is much too early!"

"I could not sleep."

"Why is that my problem?" Before he can answer, she knows why he can't sleep. She feels the small aches in her body and her stomach turning sour. The Creature is hungry, but Elan is not about to offer her blood so willingly. She will only do it when she has to. After conspiring and helping the traitor, perhaps she should let him suffer a bit, even at her own expense.

"I don't know how often you barbarians bathe, but I would like to. We have been practicing and sweating for days now."

Elan screwed up her face in annoyance. If only the binding spell had a longer leash, then she could just tell him to go to the river himself.

Elan and the Creature both get a bucket full of water from the icy river. The sound soothes her, and had she not been with the Darklandian, she would have just stayed down by the water. Elan staggers in the hut with the water sloshing. She starts the fire, putting one bucket in the cauldron then the next.

"Do you want to go first?"

"Of course. Do you think I want to use the soap after you?"

Elan rolls her eyes. "A yes or no would have sufficed." She throws soap and cloth at him in a large basin. She steps out of the hut and waits. Elan can't imagine it getting any colder, but she knows it will. The frost phase has only just started. Her arms cross as she tries to keep her hands warm. After a while, she hops up and down, trying to keep her temperature up.

"Hurry up!" she shouts. "It is freezing out here."

An audible growl rumbles the door.

But at some point, his growl is drowned out by another rumbling. The drums. A town close by must be under attack. They will need as many members as possible to ward off the danger.

Elan runs into the cabin, completely disregarding the Creature.

"I'm not done!" he seethes, trying to cover himself.

But Elan doesn't even see him. She runs into her room, grabbing her other cloak, putting on armor and finding the tiny dagger. She pulls a second green cloak from her room and a few articles of clothing.

"Here put this on. It won't fit, but it's clean." She says throwing it to him. She stays in her room to give him privacy but keeps talking. "Those drums mean that there is an attack close. The sound is coming from the West Point. That's where we have to go."

He fumbles as he dresses while Elan barks orders. After a few minutes, she comes out and observes the Creature. The pants she gave him are much too short. The green cloak isn't large enough either for his folded wings to fit. "We should get you some new clothes after this is all over."

"I don't care to fight."

Elan shoots him a fierce expression.

"I suppose I don't have a choice," he grumbles. "By all means, lead the way."

Elan runs to the west checkpoint, ready to mount a horse. The Creature's long legs move faster to keep up with her pace. Dawsley shouts orders as everyone scrambles into place.

"Where should I go?" Elan asks, her eyes bright.

"Back to your cabin," Dawsley says as he gives more orders to another member.

"But I can help you. I haven't been in a battle in over a cycle. I'm useless to you here."

"Out of the question." Dawsley turns his attention to Gallowgrave who comes trotting over.

"I sense dark magic. I must go with you, or you will be outmatched," Gallowgrave tells him.

"The word is that they are looking for Warrick. They think he has been around here. I don't know why they would think a bounty-hunting creature would be here, but they have been murdering and feasting and must be stopped. Just a little while ago our men spotted them just outside of our land," he says to Gallowgrave. Gallowgrave shoots a nervous peek at the Creature. At least Gallowgrave didn't tell Dawsley about what the Creature had told her of his identity.

Elan glances at the Creature. His eyes narrow to slits. So he told the truth. He *is* Warrick, and that would also mean he most likely wasn't working with the traitor. If creatures were coming looking for Warrick, that means she is in danger as well.

"You will need all the help you can get," Elan reasons.

"Stop. You are acting like a child, Elan. Swallow your pride and take your orders. Go back now," he booms, pointing a finger back to the hut.

Dawsley rushes off with Gallowgrave close behind. Eldon gives Elan an expression of pity as he mounts his horse.

"It's better if you stay," Jordon assures her with authority, as he catches up to Lelan who already rode off before any of them.

Elan pauses at Jordon's words. If she didn't doubt her actions before she is doubting them now. Dawsley is her leader, but she respected Jordon's judgment, always being the wise and level-headed one.

"There is no way we are going back. I would like to leave another message for my old master," the Creature whispers to Elan as Jordon trots away.

Her resolve to go solidifies at the Creature's encouragement. "And I am not putting us all in danger by hiding out here and letting them destroy their way through our land." Elan feels guilty that so many lost their lives in search of the Creature. He is here because of her. No more will die because of her mistake. If those creatures want to find Warrick, they will. But it doesn't mean that they will live long after they find him. Elan pulls up her hood, hiding her face. "With all the commotion, they won't notice us going. Pull up your hood."

The Creature obeys. She swipes swords from the armory, finds two horses and climbs up on hers. The Creature stands next to his steed.

"What are you doing? Let's go," Elan orders.

"I have never ridden one of these," he says, looking at it as though it were an otherworldly beast.

Elan gives an exasperated groan. "Just get on with me and hold on tight. The first lesson when we get back is horse riding."

The Creature clambers up, frowning deeply. Before he can even adjust himself properly, Elan kicks at the horse's side and it sprints off. On instinct, the Creature holds onto her shoulders tightly for all he is worth. She follows the other horses ahead. They aren't far. Already she can hear the sounds of destruction and the thick smell of sweat and blood. Elan had thought for sure that now that she could eat, the appeal of blood would not be as strong. She is wrong. It allures her as before. Elan slows drastically, her heart thudding in her ribs. She takes a few breaths to slow her heart.

"What are you doing?"

"You have to drink my blood, now, before we go into battle and lose our senses. We have to stay focused. Just take enough so we can withstand the bloodshed."

The Darklandian concedes. They won't be able to concentrate otherwise.

He presses against her back, trying not to fall off the horse. Lifting her elbow forward, she hangs her wrist behind her, and next to his face. He takes her hand in his to keep her arm steady. She still isn't used to his teeth sinking into her skin and squirms a bit. He doesn't pierce her flesh much, but drinks more deeply than he had before.

She feels the warmth of his mouth and the slow pull on her skin as he drinks. Soon Elan feels light headed and too detached even to notice. The Creature pulls away, closing his eyes. He gives a soft, satisfied moan, licking the blood on his lips. His unyielding posture now softens as he slightly relaxes against her. Elan takes her hand back, feeling bashful as if they shared a moment much too intimate by accident.

"Let's go," she says roughly, trying to brush off her discomfort, and kicks again at the horse.

The Creature braces himself again, and they speed faster through the trees.

Smoke and fire billow up ahead as the cries of people fighting and the clash of metal rings out through the forest. Only three creatures terrorize the town from what she can see, but they seem fearsome.

One of the creatures opens his jaw and clouds of fire billow from his lips. Elan's mouth goes dry at the sight. Her horse keens and steps back. Creatures cannot breathe fire, yet this one is! Her mind takes in the sight of him as she assesses what is happening. The fire breather's left arm bulges more muscular than the other, and in each hand he holds large makeshift knives from random pieces of jagged twisted metal.

Gallowgrave keeps trying to hit the creature with a freezing spell. Gusts of snowy ice air blow from his lips, but they merely melt when they get anywhere near the creature.

The two other creatures are just as alarming. One jumps from branch to branch, back to the ground and then to the trees again. His twig-like body moves exceedingly fast, gliding just out of reach of the members' swords. His fighting tactic uses speed, evasiveness, and surprise.

The last creature is a whirlwind of chains and spikes. He doesn't fight with a style so much as kicks and punches, pummeling anything within reach. It looks like his objective is not only to kill, but to completely obliterate.

A sound of absolute disgust emanates behind Elan.

"Friends of yours?" Elan asks as they both jump off the steed.

The other creatures don't notice the Creature beside her at all. They probably would never in a hundred equinoxes expect him to be in a green cloak. Everyone fights with such determination that they still don't notice Elan as they run onto the battlefield.

The Creature pulls off his cloak and spreads his wings to their full extent. He roars at the top of his voice.

The sound rumbles the ground beneath them. Everyone stops and stares. The enemy creatures frown, their heads tilted to the side. They appear puzzled as to why a fellow Darklandian is standing side by side with the Green Cloaks.

"Well, if it isn't, Warrick," the thin one says far in a tree out of reach. "Finally coming out of hiding. Green Cloaks! All we have come for is him. Just hand him over, and we will leave."

If Elan had any doubt about the Creature's identity before, it is confirmed now. Before Warrick can respond, someone else interrupts.

"He isn't going anywhere with you," Lelan says. He looks at Warrick with complete resolution. "Warrick is with us."

Warrick snarls at Lelan, like he wants to strike him across his face for speaking.

"This is some joke!" the thinnest creature laughs. "You working for the Green Cloaks now?"

"You have murdered and ransacked your way through our land. You are not leaving here alive!" Dawsley says to the creature, but afterward shoots Elan a death glare.

"My actions have nothing to do with anyone except myself," Warrick spits.

The thin creature throws his head back and laughs. "Maybe you should have thought that way when that useless sack of rubbish Hessero was alive. Would have saved you trouble."

Elan's mouth hangs open as she sees Warrick's face transform in the blink of an eye. She had seen him angry, she had even seen him enraged, but absolute hatred and fury contort his features. His fangs grow longer, the bones under his face sharpen, even the whites of his eyes become bright red. His claws lengthen and his face stretches forward. Unhinged madness possesses him. Faster than Elan's eyes can see, Warrick shoots up into the air, attacking the creature.

At that precise moment, all anarchy breaks loose. The other creature expels raging fires again. Elan wonders where he learned magic. The Old One must have had more than one student. The fire-breathing creature takes on five men, including Gallowgrave, all on his own, just to get to Warrick. The bald one is doing even more damage as he makes his way over.

Both Warrick and his opponent plummet from the trees. They thud to the ground. Elan runs over to them both, trying to hide that she can't be far from him. She had never seen two creatures fighting each other. It's like two ravaging animals, hacking clawing and biting. It's bloody and primal. They are reduced to the savage animals they truly are in this moment, the rabid dogs that Elan is used to fighting. The sounds of footfalls and scuffling permeate the air. They finally break away, covered in red. But Elan knows Warrick is doing most of the damage because she can only feel a few shallow slices on her side.

Elan turns her attention back to the bedlam, standing in between Warrick and the other creatures trying to make their way to him. So much is happening at once, she doesn't know where to place her attention. All she knows is that these creatures cannot be permitted to leave here alive.

The bald creature batters his way to Warrick with blunt force. Elan runs to her brothers trying to subdue this dangerous creature. Her feet spread wide and Elan sets a defensive stance, her sword held up at her side. He throws his dirty black chains, trying to tangle Elan in a web of metal. She catches the end of the chain, wrapping it around her arm and playing a tug of war with him, but he is much stronger than her. He pulls, bringing her closer to him. Elan uses her non-dominant hand to brandish the sword, hoping to at least keep him away. Others come to Elan's aid, and she lets go of the chain, putting some distance between them as they continue to fight.

Heat brushes past her as spheres of fire are hurled through the forest. Elan chances a glance at the scene around her. Most of the Order members are trying to keep up with the most dangerous creature. Dawsley's cloak catches fire, and he dives to smother out the flames.

The fire breather keeps everyone occupied, but he still makes his way to Warrick, who is still fighting. He closes in, and the flames he spits slowly become smaller. With one blast of cold air from Gallowgrave, the fire is extinguished. The creature, now without his power, pulls a jagged cut of metal from his scabbard. He fights his way through. The two Darklanders are trying to close in on Warrick.

The bald creature with the chains advances, having dispatched most of the other Order members. Elan is farther away from Warrick than she would like and tries her best to shuffle close enough so the leash doesn't affect his fighting ability, but stays on guard. The bald creature steps closer and Elan stands firm, bracing for him. Using her much smaller stature to her advantage, she stays elusive and changes through, switching her direction of attack when the beast tries swiping at her. The sword arcs as she swings with a back handed movement. The tip of the blade only grazes his side as the monster leans back, evading her.

An Order member comes up behind the bald creature and cuts his back. The beast spins around and while he is distracted, Elan plans to make the killing strike while his side is exposed when she hears Warrick spit in her direction, "Watch out to your right."

Elan is so caught up in the chaos, she doesn't react fast enough because her attention is still on the creature with chains. The one with the knife snatches her wrist and twists her arm back, causing her to drop her sword.

At the same time, Warrick lets out a groan of pain, nearly dropping to his knees.

His hot breath nears her neck as she knows he plans to feed. Elan stomps down hard on his foot with her heel. The creature yips and loosens his grip and Elan turns to kick him between his legs. He roars in pain, doubled over. Using the heel of her hand, she pushes up on his nose and hears a snap as blood gushes from his face. He should be down for a while to recover from the pain. Elan stumbles back, putting some distance between them but positioning herself to still block Warrick. Elan bends to pick up her fallen sword.

In less than a flash, the creature, who ceased breathing fire, releases a metallic roar. On instinct, Elan faces the sound. He is already gripping his shiv in his right hand and brandishing it wildly as he comes right toward her.

Something grips her shoulders and pulls her back, while simultaneously rotating her body.

A white-hot sting rips up her back. Elan hears Warrick cry out with her in unison as they both crash to the ground on their sides. Warrick is pressed against her back with his arms clasped around her shoulders. Instead of the blade slashing across her throat or chest, making a killing blow, it had torn across his back when he spun her away. She arches her back as pain zings through her and red blooms on her cape.

Elan sees the creature freeze, his eyes alight and his jaw hanging open. He saw that even though he had struck Warrick, she is bleeding as well. Elan knows he has seen what he wasn't supposed to. She can't let this creature go back and tell the Old One what has happened.

Tresdon sprints at her adversary, whipping his sword, distracting the monster long enough for her to reach down to her boot and grab her dagger. Adrenaline pumps in her veins, giving her the strength to roll Warrick away and lunge up from the battle-marred grass. The creature's attention turns to Tresdon and so he does not even see her move. The blade digs deep into his neck. His filthy hair brushes her wrists as her arms burn with exertion.

The wide-eyed shock sends a thrill down Elan's spine as he spits, dropping to the ground, gurgling in protest.

Elan falls to the cold terrain drained of all energy, still clutching the dagger tightly in her hand. Warrick and Elan are limp on the ground now. Warrick sees the small piece of metal in her hand. Recognition crosses his face, but Elan does not understand why.

An arm comes up around her. Just from the odor alone she knows it's Eldon. He lifts her as if she weighs nothing. The fabric of her cape sticks to her body, soaked through with blood. Lelan picks up Warrick as well. Lelan is short, but also broad, and throws Warrick over his back. He is conscious enough to hiss in discomfort.

"We must get you two out of here!" Eldon yells anxiously.

As the rest of the Order members continue to fight, Eldon tries to get them both out of battle.

Everything is in moments and flashes. One moment, Eldon lifts her on his horse. The next, she enters the first checkpoint. It feels like she has only blinked, but the next scene she is aware of is the bed in the infirmary. Gallowgrave is yelling something over to all the people buzzing around her. Everyone's voices are muffled. Her tired body gives in, and then there is nothing more to see but black.

Chapter 28

The scent of dust and smoke from her small front room hits her nostrils. Lying on her stomach in her bed, she shifts to stand, but a sharp spasm of pain runs up her back. She grits her teeth.

"Don't move," Gallowgrave says. "Either of you."

Elan can't see him and refuses to attempt to move again.

"You are both injured. You should have never come to the battlefield. Dawsley is furious with you, Elan. If Warrick had not acted fast, you both would be dead. At least you are both still alive, if not worse for wear."

So the Creature is being called *Warrick* now? Elan's dry mouth frowns at the use of his name.

"I have put some healing potions on your wounds, but unfortunately you both will be confined here for some time until you get better. Dawsley has also taken your armor and weapons. They will be returned to you when he sees fit."

Annoyance sinks into Elan's skin. She deserves this because she disobeyed his orders. Logically, she understands, but her cheeks still flush with shame.

"Just rest for now."

"What happened? Did the creatures die?" Elan asks through clenched teeth. Even talking moves her body slightly and hurts. Her skin stretches tight all the way from her shoulder to her lower back. They must have had to stitch her up.

"One is dead. The other badly injured, and the last retreated when he saw he was fighting alone and Warrick was gone."

"Was it the bald one who retreated? The one with the chains?" Warrick calls from the room beside them.

"Yes. Miraculously he was almost completely unharmed. But the other one you fought in the tree was quite damaged. I am surprised he did not die on the battlefield. He escaped as well."

"How was that creature able to work a spell? Is he also a student of the Old One?" Elan frowns, wondering if the Old One plans to build an army with the ability to cast spells.

"No," Warrick answers for Gallowgrave. "He would never let too many learn magic, or he would be overthrown."

Elan can't see him but hears the strain in his voice.

"He's right," Gallowgrave says. He holds a cracked glass marble in front of Elan's face. "I have rarely seen these, but they had enough power for one temporary spell. Who knows how many the Old One has given them."

Elan can hear Gallowgrave's feet walk over to the fire. The wood crackles and the fire burns hotter.

There must be an uproar among Order members. They now know Warrick's identity, and they are in danger with him being on their land.

"They are just going to go back to the Old One to get more of those glass beads." Elan says. "We can't stay here now that they know Warrick is somewhere with us. They haven't discovered our exact location, but it won't be long. They will tear through every nearby town to find us. Once we are well enough, we have to go into The Darklands if we don't want them coming back and hurting innocent people,"

Warrick huffs. "I believe that was my idea from the very beginning," he bites.

Gallowgrave grumbles. "We can think about that after you both get better. People will be by to check up on you, but many are injured, and Dawsley is sending even more members out, but calling a few back from The Darklands. Ylmore has volunteered to look in on you since he is retired. I know it is hard, but you must rest for now."

Elan anxiously wonders what is going on in the Order center. She will try to get as much information from Ylmore as she can.

Gallowgrave mumbles a few words and a silver shimmering falls on the whole space. She finds it impossible to keep her eyes open a moment longer. Elan drifts off into a peaceful rest where she dreams about being wrapped in the loving arms of Uldon.

"Elan suggested going to the expeditions into the Darklands today. We now know who the Creature really is. Maybe it's best if we get him off our lands," Gallowgrave suggests. He sits cross legged on top of his potion table wiggling his bare toes.

"With his reputation, we can't trust him here or there. But it's better he is out of our headquarters," Dawsley answers. "We should trust Warrick even less now, the Old One had trusted him completely. If he was clever enough to gain the Old One's trust and betray him, he could easily pull the cloth over our eyes." Dawsley sits in a rickety wooden chair hunched forward. His brow is low over his eyes and he rests his chin on a fist.

The only sound for a while is the bubbling of Gallowgrave's cauldron.

"Maybe even the traitor and Warrick are working together behind the Old One's back. It's not too hard to believe they have their own motives," Gallowgrave ponders.

"I wouldn't put it past him to be so self-seeking. We have to watch our backs." Dawlsey leans back and the chair beneath him creaks.

"But what about Elan?" Gallowgrave is even more unhappy about her terrible fate.

"She is safe. It's ourselves we have to worry about," Dawsley says. "The moment they heal, they are going to the expeditions."

Gallowgrave nods in agreement, but taps his fingers on his knee in a nervous tick.

Warrick crouches over the flames of the fireplace. His back stings mercilessly, but he manages to shift, changing position to poke at the flames.

A rustling and a pained groan from the Tiny Female's side of the hut alerts him she has awoken.

"So, you are awake," Warrick says just so she is aware he is in the front room.

He turns to observe her and she jolts like she forgot he existed. How she always manages to be surprised at his presence is beyond him. She struggles to prop herself up on her elbow. He sits in the main space shuffling closer to the fire.

"I don't know how you were sleeping so deeply. After a while I was getting restless."

Warrick hadn't been able to sleep. His mind had been racing thinking about the weapon she used on Snur. He recognized it as the matching pair to the dagger that injured him. So, it was the tiny female who had struck him with the blade. Without her doing that, he might still be under the Old One's control. He is not sure if he should hate her even more for hurting him or be grateful she supplied him with the resource to escape. If he ever comes up against the Old One again, he will need that weapon. Does she even know the power it has? All of her armor and weapons had been confiscated.

Warrick turns and watches the fire, but she still manages to catch him staring into nothingness before he moved. His mind wanders as he tries to plan ways he can get that dagger for himself.

Elan immediately notices there is something very different about him. The cold, snide, confident air he usually carries has transformed into something else. Neutrality maybe, even preoccupation.

"Those creatures seemed to know you," Elan begins awkwardly. "That small one even mentioned some creature named Hessero." Warrick's face winces at the name before his features turn to rage.

"Yes," Warrick begins reluctantly, irritated. "They are some of the few that know me quite well. Ichbone, the bald one, specifically knows me. We came from the same province in the Darklands."

Warrick's back faces her as he pokes the fire, encouraging it to continue. There is a blood-soaked patch between his wings spanning from the top of his right shoulder down to the middle left of his back. She must have the same one. Elan remembers if Warrick had not knocked her out of the way it could have been a strike right across her neck and they would both be dead instead of badly injured. She can't help but feel a pang of gratitude.

Elan reluctantly admits he has saved the both of them. She forces out her next words. "Thank you," Elan says, "for thinking so fast, and saving both our lives."

"Don't think for a moment I did it because I care about your life or your well being," Warrick spits, back to his old self. "I did it so I could survive."

Elan's temper flares, and she regrets her feelings of thanks, "Of course I don't think that! I was just an inconvenience to your wellbeing. I know you only did it for yourself."

Warrick flinches.

A memory comes back to Elan of that creature in the tree mentioning if only he had thought about himself to begin with, Hessero would be alive. Who was this mysterious Hessero, that even speaking ill of them for a moment put Warrick into a violent rage?

"Just as long as you know that," he grumbles before changing the subject. "That wrinkled Blood One left us new bandages and told me they had to be changed soon. I'll take care of yours if you change the bandages on me. I obviously can't reach."

Warrick moves closer to her with a fresh cloth and a minty salve. She sits up as a burning ache whips up her spine. Her skin is very tender as she moves. With the Creature coming closer, Elan holds her breath, expecting to crave the blood, but there is no reaction.

"Why don't I want your blood?" Elan asks, remembering Warrick had savored hers when he drank earlier.

"I told you, it's tainted with dark magic. We have an instinct and know what's poisonous to us."

Elan didn't like how he said "*we.*" She didn't have creature instincts. The bandages pull away, and his blood stains darker than her own. She wonders why she never noticed that during battle. His skin is crisscrossed with thick dark thread holding his wound closed. He has no other scars or marks on his back. His is smooth without flaw. Elan is both repulsed and intrigued by this fact. She scans his side where she knows the other creature scratched him. And his arm. There should be the same puncture scars that she has.

"What are you looking at?" Warrick asks, shuffling away, agitated.

"Hold still," she demands. On his side, the scar has already faded. She lifts her shirt to check her ribs. Three raw slashes remain. "Why don't you have any scars?"

Warrick moves farther away from her, with his eyes bulging and mouth twisting. "You ask the most irrelevant things. Must be the female part of you," he grumbles. "Our kind heals faster than your kind, and any evidence of past damage does not linger."

Elan had been taught for years about creatures, but didn't know these tiny details she could only get from the source. Why didn't they know that about them? Creatures are faceless to them. They never bother to look at who they are fighting, only what. An Order member would not notice that the same enemy they had injured in a previous battle stood before them again unscathed.

Elan notices Warrick curling in on himself as he scoots away. "I thought you wanted me to change your bandage," Elan says, confused about why he moved.

He returns cautiously, his back straight.

Her fingers brush up against his back, but no more, not wanting to get closer than necessary. Elan has never had the opportunity to observe a creature up close. She contemplates the texture of his wings, which look like thinly-sewn black velvet.

Reigning in her interest, she continues with the task at hand. The sticky salve keeps the bandage in place as she finishes up.

Elan knows that Warrick must be more careful than her. Her blood smells succulent to him, and he must breathe through his mouth to keep control. Elan tugs the back of her shirt up to her neck and waits for him to take the bandages.

Even though she is a Green Cloak, she is still a
female, and Warrick forces himself not be nervous getting
close to her exposed torso. His discomfort is quickly wiped
from his mind the moment he sees Elan's flesh. It is marred
with ugly scars. Her skin is raised from cuts and dents with
punctures. Some spots shine from old burns. Warrick can't
help but stare, his jaw hanging with shock. This tiny female
had been someone's punching bag and pincushion. He
wonders how many battles she had been in during her life
that would cause such damage. He pulls the bandage away
and can see the grizzly wound on her back. This one will just
be another added piece to the collection.

This one is a fighter and survivor, Warrick decides.
How many creatures have tried to do her in and she still
lived? He looks at her face, which is focusing on the flames.
Her small features portray her young age. Most females of
her kind are not fit for battle. Her body has been continually
broken and beaten, yet she goes into fights without
hesitation. Just as he had always thought, the most sinister
enemy doesn't appear dangerous at all. Many creatures must
have underestimated her only to be destroyed by her sword.
He had to be cautious. Letting his guard slip only ever led to
trouble.

He works quickly, trying not to prolong the moment.

"You were telling me the truth about who you are,"
Elan begins quietly. "You are against the Old One. If I ask
you something else will you be honest?"

"Depends on what you ask," Warrick replies
skeptically.

"Do you know who the traitor is?"

Warrick presses his lips together.

She has never trusted him before so why should this be any different? The pause stretches on, as he is not sure if he wants to answer her. He owes her nothing, but he decides to be honest.

"No," he replies with finality.

Elan's head swims, and she places a hand on her forehead to stop the spinning. They both had lost a lot of blood. She isn't sure if she believes him, but using her better judgment, she decides not to press the issue.

"We should go back to sleep and get some more rest. I don't know how much time it will take the Old One to build a retaliation team, but something tells me it won't be long," Elan says.

Warrick nods his head once and Elan sees the Creature go to his side of the house willingly for the first time. It is not long before she hears his deep, steady breathing, telling her that he has fallen into a deep sleep.

Crank limps through The Darklands to the old temple. Ichbone follows him, unscathed and unhappy. Snur had decided to use his only glass sphere in their first battle. What a waste of magic. Even with the spell, he had still died. Ichbone has no remorse for his death. It serves him right for wasting the magic.

Ichbone mills over the idea of Warrick being with the Green Cloaks. What is he thinking? And why were the Green Cloaks trying to protect him?

"Whatdaya think of Warrick'n those Green Cloaks?" Crank asks as if he plucked the idea right from his thoughts.

Ichbone doesn't move a muscle on his face. But the slight grumble of his chest is enough to express his ire.

"That's what I thought too."

The Old One isn't going to like this, and Ichbone doesn't want to be the one to give him the bad news. Maybe Warrick gave the Green Cloaks information in exchange for protection, but that doesn't sound like Warrick. He would do it just to spite the Old One, but after what happened to Hessero all those equinoxes ago, he doubted he would go to them so quickly.

Standing outside the temple, finally, they stare at the door, neither one making their presence known.

The door creaks open anyway, and Fenix stands in front of the door as he closes it behind him. Fenix's judgment of Crank's battered and bloody condition is condescending, with hard eyes and a small frown of disgust. Crank's mouth becomes a hard line under the weight of Fenix's analysis.

Crank doesn't waste any time.

"We found Warrick. He's with the Green Cloaks."

"That's impossible," Fenix replies. "The Green Cloak who is loyal to the Old One would have told us."

"Well, he's with them. We didn't know the Green Cloaks would be part of the deal. We want more magic," Crank demands.

"You aren't getting any more. Where is Snur?"

"Dead."

Fenix frowns. A small disgusted guttural sound scrapes the back of his throat.

"Stay here."

Fenix walks down the long hallway to the main chamber, then to the smaller room where the Old One lays recovering. Bowing low, Fenix enters the Old One's room. The Old One is able to sit up now. He moves within his quarters carefully, but has no strength for more than that.

"Master, I have bad news." Fenix's Adam's apple bobs.

"That is not what I want to hear."

Fenix flinches as a bead of sweat rolls from his temple.

"Yes. But you must know. The Green Cloak traitor is not as loyal to us as we think. Warrick is with them. They are keeping him. The assassins want more magic. Green Cloaks were not a part of the deal."

"Impossible!" the Old One yells. "He hates them. He would never be there."

Fenix licks his lips, his tongue becoming too large in his mouth.

"Master, the assassins are not mistaken. They saw him with them!"

The Old One roars and knocks over a bowl of blood beside his bed.

"That ingrate. I give him power, I let him dwell with me, and this is how I'm repaid? He probably is giving them information right now. He is most likely working spells with Gallowgrave against me already. And now I know I cannot trust the traitor to tell me everything. He had to have known Warrick was with them. He must have motives of his very own. You tell all the land that they may have a lifetime of spells if they catch Warrick alive and find out who the traitor is and bring them to me alive."

"You don't even know who the traitor is?" Fenix dares to ask.

"He only sends me messages through those birds. No one makes a fool out of me. They will both pay dearly. I will make sure of that."

At that moment, a caw of blackbirds cuts the air. Fenix runs to the outside, grateful he has a reason to get out of arms reach of the Old One. He rushes past a confused Crank and Ichbone as the birds observe him eerily. In one of the bird's beaks, it holds another small green bag. Fenix snatches it from the bird and clutches it to his chest. He steps back to the door, not breaking his view of the little messenger.

Crank and Ichbone follow Fenix with their eyes as he goes back and forth. Ichbone crosses his arms with indignation at being brushed aside, but Fenix has more important worries.

He holds out the small bag to the Old One with trembling hands.

The Old One snatches it and pulls back his arm as if he is going to throw it across the room. But his curiosity must get the better of him, because he relaxes his arm. He opens it, peering inside. A small chuckle bubbles from his chest.

"A peace offering, I suppose, from our Green Cloak friend. He must have had a reason for what he has done."

He pulls out the parchment and unfolds its aged corners. One of the missing pages from the Journal rests on his fingers.

"I think I like this underhanded traitor more and more."

"What should we do about the assassins?"

"Tell them they only get more magic when they return Warrick, but something tells me that our friend already has something in the works to return our Warrick to his home."

Chapter 29

Elan wakes in her room, shivering from the cold. The sun still hides behind the horizon, and the fire dies down.

Ylmore has been a great help, bringing in wood and food the last days, but he can't always be there to replenish the hearth.

Elan crawls from her bed to the dying flames. The pain from her wound aches as she moves, but it could be much worse. Warrick drank the day before, and they were both surprised at how quickly it helped speed up their healing. She blows on the embers, and they glow, producing heat that brushes past her chilled face. Drawing water from the cauldron, she swishes it in her mouth and spits out the door.

Elan hears steady, deep breathing. The Creature is still sound sleep on his side of the stone cabin. Elan steps silently to his door. She has never set foot in this space before and hovers by the entrance. Warrick's wings are cocooning his body, and his head rests on a crumpled up robe. The bed on his side has been torn open, and the soft hay and feathers were redistributed to construct a giant nest. She had never seen the resting place of a creature. Soundlessly, she slides closer, fascinated. Twigs gathered from outside stick up like thorns on the perimeter mingled in the soft materials.

Warrick exhales a deep breath then rolls onto his other side. Elan keeps perfectly still, thinking he has woken up. His eyes are shut tight, but his jaw loosens. Elan's eyes move to his wings. Again she finds herself pondering their texture. Warrick sighs, shifting slightly. His face does not express any signs that he knows she lurks beside him. His face softens, relaxed. Warrick isn't scowling or frowning like when he is awake.

Without his usual grimace, he still has sharp facial features. His hair is growing longer than when he first came to their lands. It spills across his temples the color of ravens' wings and just as glossy. Even with the dramatic planes of his cheekbones and large jaw, he isn't as grotesque as the rest of his kind. Elan doesn't know much about what creatures find attractive. Perhaps he is hideous for a Darklandian.

She clears her throat loudly. He stirs, but doesn't wake. Elan repeats the sound with more force. She doesn't want to use his name, but if she calls him *creature* after knowing full well who he is, it would seem awkward.

"If you want me to wake, Small One, why not just yell?" Warrick asks groggily, refusing to open his eyes.

She frowns, bristling at his words. "Just get up. We need some exercise. We have been in here too long."

"And just where do you propose we go? That abysmal arena?"

"You need clothes. More than just the one cloak and my largest pair of pants. We have healed enough to at least go into Rowan Oak."

His head finally lifts. "What is that?"

"It is a town close to here where we buy the few supplies we can't make on our land. If we are planning to leave after we are fully healed, we will need supplies. It isn't a far ride. We will have to go with someone else, of course, and if you stay hidden under your hood, no one will even know you are a Darklandian. As soon as they see green, they avoid looking at us."

"Why would they do that? Aren't you their heroes? I thought for sure there would be parades in the street for your arrival."

Elan frowns. She doesn't know about creatures as much as she thought and they obviously know even less about The Order. "You will find out soon enough when we get there. Nolan will be taking us. We had planned to go even before the last battle."

Warrick's face turns sour at the mention of Nolan.

"Come on, hurry up. I would like to leave early so we don't run into Dawsley."

Warrick reluctantly gets up, stretching, in no hurry.

Elan and Warrick cross the grounds to the blacksmith shop. She walks around and through the back door to a cramped corner where Nolan sleeps. It's messy with blankets, paper, his cloaks, armor, quills, ink, and a few books. On a small shelf, he has a few wood carvings crudely fashioned into various animals.

"Nolan," Elan hisses.

Nolan jumps.

"Elan what are you doing here?" he asks, rubbing his eyes.

"You said you would take us into town and I'm accepting your offer. Let's go."

"Are you kidding me? Dawsley will go into a rage if he knows you left grounds without telling him."

"Well, let's go before he finds out."

Nolan rolls his eyes.

Elan pouts before saying, "He already has my weapons and armor. I can't get into any more trouble. Besides, you can say you are keeping an eye on me."

"The things you get me into," Nolan grumbles as he swings his long legs out of his cot.

Nolan changes without any more protests and heads out with them to the south tower.

People patrol on duty, but Nolan smiles and assures them that Warrick and Elan have permission to come with him to Rowen Oak. His soft words and natural charm convince them in no time to let them go.

Nolan grabs three black horses. He coos soothing words as he pulls them along. He has a way with animals that Elan always admired. She knew it was because his family trained them so he had experience with the animals. He pats the side of the mare, and it almost kneels down to let him come up. He climbs his and waits.

"We only need two," Elan explains. "He can't ride."

"So how is he getting there, exactly?" Nolan asks, exasperation coloring his tone.

Elan jumps up first and then grabs Warrick's hand to hoist him up. Once again, he sits behind Elan. He puts his hands on her shoulders, steadying himself, but stays as far from her as the leather saddle will allow.

Before, Elan was so focused on the coming battle, she had no time to think about being this close. Now is a different story. She adjusts herself on the saddle, uncomfortable.

Nolan's face turns to disgust. "You going to let him hold onto you like that?"

Elan watches as Warrick leers cruelly at seeing Nolan's distaste, so Warrick settles in and she feels his arms circle her waist, hugging her to him.

Elan's back stiffens. Her eyes fly open, and she clamps her jaw.

"It's fine," Elan says as she elbows him hard in the stomach. She has hit him without enough force to injure him, so she doesn't worry about feeling the pain. He lets go, leaning back with a scowl.

"Maybe he should ride with me. I don't need a saddle. There will be more room to sit."

"Absolutely not," they both snap at the same time.

Elan twists to grimace at Warrick. He seems to subconsciously tighten his hold on her shoulders and almost curls himself in on her, while he stares daggers at Nolan.

"He can't ride with you, Nolan. If you accidentally ride too far from me, he could get pulled off the horse, and we would both get injured."

Nolan grumbles to himself, but does not press the issue. Instead he rides ahead of them leading the way.

They don't need to travel long before they see rooftops and smoke stretching to the sky. They slow down dramatically as they approach.

On the outskirts of the town, Warrick pulls up his hood before they get to the public stables. The man there doesn't expect payment as they approach – in fact, he doesn't even acknowledge them. Nolan dismounts and ties his horse. Elan jumps off as soon as she can. Once Warrick comes down, he tucks his hands into his sleeves, hiding them from view. The cloak hangs long, concealing his bare clawed feet.

Elan sees Warrick tilt his head to the side slightly, watching the attendant's chin turn away from their group. He focuses on the wall, his back to them.

As they leave the stable onto the busy main road, people stagger and fall silent, turning away and averting their eyes. Many part in the busy street as though the three of them have some contagious illness. The cobblestone road is lined with booths and shops.

Warrick lowers himself to Elan's ear. "Why do they slither away from you? Shouldn't they be happy their protectors are here?"

"They believe we are cursed because we have been chosen to fight your kind. They think there must be something wrong with us and we bring misfortune. The men also move away, frightened they will be chosen as well, so they hide, or turn their backs. They have even more of a reason to be frightened as of late because your kind is seeking us out and ransacking all the nearby villages."

Warrick smirks, "So, it would appear that your kind is just as disloyal and ungrateful as my own."

Elan refuses to answer, pressing her lips together. They turn down from the main road to a much smaller side street. There are only shops and no booths in this area. Nolan turns to a shop with a picture of a tunic on the outside. Before going in, he whispers, "Just stay back and keep your eyes down."

"Good day!" The woman sings brightly as soon as the door opens, but her expression drops at the color of their cloaks.

Nolan pulls down his hood, "It's only me, Delmira." Nolan gives her a full smile, and the woman relaxes to the point of melting.

Delmira is a well-fed buxom blond with far too much color on her lips and cheeks. Her brightly colored dress makes the vast array of clothing seem drab. The shop is small and dim, packed with fabrics and clothing of every kind as well as a few knickknacks.

"Why, Nolan, if you had sent word that you were coming, I would have had supplies waiting for you." The jewelry on her neck and wrists glitter as she speaks with animation.

Elan almost wants to roll her eyes at the way Delmira bats her lashes. But she supposes it is better than being pushed out the door, the way most shopkeepers would.

"It's alright, we have a new member, and he is a bit differently proportioned than what we have. We need to find just the right size. We also need more tunics and pants for the frost phase and more dye."

"We have linser wool clothing. It's very warm and durable. Or you can use something softer like hazel hair." She walks to the back of the shop, and Elan drags her feet along.

"If you can't find the size you need, you can always send me a message, and you can get an order picked up."

"That's very kind of you." Nolan smiles.

"Now, over here..."

As Delmira shows Nolan and Warrick the different types of cloth, Elan wanders away through the shop, scanning the racks. She stops suddenly at a deep violet dress with black lace. The color is so rich that Elan wants to stare at it for hours. Being brought up by men, she never really learned to appreciate such things, but she can't help the admiration, and feels silly for being so moved by it. Elan had seen many dresses, but none had driven her to such longing before. She knows a dress that lovely would look much more appropriate on someone like Delmira than herself. Her eyes drop to her person, and her heart squeezes painful in her chest. If she were curvaceous and beautiful, then perhaps a dress this gorgeous would suit her.

Maybe Uldon would have loved her.

"Elan?" Nolan's voice brings her back. "Don't you have to get a few tunics as well?"

Elan nods and carries over a few items, disappointed in herself.

"A piece of copper for each."

Nolan drops seven rectangular coins into Delmira's outstretched hand. He pulls a sack from under his cloak and stuffs the clothes in.

"Your friends don't talk much, do they?" Delmira asks, leaning to get a better look under their hoods.

Elan bows her head, shrinking away, but not Warrick. The side of his mouth curls and he parts his lips just enough to let the light gleam on his fangs. She jumps back. Her eyes glisten with fear as she stumbles back. Elan pushes Warrick through the door. Nolan follows, his face flushing darker.

231

Nolan fumes. "Look what you've done! This is the only shop I can get to sell us anything, and you spook her. I have to go back in and calm her down otherwise we will never get supplies."

"Yes, do go back in and comfort her. I'm sure that's what she wants anyway," Warrick spits, thick with innuendo.

Nolan glares at Warrick before rushing back in.

"Did you have to do that?" Elan scolds.

"I did not like her." Warrick crosses his arms over his chest, sulking like a petulant child.

"Big surprise, you don't like *another* person," Elan grouses. They keep to the shadows of the huts and watch. The villagers and the town are alien to Elan, and she is fascinated to observe people that don't have to worry about traitors and death at any moment.

Among the bustling streets, she spots a familiar face. Elan blinks and squints. Serious eyes set in an almost expressionless face. Jordon. He weaves through town without his green cloak. Before ducking into a building, he glances over his shoulder. The sign above the door reads, "Sparrow's Messenger Service." A few minutes later he slips out, appearing shaken and pulling his hood tighter around his face.

"Don't you know him?" Warrick asks as Jordon blends into the crowd.

"Yes I do," Elan says… but maybe she doesn't know him at all.

Chapter 30

Elan agonizes over her next course of action, even after milling it in her mind for days. Telling Dawsley or Gallowgrave is not an option. They would know she left the grounds without permission. Confiding in Nolan or Eldon means Elan runs the risk of them acting oddly in Jordon's presence. Confronting him may be the best course of action, but even questioning his actions feels like she is accusing him. Jordon would never do anything against The Order, he is her friend. Jordon was the first one to come and sit with her when she thought everyone hated her. He stood up for her and was loyal to their friendship. If he was out that day, there had to have been a plausible reason.

Elan halts mid-step. Her head whips to Warrick, and she staggers as if forgetting he existed. He had been practicing, but now sits on the ground silently with a perplexed expression. Elan frowns at her charge. Warrick finally wears decent-fitting clothing. Either the change of his attire or his curious expression makes him look less savage. She closes her eyes and blows a long breath out.

"Let's go. It's been a long day."

Warrick rises to his feet and puts back the wooden practice sword. Elan's mind clouds again, and her legs move automatically. They exit the training room and are only a few steps outside when a large form rushes towards them.

"Elan, report to the tower," Dawsley says as he barrels past them. "I will be there soon."

Elan sighs, dropping her shoulders, but changes her direction immediately.

Once inside, she sees a few other members rocking on their feet. She knows each face in the room. Jordon, Tresdon, Lelan, and Eldon are standing by Gallowgrave's cauldron. Elan avoids Jordon, her stomach fluttering nervously. She places her eyes everywhere else except in his direction.

"What's this meeting about?" Elan asks Eldon, but before he can answer, Gallowgrave speaks.

"This is about the expeditions into the Darklands. You will be leaving tomorrow morning. Dawsley is gathering a few more people. You will join the rest of our members there."

Elan's mouth opens and closes like a fish. Why did plans change so suddenly? Her swirling emotions can't keep up with her brain.

"All we know of the Darklands is this," Gallowgrave says as he spreads out a map on the table. There is not much detail to the drawings. Most of the land is unknown. Those who had explored the most dangerous parts of the Darklands didn't live long enough to tell what was there. "You will enter here." He jabs a spot on the map. "There will be an Order Member waiting to show you to camp and what they have learned. We know where the stone temple is but the problem is getting to it. The Old One has other creatures protecting him as well – as if he were not strong enough on his own to ward off trespassers. Only native Darklanders can even get anywhere near the temple. Most places are almost impossible to get to without flight, and we don't have wings, or the magic to fly."

"I can fly, but not while The Small One has me tethered to the ground." Every eye snaps over to Warrick, alarmed. "I know most of the defenses, but he would have changed everything, knowing I'm with you. And every Darklandian within lengths is searching for me. Not many know my face, but I'm sure the word has gotten out." Warrick spreads the map out on Gallowgrave's table. He takes a piece of coal and begins to draw out the land. He plots out the mountains, the lakes, and swamps. Most importantly, he draws the exact location of the stone temple and any known threats on its borders.

Each Order member scrunches their faces, giving each other sideways glances. Elan can see their hands fidgeting.

Gallowgrave nods, being the only one who seems pleased with the new information. "Meet at the North Tower at dawn. Pack light, and of course, before you leave, I will enchant your crests to withstand the dark magic of The Darklands. Any thing you eat or drink will be poisonous if I do not. We shall meet again."

Elan expects more of a speech. He gives no parting words of wisdom or pep talk at all to prepare them.

Everyone responds back in unison and hurries to leave. Elan's eyes follow Jordon out of the tower. Feeling the weight of her stare, he turns. Her breath catches and she averts her lowered brow. She shouldn't be the one feeling guilty. He should be. Elan treads to the door, but Warrick snatches her arm. Tugging hard, he isn't letting go, solid as a rock.

"I want to speak with you, Wizard," Warrick says once everyone is out of earshot.

Warrick releases his viselike grip and Elan almost falls over from the force of trying to pull away from him. She rubs her wrist, giving him a dirty look.

Gallowgrave nods though his eyebrows knit together.

"I am only helping you because I want The Old One dead for personal reasons. That vile creature imprisoned and tortured me for equinoxes. Once he is exterminated, I don't plan on cooperating. During my time here, I have been exceedingly well behaved. I know I have no choice but to follow the Female but that doesn't mean I can't wreak unspeakable havoc on my own."

Both Gallowgrave and Elan tense at his words.

Elan knows what she will have to do. As soon as they retrieve the book safely and the Old One is dead, she will have to take drastic measures in order to prevent his dubious plans, even if that means crippling herself to weaken him.

Elan takes her only black cloak and flint, pressing them to her chest. She spins in her room, searching for what else to grab. There is nothing else. She stands in the center of her lifeless room. If she were never to come back, there would be no evidence that she ever existed. Elan owns nothing of Uldon's and holds no sentimental keepsake or prized possession from childhood. Swallowing, her mouth dries, and a hollow ache grows stronger in her chest.

A sharp rapping at her cabin door causes Elan to jump.

Rushing over, she pushes the door open to find Nolan, his face distraught.

"You can't go to the Darklands without me," Nolan says throwing his hands out to grab her upper arms before Elan even has a chance to take in air to speak. "Dawsley has ordered me to stay behind, but it's too dangerous. Too much can happen to you there. Elan, you are an amazing fighter, but you are not ready to go there and retrieve the book."

Elan freezes, a little shocked with Nolan's strong reaction. Her shoulders come up to her ears as she goes rigid with him being so close.

"You must have known the moment those creatures attacked that I would have to go." Elan swallows. "We both knew this day was coming. Thank you for caring so much, but I don't need you to babysit me, Nolan." Her words are braver than she feels. Seeing Nolan so frantic makes her question exactly what she is doing.

"You are not going without me, Elan. I cannot stand to let you go off into the most dangerous lands while I stay here and wonder and wait, hammering metal while you risk your life. You could get hurt. You could die." Nolan finally lets her go and takes a step back. He had gotten so close to her.

Elan rubs her thumb against her index finger. She has never seen Nolan so worked up before. She freezes in place, not knowing how to respond. He had seen her leave for battles in the past. Had she not been in her current situation, she would have gone a while ago.

"Nothing will happen to the small female." Warrick's voice carries as if he whispered in their ears. He emerges from the shadows on the other side of the room, his arms folded. "I will make sure she is unharmed because I wish no harm to come to myself. There is no need for you."

Instead of calming down, Nolan's fury seems to stoke. His nostrils flare and his stance becomes wider as if he is preparing himself for hand to hand combat.

Elan sees Warrick light up with vindictive glee, watching Nolan so livid.

"They don't need two blacksmiths here. I'm not asking. I'm telling Dawsley that I am leaving with you."

Elan shakes her head, unable to speak at first. "You can't go, Nolan. You belong here. I know the only reason Dawsley is telling me to go is that the Creature knows the lands better than any of us. He needs him to reach the stone temple and The Old One. We have a mission to complete. We must get back the book. The Old One has already expanded the Darklands further out. There have been horrible attacks, and the death toll keeps rising. He orders his devotees to take men, women, and children and drag them back to feed his people. His dark magic is poisoning and enslaving."

This doesn't seem to appease Nolan – it only causes him to pace.

"I'm going, Elan, with or without Dawsley's permission."

Before Elan can protest anymore, Nolan storms out the door and into the inky night.

Elan turns to Warrick who, much to her surprise, says nothing and hides in his room.

As the sun rises, the sky turns a fiery pink. They had been riding straight for days. More Order members are coming on this expedition than those who attended the meeting. All are familiar. They had not left at the same time. They went in small groups, and all met and waited not far from the edge of the Darklands. In each group, one Order member was only there to take the horses back.

Elan aligns all the weapons at her waist, grateful that Dawsley gave her back all her armor and weapons. The dagger Nolan had fashioned for her presses against her leg, tucked secure on her boot holster.

Mosley and Serdon arrive last. Elan sighs, less than thrilled at their presence.

With Mosley's hatred of Warrick, at this point, she trusts the Creature more than him. He had threatened to get rid of them both because they were liabilities and freaks. It's easy in the Darklands for someone to go missing. It's even easier for there to be some unfortunate accident. Elan doesn't realize she is giving him a dirty look until Warrick grunts in agreement beside her. An unspoken treaty develops between them for now. They have a common nuisance in addition to a common enemy.

As declared, Nolan had made it. Elan wonders what Nolan said or did to secure his position to come but decides she doesn't want to know the lengths he had gone to get here now.

Jordon's steely gaze sets and Elan wants to know what is going on behind that stoic expression. The atmosphere thickens with electricity. Some shuffle nervously, and others become more determined. Elan's stomach knots as they wait for someone stationed in the Darklands to meet them. They have to travel as much as possible before nightfall. They can't risk lighting a fire and attracting attention right on the border of the two lands.

Eldon stands closest to the edge of The Darklands peering into the shadows, his body wound up tight like a coil.

Elan wanders over to Nolan, Tresdon, Lelan and Jordon. Being in the company of her friends dulls her anxious edge. They force half smiles to one another, staying silent and adjusting the weapons on their waists.

"I believe you were expecting me," comes a voice possessing an accent with origins from distant lands. Everyone spins around trying to find the source. Even with Eldon keeping watch, he had not seen anyone approaching.

A hulking figure emerges from the trees. His head is shaved on both sides, and long blonde hair runs down the middle. The frown lines on his forehead and mouth are deep, but he cannot be more than eighty equinoxes. The metal crest on his arm dulls with age and damage. From head to toe, gray, dirty rags and armor cover him. The dark clay of the Darkland's terrain spreads across his face and exposed skin.

"First things first," he says, holding up two large buckets of sloppy, charcoal-colored clay. "They are going to be able to smell you even before they can see you. The clay should dilute your scent enough not to be obvious. And I would suggest when we walk further in, you bathe in their water and continue to put layers of ground upon your skin."

He passes each Order member as they slather themselves in the muck. Once he reaches Elan and Warrick, his stance becomes guarded. Elan smears mud on her face and arms and even over her clothing. Warrick doesn't touch a drop. He won't have to worry about his scent.

"Dawsley has told us about your special circumstance," the man says low to the both of them. He sounds angry and suspicious as he looks Warrick over. He smirks as if not impressed with him at all. He turns his attention back to the group. "I am Relsley for those of you that don't know me. I am your guide through this nightmare. Once we reach the others, we shall discuss our next plan of action. Let's move quickly and quietly. We will cover as much ground as we can before it gets too dark to continue. Listen to my instruction closely, or you shall regret it. Whatever you think you learned about The Darklands in oacling class, it's even worse than what you were told. Keep that in mind."

He walks forward, and the others follow. Elan fills her herself to the brim with air. Apprehension and nerves start to take their toll, causing her hands to tremor. Nolan appears at her side. He gives her a stern nod, and with that, they both follow Relsley into the gray fog and black trees.

Chapter 31

The stories Elan has heard do nothing to prepare her for stepping into The Darklands for the first time. The land begins to gradually turn from emerald green to a mucky moss and then the grays and browns of a dying world. The thick fog hangs low to the ground, and with each step, the temperature warms. The trees lose their foliage, left only with thick black branches. Some trees bend as though depressed and exhausted from standing, while other branches tightly curl. Flowers cluster together, poking out of the dark clay, spiked and deep burgundy. Jagged rocks emerge, making an uneven and varied terrain. They climb, stumble, and slide on the rocks with no clear path of any kind. Only Relsley and Warrick have sure footing as they weave through the land.

The air, different than in Elan's native land, feels thicker somehow. Her lungs labor to breathe. A moist, musky scent sits on the back of her tongue. To her surprise, she finds the flavor lingering there, enjoyable.

The forest clicks, croaks and drags outside of their immediate sight, drumming a unique rhythm. Elan's skin tingles, hyperaware of every sound, but she notices neither Warrick nor Relsley draw their swords.

Now being surrounded by the specific sights and smells of The Darklands, Elan notices the sharp saltiness of their scent contrasting with the mild soil aroma. Even the tempo of their steps doesn't match the specific flow of the land.

Elan drags her feet across the rocks and picks them up only when she has to, then repeats, mimicking the tempo around her.

"Perceptive," Warrick says to her with genuine praise.

"What are those sounds anyway?" Elan asks, hushed.

"The clicks and drags are not what you have to worry about," Warrick says, tilting his ears to the timbres. "It's the gurgles you must watch out for."

Gurgles? Elan holds her breath, trying to listen even closer. No gurgling, not now anyway.

A soft thrum of paws on the land drum in the distance.

Relsley swears under his breath, "Spread out. Get low," he hisses. "Try to blend in, if possible."

A hand wraps around Elan's wrist and pulls her behind a rock. Warrick glues himself to the floor beside her, and she remains as flat to the ground as she can. Hardly into the Darklands and already they must take cover. The drumming grows louder. The sound is almost upon them.

Mangled fur and clots of blood come stampeding their way. Elan can see only what she might describe as wolves running in a massive pack. Each one holds the bloody remains of another beast. Snarling, they snap at their new kill. A howl from the very front calls more to follow. Elan realizes these things that she has named wolves have much more teeth than they are supposed to. It is not long before Elan sees their coats are not fur, but thin, sharp quills.

They clamor away just as quickly as they had come. Relsley stands first and motions for them to continue.

Elan gets up, searching the lands as they weave through the trees. Elan follows the rest of the members as tightly as she can. The air is layered with fog, reducing the front of their group to vague outlines. Elan picks up the pace because Relsley starts disappearing. She focuses solely on trying to see the front of the line. Something gossamer and sticky smacks her in the face. Taking a step back, white thread tangles in her hair and eyelashes. Pulling it away, it

242

clings to her fingers. Elan looks up, and from branch to branch and tree to tree stretch elaborate spider webs, sticky as sap. Elan's eyes follow the lines and patterns as far up as she can see. Everyone plods along as Elan stays back.

Lifting her chin, she cranes her neck, allowing her to see all the way to the very top of the trees. Just out of her sight, something jerks and crawls on the webs. Her jaw pops open at the sight of a massive insect above them. She unsheathes her sword and readies it at her side. She begins sprinting forward with her eyes round, still looking up into the fog.

"Above you!" Elan yells. They all turn up, not sure who she is addressing. As they lift their heads, an overgrown insect with a long armored body and eight sharp legs spits sticky white goo. It smacks Eldon's and Nolan's faces and hardens there. It covers their nose and mouth as they labor to pull it off, desperate for air. It moves fast, spinning them around to wrap them in liquid-like webbing coming from its abdomen. Eldon and Nolan struggle, trying to free themselves.

"It's a Larvesp!" someone yells into the thick mist.

Relsley jumps into action, brandishing his sword and running to the back of the group. The long-bodied insect slides on its belly away from Nolan and Eldon, it's four legs on each side, move the body along. It lunges at full speed at Elan with it's pinchers and teeth. She thinks fast, dropping her sword, grabbing a branch above her, and pulling her body up. Dangling from the branch, she just manages to get out of its way, the bottom of her boots still hitting its segmented back. Releasing her grip, she jumps down behind it. Picking her sword back up, she raises it high and plunges down on its rear, but it bounces off its odd rubber armor. The other Order members are trying to pull the webbing off Nolan and Eldon's faces so they can breathe.

"Go for the underside!" Warrick yells, as it jumps, trying to latch itself to him. With his sharp claws, he uppercuts with an open hand and slices its stomach. Black ooze spills out. It thrashes and begins snapping and cutting with the end of its spindle legs. Elan dodges and runs, striking her sword at its many moving legs, but inflicting no damage. Jordon tackles its back, as he holds on with his legs, trying to keep a grip. He plunges the sword down again but the blade springs back without doing any damage to the Larvesp.

As it bucks to free Jordon from its back, Serdon sprints over as its weak spot is exposed and he slashes, almost cleaving it in two as Jordon falls off. A wretched odor smacks Elan in the face. She gags then she holds her nose as more tar goop bursts forward.

Tresdon and Lelan manage to pry off the webbing from Eldon and Nolan's face. They dig their heels to the ground, looking up, making sure there are no more lurking in the trees. But they point up as they see another. It lets out a high pitched whistle, and Elan clasps her hands to the side of her head as her eardrums feel as though they will rupture from the sound.

Another one drops down. This one dwarfs the last. Its legs spin around frantically as each Order member ducks and scatters out of its reach. Relsley rushes up and swings his sword. The stealth of the insect is superior to the last and Elan has a hard time following its movements. The Larvesp speeds up, charging their group, Tresdon who is closest to the front dives, trying to get out of its way. Sliding in the grime, the Larvesp slams into him and opens its mouth, revealing rows of small sharp teeth. Even from where Elan is, as she runs toward him, she can feel the hot putrid breath of the insect blow past Tresdon's face. As one of its legs comes to spear him through, Lelan kicks hard at its stomach, so the speared end misses Tresdon.

Warrick keeps to Elan's side as they dance in the chaos. Jordon and Serdon rush over to pull off the insect's webbing from Nolan and Eldon's bodies, who are thrashing on the floor, their faces red, trying to free themselves.

Elan sees Mosley and Relsley come from opposite sides of the Larvesp and attack its sides, making the Larvesp abandon its attempt on Tresdon. Its body turns around. It spits more webbing and goop, tangling Mosley and sticking Lelan to the ground. It crawls up high above the ground. But the monster's legs still shoot down, trying to impale them. The underbelly is exposed, if they can just reach it. Tresdon grunts loudly, gets up from the floor and, jumping into the air and grabbing hold of one of its legs, pulls the thing down. Elan does the same and throws herself forward gripping a leg, but it just kicks as they cling to it.

The animal whistles and bucks.

Jordon finally frees Eldon and they join the throng, also grabbing a leg, preventing it from escaping.

Elan sweats with the exertion of holding on with all her might. She struggles to watch what is happening as Relsley and Warrick pierce the Larvesp's belly. Relsley pulls his blade up as Warrick swipes with his claws. More black malodorous blood sprays out, covering anyone nearby. The Larvesp gives one last pathetic shriek before collapsing to the ground and twitching.

Nolan and Serdon had freed Mosley and Lelan and they were all catching their breath when Relsley smiles broadly, dirty and breathing heavily from the fight, "Welcome to the Darklands, Brothers!"

He turns his back to them and keeps pressing on. The group has little time to collect themselves before they have to chase after Relsley's disappearing figure.

They walk for a long while, dodging large bugs with venom that can make one ill, animals that were once rabbits but now are vicious monsters, poisonous plants that could paralyze upon touching bare skin, and moving shadows that play tricks on your mind. Beings lived in these woods she had only read about and even more that she had not. In the last twenty equinoxes, the Old One created more monsters with the help of Kalrolin's Journal.

Elan once again feels Warrick's hand wrap around her arm, slowing her down. Nolan frowns as he walks past them. Warrick pretends to be adjusting his bag of items then begins to stroll a bit further behind the others.

Elan raises an eyebrow and opens her mouth, but he speaks first.

"What do you know about this Relsley?" Warrick asks.

Elan shrugs, her face scrunching.

"I don't like the direction he is taking us in. Not one bit. And if he has been here even a day longer than us then he should know that it is trouble going this far east. What do you know about him? What do any of you know about him? He could be the traitor, and leading us into a trap."

"Don't be ridiculous." Elan would rather not have this conversation with Warrick, because something inside of her already had a bad feeling about Relsley. The fact that he is bringing it up is causing her to examine her apprehension more closely, which is something she had been trying to repress.

"Am I being so unreasonable? Why do you automatically trust him to take you through land you have never been? Is it because he is a Blood One like yourself? Or because he is part of your little society?" he mocks. "You have already witnessed that those are not valid criteria for trustworthiness when you have a traitor among you."

"So I'm to take your word over his? You are a murderer." Elan sees something that looks like surprise or even hurt cross Warrick's features before he hardens his expression.

"In my eyes, so are all of you. Murder or not, at least I have proven to be more dependable to you than him. Remember I took a blade for you." Warrick presses out his chest as if he has made the point that would end the argument.

"Because you had to," Elan bites. She was not going to give him the satisfaction of being right, or having the last word.

"Exactly my point!" he hisses, leaning in more from his hips. "I would suffer from your misfortunes so for the sake of self-preservation, I am looking out for my best interests."

"Shut your mouths before I sew your lips together," Relsley says, now very suddenly near them.

The rest of the group is waiting far ahead of them and has stopped so Relsley could see what was taking them so long. The group peeks back at them. Some of the others are on tiptoe to get a better look at what is happening.

Elan had not even realized that Warrick and herself stopped walking to have this argument. Her face heats up in embarrassment. Now everyone is going to think that she is irresponsible.

"Why are we going this far east? We shouldn't be this close to the lakes," Warrick protests. The accusation in his voice is not veiled. He leans forward, his feet set shoulder width apart like he is challenging Relsley.

Relsley frowns, his brow coming down over his eyes. His hands are placed on his hips as though he is making an attempt to take up as much space as possible to be intimidating. "Your kind knows to avoid these areas, so we have less of a chance of running into Darklanders."

"So you would rather run into a Getch?" Warrick challenges.

"At least if a Getch escapes, it isn't going to talk. The Old One won't be tipped off to our presence," Relsley argues.

"So better dead than found?" Warrick scoffs.

"That's right. Especially in your case, a female and a creature, both are weaknesses and liabilities. Move along. Your conversations will attract attention."

Elan's stomach drops as she swallows the bile that rises at the back of her throat. She had to bite her tongue to stop herself from lashing out. She practically shakes with the effort.

Relsley pivots his body around, pacing back to the front. Serdon and Mosley don't hesitate to scowl her way, whereas Nolan and Tresdon give Relsley crude gestures behind his back. Jordon, Eldon, and Lelan give her a sympathetic tilt of their heads but no more.

Before long, marshes and shallow puddles take over where rocks used to jut out of the ground. Elan's boots stick in the soft clay, causing her feet to make a puckering sound as she lifts them. The land beneath her feet doesn't retain the print of her boot and settles back down as if the floor is more of a liquid than a solid. Soggy, green muck floats on the surface of patches of water. Elan struggles to pull her foot up when Warrick stops. His arm shoots out, pressing her back.

"You see that there?" He points to a dark iris colored puddle, different from the other dark gray ones. "That means the water is unsafe. If you get your foot caught in that then-"

A chill goes down her spine as a scream echoes in the forest. It's Tresdon. His leg sinks deep in an iris puddle. Relsley should have warned them before heading this way.

Warrick jumps to his side before any of the other members even know what to do.

"Something has grabbed hold of my leg!" Tresdon's face has lost its parlor. His usual smiling expression is worried, wide eyed.

Though the diameter is small, already half of Tresdon's calf is being swallowed up. Relsley takes hold of Tresdon, trying to pull him up, but something drags him back in with even more force.

Tresdon grimaces, letting an anguished grunt rip from his mouth as blood stains the water.

Warrick swears, and his face stretches forward, his claws unleash as he drives his hands into the ground beside the pool of water. A shriek emanates from under the ground. The sudden release of Tresdon's leg causes him to fall back. Teeth marks puncture his leather boot. Driblets of red streak down the side of his leg. The scent slams into Elan like a runaway wagon. It is so much stronger than anything around them. It is completely distinct from anything else, savory and enticing.

"Well, looks like I will need a new pair of boots now," Tresdon says through clenched teeth, trying to add levity to the serious situation.

"You're safe now," Elan says, falling beside him trying to help him up. She tries to breathe as little as possible.

"Not even close," Warrick says. "We have attracted too much attention, his blood. The Getches have scented us."

Relsley begins wrapping Tresdon's wound to stop the blood and cover the scent. It doesn't work. Elan wonders if the other Order members can smell it as strongly as her.

Warrick draws his sword in tandem with Relsley. Not even a fraction of a moment later, Elan hears what she had been dreading. A light gurgling was usually soothing to Elan's ears, remembering the flowing water of the river in her land and the small wildlife that call it home, but she knows in the Darklands this is a dangerous sound. The air around them fills with the slide of metal against scabbards.

A splash to her right causes her to whip around. A cold sweat forms on her brow. The branches of a nearby tree sway and click against each other. So that was the sound she was hearing: things crawling in the trees. Again, a low, wet gurgle resonates almost like lungs filled with water.

The branches clack again and what she sees there makes her clasp a hand over her mouth.

Bony creatures almost as large an oxenlows crawl through the dead trees. Their heads twist upside down. Their faces are similar to a hare, but the ears are mere stumps, ears and eyes fused permanently shut. Long arms and back legs bend back as they crawl on all fours with swift jerking movements. Their bodies are segmented in two and their knobby hands have six fingers each with vicious talons. Saliva drips from their teeth and lipless faces.

Most of the animals were once something normal in their own land, but had been twisted with dark magic here. Elan knew the Old One had been making pets of his own with the Journal to build an army for the day he would escape. No doubt these are newer creations.

All at once, Elan hears the labored gasps of her comrades. Five more of these things emerge from the fog.

They unhinge their jaws, gurgling a cackle. A long forked tongue darts from their mouths, tasting the air to see.

"We don't want to fight these things unless we have to. The bloodshed will only attract more attention to us," Relsley says in hushed tones. "They can't hear, but they may feel vibration in our voice if we are too loud. Just stay perfectly still so they won't feel our movement and hope that you put enough soil on so they can't smell you."

Their forked tongues lick, and they collectively move closer to Tresdon. Their jerking twitching movements coil fear in the pit of Elan's stomach as they close in on him. They can smell his blood. Tresdon holds still and Elan hopes Relsley covered his wound well enough.

"I have an idea. No matter what, do not move," Warrick says in a hushed tone.

One slinks over. Elan's heartbeat hammers against her ribs as it hovers above Tresdon. As soon as the closest Getch is almost above Tresdon's body, Warrick snatches the beast into a headlock. He holds down its mouth so that it can't give a warning gurgle to the other Getches. The animal's brood would be able to feel the vibration of his call to alert its pack. Its neck twists under his arm, its head spinning. Warrick slices the animal's throat, releasing dark blood spilling over Tresdon, whose face contorts in disgust. The Getch convulses before falling limp and dying.

As soon as the others come close, they smell the poisonous blood of a native beast. They no longer sense the fresh blood that attracted them.

Slowly, they retreat into the water or melt into the dense fog.

250

The group lets out a collective breath. But Elan can still see their pulses jumping on their necks.

"Maybe you should have warned them not to step in the puddles," Warrick accuses once he knows the Getches are fully gone.

"They should have learned that in oacling training," Relsley replies. "It is not my job to teach them something they should have learned long ago." Relsley looks down at Tresdon. "I should just leave you here. You're useless to us now, injured. You will drag everyone else down."

Elan's hands flex into fists. "I will take him. He will be my burden to bear." Elan puts Tresdon's arm around her neck and heaves him up.

"Now we have three problems instead of two. Of course, he would join you rejects." Relsley's face reddens.

"I will help carry him as well," Jordon insists, pressing out his chest and lacing his voice with authority.

"Us as well," says Nolan as Eldon and Lelan stand tall behind him.

"Suit yourselves," Relsley spits. "But we are not slowing down for the rest of you." Relsley stomps to the front of the group.

"I don't like him," Warrick says.

Elan smirks. "For once, I agree with you."

Chapter 32

After a long day, they finally stop for the night. Lighting a fire this deep in the Darklands is not a danger to them. Even if the fire was spotted from a creature overhead, they could be any Darklandian making the light for warmth.

Elan and her brothers had spent the day taking turns carrying Tresdon and helping him along. And just as Relsley had promised, he had not slowed down for them at all. Elan noticed he picked up his pace after the accident.

Relsley had hunted some sort of beast in the forest, and a few were now roasting over the fire. Most sit in silence, too weary to even speak to one another, chewing on the meat. The Darklands has taken its toll physically and mentally. Some men fell asleep without even bothering to eat. Elan learned early in lessons that great depressions were an effect of the land. A hopeless abyss of sadness had swallowed them whole.

Elan and Warrick sit a little further back from the fire than everyone else, knowing well that being too close would give them more attention than they want.

Tresdon comes hobbling over to them, limping terribly. Relsley found herbs and medicines in the forest and reluctantly bandaged him up. Both Elan and Warrick raise their eyebrows as he sits beside Warrick.

"I'm not going to make a big deal out of this," Tresdon says begrudgingly to Warrick. "But I wanted to thank you for helping me. I know you didn't have to. You could have let me bleed out or even let Relsley take care of it. Relsley probably would have abandoned me right there." Tresdon's face becomes hard, before softening again. "And you didn't."

Warrick turns his head away, frowning and refusing to acknowledge his thanks.

"Well, that's all then." Tresdon smiles even wider at his annoyance and claps a hand to his shoulder before shuffling away with his head bowed.

Warrick flinches from his touch and fumes, irate.

"You only did it so we wouldn't attract more attention, didn't you?" Elan asks.

"That's right. Saving him was just an unfortunate side effect."

"Well, now you have another unfortunate side effect coming this way." Elan smiles, trying her best to hide her amusement.

Lelan marches over, his shoulders back, and his arm extends.

"I want to applaud you for your fast thinking in saving Tresdon's life," Lelan says much too loud, obviously wanting everyone to hear. "This isn't the first time you have saved one of our own." Lelan winks at Elan. "It was brave, and you have proven to be one of our brothers despite what anyone else says."

Warrick's face flushes, murderous.

"He only did it to save his own skin," Relsley says. "Don't thank him for being a beast of survival."

"I don't believe that," Lelan says with his arms rigid. "Anyone who saves my friends is mine as well. He belongs with us."

"Shut up, child," Warrick hisses at him.

"Lelan," Elan says. "Go to sleep. It's been a long day."

"Make sure you and that monster sleep far enough away," Relsley throws out. "I don't want to find anyone drained of their blood in the morning."

Lelan bites his lips. Elan knows no matter how much he wants to say something he will not talk back to someone in charge, but he is not above giving dirty looks.

253

Elan stands and walks away from the firelight. It's colder away from their only source of warmth so Elan starts to contemplate making her own fire.

Elan believes Warrick is thinking the same thing as he begins to gather fallen branches and twigs. Only he isn't making a small pile, but a large circle around them.

"What are you doing?"

"If you feel safe enough around that lot then by all means, sleep unguarded. But I don't trust any of them not to kill us while we sleep. Especially that Relsley. He has already expressed his distaste for us. I'm making a barrier of twigs so if anything comes close to us then we will hear the sticks break. In the dark, they won't see it."

She sees him continue to make a tight circle.

"Am I supposed to sleep in the same *nest* as you?"

"This is not a nest! And if you want to make your own, be my guest. But you sleeping unguarded means I sleep unguarded. This is for safety's sake. I also believe we should sleep with our backs to one another, so nothing creeps up on us."

"You are very paranoid."

"And you are not paranoid enough. Anyone could be the traitor. Anyone. And you are playing right into their hands."

Elan is struck with the memory of Jordon hiding and sending messages in town. He is one of her closest friends, and he is keeping a secret from all of them. The Creature has a point. If Jordon could be guilty of even the smallest bit of treason, so could any of them.

Elan jumps from her sleep as the yells of her brothers pierce the night. Sights and sounds blur and flash in the chaos. Feet slip against the clay, and she hears the grunts and clashing of metal and claws. The fire has almost gone out, leaving dimming light. Warrick has his sword at the ready as he runs to greet the creatures ransacking their camp. Elan sprints, catching up.

Everything around her is pitch black and her new eye can see much better than her other. There is a flap of leathery wings that catches her attention amongst the fray. It doesn't take her long to recognize the same creatures that had attacked right outside of Order Land are here now. There are only two of them she can see, but they have the advantage of night on their side.

The smaller attacker keeps most of the members busy as the other inflicts as much damage as he can. The chains he swings slap their faces, causing them to bleed and bruise. The bloodshed attracts more of the Getches. The air fills with gurgles in addition to the clamber of battle. Elan swings around, not knowing where to place her attention with so much going on. Swords swing, and the heads of Getches roll, inky blood splattering the ground. Their jaws unhinge and snap down on what flesh they can find.

Elan runs to help Eldon as a Getch's hands grasp tightly around his neck, its feet planted on his chest, and its mouth stretches to bite. With a thrust of her sword, the blade goes right through the Getch's back, and Eldon only takes a second to stop before standing again.

Elan watches Warrick going for the bald creature, knowing that he is the one who is doing the most damage. His black chains swirl around him, but Warrick's sword skill has improved. He spins, tosses and catches the blade, like a fluid dance rather than fighting. He takes the bald creature almost all on his own.

A small marble falls from the bald one's hand. It reflects the little light. Instead of the glass dropping to the ground, it connects with the chain weaving in and out of each link. It leaves a trail of blue thread.

Elan is stunned and knows he has cast some kind of spell with the bead.

He swings the chains, causing a loud rushing of
wind. His arm raises high as the metal spins round. Elan
turns to the sound and can only see half of the beast's face
illuminated as he smiles wide. The breeze becomes louder
and louder. The wind bends and twists until the chain has
created a cyclone. A wind funnel grows as it spins, tearing
everything it touches. Warrick's eyes are wide as it grows
taller, stretching up higher. Another tornado whirls to life as
he continues to swing the chains. They howl like mad dogs
as they rip through the air. The other Order members' faces
are horror stricken as the end of the cyclone touches the
ground and rips up everything in its path.

"Run!" someone yells, barely audible over the sound.
It's Lelan. He throws himself between Warrick and the bald
creature as he physically tries to push Warrick back. His face
is anxious, his sword at the ready.

The wind uproots trees and spins out of control,
causing everyone to split and run randomly into the
darkness. Some of the Getches are sucked up into the twister
and tossed about in its force. It is utter chaos. The air
thickens with blood, sweat, and cries of all kinds. Shadows
move too quickly, and Elan can't decipher the shapes.

Warrick catches up to Elan as she runs blindly
through the woods.

"Not there!" she sees Warrick mouth because she
can't hear the words. As she watches him, confused, she
steps and doesn't hit solid ground but falls through water.
She splashes, thrashing, surprised and fighting to catch air.
Her lungs burn, and her arms flail to keep her afloat. She can
still see the wind spiraling toward her. She tries to swim, but
something has a hold of her ankle. It pulls her down. Her
hands grasp at air trying to find anything to pull her up. Her
mouth fills with muddy water as she chokes and gags.

She finally grabs hold of something, but there is a tug
of war between whatever has her ankle and what her hand
is holding on to. A few moments later, her leg frees. Pulling
on a branch, she slides out of the water in time to see a
sopping wet Warrick climb out of the water as well.

There is no time for gratitude. A second funnel boomerangs straight for them. The whirlwind shrieks and whistles as it approaches them. Tree branches, earth, and even Darkland animals spin and then hurl back out. Her heart races as they try to outrun the oncoming danger. It gains ground, barreling toward them, no matter where they turn. Warrick pulls Elan to him, wrapping his arms around her and folding his wings around the both of them.

"Tuck your head in. Brace yourself!" he orders in her ear.

Boom. The wind hits her, knocking all the breath from her lungs and she is tossed about like a child's rag doll. The creature tightens his grip so neither of them can move an inch. But even being crushed, she feels herself slipping. Locking her arms behind his waist, she thinks she must be squeezing him too hard. His wings encompass them both as debris hits and cuts. Though she has no wings of her own, the same injuries pepper her back. Her eyes press down tightly. Her stomach twists.

Then as if she were thrown out of a slingshot, they are spit out. Elan feels Warrick's wings unfurling, catching the air and slowing them down. Her stomach drops and she can feel that he is having trouble gliding on the air with how unsteadily he dips and swerves. She knows she is throwing off his equilibrium, which causes him to crash into the trees and slam hard onto the clay. Warrick rolls to lessen the damage to his body.

Her muscles throb, sore and stiff from holding on so tightly. Elan breathes hard, as both of their heartbeats thrum loud in her ears. Warrick slowly and shakily pulls away as Elan opens her eyes in the darkness. Her vision adjusts, and she gawks at him in surprise. They made it out alive. His arms pry open. He rolls onto his back, his chest rising and falling. A small whine escapes Warrick's lips. Elan can feel the scrapes, cuts, bruises and the possible broken bones. Neither of them move. Elan's limbs rest at her side like lead.

The adrenaline coursing through her veins settles, leaving her exhausted and she passes out on the cold hard floor.

The morning light wakes her. The rays are not sharp and jarring like in her land, but instead quietly benign. Elan hauls her body up as it protests. Soreness sets deep in her muscles, and her skin is sensitive from bruising. A burn reddens on the side of Warrick's body from the force of him crashing to the ground. Her flesh is also raw in the same spot. Warrick lays on his back awake and wincing, covered in mud, scrapes, and cuts.

"I don't think anything is broken," she says through gritted teeth.

Warrick groans. His wings drop at his sides as if he doesn't even have the strength to fold them back up. They both try to stand, and wobble, too weak to go far.

Warrick's voice comes out rougher than normal. "We can't stay out in the open in the daylight. I have no idea where we have been thrown or how far. I do know that we are away from the lakes. The land is much more solid and has more vegetation than the swamps. There should be caves close to here someplace. We must rest there for a little while. We cannot go very far. The best we can do is hide."

Both Warrick and Elan drag their feet, and stumble to the nearest formation of jagged stones jutting from the clay. Elan thinks how lucky they are that they had not landed on these sharp rocks. Kalrolin's magic in her crest must have protected them from that. Their bodies would have shattered to bits for sure.

They discover a small dark opening on the shaded part of the caves. It is so low they must crawl inside. But it appears large enough and high enough inside to house them for the day. Warrick ducks inside as Elan follows suit. They both get to their feet once inside. Elan trips over her feet as Warrick backs away.

In the center of the cave, a hiss echoes. Her creature eye cuts through the dark to see a snake curled comfortably in their new hiding place. But is not like any snake Elan has ever seen. It is black and gray like everything else in this land, but there are bright purple and burgundy spikes all along its body, similar to the flowers she had seen earlier. Three sets of beady black eyes shine, and its long body stretches four times the size of the largest reptile she has ever laid eyes on. It spits a liquid toward them which manages to just miss them.

As it hits the wall, it sizzles and corrodes away the stone. Warrick reaches for his sword and then pats at his side without looking away from the snake. Elan hears Warrick swear. He must have lost his sword when the cyclone hit them. He curses loudly, backing away.

The snake snaps and strikes at them, expelling more of the deadly venom. Elan pushes Warrick's arm aside, which was unconsciously holding her back. She pulls out her dagger, pushing forward. Warrick's hand reflexively shoots out toward her, but before he can grab hold of her arm, she lunges. The snake strikes, but Elan rolls away from its sharp teeth. The animal not only slides across the ground, but also along the walls of the caves and the ceiling. It slithers up the jagged walls. Elan is surprised to see it sticking to any surface it slithers over until it comes to the top of the cave, dropping its head down, snapping and striking. Deflecting each bite, the snake only takes bites of her armor or the side of her blade. The snake spits, and it burns through the metal covering her torso, but not her dagger. She pulls off her breastplate before the poison eats all the way through.

Elan isn't sure where the strength to fight comes from when she is breaking apart. Warrick takes a step forward, perhaps to intervene, when Elan runs behind it as it snaps back at her. She swings the dagger around and plunges it deep into the snake's skull, causing its body to violently jerk. Venom spills from its now punctured glands, melting its head. Once the snake has stopped moving, Elan grabs it by the tail, holding it up to Warrick. Its long body is partially on the cave floor.

"Is it safe to eat?"

He blinks and tilts his head to the side. "I believe so," he answers, shell-shocked.

"Good," Elan says. "Because I am starving."

Chapter 33

After sucking every bit of meat from the snake's bones, Elan sits in silence, allowing her body to rest. The snake's flesh had been oily, sliding around in her mouth as she ate. The small fire she had created to cook kept her warm.

Warrick had been lying still for hours now, not asleep but not fully awake. His eyes remain shut, his body pressed against the chilly stone floor to cool his pealed skin. Elan and Warrick had wrapped their injuries. Elan knows if Warrick had not thought to roll when they fell, they would have suffered much more damage. Superficial gashes and an injured shoulder and wrist were the extent. His cloak is splayed out on the ground, useless, ripped to shreds for their dressings.

"Are we going to try and find the others?" Elan asks. "What do you think is happening to them?"

"I don't know, and I don't care at the moment," Warrick replies lazily. "We have to heal. Going into this land with such a large obvious group was a bad idea from the beginning. I think our next course of action should be to rest up as much as we can then get moving to find the Old One. They already have the instructions and map I drew. We will head in the same direction, and we are bound to meet up. That is, as soon as I find out our location. I didn't like traveling with them anyway. This is safer."

Elan had always believed there was safety in numbers, but when you didn't know who to trust then perhaps less was better.

Everything is calm for the time being, Elan believes she would do well to rest up before they head back into this unknown world.

Her left wrist throbs with pain. She removes her boots and all of her armor and realizes that her clothes are still damp from falling in the water. Her bare feet reveal a swollen ankle. Elan regretfully remembers that Warrick had helped unsnag her from whatever had a hold of her in the lake. She takes her cloak and places it close to the fire. The snake's saliva has eaten away the metal on her armor it is useless.

"Use what is left of my cloak to wrap your wrist and ankle. I don't know what will happen if one of our injuries doesn't heal correctly."

Elan knows they get the same physical injuries, but don't feel the same pain. They feel each other's hunger but not each other's emotions. She doesn't know why she has a creature eye though. And now it is evident to her that they don't heal at the same rate. "Do you think if one of us has an injury and it doesn't heal properly it won't heal properly on the other?"

"I don't know, and I'm not willing to take the chance either. So make sure you do a good job."

Elan takes the leftover cloth and rewraps her wrist, giving her enough stability to dress her ankle. Every movement causes her to wince. She is now receiving twice the injuries she would have acquired compared to battles in the past. Her body can only take so much. She knows this spell is a curse so of course they would get the same injuries, but the beneficial things like healing would not transfer.

Warrick no longer has a cloak. His clawed feet remain bare. All he wears is a pair of pants bought from Delmira's shop. He is exposed to the elements without it.

"If you get an illness, will I?" Elan asks.

Warrick frowns. He crosses his arms over his chest.

_____

262

"This is quite a situation your dimwitted wizard has gotten us into, isn't it? I never thought in one thousand equinoxes that I would be forced to worry about a female Blood One and what happens to her health. Or that one would be interested in mine."

"This isn't my ideal situation either. We could be like this forever. FOREVER. And we should know as much as possible."

Warrick sits up, scowling like a misbehaving youngster.

"Well, if we are stuck like this forever, as you say, then time will tell. We have FOREVER to figure out the details," he says, trying to dismiss her. "We will find a more populated province, and with a little luck we can steal a cloak and maybe even a sword if a Darklandian happens to have thrown one out from their last meal."

Elan hates how he speaks of the death of one of her kind so casually.

Once she is done wrapping her shoulder, she broods at the prospect of just laying low for the rest of the day. After a very short while, Elan fidgets. "Maybe you can go out and get your bearings, then we can come up with a plan of action."

Warrick sits up. "Perhaps it is best we get a look around while it is light, but we should not move until after dark, just in case."

"I was thinking the same thing."

"And we have to keep out of sight. We are in no condition to fight at the moment."

Elan nods. She gets up, leaving her cloak and armor by the fire but not her dagger. Placing the knife in her back hip band, she lets her shirt fall over it.

The land contrasts drastically with where they had been a day before. Instead of the ground being soggy and wet it is almost bone dry. The vegetation fluffs and spikes in all directions and to Elan, it reminds her of squirrel tails growing out of the ground. Spiked burgundy flowers and bushes made of just black thorns clutter the landscape. These she remembers from oacling training. If you got too close, they would spring to life, wrapping around you and slicing into your flesh. You would bleed out, and the plant's roots would suck up the blood. Elan remembered never being able to think of a rose bush the same way again. Every time she saw the red roses all she could think was that they must have gotten their color from the blood the roots had possibly drunk.

The black trees are thick, and tufts of dull green leaves sprout from the branches. Elan and Warrick slowly make their way a bit further from the cave.

"I believe I know where we are about just from the land, but we could be any of three places. If only I could fly, I would be able to see the layout of the land better-"

Warrick stops speaking and halts. Two creatures fly overhead. Elan follows his eyes, scanning far ahead where another two beings descend and throw down items. They begin digging through goods they have looted.

Warrick motions for Elan to stay farther back as he steps closer to the four creatures, trying to get a better view. The Darklanders' voices bounce off the trees as they hunch over, talking amongst themselves. Elan sees Warrick creeping along the ground. He lies low, crawling a bit closer. He has almost reached the end of their tether. Warrick keeps his back toward Elan but moves away from the group of Darklanders back toward her.

A hard yank and sharp sting of her scalp causes Elan to cry out but a meaty oversized hand claps over her mouth, reducing any sound she could make to a mere groan. A creature reeking of fresh blood has a hold of Elan by the hair, and his other hand covers her mouth. He pulls her to his stomach as she struggles to get free, but his grip tightens. Elan can't see this monster's face. Warrick is well hidden a few oxenlow tails away. Elan mentally screams for him to notice what is happening.

Warrick finally turns his head toward her and his eyes become wide. Genuine fear flashes in his eyes. His gaze shifts in panic. Elan knows a Blood One this far into the Darklands only means one thing: easy food.

Chapter 34

The side of Elan's dagger presses against her back where she had put it in her waist band, sandwiched between herself and her captor. The beast lets go of her hair but uses one massive arm to cage her against himself. She twists her arms around trying to fight him off. Warrick catches her attention and imperceptibly gives her a glance of warning. She knows he is telling her not to try anything, not to move. The creature holding Elan doesn't see Warrick crouched farther away.

"Just when I thought my day couldn't get any better, a snack walks right by me," The creature's voice rumbles on her back.

"Looks like we will get to eat more than our fill today," says a broad-shouldered female with clothes poorly patchworked together. She stands beside the creature who is holding Elan tight. The female is as muscular as the male and she stands with her legs far apart. She has a haughty air to her stance.

"Let go of that one!" Warrick hisses, striding out of hiding.

Both Darklanders hunch their backs and bare their teeth, as if he is trying to rob them of their rightful possession.

"Who are you?" the male holding her asks.

"It doesn't matter who I am but what you have a hold of!" Warrick stomps over to them with large steps, his arms held away from his torso and flexing his muscles.

Both expressions turn quizzical.

"You are taking my property," Warrick spits.

Warrick takes a hold of Elan's arm and jerks it toward him like an object rather than something attached to a living person. The larger Darklandian releases his grip on her and she stumbles to her knees, but Warrick holds tight. She forces her tongue to the top of her mouth to stop herself from throwing a few choice words at him. The warning glare he gives her allows her to stay quiet for the time being. He must be up to something.

She can see the male for the first time now, and he is humongous with soft, underdeveloped features. His clothes mirror the female creature. The scent of dirt and body odor rolls off of him with each stir of movement.

"If you are going to bring it all this way just to eat it, then you might as well share," the large male says. He grabs Elan's other arm. He has his hand wrapped around the wrist of her right arm. The sleeve is being held in place by him. If he lets go, then it could fall back, and he would be able to see the crest. Elan's eyes widen.

"Did you not hear me? I said I own it." Warrick pulls her up to her feet, knowing they are a moment away from being found out if he doesn't think fast. Elan's irritation at the situation rises and she wonders if they are about to play a game of tug of war and break her in two. Warrick grips her left arm, and the other creature tugs on her right. "This is MY female."

"*Your* female?" The large male hangs his tongue in disgust.

"That's right! So unless you want to lose that arm, I suggest you let go."

"I don't believe you. You just took her now and don't want to share," the female creature says.

Warrick pulls back the sleeve on Elan's left arm, revealing multiple bite marks in different stages of healing where Warrick has taken blood. The giant male creature lets go of her, allowing Elan to quickly pull her arm to her side before the crest is unveiled.

A sound of disgust scrapes the back of the female's throat, "Such a vile practice. You should feed and be done with them. You can feed on as many Blood Ones as you want without having one with you at all times. Why anyone would keep such ugly animals as pets is beyond me," she says, giving Elan the once-over.

Elan makes sure to cast her eyes down. They might notice her eye. The female has large flaring nostrils and bumps that trail her browline. Elan twists her jaw and huffs a gust of air from her nose.

"We just arrived here last night, and it was dark. Do you mind telling me what province we are in?" Warrick asks the male.

His eyes narrow, but he answers, "Brunstway."

Elan notices Warrick blanch.

"What's your name anyway?" the female asks. "You look a bit familiar. Doesn't he, Ranku?"

"Yes."

Warrick frowns like he swallowed something bitter and his shoulders shift. His attention casts to the ground as he responds.

"My name is Phesper. I'm not from around here. I hadn't realized I was so far from home."

"My name is Jokellen," says the female, holding out her palm facing him.

Warrick takes his and places it on hers.

Watching creatures exchange polite formalities is so bizarre to Elan. She had always assumed that they shared no social interaction other than killing.

"You are injured. And you look underdressed for this weather," Jokellen says suspiciously, taking in their state of dress.

Elan sighs, relieved that her oversized clothing covers her injuries. They would have been even more suspicious.

"We have extra things from our last meal. Come." Ranku motions with a massive hand.

Warrick follows Ranku. Elan knows full well that if he tries to get rid of him, it would only increase their suspicion. They walk toward the other two creatures still shuffling through a pile of random items. Their bodies crouch low as they pick through the items, throwing some aside with disinterest.

A smaller female sits cross-legged on the ground, and the other male hunches, not as massive as Ranku, but taller than Warrick.

"This is going to be no use to us," one says to the other, tossing aside a sword and shield. Elan eyes the sword discarded on the ground and longs to pick it up.

"Look! Boots!" the new female says, who appraises the pile. "Maybe these might fit me this time." She tries to put one on. The side rips, and she frowns, tossing it.

Elan works hard not to scowl while being around so many of them at once. The hair on the back of her neck stands straight up in constant alert, ready to fight at the slightest provocation.

Ranku calls to his company, "Xelth." The male lifts his head. "Morgo." Then the female. "We have company."

They both spin around and as soon as the male sees Elan, he smiles and licks his lips. The pair is even uglier than Ranku and Jokellen. Xelth, the male, has sharp eyes and a slack jaw. The new female is much younger than any of them. Elan suspects she might be even younger than herself. Her asymmetrical face is cratered with an uneven skin tone.

"This is out to be a really good day," snickers Xelth, in a broken accented language.

"Forget it, Xelth," Jokellen says disappointedly. "That happens to be this Darklandian's female."

Morgo's face twists in disgust the way Jokellen's had when first hearing the news. But Xelth raises his brow, more interested, albeit surprised.

"Give him something to wear," Ranku says to Xelth. "I will start the fire. We will rest before going into town to trade." Xelth throws Warrick a cloak as Ranku gathers dry sticks. "Were you on your way to town, Phesper?"

"No. I am trying to get back home. I live in Hervidso," Warrick fabricates.

"You are quite a way from there. And the way you speak. It is very different. You must not be from here. Why did you make such a journey?"

Elan knows Ranku is not being polite but rather getting information. She doesn't understand why Warrick willingly sits and exchanges pleasantries with them. Elan had always thought creatures didn't trust each other and were lone beings.

"It was business. Buyers had wanted my female, but the price they had promised was a lie."

Jokellen squirms, ill-tempered at this point, "Listen to you males speaking about this! Playing with your food makes me sick. You feed, you kill. You be done with it. I find it unnatural to keep it around with you."

Elan finds it increasingly hard to swallow her words while being spoken about as if she is too dumb to understand them. And her muscles protest their locked position, with the way they talk so callously about buying and selling her kind. The only good thing about this, if there is one at all, is at least Jokellen believes in giving her victims a swift death.

"Don't tell me you are a radical, Jokellen?" asks Warrick.

"No, she isn't," replies Morgo, "but I am."

The rest of the group throw up their hands and grumble, enraged at her suggestion.

Morgo leans forward. "If we could just come to some agreement with–"

"Agreement with Blood Ones!" Xelth snarls. "Impossible. We show our faces, they slaughter us. Kill or be killed, Morgo! Up to them, they would murder all of us. We just beat them to it. You are naive."

"We must drink their blood to survive, but we don't have to kill them. It isn't easy, but I have never killed any of my food."

270

Elan jerks back slightly at her statement, really scrutinizing the smaller female with doubt at her words. Where had she gotten such an idea? Elan heard them use the word *radical*. Did that mean that there were more of them with her similar mind set?

"And how would you know, Morgo?" Jokellen scoffs. "After feeding, have you stayed around to check to see if they wake? If they are well? You have most likely killed more than you know. Besides, they would try and kill us even if they just saw us flying overhead."

"But-" Morgo begins.

"But nothing," Xelth says. "You try it one day. You go, try and talk to them. See what they do."

"So are you an extremist now, Xelth? You think we should kill for the sake of killing? Get rid of them completely?"

"Yes. We are stronger race! They are food. Nothing more. You should be worried that loyals to the Old One are listening." Xelth gives Warrick a glance. And the way he says the last sentence indicates that the case is closed and there will be no more discussion on the matter.

"You should accompany us into town," Ranku says to Warrick, changing the subject. "I don't know if you are aware, but there is a hunt out for a dangerous creature named Warrick. He is said to be traveling with a legion of Blood One males. There is a hefty price on his head as well. If you run into them on your own, and they see you have one of their females they will destroy you for sure."

Warrick looks at Ranku with his head tilted, as though debating his offer.

"That is a very generous offer, but I think I can manage on my own. I should get going now." He takes Elan by her forearm to leave when he hears Xelth.

"We gave you a cloak. Give something in return."

Warrick turns, heaving a breath as if this moment were inevitable.

"What is it that you think you deserve?"

"Your female's blood."

Elan stiffens, and all pretense of subservience dissolves.

At his response, Warrick takes his cloak and drops it to the ground. He scowls. As he pivots on his heel, Ranku stops him, holding the clothing back out.

"Take the cloak. We don't need it. I offered it to you, not him."

Warrick says nothing but nods in thanks. He accepts it and marches away, grabbing Elan's arm to play his part. He travels in the direction opposite the caves. They watch him as he goes. As soon as they are out of earshot, Warrick speaks.

"I believe Ranku recognized me. We will double back to the cave to get your cloak. I didn't want them to know what direction we were going. He was giving me a warning."

"Why would he do that?" Elan asks. "You owe him nothing."

Warrick's jaw clenches, "He said we were in Brunstway. We were thrown a very far way off. These parts are not as dangerous as where we were before, but it is more populated with Darklanders. I grew up in this providence. He must remember my face. He must pity me." Warrick says it as if he is outraged by the idea of someone showing him kindness.

She peeks over her shoulder, and sure enough, Ranku still watches them go. Elan wonders why Warrick would appear pitiful, really studying his set, chiseled face.

The terrain differs from when they were traveling towards the east. Elan wonders what has happened to her brothers and if they have separated as well or managed to stay close together. Nolan must be worried sick. He came to make sure she was alright, and now she was not even in eyesight. Tresdon must also have one less person willing to help him walk if they made it through the ordeal alive. Elan shivers at the thought. One of her brothers could be dead right now, and she would not know. She is desperate to not think about it, so instead Elan remembers something she heard earlier.

"So," Elan asks with complete disgust in her voice. "Is it normal for your kind to keep *blood ones as pets* as that female creature said?" Elan clenches her fists.

Warrick's jaw twitches, "It is not a common practice, but not unheard of. It is not something I agree with in the least. Taking anything as a slave is appalling," he says with venom.

They dredge along, Warrick picking up their pace. As they move deeper into the land, Elan does not say anything more and silently follows behind him, trusting he knows the land.

After a while, she supposes that they will start to head back now that they have gone far enough. Perhaps those creatures had left. Her thoughts had been so involved, she hadn't even noticed how long they hiked. They had been on the move much longer than necessary.

Warrick stops abruptly, and Elan's forehead knits. He stands and stares at a thick tree twisted with age. His eyes become large and shine as they glue to the roots springing from the ground. Raising a hand, he places it on his chest. Warrick's throat bobs as he swallows thickly then falls to his knees, his body sways as if he is drunk.

Elan reflexively grabs his arm to help him up but stops herself, realizing her actions. Not a single moment makes sense to Elan right now. She has never seen him or any other person in this state. It is as though the sight of the tree hypnotizes him. Thinking this is another danger of the Darklands, she refuses to set eyes on the tree.

"What is happening to you? Is there danger? What is going on?"

His eyes threaten to shed tears, but Warrick shakes his head unblinking. His jaw clenches as tight as his fists. He extends his hands, and the tips of his fingers brush the roots. He closes his eyes finally, seeming to fight something internally.

———

Elan thinks he has gone mad. Sitting back on his heels, his lids shut. His claws touch the trunk of the tree, while he again swallows a sound back. He cuts his palm with a razor edge claw. Dark blood drips slowly down to the ground in front of him.

Elan holds her hand, about to yell at him for making them bleed when he sighs through his teeth, "The reaper waits for none. Hessero. Forgive me."

Chapter 35

Warrick sat for such a long time, Elan made a fire as the day rolled to evening. He would not remove his eyes from the base of the tree. He would caress the ground beside it, the bark, then the roots. He would whisper undetectable things under his breath, once again resting his head on the ground while squeezing his lids shut.

Elan had no idea what to do with herself. For a while, she refused to watch him, paced or went as far as the spell would allow. The Order taught them never to get too emotional, to always leave displays of grief for times when you were alone. So many died in The Order that you were instructed not to dwell on the loss but move on quickly, remember them well, but not grieve. When Uldon had died, she could not have open displays of mourning. In the darkness, in the quiet, alone, she wept and beat her chest, trying to release the pain that bloomed there. How she wished she had not been alone in those times, that there was someone else to share the burden of loss with.

It has been hours, and Elan remains unaware, why this particular tree caused Warrick to be so distraught with grief. The sun had set, and Elan's skin rises with goosebumps. She rubs her hands while getting closer to the flames. She could have left long ago and dragged him away, but she couldn't find the cruelty to deprive him of this moment he appeared to need.

Curiosity gnaws unrelenting, but she has not uttered a peep.

Finally, he gets up and walks away from the tree without even giving it a backward glance. His shoulders slump. His eyes are glazed over, and he doesn't speak.

Warrick sits by the fire still lost in his thoughts. Elan didn't know these evil creatures could express such deep sadness. She did not know there was such a thing as kindness or concern like what Ranku showed Warrick by giving him a cloak. Even Morgo had wanted peace with her fellow countrymen.

"I think we should get moving." Elan finds herself using a softer tone of voice. Without realizing it, she feels sympathy for his pain.

She waits for him to be snappy, to be rude. Instead, he doesn't respond. Elan raises her eyebrows but doesn't say anything else. Elan would rather he be surly with her. That type of creature she can rationalize. Not one with emotions, hurts and loved ones.

Elan's questions burst from her lips, "What is going on? Who is Hessero? Why are you crying over a tree?"

Warrick looks at Elan and jerks up, for a split second his face twists like he is going to fight her, but then she sees his face crumble. The weariness pulling at his eyes tells her that he just doesn't have the energy to fight her. He faces her, raw and open. The tree stands behind him, but he does not look back again.

"You could have moved at any time. You could have walked away, and I would have had no choice but to follow. But you stayed here. You let me grieve. For that, I am unwillingly thankful to you." He stops and licks his dry lips. "This is the spot that I buried my Hessero. I have not been here in over twenty equinoxes. I have been too ashamed and guilt-ridden to return. But it seems as though fate has other plans."

Elan stares wide-eyed at Warrick.

"That Masked One you held so dearly to you murdered the only thing I had ever cared about more than myself, more than anything."

Elan swallows back bile at the mention of Uldon, her eyes becoming hard. But Elan does not dare interrupt. She needs to hear this, even if she doesn't want to.

"I remember it so well. I had found Hessero right there by that very tree. I was only sixteen equinoxes at the time. She was leaning against the tree, crying. She was much younger than myself, and I wondered why she had been left alone. Our kind abandon their spawn at an early age. It is to make them strong, to learn to hunt for themselves. She was much too young to be left alone though. But one look at her and you could tell there was something not right about her. It was her wings. She would never be able to fly. It was then that I noticed her arm as well. It was curled up next to her, shriveled and unable to move. Her parents abandoned her because they knew she was a risk to their survival."

Unwillingly, Elan's stomach drops, feeling sick.

"I was much too soft-hearted when I was young. I thought I would help Hessero to get by. Just to get food. At first, she stayed here by herself, and I would always bring back blood that my parents had set aside for me and give it to her. On colds days I would bring her things to keep warm. She was always so grateful for everything I gave her. So I didn't mind that giving her my portions stunted my growth and left me leaner than most.

"Then as she grew a bit older and my parents separated from me at twenty-six equinoxes, I continued to care for her. We found a dwelling and were the best of friends. She was always too gentle to hunt for herself. I had never known anyone so kind, even given her circumstances. I would bring her back blood. She couldn't travel far anyway because of her deformity. But she rarely left my side except when I went for food. Many shunned her or harassed her because she could not fly because she was different. They considered her an outcast. I started to hate my kind for being so cruel to someone so sweet."

Elan watches as Warrick stops speaking, choking on his own words before continuing.

"We were happy, the two of us. Hessero was like the kin I never had. One day, we traveled to the edge of our lands. She had been particularly taunted that day, and I would not leave her on her own. I promised that we would only go to the edge of Blood One land. She was horrified of the murdering Green Cloaks who did not kill for food or necessity.

"I should have never let her come that day. I had found a traveling merchant wandering drunkenly too close to the border of our lands. I thought for sure it would be an easy meal. I drank his blood, and after he had passed out, I placed some blood in a skin so Hessero could easily drink.

"That was when I heard the clopping of hooves. They were much too fast. There were four of them on black horses, clad in bright green. She was petrified. Her eyes widened as they came closer. I could not fight them alone, not with Hessero needing protection. They swung swords that cut my shoulder almost to the bone. I fought back, telling her to run to the woods and save herself. But she would not leave me. That's when it happened. It played in my nightmares over and over again. Her eyes were so distressed. The sword was lifted high above his head, and he swung down, slashing Hessero's neck. I could hear nothing, all I could see was her, covered in dark red, choking. I ran to her, and she died almost instantly in my arms."

Warrick's voice wavers on his last sentence, and pauses before he continues.

"I looked into the brown eyes of the man who killed my Hessero. He smiled almost proud of himself. It was a face I would not ever forget. It was long and thin. His bones beneath his face were much too defined, and it was the ugliest face I had ever seen. I wanted to destroy it. I charged at him, knocking him off his horse. And with one right swoop of my claw, I took half of his face. There was so much blood and he was screaming, his companions rushed to his aid. They beat me and left me for dead. Afterward, they took the ugly Green Cloak and the drunkard that was not dead away."

Elan claps a hand over her mouth, which lets out a small whine. Vivid pictures of that day flash in her mind's eye. She shakes her head, not wanting to believe that Uldon would do such a thing, but how could he have known? They were creatures attacking a man... he had done his duty.

"Hessero was gone, and I had no chance to say goodbye because she had died so quickly. I crawled to her. I could not leave her cold dead body in this land of enemies, and murderers. I gathered all my strength, and I wrapped her in my cloak tightly. I pulled her up on my good shoulder, and it took everything in me not to give up. To carry her all the way to this tree, where we first met. I dug with my bare hands until it was nice and deep and I put her in the ground surrounded by the roots. I stayed by this tree for days. I was so guilty. If only I had been faster or had let her stay behind, this would not have happened. If anyone deserved to die that day it was me, not her, I who had killed so many. She had never hurt a single living thing.

"After the guilt, all I could do was be angry. I was fairly certain I had killed that Green Cloak who slaughtered Hessero, but I did not know for sure. I was so resentful that I gave up my life, my land, who I was, and became Warrick the mercenary, the bounty hunter, the one no one could trust. I would kill the Green Cloaks who had hurt her, and swindle my kind for shunning and disowning her. She was no pest or oddity as some had said. I cared for her as if she were my flesh and blood.

"I recognized her killer alive that day on the battlefield and knew I had to avenge her. And though I thought I was doing the right thing, and the taste of revenge was momentarily sweet, sitting here in front of her burial ground now, his death doesn't bring her back. I don't even know if she has the knowledge that I have avenged her. Maybe it's better that she does not know. What would Hessero think of me now? I am nothing like the boy that once cared for her."

Elan sits immobile and entranced by his story. This is not what she had expected to hear. Her head reels at his story. The fearsome and horrible Green Cloak that had slain Hessero did not match up with the image Elan had of her patient, kind Uldon.

"That's not-" Elan begins but finds her words stuck in her throat. "It couldn't have been... Uldon, he would never..." Elan stops. She knows that Uldon would have killed any creatures that were found drinking blood. They are not trained to leave young creatures be. And there is no way to say Warrick had the wrong person, because Uldon bore the evidence of that day on his scarred face.

"Oh, he would never?" Warrick spits. His red-rimmed eyes finally spill over with angry tears.

"You were killing a man. He was doing his duty to protect our people," Elan defends, grasping at straws to unsully Uldon's name. But bile rises in her throat as she says it. Elan cannot help picturing Hessero. She had thought Hessero to be grown, a lover, or a fellow warrior, not a lost child. Elan imagines Hessero as herself; a lonely unwanted little girl, parentless and scared. When Uldon had saved her, how much had she cared for him and respected him, thanked him and even loved him? Hessero must have adored Warrick and he her.

"Yes, because your people needed protection from a disabled female young one!" Warrick thunders. He collapses to the ground and pounds the floor with a fist, releasing all of his anger and devastation.

The words fly from Elan's mouth before she can think twice about it, "Your kind don't stop to see if someone is young or old before feasting upon them. Don't act as though you would have done any better if the situation were reversed."

"Fool that I was as a young Darklandian, I would have! And you believe that your people are so much better than mine. It is your kind that has poisoned me. Your kind have made us monsters just as much as the Old One." His voice cracks.

Something inside of Elan splinters like thin ice. The world tilts and nothing makes sense anymore. Instead of

———

Warrick fighting back he looks defeated and guilt presses on her shoulders. She should not be feeling this way for a creature, almost like she is sorry for them, as if they matter.

Watching Warrick break down before her has left a sharp wretchedness clawing in her chest. What if Elan was killed in front of Uldon's eyes? He had already been wracked with guilt over her losing an eye. What would have he become if a creature took her life while he watched? Uldon for sure would have sought out revenge the way Warrick had. Would he have turned as twisted and ugly inside as a gnarled tree?

She knew the lure of revenge. Warrick had killed her Uldon, and in those days after his death, there was nothing she wanted more than to make him suffer. But Warrick was right on one account. His death would not bring Uldon back, and yes, it would momentarily quench the flames of revenge, but would never replace what was lost. His death would never be a balm for the hurt.

Elan does not forgive Warrick not even in the slightest bit for taking Uldon from her, but she can understand him. Lelan's words echo in her thoughts. She had been sickened when Lelan said that he understood Warrick's reasons for killing Uldon in battle. Lelan had been right about a harsh reality and accepted it.

Her teeth sink down into her bottom lip, allowing the pain to distract her momentarily from her tumultuous thoughts. Both of them are rung out mentally and emotionally. Trying to move out now would be a futile attempt. They are still severely hurt. Neither one of them are in any condition to forge on at this rate.

With her head pounding, she forces herself to speak. "We have lost too much time. There is not much daylight left and it seems safer here. I haven't seen anything in a while. We should stay here for the night and head out immediately at first light," Elan orders, making her voice sound rougher as if she is doing this begrudgingly and this is all such a bother. She will not reveal her unexpected empathy for the

Creature or her own weakness, needing time to rest and think.

Warrick nods, solemnly conceding. He wavers on his feet, coming closer to the fire that Elan had set.

"I'm starting to get achy. I can't remember the last time you drank." She holds out her wrist, keeping her head turned to the side, not wanting to find his haunted eyes looking back at her.

He needs the extra sustenance and should eat. The grieving has weakened him, and Elan can see Warrick bowing forward, holding her forearm softly. Now that she is paying attention, she wonders how his eyes are still open. Elan turns her face back to him briefly, before he sinks his teeth in. Instead of feeling the usual revulsion or nervousness, some unexpected emotion stirs in her chest. Warrick takes a few long intakes of blood before stopping. His shoulders cave in, his eyes droop, and he curls up on the ground.

In a matter of seconds, Warrick sinks into a deep sleep.

"You know Itchy, that wasn't smart to blow your one bead on something like that. You only killed two Green Cloaks in the end. And Warrick got away. He might be hurt, but we don't even know that, *Itchy*," says Crank stressing his name mockingly, playing with his marble in between his fingers.

Ichbone grimaces. His teeth threaten to crack with the force he uses to clench his jaw.

"I thought you would have tried harder to catch him, seeing how he ripped out your tongue and all." Crank smirks at Ichbone. "But who am I to say? Maybe talking doesn't mean that much too you."

Ichbone's eyes reduce to slits as he watches Crank toss the marble backward and forward.

"When I use mine. I'm going to make sure it's going to be something great. I'll get him for sure, and I will get all the rest of the beads for myself. And I think I know just where to find him. It's been so long since he has been free to go where he wants and I know exactly where he will go."

Crank concentrates on the bead rolling backward and forward in his hands. His pride inflates more and more. He is so focused he doesn't even notice Ichbone walk up behind him, holding the chain taught between each hand.

Chapter 36

A twig snaps and Elan jumps awake. Warrick's head pops up from the ground, his eyes flashing, and his body tensed to strike. Elan rubs her face, realizing that she must have fallen asleep slumped over. The only light comes from glowing orange embers. Getting to their feet, they spin around for the source of the sound. Elan scans wildly into pitch black. Her creature eye helps to differentiate the woods and shadows. Warrick moves to one side of the fire while Elan stays immobile, both trying to find the source of the sound.

Elan squints as something materializes out of the darkness. At first, it is an undetectable shadow, and then she sees a nose, a chin and finally the face of the bald creature who had tried to murder Warrick. She stumbles away, her hand groping for her dagger.

His black chains rattle as he swings them around. The iron links are colored with blood. The metallic scent of death wafts with each stir of air. The metal must have aided this creature in a fresh kill. Warrick comes to attack, and as quickly as he has come, the large creature vanishes into thin air. All of a sudden, he is at the other side of the fire, then next to them, then gone again.

Elan feels the weight of the chains slap down on the back of her head. Her skull erupts with pain like it is about to split down the middle. A cry tears from her throat as her arms reach up to guard her. There was damage done, and

Warrick groans, feeling the same. There had been nothing to see, but she had felt the cold metal crash against her scalp.

She swings around empty space. Her dagger stabs at thin air. Something strikes Warrick across his jaw. He loses his footing dangerously close to their fire, but manages to steady himself.

"It's Ichbone. He has used one of the beads," Warrick yells. "He must be invisible or using speed. Watch out for Crank too. We don't know where he is."

The chain snaps against Warrick's side where it still burns from the fall. He stifles a scream. Elan doubles over. She can feel the bruising and the possible broken ribs but not the feeling of the struck sensitive skin. That sensation of pain is reserved for him.

Elan and Warrick spin around, their backs facing each other. They know where their leash ends instinctively now. It's completely quiet until Warrick yells in anger. He fights something that isn't there. Elan bounds over to help, but she can't attack what she can't see. Warrick groans in frustration as his thigh is swiped and there are claw marks on both of their legs. Elan hopes the blackness conceals their mimicking injuries.

All of a sudden, Elan's air is cut off. Something digs into her neck. She grabs at her throat and can feel the chain and the whiff of blood but can't see anything. She falls to her knees gasping and Warrick follows suit. If the creature didn't notice them getting the same injuries before, he will notice now.

Warrick crawls to get to Elan and try and pull an invisible Ichbone from her neck. Ichbone reappears in front of Elan with his chains wrapped around her throat. Elan sees Ichbone's eyes fall to Warrick behind her. His lips must be turning blue and he is wheezing like herself.

Ichbone lets go of the chains and Elan breathes as Warrick takes a loud inhale. His vision goes from Warrick to herself and back again. He is connecting the dots. Warrick gets up now, and she can hear his uneven footsteps stumbling toward them. Ichbone tightens his hold, and

Elan's hands grasp at her neck, and then she hears Warrick coughing.

Ichbone smiles coldly. A laugh croaks from his tongueless mouth. He takes the chains in one hand, constricting Elan, she is helpless, light headed from lack of air. Elan sees him lift his elbow as it comes smashing it into her temple.

Elan and Warrick both black out.

Warrick awakes from a startling nightmare, and he jumps to a crouched position, ready to strike. His ribs burn and ache. A large bruise colors his side.

He pivots about his surroundings. His stomach turns sour, and his skin becomes cold, remembering the cell he is in all too well. Sweat creeps over his brow and the bottom of his stomach drops at the rocky interior of the stone temple. It had been his hell for twenty equinoxes, and here he was again.

He roars, battering the impenetrable walls that seem to be closing all around him. The one door remains innocently open. The only way in and out of the cell mocks his confinement. It looks like just an ordinary wide open door. You would think you could walk right out, but you can't, not unless you want to be electrocuted, thrown back, set on fire, or have spikes shoot through your feet. There were countless securities the Old One had put on the doorway. It was random, as to which horror he had enchanted it with that day. But just to keep his prisoners desperately hoping, it appears so inviting.

Warrick's lungs seize. He spins around the room searching for the dark hair and familiar eyes of the small female. She isn't there. Had the Old One broken the curse?

And if he had, was she still alive? Warrick finds himself panicked. He can move uninhibited about the room. What was happening? He opens his mouth to call for her, but holds his tongue. He cannot call her Tiny Female. He doesn't even know if the Old One is aware she is not male. He must use her name.

"Elan!" he yells from inside the door, careful to not get too close. "Elan?"

"Isn't this touching?"

The sound of the voice sends a bead of sweat down Warrick's neck. His body chills. The Old One had tortured, beaten and shamed him even when he had done the Old One no wrong. How much worse will he punish him now? He swallows back the fear. He will not let him see how affected he is.

"I would have never known that you would become so close to the Green Cloak."

Warrick wildly wonders where Elan is.

The Old One finally reveals himself in the cell, next to Warrick. He floats just above the ground, his body too weak for his legs to support him. His skin and hair droop haggard. His eyes have dark circles and puff with exhaustion. An outsider who didn't know better would never believe that this shriveled old prune would be of any danger. He moves forward, his shoulders hunched as if trying to cover his chest wound with the rest of his body.

Fenix, the Old One's long time devotee, walks through the door unharmed, holding Kalrolin's Journal within sight. Warrick had always hated him.

"When Ichbone brought the two of you here together I had no idea what he was thinking," the Old One explains. "I thought perhaps in addition to delivering you to me alive, he brought me a meal as well. But then something interesting happened. Ichbone sliced your cheek and the Green Cloak's face bled as well." Warrick touches his face, feeling the wound marks under his cheekbone.

"It was then that I noticed that you both hummed with magic. Imagine my amusement when I found out it was a binding spell. It wasn't until that moment I realized in the battle against my mercenaries, there was never any mention of you using magic against them. How foolish of you, Warrick, to get caught and have your powers turned against you. I thought I had trained you better." He smiles.

"But now I have a problem. I can't just kill this Green Cloak and have you all to myself. You might die too. And I can't have you dying on me. Not so soon when there is so much fun to be had. So I had to keep the Green Cloak alive, but out of my way." The Old One pauses. "Do you care to take a guess where that would be?"

Warrick's eyes become wide with dread.

"Elan!?" Warrick runs to the corner of his cell. There is a tiny hole in the ground no bigger than a button. He tries to look into the space below but there is no light.

"Say something! Anything!"

A small moan floats out but nothing else. Warrick knows this well also. A coffin is under the ground where Elan lays. The only light, sound or air comes from the tiny hole dug to the surface.

A memory flashes unbidden, of his voice going hoarse from screaming and his fingers bleeding from clawing relentlessly against the wooden box. The smell of desperation and fear fills the small space. His muscles ache and he gags, fighting for fresh air, panting wildly, sneezing out the dirt falling in. Warrick would go mad not knowing the passage of time in his confinement. It could have been nights or equinoxes since being able to move. The echo of the Old One's laugh rang in his ears as his only link to the outside.

"Care to see your friend?" It's as though a light goes on underground.

Warrick's heart pounds in his chest as he can see just one of Elan's eyes peering out at him, the brown one, her real eye. It blinks and rolls around frantically trying to make sense of her surroundings.

He expects to see fear, to see a red-rimmed eye worn from crying. But he is startled to see that behind her panic is not fear, but defiance. Her cheek lifts and the top of her brow comes down. She frowns, livid.

She squirms, and Warrick can feel under him the ground rumble as she bangs her shoulders and knees against her wooden box.

"I can't keep him there forever though. He might die, and then my games with you will be over."

The light goes back off but not before Warrick sees sadness as the light fades out. Warrick's head spins as it becomes harder to move his lungs. She is afraid, but her pride won't let anyone see.

"Even though you stole my book, it was returned to me. And this dagger." He pulls both daggers from his waistband. "Your Green Cloak had its pair. If only you had known just how powerful these little things are. You might have succeeded in killing me, but instead, you have only angered me. The traitor has been giving me the missing pages I need to free myself. I may be liberated as soon as one cycle. You, will be nothing, but a groveling slave at my feet."

The Old One smiles and his arms extend as burning whips sear Warrick. The barbs on his back rip through his flesh, and he screams in agony. But Elan's muffled screams barely carry beneath the thickness of land.

"Ah. Just like old times again, ay Warrick?" the Old One laughs gleefully

Chapter 37

Elan fights for air. She has struggled in the cramped box for so long, she is in so much pain, but can't see the state of her body. All she can do is labor for fresh air, not laced with the smell of her blood. At this point, she must be a misshapen mess. She had listened to the disturbing song of Warrick's screams. The claustrophobia began to make her manic as she screamed and screamed, pushed and struggled to no avail.

"Come out, come out wherever you are," echoes the Old One's voice.

One moment Elan shakes in total darkness, except for a small point of light, the next she collapses onto the dirt in a cell. She breathes deep. Crumpled on the cobblestones beside her, Warrick rocks gently. He is severely marred and painted in his own blood. Is that what she looks like too? His scars will heal but hers will not, if they live through this. Elan imagines the Old One will keep them alive forever and torture them until they become mad.

"You reek. Lucky for you both, I am tired and in need of rest. But tomorrow is when the real torture begins."

Elan hears a bucket full of water splash next to her. "Clean yourself up."

She hears his cloak slide across the ground as he gingerly walks away. Her throat burns with thirst. Elan manages to stretch her body, but whimpers.

She croaks, her voice ragged from her muffled screams, "What is going to happen tomorrow?"

Warrick barely grunts.

"They will come for us," Elan says. "I know they will."

But his eyes roll, as he slips to delirium.

Underground she was still able to hear the Old One from the small opening. "Just like old times," the Old One had said. A shudder racks her body. Warrick had been through this before. He had not been the Old One's willing servant, as she had thought. He had been tortured for equinoxes. She would have never known how much he had been through because his skin didn't show the damage.

What did the Old One plan for the next day? Something even worse than this?

For the first time in her life, she is terrified.

Elan wakes to screams for the second day. She doesn't know what the Old One is doing to him. Whatever it is, it is not all physical torture because she is not receiving many injuries.

It has been two nights since she last saw Warrick. But he has not gone any farther from her than the spell allows. She can hear him just behind the wall as she lies on her side with her knees tucked to her chest, a curled up ball in the cell. The Old One's servant, Fenix, she had heard him say, leaves rotten fruits and water that Elan forces herself to eat but they give her stomachaches.

It is dark once again and, Fenix drags Warrick's body into the cell.

"Creature?"

His eyes shift, crazed, as he shuffles into a corner and gets into a fetal position. Turning over his hands, inspecting them, he sits up and begins to rock. He wipes them frantically on his legs, and Elan's eye swells up the same as his. What had happened?

"It isn't real. It's not real," Warrick chants.

He doesn't see her. Elan places herself in front of him, but he looks right through her. Waving her hands in front of his face gets no reaction from him.

His eyes race backward and forward as he begins to tremor.

"Snap out of it. Look at me. Come back." Elan's demand turns into more of a whine sounding desperate and pleading.

Warrick's vision slowly begins to focus. But the madness does not subside. Warrick takes a deep breath, as his hands shake. He runs his fingers through his hair.

"What did he do to you? Can't you see me? Can you hear me? What is happening?" Elan yells.

"He can't see, hear or feel you," the Old One says as he softly treads into the room.

Warrick sobers at the Old One's voice. "Who are you talking to? Where did you put Elan?"

Elan does dare move, petrified by the Old One's malicious gaze. Instead of looking at him a moment longer, Elan watches Warrick as he creeps to the hole in the ground and puts his ear there.

He faces the Old One, spitting with fury. "Where is Elan?!" Elan jumps, surprised at his volatile reaction to her disappearance.

"You have become close to the Green Cloak, have you?" the Old One says curiously.

Warrick turns stark white as every bit of color drains from his face.

The Old One waves his hand, and Warrick's attention snaps to her. The intensity of his gaze lets her know he can see her now.

Warrick takes half a step toward her, his face softening, but stops. His legs strain as if he is making great pains to not move.

The Old One turns his attention to Warrick, "I do believe the spell I had been casting on you might have even more exciting results when tested on him? Don't you think?"

Warrick's brow becomes wet, and Elan sees the flash of dread before he forces the muscles on his face to appear indifferent.

"What do I care? The Green Cloak means nothing to me," Warrick says. Swallowing loudly, his face grimaces as though he had just drank poison.

Elan cannot believe that the Creature does not even attempt to help her after she had been sensitive to his struggles. She slides further back from the Old One.

The Old One stands before Elan, rendering her motionless. He places a hand on her throat to feel the pulse under her skin. For one wild moment, Elan thinks he is going to crush her neck right then and there. Elan's skin crawls. This is so much worse than when Warrick had touched her arm for the first time.

Elan blinks, and the Old One no longer stands in front of her. It is her father. They stand face to face. His dark eyes twinkle, and his stubbled face smiles proudly.

"This isn't real," Elan says aloud. "My father does not live."

"Why couldn't it be? I have Kalrolin's Journal," says the Old One, now across the room. "Don't you think there are spells in there so powerful that I can bring people back from the dead? I can. And I can do as I wish with them, after all, I give them back life," the Old One says.

Elan shakes her head. He can't bring people back. Or can he? All of a sudden everything she believes is saturated with doubt. She turns her attention inward to refocus that she is indeed in a cell, in the here and now. But observing her palms, she sees the twiggy digits of a child, and she is a frightened little girl again. The yellow dress she used to love wearing covers her torso. A loose braid of dark hair rests down her back. Touching the top of her head, she feels a soft lace handkerchief fall over her forehead.

The Old One begins to chuckle, "Now it makes sense. A female? You do have a protective streak when it comes to them, Warrick." The Old One looks her over with speculative eyes. "In The Order of all places? It can't be. My friend never told me about there ever being such a thing. But she does have the crest burned on her arm."

Warrick doesn't say a word. He swallows loudly again as if that is all he is capable of doing.

Elan tries to lock him in her gaze, to remember this is not happening. But both the Old One and Warrick plunge into darkness. She faces her father. He is flesh and bone. She can't deny his presence. It isn't an illusion. She can reach out and touch him, and Elan longs to stretch out her arms and embrace her father.

"Papa?"

He coughs, and blackness sprays from his lungs. Slowly the muscles and flesh under his skin begin to wither. He holds out his hand to her with a pained expression, his eyes pleading to save him. His voice starts to scream, but the sound deteriorates with his vocal cords. He turns to nothing but virtually skin and bone, then rotting skin. Elan stands sick as his flesh becomes green then a sickly purple until it eats away, revealing his grotesque insides.

Elan screams as she watches him deteriorate. She smells the death and decay and sees him writhing in pain.

Blackness covers her sight as another vision appears before her. She is still a little girl. Her stepmother and new lover take turns beating and abusing Elan. Every kick hits solidly on her ribs. They call her terrible names, and the man pushes her into a small room, locking the door and leaving her with nothing to eat. The hunger pains and loneliness swallow her up. She rocks, staying silent in the dark not wanting them to hear her. The pain rips through her. Everything they say is true. She is useless, ugly and unwanted. Elan hopes that they are drunk enough to fall asleep. If she remains quiet, then they will not come back for a second round. She smothers her sobs in her arms as she sits on a bare floor in an icy room curled up, trying to keep herself from freezing.

Elan's heart thumps wildly. She anticipates what's next. She backs herself into a corner as another one of her "mother's" abusive boyfriends come near. He is holding a poker from the fire. Her palms sweat and her eyes become wild as he comes close to her.

"No," Elan's small voice says.

The man swings it around, and a blood-curdling scream rips from her mouth.

She crumples on the ground, alone. Elan stands, hoping that the Old One is finished. But she knows he isn't. More is to come. She is older, but not by much. Darkness surrounds her, then she stands alone in a spot of light, as a wispy teen.

Her heart thumps wildly as a man steps into the pool of light. Serdon creeps near her. Then Mosley. Rage mixes with the fear.

"Female," Serdon spits like a curse.

"Waste, if you ask me," Mosley sneers. "Useless."

"She should be thrown out," Serdon says circling her.

"Shut up!" Elan screams.

They continue to laugh with their stream of insults.

"Stop!" Elan thunders, trying to shut out her ears but they yell louder, move in closer and spittle flies in her face. Their faces contort with rage. Hot tears spill down her cheeks without permission. She closes her eyes. Whispers repeat from the darkness, "unwanted", "waste", "ugly", "weak", "outcast"... The sounds dissolve until she hears nothing. She opens them again, and she is alone.

It fades to darkness and for a moment relief calms her as she sees Uldon. It can't be. He stands before her in the metal mask, his eyes cold. Elan returns to herself, dirty, scarred and unkempt. And she relives Uldon's rejection. The moment before he left to fight Warrick. Her feelings of inadequacy magnified tenfold in the trap of a spell. And she can't stop herself. She does what she had done that night. Elan rises on tiptoe to kiss him, and he softly pushes her away. The words repeat themselves louder this time, "unwanted," "ugly," "pathetic"...

As much as Elan tries to tell herself it isn't real, it cuts so deep she is surprised she isn't hemorrhaging blood.

Uldon's attention turns to a beautiful blonde. Elan sees the curvaceous Delmira wrapped in his arms wearing the beautiful dress from the shop. She had never seen this happen. The pain Elan feels is real even if what she sees isn't. How many times had she suspected in her mind that Uldon would have preferred someone like her? That same ache in her chest returns so much stronger than ever before. Her knees shake, unstable.

Only for a brief moment she realizes that she is back in her dirty prison. The Old One and Warrick stand in her periphery. The Old One practically cackles with glee as Warrick stands like a stone statue. Nausea and shame makes her eyes sting and her chest tight. They have seen everything, every embarrassment and hurt on full display to poke fun at and exploit.

A black fog creeps along the ground toward them. It stretches and moves with a soft screaming sound as if it is a living thing. It reaches up, winding. Her heart beats fast as the fog materializes into a figure.

A twisted, grotesque version of Warrick knits out of the black fog. This twin has eyes that glow red, his claws, feet, and teeth stretch three times larger than they have ever been. Her memory distorts under The Old One's influence. Warrick's vestige from her mind snarls and snaps like a wild beast. Boils and craters mar his skin, and his back hunches over. All of a sudden the room morphs into something else. They are no longer in the cell but in the cave where Uldon died.

Bile rises in the back of Elan's throat as the cave comes up all around her. The rock face grows out of the stone slabs, transforming the room. Warrick and Uldon fight, her most horrible memory relived. She stiffens. No. She can't live through this again.

———

Uldon turns to her. She treasures his face one last time. She knows what happens next. But it still doesn't prepare her. Warrick's hand clasps around Uldon's throat. The blood pours out, but his death is not a quick one as it had been in the caves. It is slow and painful, he chokes and reaches out to her.

Elan falls to her knees, and that's when she sees her hands. Claws bathe in shining red. Her tongue runs over the top of her mouth. Blood clings to her fanged teeth.

Now Elan kills Uldon with her own hands. She can see his frightened face. The warm flesh of his neck pulsates under her tightening grasp. His death was her fault. She might as well have been the one who killed him with her bare hands. She screams. But it does not stop. She finds herself killing all of her friends slowly, but she has no control over her own body. Tresdon falls as he screams in agony. She maims Eldon and cuts open Lelan's stomach, tissue spilling out before her. Elan slices Nolan to shreds then Jordon. She cries as fallen brothers surround her, a pile of bodies. Their irises shake with fear and betrayal. But the scene with Uldon dying keeps repeating. And she kills him in more elaborate ways. Each time is worse than the last, splitting her soul each time. She screams and screams until her voice wears raw.

Elan wants to claw her eyes out, so she never has to see these things again. Tears escape, and she doesn't try to stop them this time. She touches her face, and it has transformed. Her skin smoothes and her features contour, almost reptilian. She pulls and rips at her face with her newly made claw hands, trying to force her flesh back to its original form. They slice, but she ignores the pain. Her face burns with injury and sticky blood.

"You killed him, Elan, this is all your doing. All your fault," the Old One mocks.

Elan squeezes her eyes tight, but that doesn't stop her from still seeing it replayed over and over in her mind. "This isn't real! It's not real!"

She repeats it to herself, but she can still smell the decay and hear the agonizing screams of her friends ringing in her ears. The small cell returns to normal. Elan quivers on the ground, a ball of emotions. Thick scratches on her face remain from trying to claw her features.

The chuckle of the Old One bounces along her skin, like hammers on her nerves.

A loud cawing bird, abruptly, stops his amusement. His expression is now one of distraction as he turns to the sound.

The Old One departs from the room, leaving Elan a wreck folded up on the floor.

Chapter 38

Elan no longer cries, but her hollow eyes remain dilated with fright. Her heart will not stop racing, and her head heats feverish with anger. In the corner of her sight, every wall appears to be dripping garnet. The scent of carnage entices and frightens her. But the worst part of all this is her shameful past put on display. Embarrassment crawls up her neck as she blocks him out, holding herself tight. She had been foolish enough to think they were allies. But he had not even attempted to stop The Old One. Had it been the other way around, Elan would have tried something.

They both breathe into the uncomfortable silence. All of her insecurities and fears laid bare for the Old One and his former student. She hugs her knees close to her body too and swallows back her grief as her face stings painfully. She is going to die in this tiny cell beside a creature at the hands of the Old One. But the Old One will take his time. Elan doesn't want her life to end like this, not in battle protecting her friends, but captured and alone. Almost alone. For a long time, Elan stares with a glazed expression and mills over her thoughts of what she had just experienced before she speaks.

"Why didn't you help me?" she accuses. His face mirrors hers with slashes.

Warrick starts. He steels his body, tightly coiled. He doesn't answer.

But Elan knows why he had not helped her. For a moment she forgot the only reason they are allies is that he didn't want to be harmed. Her emotional and mental wellbeing means nothing to the Creature. He only wants to keep her safe physically.

"I know we are not friends," Elan spits. "In another situation, we would not hesitate to kill one another, but here, behind these walls, we only have each other to survive. I don't want to die here. I'm sure you don't either."

He opens his mouth to speak, but utters no words. He lowers his chin to her but jerks away.

"If you have any ideas, now would be the time to say something," Elan demands. "You lived here for equinoxes, and you had escaped. How did you do it?"

Warrick finally speaks, his voice thick and ragged.

"The method I used won't work this time. Had you not hit me with that enchanted dagger, I would not have escaped so soon. At the time, he was only recently letting me out on my own. I had painstakingly planned my escape. I had gotten him to believe that I was loyal and harmless to him. One day I was hoping he would trust me completely and then I was going to destroy him." Warrick stops speaking. He might have never gotten out of the Old One's control if it had not been for Elan trying to kill him. He continues, "I don't think he will fall for something like that again. He would know this time around I was tricking him. It had taken me a very long time for him to trust me."

Elan sits thinking for a moment, "I can get him to believe me."

"He won't fall for it twice."

"He won't fall for it twice if it is you or another creature or a male. But I'm a female. I'm seen as weaker." She stops speaking.

"He wouldn't expect it from me. Even you, who knew I was a Green Cloak and saw my fighting skill firsthand, underestimated me. Even if I can distract him for a moment, I think we can get out of here. If I can get him to trust me even just a little, he might take me into the main room, and I can get the dagger. That's our only defense against him."

Warrick worries his lip and reluctantly nods his head.

They have no other option.

Warrick cannot sleep. He lies on the uneven stone floor, wondering if this is the last night he will be alive. Elan dreams on the floor in a fitful sleep, a few paces away. She twitches and mumbles, having some nightmare. He doesn't bother to wake her. He would wake her up from one nightmare, just to be in another. Warrick will think of her as Elan now, even if he does not admit it aloud. He will not allow her to die an unknown entity. She has a name and a past even if she lacks a future.

Warrick watched in silent woe at the display before him. He had thought she was indestructible. He had never seen her break, never seen any backing down from a fight or difficulty. But even the most resilient wear down in this prison. He had seen a small glimpse of it when she grimaced in the box, and now he had seen her crack the way he had.

He never wanted to know her past, but he does now. Her father died while she was little and left her with abusive caretakers. He had seen the scars on her back and thought that they were past evidence of survival from a victorious battle. Only now he realizes that those marks were not symbols of fights won but reminders of past trauma. Then even when she went to the Green Cloaks she was still met with abuse. A flash of white anger ripples through Warrick as he pictures Elan taunted by her brothers for being female. Though the words thrown at her were not physical blows, those taunts engrave much deeper lesions.

He had thought for sure her relationship with The Masked One was agreed upon. Knowing her affections were not returned infuriates him. The callous way he had rejected her replays. Warrick hates the Masked One even more for inflicting such emotional torment on yet another. Though he may be biased on this account, he would have found any reason to hate him more.

Then he had seen himself. What she perceived him as. Her memories struck a chord somewhere deep inside him, and his heart clenches uncomfortably. He should be delighted that a Green Cloak finds him so frighteningly monstrous. He had wanted Elan to find him vile, and intimidating. But now knowing that she found him grotesque all along makes him slightly uncomfortable.

Warrick knows he is not the same Darklandian that was once Hessero's caretaker. He turned into something much darker, someone bitter and full of vengeance and hate. He faces the genuine possibility that he is going to die. And he wasn't leaving this life as himself, but a monster the Masked One and the Old One had turned him into. If he ever saw Hessero again, would she even recognize him?

A whimper forces Warrick's attention to Elan. She cries while she slumbers. The sound reminds him of another small female weeping and alone. All they have are each other here. Neither of them can trust anyone. At least they know the other wouldn't physically hurt or betray them without it affecting the other. What good would it do now to have such disdain for her? They already shared an enemy here, why add another adversary?

Elan shoots up and screams, causing Warrick to jump. Her shirt is saturated with sweat, and her eyes pop with fright as her neck snaps side to side, adjusting herself to reality.

A deeply buried reaction tells him to move closer, to comfort.

"It's-" Warrick almost says that it is alright. It isn't, not at all.

She starts to rock, covering her face with her hands. Warrick can't let her fall apart. Not now. He cannot help but think of Hessero and how Elan needs him now just as Hessero needed him then.

"Elan," Warrick says.

She stops and stares at him. He called her by her name not "Tiny Female". Her eyes lose the hazy cloud of uncertainty and she stares at him. The moment is much too long, as if she is still trying to wake from her dream. She nods, knowing precisely what he is trying to say to her without having to use any more words. Curling back on the floor, she takes another deep breath. Warrick shuffles off to his sleeping spot again. He keeps a watch on her as she closes her eyes, knowing tonight he will not sleep.

Chapter 39

Warrick hears the shuffling of the Old One's footsteps coming closer. Elan and Warrick separate as far as the room will allow. Today, they will escape or die trying. The Old One approaches and Fenix stands in the main room, watching from afar, a disturbing glee shining from him.

The Old One grins with crooked, yellowing teeth. He stretches out an unnaturally extended index finger and points it at one and then the other, backward and forward.

"Exa, Nexa, Bin, and Roose, who is the one that I shall choose?" sings the Old One. It sends shivers down Warrick's spine. He sings a song from a common children's game. That's all this is to him. It isn't their lives. He plays with them like toys.

His finger lands on Elan. Warrick's heart thuds and his limbs stiffen.

"Please," Elan whispers in a girlish lilt. "Please don't hurt me anymore. I can't take it." Elan blinks and Warrick watches as a tear slides down her cut face.

Warrick swallows back the knot forming in his throat. His hand quivers at his side.

"I promise. I will do whatever you ask of me. I will be loyal to only you. If you let me go, I swear my allegiance to you. I can't be locked in this cell a moment more. Just please let me go."

The Old One laughs as though she has told him an amusing joke. "Of course dear little girl, this is all too much for your delicate soul," he says condescendingly. "Perhaps my dear, if you were not a package deal we could have made some arrangement. But he must die, and he must suffer. You are an unfortunate tag along. But let it not be said that I'm not merciful to a lady. I can take all of this away for you. You don't have to worry about being hurt ever again. In fact, you won't even be able to worry at all." Anticipation shines in his eyes as he folds his fingers around one another.

"No. You can't," Warrick pleads to the Old One. She had succeeded in making him think she was weak. Their plan was working but with unintended consequences. Warrick knew the spell the Old One would perform. It would turn Elan into a living breathing vacant-eyed slave.

"Don't tell me what I can and cannot do, you filthy cobe. This will be so much better for her. You shall see. She will still be alive of course, but with no pain, no hurts or sadness. Doesn't that sound nice?" He directs the question at Elan, and a fresh current of terror floods Warrick's veins. "It has been so long since we have had a female guest. I'm sure Fenix would be glad for the company."

Fenix smiles wickedly outside the door.

"No," Warrick says, raising his voice. His hands tremor with more violence, and his stomach clenches. His face sharpens while his fangs begin to increase in size.

"You are in no position to stop me. This is all very amusing, but the female Green Cloak and I have an engagement." The Old One grabs Elan's wrist and pulls her toward the door.

Warrick's breath catches in his throat.

Elan digs in her heels as the Old One drags her away, her eyes wild, Fenix waits outside the door. She pulls her elbow into her body and twists her wrist, trying to get him to release her arm with no results. He still holds strong, his grip enforced with magic. It seems like whatever skill she had learned in her training has no effect on him, he still pulls her along.

Without thinking, Warrick's protective instinct springs to life, and he snatches Elan's other arm. Her tendons strain under the damp skin of her arm. "Let go of her!" Warrick roars, trying to pull her back. The Old One has a fire in his eyes as he laughs and Warrick does not think he has ever hated his captor more than he does now. The Old One's other hand conjures corrosive acid tentacles growing from the center of his palm. He presses his hand forward, and orange ropes clasp around Warrick's neck. The searing agony causes his knees to buckle. The magic dissolves his flesh as well as Elan's. He bellows, unrestrained at the same time she screams. Falling to the ground, chains connect to the floor and hold him on a leash.

The Old One continues to take her away, but Warrick will not let go. Under his hand, her skin becomes slick so he holds on to her tighter. The hairs on the back of Warrick's neck rise, and static pulses through him.

"I said let her go!" Warrick screams.

A ripple crashes through the air. Icy cold runs through Warrick as his heart stops and kicks back on in overdrive. An invisible wave pushes her back. A ferocious roar from his lungs shakes the stone slabs of the temple. The Old One is repelled from Elan, and his hand slips off her as she falls on her backside to the ground. Fenix runs to the door of the cell but doesn't dare pass the enchanted entrance. The Old One hangs his head limp, coughing dark red splashes to the floor. He wipes blood and spittle from his lips and with open shock stares at his palm, then back at Warrick. His expression shifts. The side of his mouth curls up in a smile.

The Old One spins around just in time to see Warrick shake off the spell from his neck, which disintegrates like ash. Flexing his hands, a familiar sensation runs through his body. Power hums in every vein and sinew of his body, thrumming through every part of him. His face morphs again, longer, red rimming his eyes. From Warrick's left elongated hand, blue wisps of magic stretch out from his fingers. He doesn't know where this magic is coming from and he does not question its emergence. They twist to make an elaborately carved sword that he clutches. Warrick releases Elan as he swings the steel. He sees her eyes go wide with shock as she lunges far from the two.

The Old One blocks each strike with a spark of flashing light, "You may have weakened me, but there is no way you can win. I don't know how you are doing spells, but it is no matter. I am more powerful, and I have Kalrolin's Journal on my side. There are enchantments, spells and curses you could not even dream of." He raises his hands and lava erupts around him. The Old One curls his fingers and two giant fists of molten rock materialize and begin hammering at the ground where Warrick and Elan stand. They leave pools of fire in their wake.

Warrick checks for Elan while she presses herself close to the walls as far away from them as possible. Tucking and rolling, Warrick dodges each fist He pushes against his injuries to keep moving. Blood rushes in his ears as he sprints over to Elan. He holds up the back of his forearm where bands of steel weave. They shape and shift creating a shield blocking them both from the next blow of fire. Warrick grits his teeth as he can still feel the fire heating the metal.

Dozens of sharp needles are projected from the surface of the shield, threatening to slice through The Old One. But he stops them in midair and they fall to the ground.

The Old One growls, furious. But it pales in comparison to the anger Warrick displays. They both hurl as many spells as each other as they can.

Warrick feels Elan against his back as she runs around his shield. She slips through the only opening that isn't going up in flames. Gritting her teeth, sweat pours down her face as she sprints to the exit. Warrick hits the door with a spell and it sizzles, disabling the enchantment there. Adrenaline pumps through him, his heart thundering in his chest. Warrick stumbles after her, still protecting them both.

Warrick hears a loud thud as Elan smacks into something hard. Looking up, the broad face of Fenix smirks.

She ducks as his claw tries clamping down on her. Fenix grasps at Elan and Warrick. Warrick spins his sword, lancing Fenix's skin before returning his attention to the Old One. Fenix yells, thrashing, while large drops of dark blood shower around Elan.

The Old One and Warrick continue to fight while Elan rummages about the main room for the daggers and the book.

The Old One doesn't make the same mistake twice, and the book is not casually kept by the cauldron.

"Are you looking for this?" Fenix mocks, hugging the book to his body. "You will have to take this from me, and I don't think you have it in you." Fenix pushes out his chest, expanding his wings making himself larger. His claws and teeth extend. Elan sets her face, and Warrick does not see a hint of intimidation in her.

Warrick is having a hard time concentrating. His attention shifts from the Old One and Fenix lunging at Elan, as she crouches down, slipping between his legs. Elan dodges spells that bounce off the stone walls and whiz past her. Bottles break, colored potions pop on the tables beside the cauldron. Warrick does his best to block the spells for them both. Unarmed, all she can do is evade the mountainous creature. With one hand Fenix crouches down and swipes at her again. He lumbers bulky and clumsy. Elan can slip by him easier than Warrick expected.

A spell barely misses Warrick and his determination spikes, conjuring lightning in his hands. The jagged bolts rain down, striking the floor, leaving charred spots in their wake.

It is now instinct to keep checking on Elan. He curses himself for having his attention split. He watches as she dodges behind the cauldron, and Fenix misses, hitting the edge and splashing its contents to the ground. The liquid inside begins to take on a life of its own. It turns silver and begins to rise and twist as if it is an awakening child stretching. It grabs at Fenix's leg, climbing up his calf, gluing him to the floor.

He swats at it, trying to push it off, but the liquid goes right through his fingers. The puddle reaches out and tries to do the same to Elan. But she jumps up on one of the Old One's splintered wooden tables before it can touch her.

Warrick's sweat beads down his back as he tries covering Elan and throwing spells to hold the Old One at bay. The Old One fights with such concentration to destroy Warrick that the evil sorcerer doesn't see what is happening.

Fenix tries to lift his feet, but the liquid holds on more tightly. He falls forward, still grasping the book for all he is worth. The silver liquid swallows his torso. He doesn't want it to engulf the book as well, so he lifts it above his head. Elan crawls to the end of the large table, dropping her hands to grab the book. Fenix and Elan engage in a tug of war. She pries the book from his claws when he dares to look down to see how far the silver liquid advanced. Fenix opens his mouth to scream, but the silver potion creeps up his chin and fills his mouth, muffling the sound. The silver covers his whole body, and he clanks to the ground.

As Warrick fights, his powers begin to ebb away. He doesn't know how they manifested, or why they are depleting, but he only has a little bit of time left before he and Elan can escape. Roaring and with all of his might, he digs deep within himself to cast a spell that blasts from his outstretched hand and hits its mark. The Old One is knocked off his feet so forcefully he slams into the back wall of the stone temple.

"Elan, we must get out of there!" Warrick yells as the Old One stays prone on the ground from Warrick's latest incantation. It won't last long.

"What about the daggers?"

Warrick huffs, his frustration mounting, and with the very last tendrils of magic, a red line of light weaves its way around the room, landing on a small wooden box sitting on a shelf. From the top of the table, Elan reaches up and takes the daggers, tucking them into her waist band.

The Old One gathers strength, his head moving and his body fumbling to stand. There is a small part of Warrick,

---

a very reckless and crazed part of him that wants to get the daggers from Elan to try and kill him while he is disoriented. But he has no more magic and the Old One would kill them before he was even ten paces away.

Escape to fight another day was the only option for now.

Elan leaps over the silver puddle now surrounding the table. Her ankle explodes with pain as it hits the ground and her shoulder burns. She sprints for the door, solely focused on freedom, with Warrick following close behind. The long dark hall leading outside feels like salvation. The light coming through the door calls her forward.

Elan bursts through the rickety entrance and the warm moist air of the outdoors hits her bruised and battered skin. The dim light of the open sky stings her eyes after days of darkness. She has no time to rejoice in her freedom because thrashing sounds still follow her. Warrick is close on her heals.

They scrabble their way into the cover of woods. But the Old One's magic can still reach them at this distance.

"We have to fly," Warrick frantically blurts. "The Old One can't fly after us, and I can fly fast and far enough that his spells won't be able to reach us. That's the only way out of here."

"But you can't. I have you attached to the ground."

"Not quite," Warrick says. "I have an idea from when we were spit from the wind tunnel."

In one swift movement, Warrick scoops Elan into his arms.

"What are you-?"

Before Elan can even finish her sentence, Warrick opens his wings and runs, catching the air. He kicks off the ground and flaps. He strains against gravity pushing harder.

A spell gets hurled at them, and Warrick barely dodges it. The trees around them come alive. The limbs grow longer and reach for them. Warrick flaps harder still as they ascend, even too high for the branches.

The cold, moist air slaps Elan in the face, and it quickly begins to wet her skin, hair, and clothing. She clasps the book close to her chest and remains still. The only thing keeping her from falling to the ground right now is Warrick holding her. If she squirms the wrong way, he might lose his grip.

"This is a much better way to travel. We should be back on Order land in one third the time it takes on a horse."

Elan swallows and her heart flutters uncomfortably as the land below gets smaller. She worries speaking might jostle them too much but attempts anyway, "But-but definitely not as safe."

"Would you rather do this or stay back with the Old One?"

Elan forces herself to look out instead of down, and she sees the land stretch out before her. They retreat from the dark clouds and dull landscape of The Darklands. Elan takes deep breaths and has to remind herself they escaped. Warrick had used magic again somehow, and they are going home.

As her heart rate slows and it sinks in they are out of danger, Elan begins to feel all the aches, pains and injuries. Warrick waivers in the air. He flies less steady than when they first started.

The emerald green of Solum Cowdh seems to go on forever, slightly interrupted by rivers and lakes. She knows larger bodies of water and other lands lay farther out, but she has only heard stories. Elan wonders what other places she has not seen. Something warm trickles down her shoulder. She smells the blood. Looking up her sleeve, red soaks through. Warrick has a small trail of crimson streaking down to his elbow. When did they get injured? It must have been during Warrick's fight with the Old One.

She holds the book in one arm and places her good arm around Warrick's neck so that she can hold on as well. He winces, as the injury around his neck is still raw. Elan supposes hers is just as bad.

"Don't lose your grip on that book just because you are afraid of falling," he accuses.

Elan bristles. "I was trying to give your injured arm a break. But if you insist, I will be happy to let go."

"Stay as you are," he barks back. "If you move too much it won't be good for either of us."

As time continues, she realizes that they must be close to Order land by now but can see nothing at all.

"I cannot find the towers," Warrick says, disoriented. "Are we even close to where we are supposed to be?"

Wind shrills past Elan's ear. Turning her head to the source of the sound, a thin black shadow flies past them. Before she has time to examine closer, another and then another shoot past. They miss them both only by a hair's width. They must be right on top of the towers. The Order is defending themselves.

"It's arrows! They don't know it's us. They think we are a threat!" Elan panics. "You have to get down to the ground as fast as you can before they knock us out of the sky."

Warrick's eyes widen and then reduce to slits as he dives low. Elan's stomach drops to her feet as he plummets to the ground, narrowly dodging each arrow.

The bright green grass comes up fast below them. But not fast enough. Elan feels a sharp sting and Warrick's body jerks back. Her abdomen bleeds, the arrowhead sticks from Warrick's stomach. Warrick tumbles through the air. Elan refuses to let any injury take her mind off the mission and holds on to the book with all of her remaining strength. Their bodies crash to the ground for the second time in only a matter of a few nights. She hears a crack. Bright blue light flashes behind her eyes as pain erupts from her leg. Her body presses in the dirt. Her mouth is gritty with an aftertaste of mud.

Their bodies are a mere heap on the ground, indenting the long grass. They are home, but far from safe. Her hand grasps around her, trying to find where Warrick fell. She feels smooth skin among the blades of grass. Elan places her hand on his arm and turns her head to him. They both stare at each other with weary eyes. Running up beside them, distraught faces of oaclings peer down. She blinks as more footsteps and the murmur of voices fill the quiet. Elan and Warrick refuse to tear their gaze away from one another. They escaped the Old One, they were on Order land with the book, and once the arrow was removed, they would live to fight another day.

As Elan begins to lose consciousness she whispers, "We shall meet again."

To which Warrick replies, "As though we have a choice."

Chapter 40

Opening her eyes, Elan sees a dim and blurry room. She forces her mind to push through the haze of unconsciousness. Cots lined in rows come into focus. Next, to creep into her awareness, is the overpowering scent of medicines. Her body lays under a blanket, clean and dressed in fresh clothes. The stone floor and walls are too clean to be just anywhere. She forces her head to roll to the side. Her eyes sting from the brightness of a hearth fire. The infirmary. A knot that had been tied tight in Elan's chest for nights untangles. She thought she would never see Order land again. She savors the scent of the aged cots and animal skins that fill her nostrils. The book is back and safe. Taking a deep breath, she calms her busy mind. Painfully, Elan pushes her body to its side.

Warrick lies on a cot beside her. A window lets the lunya light flood in, but the room is still dim in shadows. The outline of him stirs, he wakes as well.

Rolling on his side, he hisses through gritted teeth. His eyes adjust to the room as he surveys his newest dwelling. His head turns to meet Elan's line of sight. His brow shoots up in surprise. Grunting, he shifts, trying to get a better look at her.

"It would appear we are alive."

"If that is what you want to call this," Elan says, never remembering a time when she was so sore. The adrenaline has subsided, so nothing distracts her from every single one of her injuries.

As Elan speaks, she feels an unfamiliar tug on her skin. Touching her face, her fingertips trace long cuts made from her own nails. Her skin is tender, and her split bottom lip hurts from speaking. Warrick's face bears pink lines of partially healed wounds.

"You performed spells," Elan says, almost accusatory. "How did you do it?"

Warrick lifts his hands, examining them as if he can discover some untold secret. It had come as quickly as it had left. There was no reason, and he has no answer to give, so he remains silent.

"They must have everyone back from the Darklands," Elan says, her relief evident. Warrick flexes his fingers, lamenting the lost power. He sighs in the dark, closing his eyes. But the lamentation soon turns to the memory of their days in the stone temple. He stretches his fingers once again wishing that he had done more damage when he had the chance. Regret nags at the very back of his mind. He should have risked everything to try and kill him with those daggers. The memory of the Old One, of the things he did and said, all that had happened, fills him with dread. But more than anything else, it fuels him with a renewed sense of purpose.

Warrick feels Elan's expectant gaze. He doesn't know what to say. Unease creeps down his spine and sinks deep within him. He knows too much about her now, things he didn't want to know. And she knows too much about him. Moments away from death, it didn't seem to matter what was happening at the time. But how is he supposed to act now? He can try and pretend that he has not seen her painful past. He can try and pretend that he had never broke down and told her about Hessero under her tree, but it is a lie.

In the temple, they had both broken down and had seen each other weak. They had no choice but to rely on one another. They had been through too much together, and there is no undoing it.

Warrick has an odd feeling of responsibility to keep her from being embarrassed. Not so long ago this would have been ammunition against her. He hates the Old One even more for making him feel guilty. The thought of using her memories and hurts to manipulate her now are suddenly a vile concept. That is something the Old One would do.

Any resemblance to his enemy makes his stomach sour. No, he would not be like the Old One, throwing the past in her face. He doesn't want to hurt her as he had before. Just the idea of it is repulsive. From now on he will try to avoid it.

Elan turns away, resolved to the fact that she is not going to get anything out of him, as he is lost in his thoughts.

"Now that you have your book back, what will be your next course of action?" Warrick asks after a long silence.

"We still have a traitor to find, and we don't have the missing pages that were stolen from us. But at least we can slow him down because he doesn't have spells from the Journal. How much do you even know about the Journal? Being a student of the Old One, what did he tell you?"

Warrick shifts uncomfortably. "That is how I will be seen forever. The student of the Old One. I would prefer not to be associated with him at all. That title is a black stain forever."

There is a stretch of silence. Elan now knows that he hated being the student of the Old One, but he is right, he will be tied to that loathsome title for the rest of his days.

"There are powerful spells in that book. And the Old One could use them at will to harm his enemies to make all bow to him. Even his spells are not as effective or-" Warrick pauses for the right word, "as creative."

"Why would Kalrolin keep a record of such spells, knowing how dangerous they were in the wrong hands?"

Warrick frowns and it is a while before he says, "I wondered that myself. I believe that he was not waiting for a day that it fell into the wrong hands, but a day that it fell into the right ones."

Light footsteps coming closer to them make Elan freeze. She doesn't know why, but she feels the urge to pretend to still be asleep. Closing her eyes, she listens to the voices. They are far off, and she strains to hear them.

"Are they still out?" Gallowgrave asks someone outside the door.

"Last we checked they were still out cold," another voice replies.

"Wonder how they got out and with the book. There was only the two of them. Strange, how they were separated from the group. And the condition they came back in. I would like to hear what happened exactly."

"Wouldn't we all?" the other man muses under his breath.

Elan's heart rate picks up. They don't know anything other than that Warrick and herself had returned with the book. She wonders if anyone else has come back from The Darklands yet and how long they had been unconscious. Elan doesn't even know how to explain the situation herself. Warrick performed magic, she has to tell them, but it would cause them both problems if they ever became suspicious of him and she owed him. He saved her life more than a few times.

She peeks at Warrick to see if he is listening. From his frown, she can tell that he has heard every single word and knows the implications of their conversation as well as she does.

"It is not as though they can go anywhere," Gallowgrave says. "Get some rest. We will come back first thing at daybreak."

They pad off silently.

Elan's homecoming is not the welcoming reception she had thought.

Elan sits rigidly in her cot as she forces down a mucky wheat colored gruel. Warrick watches beside her, his face turning more disgusted with each spoonful she swallows. "What are we telling them?" Elan asks in a hushed tone, to avoid prying ears.

Warrick's brow raises, his eyes wide, "Won't you tell them everything?"

"Do you think I would tell them what happened? We don't even know what happened," Her finger taps the side of the bowl. "Just let me do all the talking. They won't believe anything you have to say anyway."

The words have barely escaped her lips when Gallowgrave approaches smiling, but his eyes shift, preoccupied.

Dawsley marches in not long after, his back straight and his eyes kind, yet cautious.

"I'm happy to see you both awake!" Gallowgrave says coming over, light as a feather.

Warrick silently watches the exchange between her and Dawsley. Elan feels like she is standing on the edge of a knife.

"You both were out for days." Gallowgrave pulled on his beard.

"That long?" Elan startles. "I'm just happy to be home and that Kalrolin's Journal has been returned," Elan says keeping her words few. A thick stillness lingers as neither one says anything more, but Dawsley watches Elan spoon more gruel into her mouth and chew.

"Yes," Gallowgrave says. "We had been sent word that you and Warrick had been swept away by a spell, and they had thought you were dead. What exactly happened? You were gone for almost a quarter cycle. They had not even been able to get anywhere near the stone temple. Most had to come back early because they were badly injured or became suddenly ill."

Warrick's eyes reduce to slits as he watches them talk.

Elan hums with agreement to everything he said. "Yes we were swept away, but Warrick and I landed, and we were able to find shelter. We tried to get to the stone temple on our own, but we were intercepted by one of the Old One's assassins. We were brought back to the stone temple and..." Elan is surprised at the reaction of the memories. Dread stops her from saying anything further.

Gallowgrave clears his throat. He looks at her slashed face, her bruises. Lastly, he stares at her left arm. Then his eyes cast down. Elan holds her breath. He knows about her arm. They had cleaned her and given her new clothes. They must have seen the bite marks where Warrick had taken blood. Her heart thumps. They think the bites are from the Old One and not from Warrick.

"Well, we were there for a while. The Old One also now knows that Warrick and I are bound. One day when the Old One wasn't looking, we chipped pieces of rock from the temple walls. From where we were, we could see the cauldron and the book. We threw the stones at his bottles of potions. It worked better than we had hoped. They cracked and fell, some were more volatile than others, and it was enough of a diversion to escape. We took the book with us.

———

We took a chance. We were desperate, and we tried whatever we could to get out of there, even if it was reckless and might not have worked."

Elan's eyes turn pleading by this point. Warrick openly stares at her in disbelief, and Elan hopes he is not giving it away that she is lying for him. Straightening his shoulders, Warrick regains his composure.

Dawsley's kind face suddenly turns hard, pressing his lips. His gaze remains on her, trying to penetrate her mind.

Elan concentrates on her gruel, "I think I could use more rest."

"Yes, of course. I left healing droughts for the both of you. Make sure you drink them."

Elan nods and both Gallowgrave and Dawsley leave the infirmary.

Before they exit the door, Dawsley looks back at Elan his brow furrows as he leans down to Gallowgrave and whispers something to him.

"I don't know if he believed me," Elan mumbles.

"It seemed like an unlikely story."

"What is less likely is that you performed spells."
Elan waits, hoping that he will say something. But his face is set in his usual hard expression. "Here, drink this. We will heal faster." Elan hands him his bottle as she knocks back her own and scrunches her face.

Warrick holds the bottle in his hands and examines it then hands it back to Elan. "You need this more than I."

Elan raises her eyebrows and takes the bottle from his hand slowly. Before she can express any thanks, he lies back down and turns his back to her.

Chapter 41

The dawn births another unfortunate day, bitter cold and almost as gray as The Darklands, but Elan doesn't care, as she steps out of the infirmary and into the crisp air. They had been cooped up for another three days after Gallowgrave had questioned them. Elan throws out her arms and catches the breeze on her fingertips. She is alive. Order land has never been so beautiful.

Now that they are healed, they have to await instruction. Elan makes her way to the auditorium. Along the way, Order members stop and stare, whispering to one another as they pass. She knows once she arrives she will see her friends, her family, awaiting her. Even on the sunniest days, the arena never let in enough light, so today leaves the building particularly dark. The floor is nothing but dirt and hay. Order members and oaclings practice. The space is filled with grunts and scuffling. Elan stretches on her toes, extending her neck to see if anyone occupies their usual spot. The distance is too far and dark to see.

Elan quickens her steps. She stays to the right of the building, walking past everyone. A heavy sinking feeling presses on her as she comes closer and sees no one in the corner where they would usually pull up stools and talk and spar. Just her, and of course, Warrick, head to a spot that used to resound with chatter and laughter. Her steps become slower as she approaches. Her brow pulls together, and her smile fades.

The sudden change in her mood alerts Warrick and he reacts with a defensive stance so quickly it is almost comical. "Is there danger?" he asks, already stepping to stand in front of her.

"Elan!"

Her head whips around as she turns to the familiar voice of Eldon. Pushing his body about, he makes his way to the corner. Her face splits into a large smile. She hears steps behind him and looks past his shoulder to see Tresdon and Lelan following close behind. "We heard that you were being released today!" Tresdon smiles, but it doesn't quite reach his eyes. "We weren't allowed to see you in the infirmary until they could make sure you were alright."

"Thank Kalrolin, you are safe and back with us!" Eldon booms.

"I can't believe the two of you faced the Old One and brought the book back yourselves," Lelan says in awe. Even as Elan listens to Lelan talk, there is something off about him. She can't place it.

"You should have seen the celebration party they threw when the book was back on our land. The party was still going on the next night," Tresdon comments. "They sent me back before everyone else, because of the injury." Tresdon drops his head as if he is ashamed he had come back before anyone else. "I guess the good news is I was here for the whole thing!"

"You did well, Elan, and you as well, Warrick," Lelan says with a proud expression as if Lelan had trained Warrick himself.

Warrick turns his head away, his back straightens, and he crosses his arms, ignoring him. But his eyes give Lelan a sideways glance before looking away again.

Elan can't help but reminisce about the last victory parties they had. There had not been many in her lifetime in The Order. But the ones she did remember filled her with a light-hearted elation. So many would be drinking to the point of enthusiastic singing and roughhousing.

"I'm sorry I missed it," Elan laments. "Where are Jordon and Nolan, not still celebrating are they?" Elan asks, imagining Jordon and Nolan waking with nasty headaches and injuries they can't quite explain.

The light from Eldon, Tresdon and Lelan's eyes snuff out in an instant. Their faces fall, and slowly each pair of eyes drop. Elan turns to ice as she takes a sharp breath. She swallows, diverting her eyes to the dirt floor as her throat tightens. Blinking more than necessary, she takes a steady breath.

"I see."

The silence presses in on her.

Eldon speaks first, "We should go. There are to be new procedures and security now that Kalrolin's Journal is back."

Elan nods and takes a chance to peek up at each of her remaining friends. Their faces twist with hurt and the awkward tension of not knowing what to do or say as they leave the arena. She hangs her head, not seeing the arena in front of her. A numb dead-eyed trance takes hold of her.

She can't cry, can't be sad, not here, in the middle of the arena. But she is allowed to be angry.

Elan clenches her fists and spins around, her shoulders set, her brow low over her eyes. After two steps, she nearly walks right into Warrick, who gives her a somewhat curious expression.

On the wall of the stadium, swords line up. Some are beautiful pieces of art and others merely blunt weapons of force. Elan picks up one crudely fashioned and unevenly weighted. She swings the sword around her and strikes the air, breathing heavily. Her throat burns and her chest aches, making it hard to take in even breaths. But having to concentrate on wielding the cumbersome thing keeps her mind busy, and her muscles strain enough to distract her from her real pain.

Elan raises the sword high above her head, about to strike down into the air when with a flash of silver light, the blade rings against another sword.

Warrick holds the sword she had seen him take the first day he came to the arena. His face is expressionless and his back straight.

Fury fuels her. Attacking Warrick, he deflects her sword. Standing back from one another, they circle each other slowly. They watch the other's eyes to see when the next one will move. Elan charges first, with a guttural cry coming from deep within her. Warrick deflects with a backhanded movement then crashes his sword down again, trying to knock the steel from her hands. Holding tight, she swings her arms, not caring about technique at all but more concerned about inflicting damage.

Elan can tell from Warrick's fighting that he is not attacking, only defending. Instead of this making her feel better, she feels resentment and more anger. She advances, pushing him further back. With each step, Warrick gets closer to the wall. Finally, Warrick's wings touch the stone wall. He intentionally loosens his grip on the sword. She easily knocks it from his hand. Her heart races and she breaths heavily as she glares at Warrick. The sword is being held at his neck only a hair's width away from his skin.

Warrick straightens his back as if he has won the fight. Offering his chin, he says with a strong voice, "You may strike me if you like."

Elan finally comes back to herself, stunned. The sudden drop in her emotions makes her feel dizzy.

Warrick's eyes never leave hers, and he waits for the impact.

Elan drops her sword; her hands shake as she turns, marching away. She had not noticed that the Order members had stopped what they were doing to watch. She feels the stares and the curious gawkers as she leaves the arena. The stir of air behind her lets her know that Warrick follows not much further behind.

Elan rounds the corner to the back side of the building. Her body shakes, and she leans a hand against the wall. Her head sags, and she clamps down on her jaw, fearing that she will retch. She chokes down gulps of cold air as her eyes sting.

Nothing distracts her from her thoughts now. Jordon and Nolan are gone. With her other arm, she holds her side as though her ribs might fall apart. Her knees buckle, and she kneels on the ground.

Warrick stands beside her, watching, but doesn't say a word.

"It's my fault. Nolan was not even supposed to go to the Darklands in the first place. I knew that there was a chance that we might not come back. But..." Elan can't finish. Clenching her fists, she forces herself not to cry and holds the pain until it burns a hole inside her. She slams her hands onto the stone walls of the building. The pain in her hands distracts her a little.

Warrick moves toward her, "If you need to scream, then scream. If you have to hit something then do it. It is a tragic thing when one you care for is gone, and you feel as though you had a hand in their demise." He breathes heavily, and his feet shuffle before speaking again. "You let me carry on in front of Hessero's grave." Warrick swallows. "I will, this once, give you the same courtesy."

Warrick walks away with his back toward her. He goes as far as the spell will allow.

She sniffles as her breath becomes uneven. The pressure that was in her, all at once breaks. A pained high pitched whine emits from her open mouth as hot tears spill over in her burning red-rimmed eyes. Her nose runs and she knows she looks pathetic and undignified but she doesn't care.

It is a relief to weep, to let go of the tightly-held reigns of her emotions. Her sobs are loud and rack her small frame as her arms wrap around her torso.

A small weeping carries across to him. Warrick's hardened heart feels as if it is cracking. An ache slowly unfurls. He grits his teeth, shuts his eyes tight and clasps his hands over his ears, to muffle out the sound. But he can still hear it. Now that he knows the sound of her crying, it haunts him, echoing in his mind. He thinks of Hessero all those equinoxes ago, leaning against the tree and whimpering sadly.

Pressing his eyes tighter and shutting up his ears even harder, he feels a single tear roll down his face. Warrick despises himself because he knows that he is not only sad about Hessero.

Chapter 42

The Old One has been thrashing for hours. Fenix is utterly useless to him now with his whole body encased in silver. He is alive but entrapped, never to move again. He will waste away and die inside his metal shell. The potions must have fallen while he was fighting and created this concoction. Warrick should not have been able to do any magic, but he somehow had. There is no explanation, and the mystery of it has him going mad.

Massive feet stomp across the Old One's land. Ichbone comes into the stone temple with his bag of beads rattling at his side.

"How dare you keep me waiting!" the Old One snaps.

Ichbone frowns, his distaste obvious. The Old One knows he will not disrespect him however. He would crush the bounty hunter with a snap of his fingers.

"You will get me every degenerate, immoral, cutthroat you can find and you will bring word for all to come to the stone temple." The Old One points a bony gnarled finger at Ichbone. "I am going to make them more deadly and powerful than any creature has ever been. You tell them that they are going to lead thousands of creatures into Blood One land. Getch, Darklander, Larvesp and all beast alike. We are going to wipe every Blood One village and reduce them to nothing more than cattle. I have been too merciful and kind. I am arming myself and will lead you all to war. I was not so foolishly prideful as I was before. I kept the loose pages that the traitor sent me separately, and still possess the spells to free myself. Once I have all the Order enslaved, I will have every single incantation, and no one will stop me. The Order, with all Kalrolin's protection, will be no match for me," The Old one spits with fury. He turns to a pile of pages, scribbled aged and torn. Shuffling through them, he bares his teeth when he finds the one he is looking for.

"I have one more special thing I need you to do for me." There is a sick twist of satisfaction as the Old One hands Ichbone the written instructions.

Ichbone's eyes become wide as he reads what the Old One is telling him to do. His hand trembles and fear shines behind his eyes. His once haughty expression is now like a cowering seedling. Without even thinking about refusing, he leaves, clutching the paper in his hands.

It is only a few moments later that the Old One hears the familiar cawing of the blackbirds. He runs to the doors of the stone temple. In front of the stone temple, three black crows caw and fly in the gray sky. A large dark figure emerges from the twisting trees of the forest. He is clad in all ebony, and black bandages cover his face. He wears massive leather boots and is armed with all manner of weapons. Thick gloves cover his hands. This is undeniably a Blood One.

As the man gets closer, he sees that this Blood One is more substantial than average. He has no skin exposed at all except for his large eyes. And the Old One can't help but admire how they are the perfect shade of river blue.

Elan opens the doors to their cabin and it creaks open. She thought she would never see her home again.

Stepping inside, she touches the fabric covering the opening to her room. It is coarse under her chilled fingers. Turning to start the fire, she pauses, noticing Warrick already there, coaxing a small flame to grow.

"I'm thirsty," Warrick says as he hunches in front of the hearth, stoking the fire.

"I know," Elan says, rubbing her shoulder. She is surprised that they had lasted this long. They have both been trying to ignore it, but it is growing stronger every day.

"We lost a lot of blood these past quarter cycles. I don't know if I can give you much."

But Elan knows, even without Warrick saying anything how desperately he needs to feed. "Will the little I am able to give you even help?"

"I don't know. We have to try. We can't go back to the way we were before. The illness, the madness."

Warrick is right. Even if her crest was exacerbating the situation before, all it did was speed up something that would have happened anyway. It will be only a matter of time.

Elan swallows.

Pulling back the sleeve on her arm, puncture scars scatter up and down her forearm. Even if the severe blood loss doesn't kill Elan and she lives to be as old as Ylmore, her arms will be forever covered in bites. He will be feeding from her for as long as they live.

Warrick walks over. He doesn't tear his eyes away from the imprints of his teeth, the scars he has left behind. Elan watches as Warrick's face twists into something that looks like a mix of disgust and guilt. He ties a piece of cloth tightly to his arm to keep himself from bleeding. Warrick closes his eyes, and it strikes Elan as so odd. This is the first time he has shut them, almost as though he were ashamed of what he was doing.

With one draw of blood, Elan's knees become unstable, and her head spins. They both know it is too risky to take another. Warrick helps steady her, not feeling stable enough himself. Elan clamps a hand over her wound. Warrick's mouth stains.

The door creaks. Both of their heads snap to attention to the front of the hut. They hadn't noticed they left the door ajar. Through the crack, a hazel eye opens wide.

Both Warrick and Elan sprint for the door, nearly ripping it from its hinges. Outside, one of her brothers escapes, but Warrick is faster. He reaches his long arm out far enough to catch the end of the cloak. Pulling it back, the Order member falls to the ground. Warrick blinds him with his hood as Elan helps keep him down.

"Get him inside!" Elan orders as she frantically spins around to see if anyone is watching.

They have not gotten too far from the hut. The center of Order land is far enough away that she hopes no one can hear him.

The Order member thrashes violently with muffled screams as he tries to get free. Shoving him inside the cabin, Elan latches the door behind her.

Warrick pulls back his hood to reveal the spy's face.

Elan swears under her breath.

A panicking, sweaty, yet defiant Lelan has his arms being held behind his back by Warrick.

A sneer touches Warrick's features. "It's that boy."

"Lelan, calm down. We won't hurt you! What are you even doing here? Warrick, let him go."

Warrick pushes him away, and Elan is amazed that he listens without protest. Lelan moves back, trying to put as much space between himself and them. A sheen of sweat shines on his brow. His eyes wildly look at the blood smeared on Elan's arm and the fresh crimson on Warrick's teeth.

Elan floods with shame. She can't even bring herself to lift her head. Panic and hurt mix with a deep self-loathing. The evidence damns her, and no argument or excuse will undo what has happened.

Lelan turns his back on them both. His body trembles as he asks, "How long? How long have you been lying to us and letting the Creature feed on you?"

Elan can hear his voice breaking.

"I'm so sorry Lelan, we just, we were so hungry," Elan pleads.

Lelan gives Elan his attention again shaking his head in disbelief.

She realizes after the words have left her, she had said "we" not "Warrick." She knows she has to come clean. Whatever Lelan decides after she tells him the truth, she will accept it. She has no choice. Closing her eyes she lets the words tumble from her mouth, "When the Creature doesn't drink, I crave blood too. It's been…" Elan doesn't continue. With her heart in her throat she finally takes a chance to see her friend's reaction.

Revulsion takes the place of the wide-eyed shock he had moments before. He knows now. He knows that she craves blood as much as Warrick. Elan can't speak. She can hear Lelan's heart thumping wildly. A strange wave of desire crashes into her, because Warrick is still hungry.

Lelan clasps a hand over his mouth, looking so heart broken. First he loses his mentor and now he knows his friends have been keeping secrets from him.

"Lelan, you don't understand – we were going mad," Elan practically begs. She can't stand the way he stares at her, like she is a stranger.

"How long has it been?" he asks louder. His hands quiver as he curls them into fists.

Warrick's back gets straight, he jerks his chin to the side, warning her not to speak. Elan wrings her hands.

"Since the beginning," Elan admits.

Warrick's jaw clenches.

"Ever since the spell bound us." She feels lighter as she confesses.

"You have been letting the Creature drink from you for that long?" he asked softly. His words sound hollow.

Elan wishes more than anything that she can see his face. Elan moves forward to get closer to him but knows he probably doesn't want to be anywhere near her. She is a liar. How many times will she fail them, time and time again?

"I know you are going to tell Dawsley," Elan says, knowing she deserves whatever punishment they dole out. "And I am not going to stop you, but-"

"All this time you never told any of us what was happening," Lelan says softer dropping his chin.

She can feel the betrayal in his tone.

When he lifts his face, Elan blanches at his expression, one of hurt, not of anger or revenge. He pulls back the sleeve of his right arm, exposing the soft side of his forearm.

"You can drink my blood. You are both my brothers in arms. If you suffer, I suffer as well."

Elan stares blankly.

"Elan, you should not have had to go through this alone. Over two cycles of giving Warrick your blood. It must have been hard for you to give so much. I thought we were closer than that."

Both hold their breath as Lelan speaks. His eyes swim as he holds her gaze. He then turns to Warrick, his face set.

"Go on, Warrick. You are our brother. And if this is what you need to survive, then I will help you. You have saved us many times already."

"Lelan," Elan begins.

"Don't argue with me, Elan. You both have lost too much blood. I'm not going to let him drink from you when you both need it. Let me do this for you. Let me help you," Lelan's face burns with resolve. And Elan cannot turn him away, as much as she wants to. They both need this, and if he is willing to give, then they will take it, but just this once.

Warrick looks to Elan to see if she is honestly going to let him take his blood. She nods once.

Warrick takes Lelan's arm.

Lelan jerks back. A normal reflex. "He isn't... You will be careful, won't you?" Lelan asks Warrick.

They both know what he means. If Warrick isn't careful, he could kill Lelan. It isn't the same as with Elan, where Warrick's own life is at stake. Lelan is taking a creature's word that he will not be harmed.

"I assure you. I will be cautious."

It doesn't escape Elan's attention that Warrick said he would be cautious, not that he would not kill him. There is a tangible possibility of that. He looks nervous at what he is about to do, but he remains unmoving and keeps his attention on Lelan's arm, not looking away at what is about to happen.

Warrick sinks his teeth in, taking a large pull of blood, then one more and another. Warrick can finally drink his fill. Taking from one person meant that he could only withdraw very little at a time. The muscles under Lelan's arm tense. Elan watches closely as Lelan's face begins to wane in color.

Elan shoots her arm out to stop Warrick before he harms Lelan. But before her fingertips can even make contact, Warrick pulls back. He licks his mouth. Lelan wobbles as he puts pressure on the spot where Warrick drank.

Warrick can feel the effects of fresh blood almost instantly. His stiff body now loosens, and he feels energized. He had wanted more. His instincts told him to drain him but he managed to tear himself away.

Even he can see Elan's relief. She never had this much blood. The effects are instantaneous. The boy had helped them. From what he had said he would have helped them all along. Warrick knows it is a good thing he had not offered his help sooner. Had he volunteered much earlier, Warrick would not have bothered to stop.

"You have been generous," Warrick states. "Besides Elan, with our special circumstance, I have never known a Blood One to give their blood freely to our kind."

"But you are not their kind anymore," Lelan says. "You are not a Blood One either, but you are an Order Member. That surpasses everything else to me."

The statement floors him. Warrick meets his's gaze, and there is nothing but pure honesty in his words. A newfound respect for the annoyingly persistent boy grips his chest. He admires his dedication to his brothers even if he, himself does not share the same devotion. If he is not careful, he may come to not hate this… *Le-land* ?

"What are you doing here, Lelan?" Elan asks more softly than she had before.

"I came here because there was something I wanted to tell you. Jordon. He…" Lelan stops and takes a deep breath before continuing. "A messenger bird came into town with a letter made out to him. 'To Jordon the Green Cloak' it said. The man in the sparrow shop gave it to Crosley. And then Crosley gave it to me. Jordon didn't tell me. He didn't tell anyone," Lelan sounded hurt by the last statement. "He was looking for another sorcerer, anyone that might be able to break the bond between you and Warrick."

Elan can't believe what she is hearing, closing her eyes and shaking her head. It can't be right. Conductors of magic are rare. Sorcerers who study and can wield spells were almost impossible to find. Elan knew only of the Old One, Gallowgrave and now Warrick. The practice almost died out because people were far too irresponsible or greedy.

Elan's heart races with the prospect of being free, but her mood quickly turns as she remembers seeing Jordon in town. She had thought that he was the traitor. When all he was doing was trying to find a way to help her. Elan thought it was impossible to feel a deeper layer of guilt than she already had, but she is wrong. A bone deep self-hatred sinks in.

"Did he find anyone at all?" Warrick asks, his eyes alight with anticipation.

"It seems like there is a rumor of an old wizard. A hermit."

"But they are only rumors, right? Did Jordon find anything?" Elan asks eagerly, but her voice snags on his name.

"If there is a chance that there is a sorcerer out there that can free us, wouldn't you take the risk?" Warrick asks anxiously.

Elan touches her left forearm.

"I'm willing," Elan says. "What do we do now?"

Elan saddles her horse as Warrick stuffs a few bags with provisions. Elan is fully armored and clad in her green cloak.

Warrick wears the clothes they had bought from Delmira's shop. His hood casts his face in darkness. Elan puts two swords in her holster before climbing up.

The other ebony horses trot impatiently, ready, each with their rider. Some are her friends, Eldon, Tresdon, Aldon and Lelan. The others, Mosley, Serdon, and Kingsley she knows are only there to keep an eye on herself and

Warrick. They told Dawsley they wanted to stay on the move, to be decoys so the Old One would not know what they were planning. Really, they would follow clues that would lead to the unnamed sorcerer. She knows that Dawsley would have no objections to them leaving. Being away kept her and Warrick as far from the book as possible. And since a bounty remains on Warrick's head, staying on Order land is not prudent.

Elan lends Warrick a hand as he joins her.

How odd a feeling, to have a Darklandian directly behind her and she does not flinch. Her muscles don't tighten. She searches for suspicion of any kind, but she does not feel it. The sun begins to wake. The damp air causes her breath to rise. She touches her side pocket where she is hiding a map and a letter from a far-off place.

"Aren't we going?" Warrick sneers from behind her.

Elan frowns before covering her face, shielding it from the wind. She kicks hard, and her horse sprints forward.

The sun is to her back and hope lies ahead.

"Don't repay evil for evil. Don't retaliate with insults when people insult you. Instead, pay them back with a blessing. That is what God has called you to do, and he will grant you his blessing."

- 1 Peter 3:9 (NLT)

Made in USA - Crawfordsville, IN
59349_9781696782487
01.24.2020 1514